CHEROKEE SUNDOWN

Standingdeer's smile spread to his eyes and made them as soft as brown velvet. They caressed her, from the fringes across her breasts to the long, tight leggings beneath.

"You look fierce in your buckskins, Tiana," he said. "Like a Beloved Woman ready to go on the warpath." His heavy-lidded gaze moved lazily over her once more, then lingered on her lips.

The powerful pull of his dark-burning eyes lifted her feet from the floor. She took a step toward him. Then another.

He reached across the lantern light to cup her cheek. With a trembling sigh she leaned into the cradle that his hand made for her head and opened her mouth to his with no holding back.

FOR MORE F...
INDIAN...
BY GEN...
BE SURE...
CHEROK...
and
CHEROKEE NIGHTS

CHEROKEE SUNDOWN

GENELL DELLIN

AVON BOOKS ⟁ NEW YORK

CHEROKEE SUNDOWN is an original publication of Avon
Books. This work has never before appeared in book form. This
work is a novel. Any similarity to actual persons or events is
purely coincidental.

AVON BOOKS
A division of
The Hearst Corporation
1350 Avenue of the Americas
New York, New York 10019

Copyright © 1992 by Genell Smith Dellin
Inside cover author photograph by Glamour Shots
Published by arrangement with the author
Library of Congress Catalog Card Number: 91-92435
ISBN: 0-380-76716-3

First Avon Books Printing: June 1992

AVON TRADEMARK REG. U.S. PAT. OFF. AND IN OTHER COUNTRIES,
MARCA REGISTRADA, HECHO EN U.S.A.

Printed in the U.S.A.

RA   10   9   8   7   6   5   4   3   2   1

For Jean Hager, who never let me quit
and never let me down

Friend of mine and Friend of Thunder

Ha, then! There is no loneliness!
Like the red lightning strikes from the sky
Like horses race above the treetops
You have just come to draw out my soul.
                    —Inspired by
                      traditional Cherokee
                      incantations

Prologue

Cherokee Nation East
February 1833

Tiana Tenkiller ran down the alleyway of Pine Grove Plantation's slave quarters and up to Fawn's cabin, the blood pounding so loudly in her ears that she could barely hear her own ragged breath.

"Fawnie!" she called, keeping her voice low. No answer came, so she pushed open the rough door and stepped in.

Her best friend's face didn't change expression when she saw Tiana. It couldn't. Every inch of it had swollen until the skin threatened to burst.

"Oh, dear Lord!" Tiana cried, rushing to her. "Fawn, he used the whip on your face!"

The cut had turned Fawn's top lip nearly inside out; without moving it she mumbled, "Tobacco Jack ... devil ... liquored up."

"The Devil *take* him!" Tiana said, jerking out her handkerchief to dab at the oozing wound. "Dilcey told me he'd beaten you, but I had no idea!"

Her ministrations only made the festering fluids seep faster. She snatched a quilt from the narrow bed that occupied a corner of the small room.

"This is all Gray's fault for selling you away

from home in the first place," she raged, running back to Fawn and wrapping the quilt around her shoulders. "As soon as I get you to Running Waters, I'm going to write to Chief Ross in Washington City and ask him to send Papa home."

"No!" Fawn muttered, her voice full of fear. "Tobacco Jack . . ."

"I'll return the money he paid for you," Tiana said firmly. "If he wants more I'll meet his price—if I have to sell a horse to do it."

She guided her friend to the door and outside, supporting her with both hands as they started down the alley. Fawn barely had the strength to stand, much less walk.

"I hid Jane Hunt in the trees," Tiana said, knowing that the mention of Fawn's favorite mare would spur her on. "She's really missed you since you've been gone."

Fawn nodded. Her listing gait quickened.

Then she froze. Tiana looked up.

A round form sat huddled on the stoop of the next cabin. Old Sudie.

The girls waited, not daring to move, but the ancient black woman never looked up. She was asleep in the poor warmth of the winter sun.

They slipped along in front of her, Tiana not making a sound, and Fawn, in her weakness, shuffling her feet against the hard-packed earth. Finally they had passed the danger.

They came to the last cabin. Ahead lay a slight dip, then a rise to the pine-topped slope where Jane Hunt stood waiting. Tiana led Fawn out into the open.

A shadow fell across their path. Tiana's feet slid to a stop on the frost-covered ground.

"Where y'all think you're goin'?" The harsh voice belonged to Tobacco Jack.

Fawn's body turned to stone in Tiana's hands.

"I'm taking Fawn home with me." Tiana cleared her throat and forced herself to look from Tobacco Jack's shadow to his boots, then up over his disheveled clothing to his flushed, fierce face. His eyes burned with a crazy fire. He hadn't sobered up yet.

"That gal stays here. *You* go, Missy."

Tiana's fingers tightened around Fawn's arm. "I'm buying her back," she said. "My brother never should have sold her. I'll return your money the instant we get to Running Waters, Mr. Tuskee."

The man crossed the space between them in two strides and hit Fawn across her swollen face with the flat of his hand. She fell, her limp body tearing loose from Tiana's grip.

He bent to hit her again.

Tiana tried to beat him back, but she couldn't even slow him down.

Screaming, she whirled away, wild for a stick, a rock, anything to use for a weapon to fill her empty hands. Her eyes raked the passageway between the cabins, but it had been swept clean: the only rocks were those that made up the foundation beneath the corners of the houses; the only sticks were attached to the trees that looked miles away.

Then Tiana spotted a hoe that leaned against the wall of the cabin on the end.

She ran to grab it, turned in a swirl of skirts that nearly tripped her, and rushed back to Fawn, lying limp at Tobacco Jack's feet. He raised his huge fist.

Tiana lifted the hoe over her head and, with all the power in both her arms, swung it at him.

His body dropped across Fawn's like a felled tree.

Tiana sank to her knees. Tobacco Jack's long gray braid swung sideways, showing the mark the dull side of the hoe had made on the back of his head.

Fawn moaned.

Tiana scrambled around to hold her head. "Are you all right? Oh, Fawn, talk to me!"

"Listen!" Fawn commanded in an eerie, loud tone.

"I'm listening, Fawnie. I'm here."

Fawn sighed and began to mumble. Tiana bent over her.

"Bluford," Fawn said softly. For one terrified instant Tiana looked over her shoulder to see if Tobacco Jack's son had come up behind her. No one was there.

Fawn made a horrible gurgling sound. "P . . . pony," she gasped, and turned her head to one side. Her body jerked once and then went totally still.

As still as Tobacco Jack's.

Tiana stared. Fawn was dead.

And so was Tobacco Jack.

Chapter 1

Tiana squeezed Coosa's hot sides with her thighs and lifted her face into the wind, willing the race never to end. The thunder of his hooves surged in her blood, swelling up through his long, strong bones like a mighty heartbeat. He was lightning; she would ride him across the sky.

She wished. That way she could escape.

The silver-colored stallion raised his head, too, and began to slow, tossing his mane so that it rippled down along his neck to sting against her hands. He wasn't the champion running horse of the Cherokee Nation for nothing. He knew when he had crossed the finish line. And when he had won.

She let him check his speed and carry her back into the real world. Shouts and cheering beat against her ears. She opened her eyes.

The noisy crowd of racegoers swirled across the skinned-earth track and onto the open, grassy area at the foot of Talking Rock Mountain, coming closer to her with every stride Coosa made. Voices chanted, "Coosa, Coosa, Coosa!" like a drumbeat. He dropped down into a long, slow gait that fit the rhythm of the crowd's calls, swung in an arc around the end of the field, and, head tossing, cantered to meet his admirers. The horse was dancing—he loved attention as much as her brother, Gray Fox, did.

Gray, dressed in his newest fancy white suit, was pushing his way through the crush to claim them, smiling as if the victory were all his doing, intending to lead Coosa into the winner's circle, of course. Well, that was fine with her. Let him be the center of attention. Ever since that awful day in February, Tiana didn't like to look at herself and she didn't want anyone else to, either.

The minute her brother took Coosa's head, she gave a little sigh of relief, kicked away her stirrups, and, throwing one leg over his withers, started to slide to the ground on the off side. But a glimpse of a familiar buggy sitting at the very edge of the meadow stopped her. She lifted her hand in a quick gesture of greeting, and across the wide space, over the heads of the crowd, Papa waved his buggy whip and Mama her handkerchief. They *had* returned from their tour of the southern part of the Nation in time to see the race! They had seen her win!

Tiana's heart lifted, then fell again. It was so wonderful to have Mama and Papa home from Washington City, but she couldn't relax and enjoy it, for tomorrow morning they would be leaving to go there again. After being home only two short weeks! And most of that time, touring the land to talk with people from all parts of the Nation about the negotiations in Washington City.

They began climbing out of the buggy to make their way toward their children, and Tiana vaulted from Coosa's back to the ground to go meet them. Gray Fox took no notice of her, or them, as happy bettors surrounded him, chortling in satisfaction at the outcome of the race.

The crowd soon turned to look for Coosa's rider. Tiana knew they wanted to congratulate her, as they always did after she won, but she could not bear it. She wanted no attention except from Mama and Papa.

She moved away from Coosa and tried to work through the crowd, but people pressed tight around her and she couldn't make progress away from the horse. Someone bumped her arm and a harsh sound grated in her ear. "Missy Tenkiller!"

The voice was strange. And full of hatefulness. Tiana looked up to find its owner; somebody else pressed close against her on the other side. A sudden, stark fear tightened her throat.

Two white men flanked her, men she'd never seen before. One tall and one short. Both hard-eyed.

"Yore brother owes us a pile of money," the taller one, who had the raspy voice, said. "If he values his health, and yores, Missy, y'all will give us that purse ye jist won."

The purse. The purse from this race was to ransom the bloodstock mares Gray had lost in a bet and keep them at home, in the pasture at Running Waters. She had no other way to save them. Thanks to Gray's powers of persuasion, James Dalton, the man who had won that bet, had promised not to come and claim Jane Hunt and the other mares while Papa was at home. Now she could get them back permanently.

But the two strangers were demanding that she give the money to them. How dare they?

"I have no idea what you're talking about," she said, trying to sound haughty enough to cover her fear. Just the mention of Gray Fox and money in the same breath was enough to terrify her, not to mention the sinister air of these two men.

She tried to push past them, but the tall one stepped directly into her way.

"Gray Fox Tenkiller has lost bets to every gambling man in the Nation as well as most of the ones in the saloons across the Chestatee River in Georgia," the short one said, patiently, carefully, as if he were a teacher explaining a lesson to a dimwitted pupil. His voice was surprisingly soft and well modulated. "We are asking only that we get *our* money before his other creditors collect theirs. He must have a dozen of them, at least."

She stared from one of the white men to the other while anger began rising in her veins to wipe out her fear. They saw it in her eyes.

"Tell your brother to give us the purse or I'll break your pretty neck, Missy," the tall one croaked. "After I sample what's beneath them boy's britches there."

Tiana's face flushed hot. Who were these ugly, dirty *yonegas*, anyway, to appear out of nowhere and talk to her this way? She wouldn't, she *couldn't* let them have the Council Oak purse.

"*I* don't owe you money!" she snapped. "Get away from me!"

"*You* may not owe us, perhaps," the polite man said, "but your brother does. And we hear you have a great deal of influence on him."

"You had better," the crude one snarled, "or before you know it, you won't have no influence a'tall. No brother, neither."

"Let's go see Gray together," the short one said soothingly, doffing his small, round hat. "And you can encourage him to do the right thing, my dear. I'm Jonah Walters, and my partner here is Owen Sykes."

His false politeness made Tiana's blood run cold. The tall man started to take her arm, but she jerked it away and stepped backward. A large woman in a buckskin dress came between them; Tiana turned and thrust her way through the mass of people.

She used her hands and her elbows and her eyes to keep forcing a path to open ahead of her toward selfish, lazy, *stupid* Gray. He had brought these vultures circling down around both their heads. How many more of them existed? That man had said a dozen!

If Gray Fox kept on losing, making more debts, they'd never get them all paid off, even if she continued to work like a field hand training and riding their running horses as she had done all this spring. Well, she wouldn't let him give this purse to those low-down scoundrels, no matter *what* they threatened.

This purse was to pay off the bet he had lost when he wagered the bloodstock mares, and Tiana would see to it that that happened. She couldn't bear to lose Jane Hunt and New Chowa and Hiwassee Lady. And neither could Papa—his heart would be broken. Poor Papa. He had certainly been wrong when he'd said that leaving Gray in charge of the plantation would force him to grow up.

But Papa mustn't know. It would worry him so, he wouldn't be able to concentrate on his crucial task of persuading Congress to let the Cherokees keep their homeland. He *must* succeed at that!

Finally she broke through the crowd to Coosa's head. She grabbed Gray Fox's arm.

But he didn't even turn toward her; he was drifting over to the winner's circle, talking to someone on the other side of him. Tiana took two running steps to catch up, to see who it was.

Gray Fox stopped in his tracks and held Coosa's restless head still and high. "The Coosa Evening Star!" he shouted in his naturally booming voice, making a hush fall over the crowd. He looked around, grinning that grin of his that could charm a snake out of its hole. "Winner of a two-out-of-two-heat run, winner of the Council Oak Match Race!"

Behind Tiana, amidst the cheering, a voice yelled, "That stud coulda beat ol' Eclipse hisself!"

Tiana barely heard the words. She could do nothing but look at the man beside her brother.

He had a powerful stance, sure and easy as if he knew every inch of the earth beneath his feet. When he turned and stepped back to run his hand along Coosa's neck, he moved with the wild grace of a buck deer in the woods. Yet he was heavily built: even the full cut of his traditional Cherokee hunting shirt couldn't conceal the massive muscles of his shoulders and chest. He was taller than Gray Fox by four or five inches, and in their faces there was no comparison.

This was a man grown, a man who knew what he was about, a man whose rugged, very Cherokee features spoke silent volumes. He must be a full-blood. *Who was he?*

Gray and his companion started Coosa walking again and the crowd swirled in, sweeping Tiana along toward the huge, ancient Council Oak tree that served as both finish-line marker and winner's circle. Callace Stones, who had arranged the day's meet, waited in the shade of its high, spreading branches to present the prize purse.

He shouted, "The Coosa Evening Star! Owned by the Tenkillers of Running Waters Plantation. Ridden by Miss Tiana Tenkiller!"

Tiana didn't feel her usual surge of pride at those words—her fascination for her brother's companion was too strong at that moment to let any other emotion take hold. She couldn't stop looking at him.

With a gracious nod of thanks to Callace, Gray took the heavy sack of coins, then immediately raised it high, lifting the stranger's hand with his. The leather bag swung between them.

That broke Tiana's entrancement. Her heart stopped. What was Gray Fox *doing?* Giving away the money? Sharing it? He couldn't!

"Our partner in The Coosa Evening Star!" he cried, smiling as proudly as if he himself had produced the mysterious man beside him out of thin air. "The Paint!"

Tiana stood stunned. No. No. This could not be true.

The gathered Cherokees went mad. They sent up an enormous cheer, repeating the famous name over and over; it beat at Tiana's ears in staccato bursts of excitement. "The Paint! The Paint! He's come home!"

The Paint. Standingdeer Chekote. Tiana listened as if from a far distance. She couldn't feel her body; her mind must have gone away.

Then it came back, bringing nothing but pure terror to run in her veins. From a spring in the pit of her stomach it bubbled up and rushed outward, changing her warm blood to cold water. The top of her head felt suddenly as light as air.

She had heard of The Paint in every story Papa or any of the other men ever told of the Battle of Horseshoe Bend, in which the Cherokees had defeated the Red Stick Creeks for Andrew Jackson. Standingdeer Chekote had painted for battle with tremendous zeal and fought like ten men that day, they said, even though he had been only fourteen years old.

Tiana had been born just after that battle and was too young to remember when her boy-warrior neighbor had gone away a year later, to travel alone to the Western Cherokees. She calculated quickly. He must be around thirty-three years old now. It would have been eighteen years ago that he left Pine Grove.

He left Pine Grove. The man who had captured her eyesight and dulled all her other senses, the man whose mere *appearance* this day intrigued her more than the continued company of any man who had ever come courting her, was Standing-deer Chekote—the favorite nephew of Tobacco Jack Tuskee.

She had killed the only parent this national hero had ever known.

Tiana felt sweat suddenly cover the palms of her hands. What would he do to her if he knew what she had done? Would he want revenge? The man was a great warrior. He would want revenge.

Would he find out? Her body swayed, and she wished she were near a tree so she could lean against it.

He wouldn't find out. Surely not. Not so long as Bluford believed that Fawn had killed Tobacco Jack and then died of her own wounds.

The Paint was saying something to Gray. A crazy, headlong desire stabbed through Tiana: she wanted to hear his voice. She felt desperate to hear it. Was it rich and deep? Or light and whispery, like the voices of some men who lived in the outdoors?

She jammed her fist against her parted lips, biting down against her knuckles until they hurt. She had to get away from The Paint and the threat he represented, yet her feet felt rooted to the earth.

Gray Fox lowered the sack of money and he and The Paint opened it, holding it out between them. Her rogue of a brother *was* going to share it! Or gamble it. People edged nearer to look at the shining pile of coins.

Was Papa close enough to see? Did he know about this?

Tiana's nails cut into her palms. She needed that money! She had to get her hands on that purse and on Coosa and take them safely home. And take *herself* safely home.

She ran across the dirt of the track toward her brother. "Gray Fox!" she called. "I need to speak to you . . ."

However, by the time she reached him, his old friend Early Vann had caught Gray's attention. Early was talking to Gray so intensely that Tiana knew he was proposing another race.

She had to stop them before the wager was set. The Tenkillers must go home.

She pulled at her brother's arm. "Gray . . ."

But it was Standingdeer Chekote, The Paint, who turned to her, the precious bag of coins dangling loosely from his fingers. Tiana wanted to hide her face, snatch the bag, and run.

But she couldn't move. Not one muscle. His compelling dark eyes took her captive, made her unable to stop looking into his rugged, gorgeous face. He smiled at her.

A new kind of warmth flooded her body, a deep-seated pleasure stronger than holding her hands to a fire after riding for miles in the cold.

How could she have such feelings about him? It was almost a sin to be so attracted to the nephew of the man she had killed.

"Nice race," he said. His voice *wasn't* the feathery, dry kind; it had a rich timbre like the rumble of faraway thunder.

Tiana waited to hear it again. The warmth inside her grew to a bewildering heat.

Until his smile vanished as suddenly as it had appeared. She felt as if a cloud had covered the sun.

"You handle Star right," he said briskly, as if he'd just remembered that they were not friends, but strangers. "We'll definitely enter him in the Dahlonega Gold Stakes with you up."

Tiana listened to the rhythmic tones in his voice, as deeply moving as the sound of a drum. Then, after four long heartbeats, the meaning of his words sank into her brain.

"Who are you to say where he'll run and who'll be up?" she demanded, forcing her mind to work. "Besides, we call him Coosa."

"Coosa," Standingdeer Chekote agreed.

She locked her gaze with his.

"How can you say he'll run at Dahlonega?" she repeated.

The Paint reached up and, with one finger, pushed the wide-brimmed hat back from his forehead. His black hair caught the sun like a raven's wing.

"Didn't you hear your brother say I was his partner?" he drawled. "I own a half interest in this Coosa horse here. Won 'im last night in a card game."

"No!" Tiana blurted, although a small voice inside her shouted that there was no doubt The Paint was speaking the truth. "You *can't* have half! Gray Fox has made debts . . ."

"I won him fair and square," Standingdeer Chekote said.

"Oh, I don't doubt that," Tiana cried in despair. "Gray is a terrible gambler, even if he does practice at it day and night! It's just that Coosa isn't his to risk."

"Now, now, Miss Tiana, what do you mean?" a man asked from behind her.

She didn't turn around. The very sound of Bluford Tuskee's voice paralyzed her. The thought of him had haunted her ever since that horrible day in February when he had galloped into her yard looking for the "runaway" Fawn.

"Coosa belongs to all of us, Mr. Tuskee," she said through lips gone suddenly stiff. "Gray Fox has no right to gamble with him."

She felt foolish the instant the words came out of her mouth. Both these men, *anyone*, would know that twenty-two-year-old Gray could do as he pleased.

"He may belong to all the Tenkillers, but you're the only one who can ride him," Bluford said gallantly, stepping around to tip his hat to her. "You could put that horse through a flaming hoop."

Tiana tried to smile at him without looking into his eyes. "I don't know about that."

"It's true," he insisted. "I always like watching you ride—you're as beautiful as you are a good rider." He winked at her and turned to Standingdeer. "Don't you agree with that, Cousin Stand?"

The Paint nodded, one black eyebrow raised as his keen glance flashed from Bluford to her.

"You flatter me, Mr. Tuskee," Tiana murmured, uncomfortable as always with the man's flirtatious ways.

Bluford smiled broadly at her and said, "Daddy always declared that there hadn't been a horsewoman in the Nation as good as Tiana Tenkiller since his mama was alive."

The mention of Tobacco Jack made Tiana cringe inside. It brought a softening gleam to Standingdeer's eyes.

"Uncle Jack knew a real rider when he saw one," he said, "*and* a good horse. I'll never forget him helping me break my first young one."

"I wish I knew who killed him," Bluford blurted with a sudden, fierce intensity, his face somber.

Tiana's gaze flew to meet his. Her heart skipped

a beat, then stopped. *He didn't know who killed To-bacco Jack?*

"I thought everyone knew Fawn killed him," she said.

He stared down at her with tortured eyes, shaking his head, all his flirting forgotten. "I rode straight to Running Waters when I found Papa's body," he said, "because Fawn had run away and I knew she'd come back to you. But I only wanted to question her."

"Yet you said she'd had reason to kill your father because he beat her!"

"And I said she had the disposition to do so because you Tenkillers had raised her in the house and caused her to be arrogant," he said. "That's true. But I knew then she didn't do it."

The blood drained out of Tiana's head in one great flood. The branches of the oak swayed in the breeze, their leaves whispering together overhead as if they were telling her secret. The sun peeked through them, moving as the leaves moved, hitting Bluford's face with spots of light.

She forced herself to look at him, searching his face for his innermost thoughts, fighting the dizziness that threatened to overwhelm her. If he knew Fawn was innocent, did he know that Tiana was guilty? Was he trying to make her confess?

Neither his bloodshot eyes nor his set expression told her anything. He looked worse, much worse than he had on that awful day last winter: dark circles lodged beneath his eyes like pools of pain; the muscles of his face tied themselves into knots that jumped and scattered beneath his loose skin. He had lost at least thirty pounds since she had last seen him.

"When you found Fawn that day, dead and just laid out there on my porch," she said, nearly choking on the words, "you . . . glared so angrily at her body, jerked your horse's head around, and galloped away. I thought that meant you were furious because you couldn't take revenge."

"I was furious because she couldn't answer my questions."

At that moment his voice sounded as dead as Fawn.

That horrible frosty day flashed back through Tiana's mind in a rush: the desperate struggle to lift Fawn's body onto Jane Hunt's withers and hold it there while the spirited mare snorted and resisted all the way to Running Waters; the terror that the Tuskees wouldn't believe her story that Fawn had run from the beatings back to Tiana and her old home and had instantly died there on the porch.

Bluford said again, flatly, "The girl didn't do it. I know that for a fact."

"*How* do you know it?" The Paint demanded.

Those were the very words Tiana would have spoken if she could have moved her frozen tongue.

"Old Sudie told me she saw Papa alive after Fawn left her cabin and disappeared in the direction of Running Waters," Bluford said, his voice breaking a little. "But when I asked had she seen anyone else, maybe the killer either coming to Pine Grove or leaving it, she said no."

Tiana's legs went weak beneath her. Old Sudie hadn't been asleep? She'd been watching?

Then Sudie knew that *Tiana* had killed Tobacco Jack.

But why hadn't she told Bluford the truth? Was she protecting Fawn, or did she have another reason?

Well, Tiana couldn't think about that now. She looked from Bluford's ravaged face to Standingdeer's handsome one.

"Somebody was on Pine Grove that day, and whoever it was killed Papa Jack," Bluford said, twisting his hands in anguish. "I can't rest till I find out who."

He touched Standingdeer's arm with fingers that trembled.

"My daddy's spirit is haunting me," he said. "I can't sleep—I can't close my eyes at night."

His torment caught at Tiana's conscience. She ought to confess. She should explain to Bluford that Tobacco Jack's death had been an accident and that she was the one who had caused it. No, the man's own drunken cruelty had caused it. Maybe knowing that would help put Bluford's mind at ease; maybe it would stop his hands from shaking so.

She opened her mouth to speak, but Bluford's next words stopped hers on her tongue.

"Tobacco Jack Tuskee's spirit *will* go to the Nightland," he said, his voice rising louder over the noise of the crowd with each word he spoke.

He threw back his head and shook his fist at the sky. "I aim to find out who killed my daddy, and when I do, I'll invoke the old blood law."

Icy trails of panic ran up and down Tiana's backbone. He meant it.

Instinctively she turned to Stand.

His dark brown eyes had gone to shiny black, glittering hard as marbles. They locked with Bluford's, vowing brotherhood. "We'll find the murderer," he affirmed, "and when we do, we'll kill that dog."

Chapter 2

The bright day narrowed around Tiana, closing in on her and then vanishing as if a giant hand had clamped out the sun. She stood still in the dark.

They would kill her if they knew. Would Old Sudie ever tell?

Worse than the fear of dying, though, was the realization just dawning, washing a new, sick feeling through her veins: The Paint, the wonderful Cherokee hero, The Paint, had just become her sworn enemy. And there was not one thing she could do about it.

Nor about anything else. Even Coosa, her only hope, was being wrenched from her hands! *O-oh*, Gray Fox should be whipped like a thief and locked in the root cellar until he was an old, old man! How dare he gamble even half of Coosa?

And to Standingdeer Chekote, of all people!

The Paint's rich voice rumbled, just outside the circle of gloom that enclosed her, and her foolish, impetuous heart lurched toward its music, even knowing what she knew.

Bluford answered. Standingdeer's deep words gathered, rising and falling, coming closer, then going away, like a swarming hive of bees. The sound of him, strong and tangy as a mouthful of

19

wild honey, melted something inside her as the sun would melt that nectar—enemy though he might be.

Enemy he *was*, and she'd better not forget it. Not only because of Tobacco Jack, but because of Coosa. Hadn't he already started trying to dictate where and when the stallion would run?

Her teeth clenched so hard it made her jaw hurt. What did *he* want with half of Coosa, anyway?

"Tiana! Let's have one more ride before the crowd breaks up today!"

She opened her eyes and turned to see Gray Fox and Early Vann beaming at her. They had been so busy with their plotting that they'd left Callace Stones still holding Coosa.

"No!" she said, trying to think, fighting to get her mind away from The Paint. "He's run four heats today, one full out. That's enough." By Thunder, she would keep *some* measure of control over the horse!

"Now, Sister," Gray Fox said, turning on the full force of his cajoling grin, "Early's slandering Coosa's good name, swearing that that new Blackburn's Whip mare of his can beat The Coosa by at least two lengths."

For one unguarded instant, Tiana's blood rose. The mare couldn't do it. Nothing on four legs, at least nothing in the Nation, could beat Coosa by such a distance.

Early nodded. "She can," he insisted. "Lightfoot Lady has wings."

Tiana pushed down her pride and bit back a contradiction of his words. Coosa had already run plenty of distance for one day.

She took a deep breath, looking from Gray to Early.

"You all know me too well," she said, trying for a light tone that would dismiss the subject out of hand, "but that old trick of a double dare won't work this time. Coosa's earned his rest."

She fastened her gaze on Gray Fox's face. "Besides," she warned, "Papa and Mama are here, and some other people are looking for you. We need to go."

"We saw Papa and Mama right over there, surrounded by people talking politics, as usual," the unperturbed Gray answered. "They'll be there all day, and forty dollars would be mighty nice." He signaled Tiana with his eyes that the money would be more than nice. *Remember*, he was telling her silently, *remember how worried you are about keeping the mares.*

He jingled coins in his pocket; he must've taken the Tenkiller share of the purse when he and The Paint had opened the pouch. He certainly hadn't had any money this morning.

"Add that much extra to our winnings today," he said, "and we'd have a tidy little sum."

Early bragged, "*I'll* be the one with the extra forty. This mare of mine beat Corntassel's bay gelding in three heats last Saturday."

"Corntassel's bay gelding is slow as a turtle," Tiana snapped. "You oughtn't to say his name and Coosa's in the same breath."

"I haven't," Early said. "Yet."

Tiana clenched her fists until her nails cut into her palms. Oh, how she hated to refuse such a challenge! Early and Gray did, indeed, know her well.

But she couldn't let them ruin Coosa. If they did, all future challenges would go forever unmet. Besides, she loved the big silver horse too much; better damage his reputation than his body.

Gray and Early waited for her to rise to their bait, grinning like possums, believing they had succeeded in manipulating her. Dimly Tiana became aware that Standingdeer and Bluford had gone quiet at her back; they, too, were waiting for her answer.

"Coosa won't run again today," she said, fighting for a tone of cool authority to cover her sudden, growing fear. What if The Paint contradicted her? He was a full partner, he owned half the stallion. What if he agreed with Gray?

Tiana swallowed, hard, and forced herself to return Early's confident smile. "We'll race your mare next Saturday, Early. How about here at the Council Oak?"

"Can't come next Saturday," Early said. "It's now or never."

"Then it's now!" Gray Fox exclaimed loudly.

"No!" Tiana cried. "It's never!"

Gray's face twisted. "What's the matter with you, Tiana? We can't let Early get away with these brags of his! Now, you listen to me. Forty dollars—"

"Forty dollars couldn't buy a ride to town on our Coosa."

The Paint's languid voice, supremely assured, sent a liquid thrill tumbling down Tiana's spine.

Then she realized what he had said. Their new partner, her unknowing enemy, agreed with her! He was on *her* side!

She whirled around to flash him a grateful smile. His eyes glinted darkly into hers from beneath the brim of his hat; one laconic nod of his head acknowledged her thanks.

"Now, see here, Chekote," Gray Fox said, frowning at The Paint as intensely as he had smiled at him a few short minutes ago. "Don't mind my sister. It's the two of us"—he gestured from himself to Standingdeer—"who should decide—"

"Looks to me like it's the three of us," The Paint

interrupted lazily. "And Tiana and I say Coosa won't run again today."

He turned back to Bluford as if the matter were settled.

Tiana and I. Her name on his tongue teased her senses. It floated softly, like dandelion fluff dancing on air, through her veins into the core of her body and settled on her heart.

"They wanta see you?" Early's furtive tone, then the movement of Gray's violent start, wrenched Tiana's gaze back to them from The Paint.

Goose bumps broke out on her arms.

Those awful men, Sykes and Walters, were coming across the track through the dappled sunlight; Sykes had his narrow eyes fastened on her. Without thinking, she took a step backward, closer to The Paint.

"I'll see you tonight, Cousin Stand," Bluford was saying. "Maybe if I go home now I can rest a little—while it's daylight."

"Good-bye, Miss Tiana." He inclined his head to her and turned to go without attempting to take leave of Gray and Early. The hateful *yonegas* had approached them.

Sudden shame brought heat to her cheeks. The Paint mustn't know what a disgrace Gray Fox was creating. She could not bear it if he knew!

"Come and watch Coosa move while I walk him," she blurted, already edging away from her brother to lead Standingdeer toward the horse. "I was worried he might be coming up lame when you and Gray led him into the winner's circle."

Thank goodness he couldn't read her mind. Coosa could have crawled his way to the winner's circle and she would've seen nothing but the long, free stride of Standingdeer Chekote, covering the rolling, grassy ground as if his moccasined feet had grown from it.

"I think I would've noticed," he said, following her as she rushed to Coosa's head and took him from the relieved Callace Stones. "Where'd you see him limp?"

"He seemed to be favoring his left hind foot," she lied. "He hurt that hock when he was a baby."

With Standingdeer walking beside her, she led the stallion across the dirt track onto the grass of the narrow valley and trotted him around in a large circle. When she stopped, she chose the point farthest away from Gray and his seedy associates. She threw a quick glance at them, though. If Gray Fox took that money out of his pocket to give it to them, she would stop him. Somehow.

Her eyes also made one quick sweep over the crowd looking for Papa and Mama, but she couldn't spot them.

Stand strolled over to her, shaking his head, his eyes on Coosa. "I don't see anything."

He approached the horse and loosened his girth first, letting the stallion get used to his nearness, making friends by bringing him comfort. He stroked his neck, his back and croup, murmuring to him in soft, rumbling tones that made Tiana's hand tremble on the bit. She would trust that voice, she thought; Coosa was bound to do so.

And he did. He let Stand run his hand down his hind leg, then pick up his foot and examine it as if he'd known him forever.

While The Paint was occupied, Tiana stole another glance at Gray. He and the horrid white men appeared to be arguing. Gray was adjusting the bow of the soft silk tie at his throat, worried about his appearance as usual, trying to build his confidence.

Early had disappeared, fortunately, and she'd brought Stand a far enough distance away so that the shouts floating from the track to the horse owners at their wagons by the edge of the woods drowned out Sykes' and Walters' apparently heated words. Maybe, somehow, she could get Gray through this crisis without Mama and Papa and the whole Nation knowing what dire times had come upon the Tenkillers.

Tiana sighed, narrowing her eyes against the afternoon sunlight, staring at Gray Fox in his white suit bright and slim as a candle against the huge dark trunk of the tree. She sent him a message with her thoughts, as they used to do when they were children: he had better hold his own with those parasite gamblers. He had better keep that money, and he had better do so quickly and discreetly.

Not only would it be horribly embarrassing for people in the Nation to know how desperate their troubles were, but if Papa and Mama happened onto this scene, it could be disastrous. They might not leave for Washington City tomorrow, and much as she would love to keep them home, that would ruin the delegation's chances at persuading Congress to repeal the Indian Removal Act. The Principal People *must* obtain permission to keep their homes and their land, and Papa was the most diplomatic negotiator in all the Cherokee Nation.

"There's nothing wrong with this horse," Standingdeer declared.

Tiana's gaze flew back to him. He set Coosa's foot down, straightened up, and looked at her, his gliding motions as captivating to watch as the flight of an eagle. His heavily muscled arms and shoulders moved with that same graceful power.

The cold knot re-formed in the pit of her stomach. Just a few moments ago, this man had sworn to kill her.

Yet as he stepped toward her, she had no desire to run from him.

The pale yellow of his hunting shirt, open in a buttonless deep vee on his chest, made his skin look like molten copper. Her fingertips tingled, wanting to touch its warmth in spite of everything her mind was telling her.

"What you may have seen is a spot of soreness in his stifle," he said. "That comes from asking him for more speed in the race for a longer time than you've done in his practice runs."

He nodded briskly. "I'll let him rest a day and then give him a good, slow gallop," he said. "Every time after that I'll push him a little harder."

Tiana's blood roared in her ears. Could she possibly have heard him right? Her gaze froze to his. "*You*? You'll do nothing of the kind."

"I surely will." Standingdeer reached back, turning sideways to her to run a possessive hand over Coosa's hip. "It's only six weeks until the Dahlonega Stakes."

She rushed forward to lay her hand on the stallion's withers. "I have not yet said that this horse will run in the Dahlonega Stakes!"

Standingdeer pivoted to face her. "But I have." He spoke in the flat tone of absolute authority.

He pushed back his hat and looked down at her, his dark gaze hard and steady. He had spoken, and that was the way it would be.

Fury raced through Tiana like fire before a wind. Conceited wretch! Insufferable boss! Who did he think he was?

She couldn't talk fast enough to put him in his place. "And what do you mean, criticizing my training of him? What do *you* know?"

"I know you haven't pushed him fast enough, far enough every day," he said. "I just told you that."

Tiana wanted to fly into his face and flog him. Words popped from her mouth like rocks hot from a fire. "I suppose you were hiding in the bushes watching me work him."

"I didn't have to. I can see it just as plain by looking at him now."

Tiana moved forward so fast that Coosa snorted and jerked his head. She stood toe-to-toe with The Paint, all fear of him forgotten.

"For five years," she said, biting off each word, "since I was fourteen, I've been training the Tenkiller running horses, as well as some for other people. And they have been winning. My reputation among the many good horsemen of this Nation is my greatest pride."

She forced her teeth to unclench. "Exactly how many horses have *you* trained to run, Mr. Chekote?"

"This'll be my first one," he replied.

And gave her a taunting grin!

"Over my dead body," she said. "*I* campaign this horse. I raised him, I train him, I campaign him."

"Well, Tenkiller or no, you need help with him," he said with sarcastic certainty. "You've been afraid you'd make him peak too soon, but he can take it. You'll be surprised—he can likely run even faster than you think."

And then, *of all things in this world to do,* he lifted one muscular arm and leaned on Coosa, lounging against him with one elbow resting on her saddle! As if he were taking possession of him!

She clenched her fists and shouted, "*You* can likely run even faster than you think! I'm taking after you with a riding crop if you don't get away from this horse—at that card game you won *half* of what Coosa wins, not *all* of the right to train him!"

The Paint threw back his head and laughed. A

deep, rolling belly laugh that echoed across the open field and into the trees that surrounded it.

That insult added to the others was too much to bear. Tiana, dimly aware but past caring that people all around them had turned to look, dropped the reins and began pounding on his chest with both fists. She might as well have pounded on a brick wall.

She might as well have thrown her entire body against the granite cliff on Whitebird Mountain.

She might as well have thrown herself *off* that cliff, for Standingdeer Chekote grabbed her wrists with his huge hands.

His callused fingers stilled her arms effortlessly, using a deep, easy strength that made her heart stop.

She tried to pull away but he held her helpless, his hands moving lightly against her arms, cradling her skin, her muscles, her very *bones* into his warm, hardened palms. Their delicious roughness threatened to rub the stone of her anger into dust.

Tiana fought that, trying to keep her fury whole and hard and hot inside her, but she couldn't. Because she couldn't stop looking at his face. His eyes burned like dark, glittering stars; his lips curved full and sensuous across even white teeth. A lock of shiny black hair fell across his forehead.

She wanted desperately to reach out and brush it back.

"I grant you can train a horse to run, Miss Tiana, but this is my horse, too, and you still have a great deal to learn."

He was so sure of himself she wanted to slap him.

Yet beneath his certain, calm exterior a pulsing tension had begun to surge. She heard it now, throbbing in the music of his voice; she saw it leaping in his eyes.

The man was a deluded *una-sti-ski*, a crazy person. She must remember that.

"And you think you're the one to teach me?"

"I am," he said. "Listen to me and you can throw away your riding crop."

"You talk as if I beat my horses!"

She jerked her arms against his grip. He held them. Could he feel the skipping of her pulse beneath his thumbs?

"You were talking about beating *me*," he drawled. "I naturally might think that's how you treat your horses."

Tiana gritted her teeth. "I was *not* talking about beating you."

One of his black eyebrows shot up. "You planned to chase me with a crop to see how fast I could run, but you wouldn't beat me with it?"

His half grin made a taunting slash of white across his coppery, weathered face. "No wonder you need help with your training program, Tiana! Haven't you learned yet that empty threats never work for long?"

"Overbearing, high-handed, arrogant *galagi'na!*" she cried. "Vain buck deer! I'll show you empty threats! You aren't my master. Turn me loose!"

He did. And as she got her wish, a strange disappointment shot through her, beneath her pounding anger.

"I'm not your master, Miss Tenkiller," he said, his tone suddenly invested with a sharp edge she hadn't heard in it before. "But, like it or not, I am your partner."

She straightened her back and used her haughtiest voice. "I am weary of your insults, jolly though they may be, Mr. Chekote," she said. "I can train a horse that'll run circles around any one you train. I challenge you. Your choice. Any two-year-old at Running Waters."

"No," he said. "Six weeks is all we have."

They were almost touching. Her hands shook, she couldn't seem to control them; her breasts came too close to brushing his chest. His hard-muscled chest that was strong as the mountains themselves. She needed to get away from him.

"Six weeks?" Her voice came out light and shallow. She cleared her throat. "What wampum belt says six weeks is all we have?"

A trace of that mocking grin touched his lips again, but his voice sounded hard as granite.

"*My* wampum belt. I never stay long in one place. Looks like this trip we'll have to share the same horse."

"That's insane! Do you want to ruin Coosa?"

"I'm going to improve Coosa."

She stepped back and slipped her arm around the stallion's neck. Reason. She must try to reason with him.

"Evidently you do own half this horse," she said with a desolate sigh. "And Gray Fox and I will certainly halve his winnings with you. But I'm the one who'll oversee his training—I've raised him from a baby and he won't run for anybody but me."

The Paint's dark gaze was relentless. "We'll see. Most of 'em give their hearts to me after a time or two."

I'll bet they do, she thought as her strength began to bend before the force of his. *I'm not a gambling woman, but that I would lay a wager on. And not just horses, either.*

He said, "We'll work with him together."

The rich depth of his tone set Tiana to thinking about the feel of his hands.

"Stay away from us!" she burst out. "Coosa's the only chance I have!"

"Chance for what?"

Her eyes darted away from his; she half turned to look at Gray Fox. Her heart dropped. He was gone! He and the two *yonegas* had completely disappeared!

Probably to go out behind the wagons somewhere so he could give them the Tenkillers' half of the purse money without her—or Papa—seeing him. She had to stop him before they could get the money and be gone!

"Chance for what?" The Paint repeated.

"Chance to keep all my horses," she cried over her shoulder. She led Coosa forward so she could tighten his girth without going near Standingdeer again. "Excuse me. I must go now."

But he strode nearer, to help her mount, his intent gaze capturing hers.

"I'll be at Running Waters shortly after sunup day after tomorrow," he said. "To ride before it gets too hot."

She pushed the horse from him and flew onto his back to escape Standingdeer's troubling touch.

"No! Don't come!"

He stepped backward, caught Coosa's bit, and held it. Then he flashed her that infuriating grin. "Whatever happened to the famous Cherokee hospitality?"

Then his face went hard and solemn as he added, "The *Tenkiller* hospitality?"

"Let me go!" she cried, terrified by the storm of mixed fear and desire rising in her. "Stay away from Running Waters. You'll get your share of the winnings."

"I don't doubt that, Tiana," he said harshly. "That isn't the reason I'm going to help with the horse."

"Then why are you?"

"Because he's half mine and I don't intend for you Tenkillers to have complete control," he snapped, "and because I intend for him to win at Dahlonega."

"He isn't *going* to Dahlonega! How many times do I have to tell you?" Frantically she tried to think of something to say that would stop this insanity once and for all. "I entered him in a match race two days before that at Pinetown."

"Scratch him. The Dahlonega purse is much bigger."

"And we'd have to run the gauntlet of gold-crazy scoundrels and Indian-hating Georgians to get a chance at it! You don't strike me as the kind of man who'd risk his horse and his life for nothing but money."

"I'm not scared of the chicken-snake Georgians."

"Neither am I! I just don't care to have anything to do with them." With her heels and her hands she signaled Coosa to back up.

"I'll protect you, Tiana."

The unexpected words, even said as a mocking challenge, stopped her still. They struck all the way to her worried, weary soul. She looked down at him for a long, long minute, wishing, *yearning* that they could be gently spoken and true.

The Paint would protect her!

He'd be making a different cry if he knew she was the killer who'd taken from him the only family he'd ever had.

"I must hurry!" she cried. "Drop your hand and let me go."

She swung away from Standingdeer, fast, and he watched her head Coosa across the meadow at a trot, the frantic tone of her voice ringing in his ears. He closed his mind to it; he opened his hands and wiped the palms across the tail of his hunting shirt to rid them of the feel of her delicate wrists. The beautiful, fiery, frightened Tiana was a Tenkiller.

But still he watched her ride away from him, her slender, curving body sitting the magnificent horse with as much natural skill as a Comanche. She had ridden all the way to the edge of the trees before he could will himself to turn away.

Only to come face-to-face with her father.

From less than ten yards away, Nicotai Tenkiller was hurrying straight toward him, accompanied by a dozen or more men. As they surrounded Stand, the old, half-forgotten rage began to build in his gut like that of a bear in a trap. His hands clenched into fists. He had hoped to live the rest of his life without ever seeing this man again.

"Standingdeer," Nicotai said heartily, holding out his hand, "so good to have you home at last! We need to talk."

Stand ignored the hand Tenkiller offered. Nicotai clapped him on the shoulder, anyway.

"Otterlifter here has just had the best idea!" he boomed. "You should come to Washington City with me and help the new delegation convince Congress to repeal the Removal Act. We're leaving tomorrow morning."

Thick, hot anger boiled up and outward into every one of Standingdeer's veins.

I wouldn't go to a dogfight with you, Tenkiller.

Yet somehow he managed to be cold and civil. "I only arrived three days ago after traveling fifteen hundred miles," he said, glancing from one welcoming, smiling face to another without giving a trace of a smile in return. "I have no desire to go anywhere, much less to Washington."

He could not resist adding, as his gaze came

back to rest on Nicotai Tenkiller's bright and hopeful one, "Particularly with you."

Tenkiller's expression changed to one of puzzlement, but before he could reply, a short, skinny man in the group cried out, "But you would have much influence on Congress—you're The Paint, you're a great hero!"

Another man called, "Yes, you could remind Andrew Jackson that you whipped the Creeks for him at Horseshoe Bend. Make him feel guilty. He owes you, he owes us all!"

"Andrew Jackson has no conscience," Stand and Nicotai Tenkiller said, speaking at the same time.

Stand clamped his mouth shut and gritted his teeth until they hurt, galled to the bone at agreeing with this man he detested. He turned his back and pushed his way out of the circle of eager faces, but before he had gone a dozen steps, he felt Nicotai at his elbow.

"Leave me alone!" he growled. "For God's sake, man, what do you think I am?"

"A hero who might save his Nation if he tried," Tenkiller answered quietly. "The very one of all the Cherokee who might stop the United States government from giving our homes to Georgia and forcing us to move West."

"No power on this earth can stop that," Stand said, his throat raw with grief. "Just as none could save my mother from you."

He got a fleeting moment of satisfaction from the shocked surprise that suffused Nicotai Tenkiller's face.

"You knew about . . . your mother and me?" he asked. "How old were you then?"

"Old enough," Stand shot back, the ancient bitterness welling up. "Old enough to see you kissing her one night in the grove of pines beside the pond. Old enough to wonder about that lying

story you told of her being thrown from your
buggy as you supposedly drove her home from
nursing your sick wife. Old enough to know you
were responsible for her death!"

"I didn't kill her. I loved your mother."

Stand snorted his disbelief.

Nicotai made a motion as if he would take him
by the arm, then seemed to think better of it and
turned to wave away the group of men behind
him. "I'll talk to The Paint alone," he called to
them. "Meet me later at the Oak."

The men reluctantly drifted away while Stand
stayed rooted where he was, wanting to leave this
man he hated, but wanting more to hear about the
mother he'd lost when he was twelve. Nicotai
Tenkiller looked at him. Unjustly, the man had
hardly aged at all in the past eighteen years, Stand
thought.

"A man can love more than one woman,"
Nicotai said quietly. "And a woman can love more
than one man."

He paused—expecting agreement, Stand supposed. But Stand waited in silence for him to go
on.

"My wife was sick and fretful with childbed fever for eighteen moons after birthing our first
baby, who died. Your mother was living in her
brother's house, heartbroken by your father's de-
sertion. She began to spend much time with us—
she was a wonderful nurse to my wife. We were
two lonely people who took comfort and found
joy in each other."

Resentment rose in Stand like a storm rising
over a mountain. "And she found death. If you'd
left her alone, she'd still be alive."

"Her death was an accident that could've happened anytime, anywhere. The horses shied beneath a low-hanging branch, and she was dragged

from the buggy and thrown to the ground. It broke her neck."

A memory he had suppressed for more than twenty years floated into Stand's vision: the sight of his mother's body, seemingly unharmed and breathtakingly beautiful, being carried into the house at Pine Grove, with Nicotai stumbling along behind it, tears streaming down his ashen face.

But he pushed it away again. *Somebody* had to be responsible for that lonely little boy's grief. Tenkiller.

"Get away from me," he said harshly. "And don't mention your hopeless politics to me again. I wouldn't travel across this meadow with you or anybody else named Tenkiller."

"I thought you'd gone into business with 'us Tenkillers.' What was all that I heard from the winner's circle about our being partners in Coosa?"

"That was a fluke. I'd never have sat down at the gaming table with Gray if I'd known who he was."

"Don't be irrational, son," Nicotai Tenkiller said softly. "Your mother's death was a horrible, senseless accident, and in your heart you know that. We Tenkillers want to be your friends."

"Well, that's not what I want," Stand said, craving escape from that incessantly kind, reasonable voice. "The only dealings I intend to have with your family are business ones—half of that stud horse is mine."

He turned on his heel and strode off, making his way blindly away from the crowd, which was madly cheering the horses on the track. He meant what he had said and he intended to live by it every minute he spent here in the Eastern Nation. Any contact he had with any of the Tenkillers would be purely business, and that included Tiana.

The closer Tiana came to the grove of red oaks where a dozen or so carriages, including hers and Gray's, had been left in the shade, the surer she was that the blur of white flashing intermittently among the shining black vehicles was Gray Fox's suit. She sent Coosa around the end of the line of buggies at a lope.

It was his suit. As she rode up behind the two hateful *yonegas*, Sykes, the tall one, raised a stick and hit Gray, who fell, trying to deflect the blow with his arm.

She sent Coosa straight at the man, screaming, "Leave my brother alone! I'll have the whole Nation down on you. Get out of here!"

Walters, who was closer to her, scrambled awkwardly out of her path, as did Sykes; she brought Coosa around in a tight, quick turn so she could see both of them.

"Get away," she shouted, "or I'll run you over! What do you mean beating on him, two against one?"

"He owes us!" Sykes yelled. "And he'd better pay!"

"I *did* pay!" Gray said, getting to his feet, brushing dirt and leaves from his white suit.

"You can hardly say that," Walters disagreed in his smooth voice. He took a few quick steps so he could stand a step behind Sykes. "If you'd had the *whole* purse, you couldn't have paid all you owe us."

"You people have no business in the Nation in the first place," Tiana said, riding right up on them again before she stopped, making them move back from Gray. "You had better leave it while you're still in one piece."

Walters chuckled and looked at Gray Fox. "Your little sister shows more courage than you do, Mr. Tenkiller."

"Yeah," Sykes sneered. "She's the one with the guts!"

"Both of you," Tiana interrupted, "listen to me. Stay away from my brother. Don't ever come near him again."

Sykes growled, "We'll come near him, all right. We aim to get the rest of our money from him."

"He has no more money," she snapped, sick at heart because Gray had already given up their half of the purse. Without a weapon to use to threaten these white men, she couldn't hope to get it back. "You can't get blood out of a turnip."

"But we *can* get blood out of a Red Indian," Walters intoned, taking a step toward her. The cruel edge in his otherwise soft voice made goose bumps spring up on Tiana's arms. "And that we will certainly do if he doesn't deliver one hundred and fifty dollars to us sometime during the next ten days."

Her whole body chilled. A hundred and fifty dollars! It might as well be that many thousands! And they still had nothing to ransom the mares!

"That's out of the question," she said, keeping her voice steady and her chin up through sheer force of will. "Your expectations are not reasonable in the least."

"Yeah," Gray grumbled. "I told you I'd need time."

"Ten days," Walters said smoothly. "No more."

"I *will* ride out into the crowd and get help," Tiana said. "If you men don't leave here immediately, you won't leave at all."

She met Walters' cool blue eyes again, and then Sykes' narrow, cruel ones, the color of moss on a rock.

Walters made a gesture with one plump white hand: Sykes dropped his stick.

"Before we go, my dear," Walters said, "you should know that we are perfectly serious about collecting the remainder of our money."

"Good luck," she said, trying to sound tough enough to conceal her panic. A hundred and fifty dollars!

"You've got ten days—sweetheart," Sykes said nastily as they began edging toward the woods.

"Don't give me orders," she said. "Get out."

When the huge oak trees had concealed them, Sykes' raw voice floated back out into the clearing. "We'll *make* you take orders, Squaw Gal!" he yelled. "Jist you wait!"

He sounded like an angry child screaming at a playmate. If only he were no more dangerous than that!

"How could you do this to us?" Tiana demanded, throwing herself off Coosa to run to Gray Fox, torn by the equal desires to hug and to pummel him. "Where can we get a hundred and fifty dollars?"

"Stay out of this," he muttered, holding her at arm's length, still brushing himself off, obviously not badly hurt. "I'll take care of it."

"Stay out of this?" she repeated with a small, hysterical laugh. "If I'd stayed out of it, you might be dead right now."

He didn't respond as she turned back for Coosa and led him to their carriage at a hurried trot, her mind whirling.

"Let's go home by ourselves so we can figure out what to do," Tiana said as she brought Coosa to a stop at the tailgate. "We'll load up, find Mama and Papa, and tell them we'll meet them at Running Waters."

"All right," Gray murmured absently. Finally he

added, "You were a good distraction. Thanks, Little Sister."

Helpless frustration choked back all the words that rose in her throat; she clamped her lips tight and threw herself into searching behind the seat for Coosa's halter.

"Sykes and Walters wouldn't kill me," Gray assured her as he went to get the team and hitch them to the carriage. "They just want to scare me into getting the rest of their money."

"And you can't do it!" Tiana burst out, throwing the lead around Coosa's neck and untacking him. "You had no right to give them even half of this purse—that money was to save our mares!"

She untied Danny, the other horse they'd raced that day, from his tree and took him to the side of the carriage opposite Coosa. "Did you give them *all* of our share?"

"I had to! They threatened to hurt you, Sister, if I didn't."

"Don't use that excuse! They'd never have known I existed if you hadn't been gambling with them. Gray, *when* are you ever going to learn?"

Her fingers trembled with rage while she made sure both racehorses were securely tied to the back of the carriage; then she loaded the saddle behind the seat. She might as well save her breath, and she knew it. Mere words would never be strong enough to pull Gray Fox away from gambling.

She bit her lip and forced herself into silence as she climbed up onto the seat. Gray settled himself beside her and took up the lines. He shot her a pleading look which she ignored.

Ten days! One hundred and fifty dollars! And *more*, if she still wanted to save the foundation mares!

She did. Oh, dear Lord, she had to save them for Papa.

But ten days would be gone before she knew it, and this one certainly hadn't brought her any closer to paying the note on them. The low-life gamblers had half of her purse and The Paint had the other.

She and Coosa had worked like the *U'tlun'ta*, the Old Spearfinger, was after them, and they had absolutely nothing to show for it.

Except a new partner so powerfully troubling he could bring her whole world crashing down around her head.

She gripped the side of the seat until the brass trim bit into the palms of her hands. Oh, how could she be so drawn to him?

Standingdeer Chekote was someone she had to leave alone.

And he had to leave her and Coosa alone if they were to keep winning. But how could she make him stay away?

The futility of her argument with Stand washed over her in a wave.

"And another thing," she said tiredly, turning to look full in Gray Fox's face. "You ought to be whipped for gambling away an interest in Coosa when I didn't know a thing about it!"

"I almost won that hand," he said thoughtfully, shaking the lines over the horses' backs. "If I'd had another queen, I'd have won The Paint's money and kept all of the horse."

"If, *if!*" she cried. "Well, one thing is for certain. The Paint would never gamble all he had on one hand. You might take lessons from him."

"Um-hmm," he said, his eyes straight ahead as they drove slowly into the edge of the crowd to look for their parents. "Speaking of The Paint, Sister . . . I have a plan."

"I hope it has nothing to do with gambling. And I hope it has nothing to do with the emergency money that Papa keeps in the safe for us. We are *not* dipping into that—we might need it desperately later."

"No. My plan has to do with making more money, fast."

"Thank goodness!" she said dryly. "Then those no-good cohorts of yours won't kill you and maybe me, too, and we won't lose the best broodmares in the Nation and break our papa's heart."

She turned around to see if the racehorses were moving along smoothly behind the carriage as they wound their way toward the spot where Gray had last seen their parents.

"I know, I know," he said, his voice heavy with regret. For an instant her heart went out to him, to the sweet big brother she had once adored. Guilt stabbed at her for talking to him in this way that was so mean.

"I'll save the mares, Ti, I promise. Now, don't worry. As soon as we get home I'll send a message to Corntassel. He'll race at the drop of a feather, and Coosa can beat anything he owns."

He shook the lines over the team again and pulled them to the side to avoid one of the racehorses on its way to the track. His worried eyes almost met hers.

"The only trick is that we must make sure that The Paint doesn't get wind of it," he said. "If he doesn't know Coosa has run, we can keep all of the purse."

"He *will* know," Tiana said between clenched teeth. "The entire *Nation* will know within half a day after you set the race. You know that, Gray. You've lived here all your life. And lower your voice, or someone'll hear you now."

"Maybe not," he pleaded. "Maybe we can keep it a secret."

"Now, you listen to me," Tiana said in a furious

whisper, although no one seemed to be paying the slightest attention to them. "I will not have you disgracing the Tenkiller name any more than you've already done. That kind of dishonesty could ruin our standing in the community—and after Papa has worked so hard for the good of the Nation! No. The answer to that suggestion is Absolutely Not."

"So you'd rather let Sykes and Walters kill me?" he asked in a pitiful voice.

"You just told me they won't kill you."

"I said they weren't trying to kill me today. Ten days from now, if I don't have the money, they might."

Tiana gave him a hard look, then heaved a great sigh and slumped back into her seat.

"I'll think of something else, Gray," she said. "Don't send a message to Corntassel. I'll think of something."

Chapter 3

∽◡◠◡◠

Two mornings later, Tiana went outside even before Grandmother Sun had lit the sky over Hiwassee Mountain with the first pale streaks of Morning Red. Running Waters lay without stirring in the deepest blackness of the night, the impenetrable dark that gathered, always, just before she, Grandmother Sun, came up there. Tiana stood without moving on the back porch.

Even through the thick darkness she could feel the spirit of the day beginning to grow. This wretched night would soon be gone, thank God in Heaven and Friend Thunder.

One of the dogs sleeping beneath the veranda stirred and groaned; the leaves in the big magnolia at the side of the house rustled and whispered— from a restless bird, no doubt, not from the wind. There wasn't even a hint of a breeze.

The heavy, sweet scent of magnolia blossoms mixed with the fainter one of Mama's white roses. From a bit farther away she could smell the fresh-cut hay in the fields and, from even farther, surrounding the whole world, the rich, damp fragrance of the slumbering mountains. She held out her arms and stretched them high to draw in a long, deep breath.

Home. No place else could ever be home.

Wake-up pricklings ran along her limbs; she dashed across the porch and down the steps. The smooth, sawed planks beneath her bare feet gave way to the hard earth of the drive and then to the dewy grass of the yard. Its cool wetness sank between her toes and drenched her to her ankles.

She stayed in it, though, long after she could have taken the path, enjoying the sudden, alerting sensations it sent spreading through her. The dragging fatigue of the worries that had kept her awake until long after midnight fell away. Today would be a better day than yesterday and the unsettling day before had been.

Her feet found the trail that ran from the two kitchen buildings up to the house. It was still too dark to see clearly, but she could picture the worktables, the crocks and the pots and skillets inside them, the cooking-hearth fires banked to nothing but ashes and a few hot coals.

Just as she could picture the horses sleeping or munching hay in the dark stables and the crocks of milk and butter standing in the cold running water inside the springhouse. And the servants in bed in their cabins in the quarters, dreaming their last dreams of the night.

She could see Poor John, the rooster, opening one yellow eye in the chicken roost to see whether day had come.

Tiana pulled all those visions to her and wrapped them around her like a soft, warm quilt. She would keep them all, exactly as they were this morning, forever.

Her right foot dipped into the low spot in the path where rainwater sometimes stood, and the left one hit the gentle rise in the packed earth that signaled the fork in the path. Every morning she took the left branch, which led to the barns and stables; that was the first place she went every day of her life. But this day would be different. This day she would go to the springs.

This day she needed help from the waters under the earth—and from the earth itself, and from the heavens above the earth—help to do what the elders called "be of good mind." She had to learn how to take what was done and turn it on to a better path.

Tears stung her eyes as she thought of her parents' departure at dawn the day before, a too-quick departure after a too-short visit, one filled with other people anxious to have their views represented in Washington City and more travel to go to the ones who couldn't come to Running Waters. Soon, surely someday *soon*, all that would be over and the Tenkillers' family life on the plantation would return to normal.

Soon Papa and Mama would come back to the Nation victorious, with a guarantee that the Cherokees would not be forced to move West. Then, if the Tenkillers' bloodstock were still grazing in the pastures of Running Waters, and if Gray Fox was working the plantation with her training and running the horses, and if the emergency money was still in the safe, everything would be the way it used to be.

But for that to happen, Gray had to stop carousing, gambling everything away. If he kept it up, he might be dead when his parents came home, murdered by those low-life strangers.

And she must rid her conscience of the accident that had killed Tobacco Jack. No one else must ever find out.

These thoughts lent wings to her feet; she flew toward the quickening sound of the bubbling, purling waters, the *Tanta-ta-rara* that gave the plantation its name. How could she, one nineteen-year-old girl, turn the terrible things that she and Gray had done onto a better path?

And how could she turn these wild, opposing, bewildering feelings for The Paint, still roiling inside her, undiminished by the long hours of the night, onto a better path? That question sent a shivering through her whole body.

Oh, what she would give to be able to ask Mama—to look out across the river after the sun came up and see Mama and Papa in their road carriage, hitched to the team of bay geldings, floating toward home instead of away from it on the ferry! And then rolling up the long, curving driveway to stop beneath the portico!

Papa and Mama would climb down and hug her (and hug Gray, too, of course), and then, their faces beaming, they would announce that the delegation from the Cherokee Nation to the United States Congress had been a great success. The Indian Removal Act had been soundly repealed, they would say, and Georgia had been told to take back her land- and gold-hungry citizens and keep them within her old boundaries, because all the Cherokees would stay in their homes forever.

The Nation would remain at the Center of the Earth. Oh! That would be the heaven the missionaries talked about!

The ground around the springs sloped downward; Tiana's bare foot slipped on the trail, damp from the spray of the water. She was here. In good time. Grandmother Sun would give her the answers.

She felt her way downward, slowly, creeping through the heavy dark air filled with the spray and the noise of the springs, down and down to the place where the talking waters bubbled up out of the earth. Reaching out with both hands, she found the rocky ledge she remembered, sat down, and crossed her legs under her, facing the east.

When Grandmother Sun rose, creating that magic moment in the day when the dividing wall between the natural world and the supernatural one was weakest, she, Tiana Tenkiller, would be here to greet her. And to ask all the Spirits, Cherokee and Christian, what she should do.

The dawn came creeping, pearl-gray, into the land. Mountains piled upon mountains took slow shape before Tiana's eyes, then hill upon hill. Pale mist concealed the valleys below.

Grandmother Sun slipped up over Hiwassee Mountain and stuck her finger through the fog. One at a time, a dogwood tree, a rock overhang, a gushing burst of the springs lit up in green, red-brown, and silver, bright as paint. They gleamed hot as the colors in a fire.

But still, some cool, heavy vapors remained. They hung white and thick in the valley and over the springs, in all the low places nearby.

Tiana peered into them but could see nothing. They shifted and remade themselves and drifted some more, forming shapes with no meaning, figures with no name. Then, finally, as the sunlight took possession of more of the earth and its power began to throw heat against her face, she glimpsed the long, moving shape of a horse.

It was running. Then it stopped and threw up its head. As she stared at it, the fog that formed its feet broke off and floated away; gradually, its body, too, disappeared. Only the rippling mane was left, for a moment; then the horse was gone completely.

Tiana watched that spot for a long time after, and listened with her whole self to the springs, but no words came to her ears out of all their talk. Finally, as Grandmother Sun drove the very last shreds of the mists back into the night, Tiana rose to her feet.

Coosa. It must have been Coosa. That was all she had seen.

How could she use Coosa to turn Gray onto a better path? Or her feelings for The Paint? How could a horse hide her secret and assuage her guilt?

The path took her back to the house the same way it had brought her from it, but now everything was different: the plantation was awake. Smoke rose, curling gray into the air, from the chimney of the summer kitchen. Poor John and the other roosters crowed over and over again. Voices floated out from the quarters and from the barns. The broodmares and their babies shone, moving quietly against the green of their pastures like loose jewels on a velvet cloth, white and red and black and brown.

Home. She could never live anyplace else. Ever since the first boy had ever come courting her, she had had a secret plan: she would marry a man with no land and no family so that he would have to live here with her. By that time, though, she would probably want her own house. There was a fine site for building on the south side of the plantation, on a hill rising high in a bend of the Coonasauga River.

With one last glance at the mares Gray had gambled away, the mares she was determined to save, Tiana left the path and ran toward the stables through the high, wet grass of the hay meadow; when she got there, she ducked between the boards of the fence to get into the south paddock. It was empty—none of the horses they stalled at night had been turned out yet. Here the nighttime quiet held fast.

But when she'd crossed the big pen and come into the grove of maples that shaded the stables and the small hay barn set at right angles to it, she saw that the bottom half of the double doors stood ajar. The iron latch dangled, knocking lightly against the wood.

Gabriel must have gotten here before her, but she found that hard to believe—he was a notorious lie-abed. Papa might have sold or traded him years ago if he hadn't had such a gifted hand with the horses.

She pulled the doors all the way open and stepped into the gloom. The morning was heating up fast; the stables' coolness was already fading away. The stillness felt so complete that, for an instant, Tiana thought somehow the horses had gone.

"Gabe?" she called.

Coosa nickered and kicked at his stall. Danny whinnied and hung his head into the aisle to look for her. Gabe didn't answer.

Tiana ran the length of the aisle to prop open the doors at the opposite end. Then, in the sunlight that poured in, she opened the feed room, filled the small, oak-splint buckets, and went from stall to stall, dispensing oats, stroking noses, inspecting legs and feet, talking to her pets.

"You all are such good horses!" she crooned again and again. "We'll get the right races and save our mares yet!"

She slid open the door to the big stallion's stall and went in, letting him have a bite from the bucket before she poured the feed into the manger on the wall.

"Surely The Paint won't actually come here today," she whispered, stroking the long hairs of his mane while he ate. "Surely he won't. I *have* to keep control of you—the sign I saw this morning at the springs told me so."

Her hand went still on Coosa's silky neck. "Yet I wish he would come," she admitted in a desperate whisper.

By the time Gabriel arrived, she had the horses all turned out and was sitting on the fence watching them find their freedom again.

"You early, Miss Tiana," the servant said, as he did every day. Then he added, "I reckoned you and that Coosa wanta rest some more."

"You're late, Gabe," she said, as she did every day. "I'm only going to lunge him to get the soreness out."

The man, who'd been stable boss at Running Waters for as long as she could remember, leaned on the fence beside her; they talked about plans for each horse until the sun was halfway up the sky. Tiana's stomach growled.

"I'm going to lunge him now," she said, climbing down from the fence, "and then I'll have breakfast before I ride The Butterfly."

"You takes that there hoss right on to the round pen," Gabriel said, moving away to go get a halter and lunge line. "I be there jist shortly with the 'quipment."

Coosa led with only Tiana's hand beneath his throat, as he had since he was a baby. Gabriel brought the halter, line, and long buggy whip down the hill to her and then returned to the stables to go about his business.

Tiana had the stallion up to a canter in the second direction, there in the open round pen, when a heat even hotter than the sun on her back fired her skin. She slipped the loop of the line over her wrist, lowered the long whip, and turned, already knowing who was there.

The Paint.

He was leaning on the plank fence, one booted foot planted on the bottom rail, his big, powerful arms crossed on the top one. The wide-brimmed black hat was gone: his hair glistened like cut coal in the sun's light. Tied in a long club at the back of his neck, it threw his face into stark relief, like a living sculpture in wood.

"I see you've got your whip," he drawled. "So you're all ready to do some professional training."

Instant fury mixed with the pull she felt toward him. Good!

An angry order for him to get off the place sprang to her lips, but she bit it back. That wouldn't be sufficient—at the race she had told him not to come, yet here he was.

She tried for the same devil-may-care kind of tone that he had just used, calling back, over the rhythm of Coosa's hooves striking in the soft, sandy ground of the pen, "Oh, but I haven't hit him yet!"

She waved the long braided whip and popped it over the stallion's croup. He picked up speed, cantering around the circle to come between her and Standingdeer.

"You see!" she said when he had passed. "Threats *do* work."

But as the words left her mouth, the horse slowed, then slowed again. He always knew when her attention went elsewhere.

Tiana popped the whip in the air behind him. She would *not* give over control. Not to Coosa, and not to her feelings for The Paint.

Coosa, the turncoat, slowed and broke to a trot.

The Paint's dark gaze flicked from the rebellious horse to Tiana; he laughed. "What were you saying about threats that work?"

It made her so mad that she popped the whip

again and yelled at Coosa. For good measure, she kicked dirt at him.

The Paint, still grinning, shifted his weight to his other hip in an easy, powerful gesture that flexed the long saddleman's muscles along his thighs. The sight made her blood run hot.

It destroyed the fragile hold she had on her nerves and her tongue.

"What're you doing here, anyway?" she snapped.

"I told you I was coming."

"Yes. You did. Have you ever heard of *asking* instead of telling, or are good manners not the custom in the West?"

Coosa came between them again, but The Paint's low chuckle floated to her, anyway, as disquieting as his slanting half smile.

"Out West, I'm not around people very often," he said. "I guess I've forgotten my manners."

His tone sounded very matter-of-fact, but underneath it, so deep he probably didn't even know it was there, she heard a trace of loneliness. What a forsaken way to live!

She fought down the twinge of sympathy. "Maybe if you weren't always teasing and taunting and picking a fight, people would want to be with you more," she said tartly.

Standingdeer raised one eyebrow and cocked his head in mock amazement. "I'll bet you're right," he said in his slow teasing way. "I never once thought of that."

Coosa laid back his ears and cranked his tail as if to say that he had traveled enough monotonous circles around this pen for one day. He stopped.

"Better threaten him again," Standingdeer said.

"You have run that jest into the ground," Tiana said, gritting her teeth, grasping for some semblance of dignity.

She wanted to pop the horse on the croup with the whip, which he well deserved and he knew it, but after all she'd said yesterday about not beating her horses, that would only give Standingdeer another arrow for his joking bow. She reached for yesterday's lie.

"He's still sore. I'm laying him off for a couple of days."

"So you've come to agree with me about the stifle," The Paint said dryly.

Tiana bit her lip, but she wanted to scream with frustration. How could he make it seem that he was always right?

"Not exactly," she said hastily. "At least I don't agree with the intention you had to ride him today."

Holding her back very straight, she gathered the line into her hand until she had reached Coosa's gray velvet nose, taking her time with each loop, delaying as long as possible walking toward Stand, trying to give herself a chance to think. How could she get rid of him?

Finally she led the horse toward the gate. The Paint didn't move. She tried not to look at him, but she couldn't help noticing that his thin breeches fit him as tight as skin.

After a lifetime had gone by, during which he didn't take his eyes from her, he dropped his foot to the ground, stepped back, and swung open the gate.

"It won't hurt for me to take him around your practice track," he said. "Loosen him up."

"No!" she exclaimed. "Anytime he's been sore, he's done better with rest than with exercise. Besides, no one can ride him but me."

She clamped her lips shut. A direct challenge was the wrong way to deal with The Paint. When would she learn?

Sure enough, he said, "I can ride him, and I will."

She led Coosa through the gate, then around in a looping circle as she watched The Paint close it. He picked up the latch and dropped it into place with one smooth motion, then fell into step by her side, walking so close to her she could smell the musky, masculine scent of his skin.

She wound the lunge line more tightly around her hand. She had to distract him; once he rode Coosa, he'd definitely try to take over his training.

"Would you like breakfast?" she asked, before she even knew what she would say. "I was about to have some."

"No, thanks. I'll wait here."

Tiana stopped walking as abruptly as he'd spoken. Coosa's nose bumped her back as she turned to stare at Stand.

"Don't be ridiculous!" she cried. "I couldn't eat a bite with a guest of Running Waters waiting at the barn! Why, if Mama and Papa were here, they'd throw a fit!"

"They're gone?"

"Yes, they left early yesterday morning." Her tone lifted into a question. "Papa said you refused to go."

The skin went taut over his high cheekbones. "Right," he said. "I did."

I refuse to go two steps with your treacherous papa.

But she was looking at him, her dark eyes huge with the question of why he had disagreed with her *precious* papa. She wasn't very old, hardly more than a child—she never had to know what her father had done long ago.

So Stand forced his thoughts away from Nicotai's past sins and onto his mission in Washington City. He said, "I refused to go grovel and beg."

"They aren't groveling!"

"Of course they are. Last month the United States Congress passed a law saying that all Indians must be removed, by force if necessary, to new lands west of the Mississippi. There's nothing left to do now *but* grovel."

"You'd better not say that about Papa!" she said fiercely. "He went back there to get that law repealed!"

Standingdeer Chekote cocked his head and gave her a look so sharp and straight that it struck a strange terror into her heart.

"That law won't be repealed," he said. "Too many powerful men, President Andrew Jackson included, have worked for years to get rid of us; they won't give up the victory."

The words shocked her as deeply as his look had done. "It *will* be repealed! Papa can prevent removal. Why—"

He interrupted her with such a scornful tone in his voice that she felt he had slapped her. "Your papa knows better than that. Think about it. Look at our history and *think*."

"Our history shows we are still here," Tiana shot back. She turned on her heel and started hurrying up the hill to get away from his horrible words.

But in an instant The Paint was beside her, shortening his long strides to match hers.

"Tiana," he said, "you need to prepare your mind. That law gives us five years to move ourselves West, or they will send the United States Army to move us."

His quiet tone stopped her in her tracks and lifted her face so that her eyes would meet his. Suddenly, she could name what she saw there, the quality she'd seen at the Council Oak that made him different from other men.

Truth. The Paint was a man who faced the truth.

But in this case, she couldn't bear for it to be so.

"Papa and the others will find a way to keep us here in the Center of the Earth," she cried. "They will!"

Coosa dropped his head to nuzzle at the grass at their feet. Without looking down, Tiana thrust her hand into his mane and twisted the strong hairs around her fingers.

"For a hundred years we've searched for a way to stay here," Standingdeer said gently, his eyes never leaving hers. "First we took the whites in and made friends; then, when they kept coming and coming, we fought to keep them out. Then, outnumbered and outgunned, we ceded parcel after parcel of land."

"Yet we kept the Center of the Earth . . ."

He went on as if she hadn't spoken. "Finally," he said, and his voice became harsh as a crow's cry, "we began the groveling: if we would live in houses, raise crops instead of hunting, spin and weave cloth and keep herds of animals, speak English, become Christians, send our children to Eastern universities, set up schools, publish a newspaper, write a constitution and model our government on that of the United States, we thought, they would not run us off, they would let us live beside them."

"But the old ways were outdated—" Tiana began.

The fire in Stand's eyes stopped her words. "The old ways were born into our hearts and our bones and our blood and our brains," he said. "And we gave them up, threw them away, because we loved this land *that much*, these Mountains of the Blue Smoke, our home. But even that sacrifice wasn't big enough. We must move."

Tears made a lump in Tiana's throat. She

reached for the comfort of Coosa's warm skin and stroked it.

"Don't you see, Tiana?" The Paint asked gently. "If giving up our brotherhood with the animals and our rhythms with the earth, our language and our medicine cannot keep us safe at the Center of the Earth, then nothing can."

Tiana swallowed her tears and lifted her chin.

"My papa and Chief Ross will keep us here," she said, telling herself that The Paint didn't know the truth after all.

"Not for long. As soon as that little boy discovered gold on the Chestatee River, the fate of this Nation was sealed. The whites covet land with gold on it even more than they covet land with Indians on it."

"Papa said . . ."

"Papa said, when he left yesterday, for you to be careful, didn't he? He said there are more raids on the Cherokee every day, more intruders in the Nation raping and pillaging, stealing horses and cattle, burning homes, jailing the *white* missionaries, even. Did he say that?"

Reluctantly, she nodded, the knot in her throat swelling until it felt large enough to choke her.

The Paint made a sharp motion with one big hand. "Think for yourself, Tiana. Your papa should be here instead of in Washington City, *here*, loading his wagons, because you are all going West."

Tiana's anger blossomed inside her like a morning glory opening in the sun. She squeezed the woven canvas lunge line so hard that its edges cut into her palm.

"Then what are *you* doing in the Cherokee Nation East, Mr. Standingdeer Chekote, if our situation is so hopeless? You were already in the West.

Why didn't you take your own advice, stay there, and save yourself a trip?"

The Paint's hard eyes never wavered. "That's what I should have done, but I'm a sucker for a last request."

Her hand froze on Coosa's hide. "*Whose* last request?"

"My uncle Jack wrote to me shortly before he died, saying he wished I'd come back and try to straighten Bluford out. After his death, I felt I had to honor that."

"So," Tiana said, her stomach contracting as it always did at the mention of Tobacco Jack, "you needn't criticize Papa. You've taken on a task more hopeless than his."

Stand asked quickly, "What do you know about Bluford?"

"Only rumors," she replied, making her feet move, turning to head for the stables again, rushing away from the question, from anything connected with Tobacco Jack.

But he kept up with her. "What rumors?"

"Oh . . . that he drinks a lot and flirts with girls and gambles almost as much as Gray Fox does."

"Who does he run with?" he demanded, catching her eye across Coosa's moving withers. "Uncle Jack mentioned bad companions."

"How would I know?"

"At Council Oak you and Blu seemed pretty friendly."

"I *told* you, he flirts with all the girls. I don't know him well."

Desperate to get away from his questions and his dire predictions, she ran faster toward the stable, calling, "Gabe! Gabe, can you take Coosa, please?"

Standingdeer followed her into the coolness of the barn at the same time Gabe's helper, Moss, appeared from the other end of the aisle. Tiana gave Coosa to him.

Then she turned to Stand, brushing back the wisps of hair that had come loose from her braid, wishing she could remove him from her presence that easily. His awful talk was making her heart pound like a trapped thing inside the cage of her ribs.

Or was it the *sight* of him that caused her agitation? He had leaned back against a stall front, hooked his heel onto its bottom board, and started looking over the stable as if he owned the place. Anywhere she'd ever seen him, he looked as if he had belonged there forever and was Principal Chief.

Tiana glanced away from the heavy muscles of his chest and arms rippling beneath his red-and-white print shirt, cut in a buttonless, high-collared vee like his yellow one. Her gaze dropped to his flat stomach and long legs; she jerked it up again to the woven sash tied at his slim waist. Its fringed ends swung gently against the tight, faded blue denim of his pants, reaching almost to the tops of his shining boots.

Well, he wasn't chief of Running Waters and he'd better not be waiting to pounce on Coosa and ride him!

"Are you coming to the house with me, or do you still prefer hay and grain here at the barn?"

He slanted his mocking glance at her. "For someone with beautiful manners, you didn't make that invitation sound terribly gracious."

"It's the only one you'll get," she retorted, and turned to Moss. "Where's Gabe?"

"Gabe, he over to the hay barn," the boy told her, " 'cause he done heered somethin' in thar."

"Heard what?"

"Reckon that skunk been tryin' to nest in hyar," Moss said. "Gabe, he gone kill it."

"Well, rub Coosa down and take him over to the east paddock to turn him out," Tiana said. "And stall The Butterfly in here. I'll work her right after breakfast."

She turned and left the stable; The Paint walked beside her. They started up the graveled drive toward the house.

"So," she said, trying to keep her voice calm and her eyes away from him, "you choose biscuits and ham over alfalfa and oats?"

He shrugged. "I didn't want to ruin your bribe—I know you're trying to stuff me so full I can't ride our horse."

"What! I am not ..."

But her voice trailed off in her dismay that he could read her so easily. Disaster would be upon her if he learned to read all her thoughts.

"Is The Butterfly another one you're running?"

"Not yet," she said. "She's just a two-year-old. I'm breaking her and three others this year."

"How many do you have on the track?"

"Four, counting Coosa."

"And you're doing all the work yourself?"

"The training and the race riding, yes. Gabe and Moss both help me with warm-ups."

He turned sideways to look her full in the face as they walked. "So," he said, "you ought to be glad to have my help with The Coosa."

"I can do it alone," she said stubbornly. "Besides, no one can ride Coosa but me."

The corners of his mouth lifted. "Tiana, I catch and break wild horses for a living—horses that have run loose on the plains without ever *seeing* a human being until they are three and four years old. I can pretty well ride 'em all."

His tone was so incontestable that it scared her half to death. This was a man with his mind made up.

"Not this one! He's mine!"

Stand caught the scent of her terror on the breeze; it shook in her voice and raged in the wild, dark forests of her eyes, just as he'd seen it in many a mustang filly. She didn't trust him for a minute, and she was terrified of losing the stallion. Stand's very presence here was frightening her.

He ought to give up his claim on Coosa and go away. Really, he didn't care what the stud might win; money for its own sake had never called to him that strongly. He had everything he needed for his wandering life.

Yet if he left the horse, he'd be letting the Tenkillers take one more thing away from him. A knot tightened in his gut, the knot that had formed when he'd first set foot on Running Waters that morning. His share in the stud was the most valuable possession he had, and he'd be damned if he'd turn it over to them.

But as he climbed the steps beside her and they washed in the basin on the back porch, as he walked behind her into the house and down the hall into the dining room, wondering why he was accepting hospitality in Nicotai Tenkiller's house, he wondered, too, if there could be another reason for his clinging to Coosa. Tiana's hair, braided down her back and then tucked halfway up again to be tied with a narrow ribbon of shiny purple satin, smelled like the wild Cherokee roses. Her tiny waist and pretty, rounded hips beneath the boy's breeches that she wore called to his empty hands.

He had better not spend much time with Tiana Tenkiller. He would let her do whatever she liked with the horse.

Yet, to his own consternation, when they were seated across from each other and the servant was filling the white-clothed table with fragrant platters of cured ham and fried eggs, along with steaming bowls of grits and baskets of beaten biscuits, he said, "I'll agree to your being the only rider on Coosa if you'll agree to work him my way."

Her huge eyes flashed up to meet his. "Absolutely not!"

He couldn't look away from her. Her passions were right there, all the time, just beneath the surface of her beautiful peach-colored skin. A man could almost see them simmering.

Stand took a biscuit and buttered it, then added strawberry jam from the crystal dish in front of him.

"Tiana," he said, "I know more than you think I do about running horses."

"That's exactly what I keep telling her about me!" Gray Fox said from the doorway. Smiling from one of them to the other, he swaggered into the room and took the chair at the head of the table. "But she never listens to me, Stand. Maybe you'll have more luck with her."

His cheerful effrontery cut through Tiana's deep irritation with him. Gray Fox was absolutely impossible. He always had been. She smiled back at him in spite of her resolve to be constantly stern with him in hopes of keeping him under control.

"There's hardly any comparison here, Gray. At least, Standingdeer works with horses all the time—you never touch one except to leap on its back and go galloping off to a card game."

"Sister!" Gray said, pretending to be terribly hurt as he loaded his plate with generous helpings of ham and eggs. "That isn't true. Sometimes I ride all the way into Augusta and sell cotton and corn. I've even been known to bring gifts back for you."

She made a face at him over her steaming cup of coffee. "Thank you, Brother," she said.

"And I thank you for getting the admission from Tiana that I actually know what I'm doing with horses," Stand said dryly, saluting Gray with his cup. "My ears could hardly believe it."

"What!" Tiana gasped, staring at him until he moved his gaze from Gray Fox to her. "I did *not* say that! I only meant . . ."

The exaggeratedly innocent look he gave her made her burst out laughing. Her finely boned face was even more beautiful when she smiled. It was wonderful.

"You're welcome," Gray Fox interjected, sketching a bow to each of them and flashing his own charming smile. "I'm so glad I got up for breakfast today. I haven't felt this useful in a long, long time."

They all laughed then, and frequently again throughout the meal. Dilcey had brought in the third pot of coffee and gone back to the kitchen, and Gray was in the middle of telling Stand about the last *chungke* game he had attended when pure commotion drowned out his words.

Outside in the back yard, the plantation bell began to ring, its iron tongue clapping from one side to the other in a frantic rhythm of alarm. Inside, in the hallway, sounded the noise of pounding feet and a piercing scream.

"Fire! Barn fire!"

The words jerked the three of them to their feet. Moss dashed into the room, his face frozen in a look of terror.

"Stables on fire, Miss Tiana! Massa Gray Fox! After I done put The Butterfly in like you said. That filly in dar, she is."

Tiana threw her napkin on the table and darted past him, vaguely aware that Stand and Gray were at her heels. She ran totally on instinct, not seeing the hallway or the veranda or the steps, the driveway or the trees that lined it, for the image of the burning stables filled her eyes even before she had rounded the curve to see its reality.

And The Butterfly's terrified screams filled her ears.

The back end of the stables was the part already in flames; they licked from the windows and from beneath the eaves, curling up into the limbs of the maple trees like greedy, long tongues, hungry for food. Tiana ran for the front doors, which were gaping open like a monster's mouth.

Inside its hot belly was nothing but smoke. And one beautiful, sweet, *fast* filly, kicking and whinnying, going completely mad with fear.

Tiana bolted into the building, jerking at her shirt collar, pulling it up to cover her nose, feeling with her other hand for the walls of the stalls. They were already getting warm to the touch.

She must hurry. Had Moss put the mare in her own stall or in one of the others he hadn't yet cleaned? Oh, *why* hadn't she taken the time to ask him?

Tears stung her eyes and smoke scratched her throat; she coughed and blinked and wiped her face on her shoulder in an effort to see. There! In the stall next to this one: a glimpse of a big, rolling eye through the thickening smoke. The loudness of the next terrified whinny confirmed The Butterfly's location.

Tiana pushed on until she could reach the latch, then, when she touched it, pulled out her shirttail to protect her hand. If only she were wearing a dress!

Finally, the metal burning her fingers through the cloth, she twisted the catch free and pushed back the door to the stall, which vanished in the gray haze. She glimpsed the shining black hide of the horse and rushed in, gasping for short breaths of air and grabbing for Butterfly's mane.

The filly threw up her head and refused to be touched. She backed away until the corner caught her, then dashed past Tiana.

But she wouldn't go out. She whirled and came back straight at Tiana, heading for the corner again, desperate to stay in her familiar stall, which had always been safe.

Tiana lunged for her neck. Butterfly, like Coosa, would usually lead with an arm under her throatlatch, but not now. She huddled in the back corner while Tiana, taking shorter and shorter breaths, managed finally to put her arm around the filly's neck. She pulled, and petted her neck, and gasped out a pleading word or two, but Butterfly refused to budge.

Tiana's throat and lungs burned hotter now; she swayed on her feet and came up hard against Butterfly's shoulder. She grabbed a handful of mane, put her foot against the wall of the stall, and used the last of her strength to push and pull herself onto the filly's back.

By some miracle, the mare moved forward. Tiana wiped her eyes on her sleeve and peered through the dense, gray-black fog. Stand was looming there, at Butterfly's head, fastening a halter around it.

Tiana's body felt like it was melting to the mare's hot flesh. Oh, Lord, he could be killed! Smoke was boiling up behind him, and soot and ash were falling like rain onto his hair. Some of the fragments were still on fire.

He pulled the filly's head down and spoke into her ear. Tiana found one more shred of energy and kicked her in the sides. Stand urged the filly toward him.

Though still whickering with fear, Butterfly let him lead her into the aisle. Beside him, she began to trot down to the doors, and while Tiana held the one tiny puff of breath that was left in her lungs, the filly ran outside.

The Paint led The Butterfly across the stable yard through the milling, shouting servants to a spot on the grassy hillside across the driveway from the house, shaded by red oak trees. He dropped the lead rope, stepped back to Tiana, and pulled her off the filly's back, gathering her into his arms.

She fell into them, her hands frantically brushing at his hair and his shoulders. Then she buried her face in the hollow of his neck, wound her arms around him, and clung there, trembling. It took him a minute to realize that she was racked with sobs.

His own legs began to shudder. He braced his feet farther apart, his boots sliding a bit on the grass.

"You little fool," he growled, squeezing her harder against him, "you're too brave for your own good. You could've been overcome by the smoke, or hurt by the horse, or trapped in the fire!"

"So could *you!*" she cried, and pulled back to stare at him.

His heart stopped. His eyes couldn't look at her enough. If he stood right there and gazed at her for the rest of his life, he couldn't look at her enough.

The bones of her face showed delicate and strong through the smoky grime that layered her skin; her tears streaked through it, falling from enormous dark eyes that burned with the same accusing concern he was feeling for her.

The emotion trembled between them, so fervent

that if he reached out, it would be real to his touch. He had been so *scared* when he saw her run into that fire; he still felt hollowed out inside by the power of that fright.

And she had been afraid for him.

He could hardly take that in. It had been years, long years, since there had been anyone to care about him.

She whisked a last burning ember from his hair.

"I couldn't even make her budge from that stall," she said wonderingly, "but you did."

Then she gave him a smile as rich and as unexpected as thunder in a snowstorm. A smile that wrapped the two of them together as warm as a mink-skin robe.

"You'll do anything to prove that you have a way with horses, won't you?"

His heart lurched and began to beat again, so hard that it hurt against his ribs.

He returned the grin. "I will," he said, "and don't you forget it."

But the words rasped from his throat the way the beating of his blood rasped through his aching heart. How could his pulse leap this hot and wild over Nicotai Tenkiller's daughter?

Chapter 4

It was three days after the fire, and sundown found Tiana still pacing the veranda, fighting the panic rising in her throat. If Dilcey weren't sticking so close to her, she felt she would lose her mind.

"I wish I'd sent Moss out sooner," she said for the dozenth time. "Do you think he'll find Gray?"

Dilcey always gave the same comforting answer. "Sho' will," she said, nodding as she swept her broom back and forth in the dim twilight. "All unhurt and 'thout losin' nothin' else in a wager."

"Mostly I just want him to be unhurt," Tiana said, stopping to stare through the dusk toward the road. "Those horrid men who set fire to the barn could be anywhere. They could kill him."

"He be fine," the servant woman comforted.

But Tiana shivered. The chilling sounds of The Butterfly's screams, the bitter smells of smoke and ashes, the smothering sensation of no air in her lungs still haunted her.

As did the turbulent feeling of The Paint's hard arms around her.

And the soul-deep look that had passed between them.

She turned on her heel, away from those thoughts, and stalked back toward the east end of the porch. Hadn't she promised herself a hundred times in the past three days that she would forget all that?

There was no need to drive herself crazy trying to find a reason that, after they'd run out of the barn and it seemed as if there was so much left unsaid, The Paint would so suddenly lay her down on the grass, turn away without a word, not even a good-bye, and go help the others who were battling the fire. And, after that, take his silent leave for home.

No need at all. Gray was enough to worry about.

"If Gray *is* all right, he'd better not have been gambling!" she said. "We only have seven days."

"Till what?" Dilcey murmured, barely louder than the swish of her broom against the planks of the floor.

"To pay those awful men for Gray's gambling debts! And it just breaks my heart to use Papa's emergency money, especially after I told Gray we never would."

"Sounds like this here's a 'mergency."

Tiana heaved a mighty sigh. "It is, Dilcey. It is. But even with Papa's five hundred dollars, I can't pay those men and still ransom the mares. James Dalton'll be coming to get them any day now."

Dilcey began to hum a mournful hymn, a sign that she could bear no more worrisome burdens now, but Tiana couldn't hush. She had to talk through *all* her troubles.

"Mama's jewelry is the only other thing I can think of to sell; none of the young horses would bring enough, and we must keep the racehorses. They're our hope."

"Yo' mama'd give her jewelry quick, fo' to save Gray," Dilcey offered in the middle of her song.

"Yes, she would!"

Yes, Tiana thought, stepping around Dilcey to pace even faster. By breaking all the rules, she could save everything and everyone. Barely. Papa's five hundred to James Dalton for the mares, a hundred and fifty from the jewelry to Sykes and Walters.

At last, long after deep darkness had fallen and Dilcey had gone into the house, just before Tiana decided to light a torch and ride out on the search herself, she heard the rumble of wheels coming up the drive. It sounded like the gig that Moss had taken. Thank God!

She ran down the steps and along the drive beneath the maples to meet it. Moss slowed, and she ran to the opposite side, her blood singing with the thrill of relief.

"Gray Fox!" she cried. "Moss found you!"

"Yes!" her brother shouted over the crunching of the wheels. "And a good thing, too, 'cause I was afoot!"

"Why in the world? What happened?" she called back, ready to order the stupid boy, Moss, to stop the gig and let Gray Fox get down.

But when Moss pulled the team to a halt at the foot of the steps, she saw why he'd driven Gray all the way to the door. Her brother was roaring drunk, too drunk to stand up.

Moss dismounted from the driver's seat and came around to help him down.

"Sykes and Walters stole my horse, that's what!" Gray shouted indignantly. "Jerked him right out from under me, the bullies, and I didn't even agree to wager him!"

Tiana's blood turned to water. Icy water. He'd been *gambling* with those barn burners again! When she'd thought they were killing him!

"Who, Gray? Which horse were you on?"

"Skip."

She let out her breath. Skip had never lived up to his breeding.

"What else did you lose?" she demanded, following across the driveway and up the steps as Moss led him to a cane rocker on the veranda.

"Ran up a bill at Horn's Tavern. And another sum to Sykes and Walters. They said to meet them a week from today," he told her, as openly and cheerfully as if he'd been relating a compliment he'd overheard. "At the sycamore bend on the Federal Road with three hundred dollars."

He made a rueful sound. "We cut the cards, double or nothing. I nearly saved us the hundred and fifty, Tiana. I came so close! Mine was the jack of clubs . . ."

"Three hundred dollars!"

"Or else they'll burn the house," he said, nodding agreeably. "They *are* the ones who set fire to the stables."

For the first time in her entire life, Tiana wanted to faint. She *willed* herself to faint. She could not bear this; she had to escape it, escape it this instant. She would pass out of consciousness and fall on the floor.

But she couldn't. She stood right there on the veranda in front of Gray Fox while he lolled in his chair in the lamplight from the window and told her every detail of the story. As pleasantly as if telling a soothing bedtime tale.

Then he got up, straightened his shoulders, and walked past her, over to the balustrade. He leaned over it, stiff as a puppet, and vomited into the spirea bushes.

Tiana walked past him, across the veranda, through the doorway, and into the house. Dilcey was in the dining room, laying out places for breakfast, fitting each plate carefully upside down over its knife, fork, and spoon.

"Dilcey," Tiana said, "Moss has gone to see to the horses. When he comes back, would you have him help you put Gray Fox to bed? He's drunker than I've ever seen him."

Then she went out the back door and down to the *Tanta-ta-rara*, where she stayed the whole night.

In the morning, Tiana came back into the house just after good daylight and went along the silent hallway to Papa's study. She opened the heavy oak door, slipped inside, then closed and locked the door behind her. Gray Fox was still passed out completely, no doubt, but she was taking no chances on his getting his hands on *this* money.

"Help me, Papa," she whispered, turning from the door to stare at the portrait of her father that President John Quincy Adams had had commissioned as a gift during another, long-ago trip to Washington City.

Papa's kind, loving eyes stared back at her. Oh, dear Lord, what she would give if he could speak to her and tell her how to get out of this mess!

Papa couldn't speak, though. Papa wasn't here.

But The Paint was here. Only a mile or two across the hill at Pine Grove. The Paint's arms were strong; they could hold danger away.

But she could not go to him with these troubles. She would be mortified if he knew what a degenerate Gray Fox had become.

Besides, *why* had he left her there with The Butterfly beneath the red oaks without even a good-bye?

And after running into the stables and bringing her out to safety! After holding her so close!

Maybe he hadn't been so worried about *her*. Maybe he was just being The Paint, doing heroic deeds, no matter who happened to be in danger.

That thought, which she'd been holding at bay with the full force of her will, nailed her feet to the floor. It came crushing down on her as heavily as a boulder rolling off a mountainside, one that she'd been running away from for three whole days.

But what other explanation could there be?

The Paint's handsome, weathered face floated in front of her for a moment, blanking out Papa's portrait, and she closed her lids against it. She wouldn't think about him anymore. They were enemies, anyway.

He'd simply gotten her out of one scrape that she should've been able to take care of for herself, and she wouldn't permit him to do it again. She could take care of herself and her own plantation.

Besides, how could he help her this time? Only by lending her money that she couldn't pay back.

She would not be so beholden to him. If she were, she'd certainly lose all control over Coosa to him.

Tiana opened her eyes and turned away from the picture. She sank her bare feet into the luxurious rug and walked slowly to Papa's huge rolltop desk, opened the secret cubbyhole and took out the paper that contained the combination, read it, and replaced it in its hiding place.

Then she went to one corner of the rug, turned it back, and opened the safe. For a long, long time she stared into its shining depths before her mind would take in the fact that it was empty.

Empty! Some papers were there, true, at the bottom, but the leather sack that had held the money huddled in on itself limply, lying in a forlorn heap. She snatched it up, turned it upside down, and shook it, but nothing came out, not even dust. Gone! Every cent of cash on the plantation was gone, and she knew where.

If she'd had the sense of a guinea hen, she would've known it before she ever came sneaking in here so hopefully. *Of course* Gray Fox had taken the emergency money! Probably months ago!

She hit the floor with her fist, then let the bag drop, closed and covered the useless safe. Her pulse pounded like hundreds of hoofbeats in her ears.

She rushed out of the room and headed for the stairs. Mama's jewelry was all that was left; she would have to sell every piece and try to stretch the money. *If*, a voice screamed from the back of her mind, *if Gray hasn't taken the jewelry, too.*

He had.

Tiana stood in front of Mama's carved dresser with its attached mirror framed in matching golden oak and stared down into the lacquered jewelry box, as unbelievably empty as the safe. All the strength left her body. They were all lost. She and Gray and the mares, this house, everything was lost.

But why should she be shocked? She should have known that if Gray had the nerve, the unmitigated gall, to sell *Fawn*, he would do anything.

The thought of her friend roused her spirit. She picked up the box and shook it as she had the money bag, but the result was the same. She set it to one side and, desperate, bent to peer into the space between the hinged mirror and the dresser top. A glint of gold caught her eye.

Thank goodness! There *was* something Gray had missed!

She managed to get hold of it with two fingers, and finally, in spite of the fact that she was trembling all over, pulled it loose and into the palm of her hand.

It was the brooch, the gold-and-diamond brooch!

With shaking hands, she opened her blouse and fastened the pin to her chemise, hiding it. Then she rushed from the room, her mind whirling. Even with the valuable brooch, she would have to sell some horses.

But before she made another plan, before she gave up a horse that she loved, before she did another hour of grueling work, she was going to put the fear of the Devil, the *asgina*, into Gray Fox Tenkiller.

He was asleep in his bed, sprawled on his back with the sheet over his face. Tiana jerked it away.

"Get up!" she shouted. "Get out of this bed and out to the fields. You have a hay harvest to bring in."

Gray groaned and rubbed his eyes. "Ti?" he muttered. "Go away."

Without another word she stalked to the dry sink by the window, lifted the pitcher full of cool water from its bowl, and dashed half of it directly into his face.

He came up spluttering and yelling. "What'd you do that for? My head already feels like a watermelon about to split open!"

"Get up," she said. "Saddle a horse and go to the hayfield."

His eyes popped fully open; he wiped water from his face. "Are you crazy? I'm not able to go anywhere, much less to the hay field! Why, it'll be hot as hell today!"

Tiana stood over him, holding the pitcher ready. "Then prepare for a worse hell. I'll send a letter today and Papa will be home within two weeks."

"You wouldn't! He won't come back! You know the Nation needs him too much."

"He'll see how foolish it is to try and save the Nation if his own home is in ashes."

"Tiana!" her brother wailed as he looked into

her eyes at last. "I'm sick. Gabe'll supervise the hay hauling. Moss will—"

"Gabe and Moss have horses to ride. Thanks to your selfish squandering of Papa's emergency money and Mama's jewelry, we'll have to enter every race that's run for miles around this week to try and pay off those barn-burning vulture friends of yours."

"Then," he whined, "I need to arrange some match races. Today, Ti. That'll make up for the trouble I've caused."

"I'll do all the arranging from now on," Tiana said, shocked at her own cold voice. "I have all the responsibility, so I'm taking the authority, too."

She shifted the pitcher into both hands. "Get to your feet, Gray Fox, or, I swear, I'll drown you in your bed."

Tiana wrote out the invitations that morning in a hand she made steady and ornately beautiful through sheer perseverance. *Come to a social at Running Waters Plantation,* she wrote, *on the evening of June 10. For a celebration of The Green Corn Moon.*

"Everyone will come," she told Dilcey. "They're starving for a summer like we always have, with lots of horse races and ball plays and dances."

"You knows it, Miss Tiana," Dilcey muttered as she lumbered grumpily around the parlor placing vases to hold cut flowers. "Folks is sick of intruders and beatings and killings and throwing th' missionaries in jail in Georgia, and all them plantations bein' lost in the lottery. They'll come in droves and we 'uns'll have to cook bushels o' food."

"And they'll buy some horses, I hope," Tiana said, ignoring the grumbling while she copied her message over and over onto the lacy-edged notepaper Mama had given her. "But don't mention that to Gray. If he knew I'd decided to give any of them up, he'd be leading them around to card games all over the country, gambling them on the hoof."

"So *that* th' real reason for havin' a social with yore folks gone," Dilcey murmured. "I be wonderin'."

Tiana looked down at the invitation she had just addressed. She had another reason, too, but that one she wouldn't tell, not even to herself. The neighbors at Pine Grove were, of course, included on the list of guests.

On the day of Tiana's social, Grandmother Sun and *Nungi-tsunulay'*, The Four Winds, conspired to help her. The evening of the party arrived with a south breeze and a golden light that made the grassy lawns of Running Waters and the house itself glow with a welcoming warmth. Inside, the cherry floor of the hallway gleamed red-gold and handsome, inviting guests to cross from the veranda to the long double parlor, its furniture pushed back against the walls for the dancing.

Tiana wandered through the house, breathing in the light, clean scent of lemon oil and the heavy, sweet ones of freshly cut pink roses and creamy white magnolias, loving the shine of polished woods and the shadows thrown across them by the stiff-patterned curtains of starched lace. She shivered with pure delight. Running Waters had to be the most beautiful house in the entire world.

In the dining room, in front of the gilt-framed mirror that hung over the long buffet, she stopped. She hardly knew the young woman staring back at her; it had been weeks, endless weeks of constant working with the horses, since she'd loosened her hair from its braid and worn a dress.

And such a dress! Dilcey had said, when she

was fixing Tiana's hair, "Pretty. Draws th' eye t' yore bosoms, that satin bindin' there."

It did. The low cut of the neckline and the tiny puffed sleeves that ended even with it were trimmed in a rolled satin ribbon a shade darker violet than the finely woven lawn of the dress. The richness of the ribbon shone against her skin and made it gleam.

Was the bodice cut too low?

The Paint had never seen her in a dress. What would he think?

"Miss Tiana," said a soft voice behind her, "folks drivin' up now."

She turned and hurried out into the hallway, past the servants laden with tea cakes and fruit plates and pitchers of tea and blackberry punch. She couldn't think about The Paint now. She had to think about selling some horses.

When she reached the veranda, however, only her parents' best friends, the Swimmers, were there. Then, like pine needles floating into a drift on the ground in a rising wind, carriages and horses filled the circle drive.

But The Paint on his shining, pale buckskin horse wasn't among them.

Gray Fox came downstairs then, resplendent in yet another new suit, exactly the blue of the summer sky and made by the best tailor in Augusta.

"*Osiyo*, hello, welcome to Running Waters," he greeted the guests expansively.

Tiana smiled and talked and moved among their friends, wondering which of them would help her save her brother.

She must get the best price, she thought as everyone began drifting into the house toward the laden tables of refreshments. And to do that, she mustn't give a hint that she was desperate.

How did Papa do this, anyway, buying and sell-

ing and trading horses? All he'd ever told her was
never to put a price on any animal she didn't want
to sell. No matter how ridiculously high it might
be, he'd said, some silly fool might meet it.

Well, she certainly hoped that silly fool was here
tonight. And that she had sense enough to find
him.

She chatted with Sally Dove and Cahtahtie
Campbell, her old classmates from Springplace,
the Moravian missionary school, and shouted a
greeting into Aunt Polly Hurt's good ear while she
watched Cahtahtie's father, Etuwee, walk up to Joe
Raincrow and Thomas McDonald. Those were
three of the most prominent horsemen in the Nation, and they all had expressed admiration for the
Tenkiller bloodstock. And they all had plenty of
money to indulge a whim.

If she could get a competition started among
them . . .

But how could she join a group of men and in-
terrupt without appearing immodestly bold? They
could talk for hours: politics, removal, crops,
weather. How could she turn the conversation to
horses without arousing their suspicions?

"Let's go into the parlor," she called out over
the contented buzzing of many voices. "Simon,
please give us some music for dancing!"

She stayed by Cahtahtie's side and kept one eye
on Mr. Campbell's whereabouts as everyone
slowly milled around and wandered across the
wide hall into the parlors. The fiddles began tun-
ing up. A few of the men went out the front door
to sit on the veranda and smoke and talk, but no
one came in.

The Paint, riding horseback beside his cousin's
carriage, looked down at Maud Tuskee with a
frown.

"You decided to come with us after all, Standingdeer?" she was asking. "Bluford said you might not."

"I don't like accepting the hospitality of Nicotai Tenkiller, even when he isn't at home," he said with a shrug. "But I let Blu talk me into it."

"You might as well," she said, speaking in her habitually sharp, bossy tone. "And give up that grudge. Nicotai never caused Kinnea's death."

"I'm not holding a grudge, Maud," Stand said, giving her a glance so full of irritation he hoped it would make her close her mouth. "I just don't want to have anything to do with anybody named Tenkiller."

"How about Miss Tiana?" Bluford said, shaking the lines over the backs of his team of gleaming black horses. "You might want something to do with *her*."

Maud jabbed him with her elbow. "Well, *you'd* better not!" she snapped.

Bluford went on, talking to Stand as if she hadn't spoken. "Tiana's the prettiest girl in the Nation."

At Maud's loud gasp, Bluford turned to her and smiled. "But you, my dear wife, are the most beautiful woman."

"Pay some attention to me at the social, then," she said, obviously only partially mollified.

She looked abruptly from him to Stand. "Tenkillers or not, at least you'll be in company this evening," she remarked. "You're alone way too much, Cousin Stand."

"I like the way I live, Maud."

"But it'd be better if you had someone," she persisted. "Whatever happened to that woman you wrote to us about that time? I thought you planned to marry her."

Stand gave a short, bitter laugh. "Turned out

Elena was already married. That's when I learned for sure that you women can't be trusted."

Maud snorted and put her hands on her hips, ready to enjoy an argument, but he spoke before she could get out the first word.

"Don't you ever forget anything, Maud? That was *years* ago."

"She never forgets anything that has to do with another woman," Blu said, flicking the lines on the horses' backs.

"It's *your* other women I remember, Blu," Maud said.

"I don't have any other women!" Blu said through clenched teeth. "How many times do I need to tell you?"

"You used to—" Maud began.

"Come on, Blu," Stand interrupted, putting his heels to his horse. "Speed up your team. Let's get to this social and get it over with."

In the parlor, with the lively strains of "Hi-wassee Town" beginning to stir, Tiana positioned herself near Mr. Campbell and Cahtahtie.

She waited until he'd given some instruction or other to his daughter, then asked, "How is Black Maria, sir? Is she running anywhere soon?"

He turned to her with a smile. "At Ellijay on Sunday," he said.

"Ellijay? That's a good distance from here."

"Yes, but I think it'll be worth it. Crittenton and his bunch got up a meet, just on a whim. They'll go as high as a thousand dollars a side, five hundred to forfeit; money added, of course."

Tiana's heart leapt. Every thought of selling some of her darlings flew out of her head. Perhaps she could *win* the money she needed!

"No one told me!" she cried. "I want to take Coosa!"

"Come and dance," he said. "I'll tell you about it."

Thank the Great Protector, she thought as she took his hand and whirled out onto the floor. Maybe she wouldn't have to sell a single head after all.

But when the dance had ended and Mr. Campbell started leading her off the floor so they could talk further, she lost all interest in horses and races. Just beyond Bluford and Maud, who were entering the room, Tiana could see The Paint standing in the wide opening of the doorway.

His stillness and his dress—stark, bold black and white—gave him the air, somehow, of having been there for a long time, as if he were posing for a formal portrait in the frame of the dark cherry woodwork. But his eyes swept the room like a hunter's.

Like an eagle's. They passed over Gray Fox and Sally and Cahtahtie and Mr. Campbell. To light upon Tiana.

His glinting gaze narrowed, then, as if he'd found his prey, blazed at her like a flame from a fire.

But he didn't smile.

And he didn't come to her.

An excited buzz rose in the room as others noticed him and people moved between them. Mr. Campbell drifted forward to meet him, too, leaving Tiana standing alone, but she didn't care.

Standingdeer Chekote was here.

Gray Fox went up to him and took his arm, chatting away as if they were lifelong partners who had never had a disagreement over when to race their best running horse, and drew him into the room. The Paint greeted people graciously, but almost immediately he said to Gray in his deep, strong voice, "We didn't mean to stop the dancing. Let's have music again."

Tiana's eyes couldn't leave him. Did he mean to dance? Would he dance with her?

Cahtahtie and Sally and several other girls must have had the same thought, for they floated up to him, greeting him with muted talk and many giggles. The Paint smiled and nodded and made his way through them.

Tiana's throat tightened in anticipation.

Simon lifted his fiddle and signaled the other musicians. They started the sweet strains of a waltz.

But The Paint didn't come to her. Mr. Campbell did, and numbly Tiana let him whirl her out into the middle of the floor. His low voice sounded in her ear about the Ellijay races, but she didn't hear a word.

The Paint was working his way through the crowded room. Finally he stopped in the curve of the bay window that jutted out into the rose-colored evening. Several people, including Bluford and Gray, gathered around him, but even when he turned back to them from looking out over the lawn, he seemed to hold himself apart.

I'm not around many people out West.

A hidden loneliness might have been in his voice when he said that, but solitude suited him. At this moment he would have preferred to be alone; Tiana could read that feeling in every line of his perfectly proportioned body. He was sorry he had come. He wanted to be outside this house.

Except . . . his eyes were following her, Tiana.

Mr. Campbell turned her around and she lost sight of Stand for a moment, but when she could see him again, his gaze was waiting for hers. Hot as Table Rock in the summer.

Tiana trembled. Every inch of her body could

remember how it had felt to be held so tight in his arms.

"Are you chilly?" Mr. Campbell asked. "Can I get you a wrap?"

"No, thank you," she said. *Get me a new partner. Go and get me The Paint.*

Simon and his band played four more songs. Four more endless, beautiful, lilting songs. Songs perfect for dancing.

The Paint stayed where he was, talking and listening, mostly listening. He never danced, not once.

Tiana could bear it no longer. She had to be near him at least for a moment. She had to hear his voice.

She signaled Simon to stop playing and invited her guests to have more refreshments. The group in the bay window still did not move. Maud and Mrs. Campbell followed Cahtahtie over to join them. Dilcey passed through the guests with a plate of sugar tea cakes; Tiana took it from her and walked toward them.

"That lottery ought to be all the sure sign you need," The Paint was saying. "Georgians winning whole Cherokee plantations by simply drawing a number proves the whites won't rest until they've taken possession of every inch of this country."

"No!" Tiana burst out, lifting horrified eyes to his face. "Do stop that doomsaying! We'll never give up Running Waters, never—this is home!"

Other voices rose in agitated agreement with her, and Etuwee Campbell said teasingly, "Watch out, now, Standingdeer. You'll be accused of talking pro-removal!"

The Paint's only response to that was a lifted brow. He glanced at Campbell, but then he turned and gave Tiana one of his long, straight looks.

"I'm sorry," he said. "I don't mean to upset you,

but the only power the *Tsa-la-gi* have now is to face the facts."

She returned his level gaze. "We don't agree on what constitutes the facts," she said, "and this is a social." She smiled at him. "Welcome, Standing-deer."

"Thank you for the invitation, Miss Tiana."

A teasing remark about his good manners sprang to her tongue, but she bit it back. Because, *still*, he hadn't smiled at her.

Her blood chilled. *Had Old Sudie told?*

No. If she had, then Bluford would know, and his behavior was the same; he had given her a surreptitious wink as she'd entered the group. Then Tiana again remembered Stand's behavior when he'd left her the day of the fire.

She offered the plate and he took a tea cake.

"I believe Papa and the others will persuade Congress to repeal the Removal Act," Gray Fox said, and everyone agreed with that, too.

Except for The Paint, who didn't seem to hear him. He lifted the cake to his lips, and his even white teeth bit into it. Tiana thought she could taste the sweetness.

Then Thomas McDonald demanded, "How can our delegation persuade Congress to do anything? All the officials and politicians and Lighthorsemen of this Nation can't even keep the *pony clubs* out of here!"

Joe Raincrow agreed. "They're rampaging, driving off more cattle and good horseflesh nearly every night."

"They're really bad right now up near Ellijay," another man said. "I don't know if I'll take my horses to the race Sunday or not."

The race at Ellijay again. A good change of subject. And she must ask The Paint if she could take Coosa.

He raised his hand again and took another bite to finish the tea cake. The white cuff of his shirt stood out from the bronzed skin of his wrist. How would it feel to run her fingertip up underneath it, between his smooth flesh and the stiffly starched cloth?

She tightened her grip on the crystal plate as Etuwee Campbell gave a derisive snort.

"Might as well go to Ellijay as anywhere else," he said. "There's been plenty of pony club raids all over, excepting right here in this valley," he said. "Other than here, the highest peak and the deepest cove in the Nation aren't safe from them."

"In this valley, we have been lucky," Joe Raincrow said.

"That's right," Gray Fox said. "The thieves take all the best stock, too."

"You know," Etuwee said thoughtfully, "sometimes I think it must be that a turncoat Cherokee points out the good stuff."

Someone at Tiana's elbow knocked into her and jarred the plate almost out of her hands. The cakes slid sideways; she would've dropped them, and the plate, too, if she hadn't already been gripping it so tightly.

She turned to see Bluford staring fixedly at Etuwee. He seemed completely unaware that he had touched her.

"Surely not!" Joe Raincrow said. "There's factions in the tribe, but nobody . . ."

"Speaking of that," Bluford blurted in a tone so loud it rang in Tiana's ears and made Cahtahtie and Sally, sitting on the settee by the wall, turn to stare. His bloodshot eyes met Tiana's for one startled second while he cleared his throat.

"Speaking of factions," he said again, "I've heard it said that somebody saw Willie Ragsdale on the road to Pine Grove the day my daddy was killed. Any of you heard that talk?"

"Yes. And in my opinion, Willie could be the man that killed your daddy," Joe Raincrow said bitterly. "Tobacco Jack hated him for his secret pro-removal work, and Willie knew it."

"*Everybody* knew it," The Paint said, pulling a handkerchief from his pocket to brush away the crumbs from his fingers. "And everybody knows, too, that Uncle Jack raved against a lot of people when he was drunk, yet considered them his friends when he was sober."

"Yes," Bluford said, "Papa was a different man when he was drunk, but he hated Ragsdale and removal, drunk *or* sober."

"Tobacco Jack was a devil when he was drinking," Etuwee Campbell said, nodding agreement. "He threatened me with a pistol one time when he was in his cups, and us fast friends since we were young 'uns."

"You said he'd been on a three-day drunken tear when he died, didn't you, Blu?" Joe asked.

"That's right."

"But that's no proof that he and Ragsdale got in a fight or that Willie's the killer," Standingdeer said.

"Who needs proof?" Thomas McDonald cried. "Willie's a sneaky young traitor who deserves killing before he talks half the Nation into giving up this land. You ought to take care of that for us, Bluford."

Tiana's stomach tied itself into a knot. Willie Ragsdale might be sneaky, and pro-removal, but he was also a handsome, intelligent young man. And he was innocent of killing Tobacco Jack.

"Yeah," Etuwee Campbell said. "Willie's a traitor. He's being paid by the Georgians, I'll vow."

"He oughtta ride into an ambush some night," another man said.

"If he's the one we're after, we'll face him down in broad daylight," The Paint said in a dangerous voice.

"No!" The word burst from Tiana before she could think of what else to say. "He isn't—Willie, I mean—surely he isn't the one! *Anybody* can see Willie's not a killer!"

She spoke in a tight, tinny tone that bore not the slightest resemblance to her usual voice. It was so loud it echoed in the room.

Everyone in the group stared at her. Slowly she forced herself to meet one questioning gaze and then another while her feet glued themselves to the floor. If only she could sink through it and disappear! *How* could she have made such a spectacle of herself?

The Paint's eyes bored into hers. She dropped her lashes and looked away so he wouldn't see the truth.

"I don't want to kill the wrong person," Bluford said wearily, turning away from her to let his bleary eyes roam over the rest of the company. " 'Cause that still wouldn't send Papa's spirit to the Nightland. But I've got to do something soon; I can't stand to be haunted by this much longer."

"Get rid of a few of these traitors like Ragsdale," Mr. Campbell insisted, "and the whole Nation'll sleep better. They're haunting *us* with the threat of losing our homes."

"That's right!" Joe Raincrow said.

"Ha! Now, listen!" another man agreed, strolling over from another group to join them. "Ambush all traitors!"

"Let's talk about something else," Tiana suggested. She tried to think of another topic. The plate tilted in her hands; she straightened it and

cried, "Horses! Mr. Campbell tells me there's to be
a big purse at Ellijay this Sunday."

She could feel The Paint's eyes on her; they
hadn't left her face since her outburst about Willie.
Why wouldn't he stop staring at her?

Fighting to get her mind on the horses and only
on the horses, she forced her gaze upward to meet
his. She couldn't read one definite thing in his
eyes.

Mr. Campbell and Joe Raincrow immediately
began discussing the terms of the race, getting
more and more excited as they talked. Cahtahtie
and Sally got up and came over to them, inter-
jecting pleas to be included, perhaps even to have
picnics and dances at Ellijay.

At the first pause, Tiana said in an offhand way,
looking at Standingdeer, "I'm thinking we should
enter The Coosa."

He gave no sign that he had heard.

"You should!" Etuwee Campbell said.

Cahtahtie chimed in with "Oh, yes, Tiana, do
go! Papa," she said, turning to her father, "do let
me go and watch The Coosa."

Tiana continued to stare at The Paint.

Finally he said, in an implacable tone, "Ellijay's
too far."

Tiana's fingers squeezed the fluted edges of the
plate. Nothing, *nothing* was more infuriating, more
humiliating, than having to ask permission to do
what she wanted with her own horse! She had
been making this kind of decision for years! She
ought to hurl this heavy plate at Gray Fox, whose
fault this was!

"The trip would toughen Coosa," she said, looking Stand straight in the eye, but keeping her tone
light. "You said yourself that he needs experience
on different ground. We could leave tomorrow so
we wouldn't have to rush."

Gray Fox spoke up in favor of the plan; the Campbells and the Raincrows and half the other people there vociferously urged Standingdeer to go. Everyone speculated that Coosa, no doubt, would win his match pulling away.

"Oh, Mr. Chekote," Cahtahtie said prettily, sidling closer to smile up at Stand, "please do decide to come! Races away from home are like one long social occasion!"

The Paint reached out with one big hand, took the plate of tea cakes from Tiana, and gave it to Cahtahtie. His other hand closed around Tiana's bare elbow.

"We need to speak privately for a moment," he rumbled, turning her to face the door, already moving to make way for them out of the group. "Please excuse us."

Before they had finished crossing the crowded parlor, his callused, forceful fingers had traveled up from her elbow to the bare skin of her upper arm. They burned their shapes into her flesh as he thrust her through the flower-scented air toward the hallway and the open door to the veranda beyond.

"You can turn me loose!" she said as soon as they were out of the room. She flashed an angry look at him. "I'm not going to run away."

He didn't return her look, nor did he answer her. With his jaw set, he simply guided her down the length of the hallway and out the door, across the veranda, where several people were smoking and chatting, down the steps, and out onto the lawn.

Tiana's anger was boiling by now, but she would not make a scene at her own social. All that talk of killing in there was already enough to ruin it.

But as soon as they were out of earshot of the

people on the porch, she jerked her arm against his grip and demanded, "Let me go!"

He dropped his hand and kept walking. Without even thinking of doing otherwise now that she was free, Tiana followed him. He stopped at the side of a large magnolia tree where the pale moonlight shimmered through the leaves.

"Don't try this," he said, his voice as harsh as the crack of a whip.

"Try what? What are you talking about?"

He stood perfectly still, his handsome face looking as if it were chiseled in stone, and stared down into her eyes.

"You know what I mean. Getting your way by having the whole Nation cajoling and wheedling at me. Listen, Tiana. Nobody, certainly no bunch of busybodies, tells me what to do."

Sheer surprise drained the anger from her veins. Was *that* what had made him so furious?

"I'm not! They aren't! Stand, that conversation wasn't planned ahead of time—I only heard about the race tonight!"

She lifted her face to him with the innocent eagerness of a rose blossom seeking the sun. She was easily the most beautiful woman ... girl ... no, woman ... he had ever seen.

She smiled at him, her wonderful smile that set a light in her huge dark eyes, now deep as pools in the night shadows.

"Think for a minute and you'll know that talk about Ellijay wasn't a plot against you, Stand," she teased. "*That* many Cherokees couldn't agree on anything, not even a horse race!"

Her words knocked the quick fury out of him as fast as it had come. He laughed.

"You could be right. Not even someone as persuasive as you could accomplish that."

She laughed, too. "You just aren't accustomed to

dealing with a group of people," she said. "Nor any people at all. You're used to making all your decisions alone."

Like me, she thought.

The hard knot in the pit of his stomach fell apart. A new, warm satisfaction spread out from it through every limb of his body. How long had it been since another person had looked into his heart that way? Forever.

She was waiting. But he couldn't reply.

The moonlight hit the shining ribbon that ran so faithfully close to the curves of her breasts. It made her skin gleam like peach-colored satin.

Her mouth pouted, slightly opened, for all the world exactly as if she expected to be kissed. He tried to take his eyes from it.

But they clung to it, instead. His hand lifted, of its own volition, and went back to its place on her arm.

He let it slide slowly along the warm silk of her skin, down to caress the warm hollow inside her elbow, then down again to clasp the fragile bones of her wrist.

Her pulse beat like a frightened bird's wings beneath his thumb.

Right. You are right to be afraid, the beautiful Miss Tiana Tenkiller.

For his own instincts, honed to a razor's edge from years of living alone in the wild, were screaming danger, too. This kiss would not lead to one of the fleeting encounters that were all he had known or wanted for such a long time now.

This kiss could lead to a loving that would tear apart his heart.

Chapter 5

The night wrapped around them like the warm waters of a pool. Tiana could feel the energy and heat of Standingdeer, and, without moving, she felt as though they were moving closer and closer to each other.

Only his hand on hers kept her body upright. Only his mouth, coming nearer and nearer, offered her lifesaving air.

She brought hers to meet it in a rush of sweet need.

Which he reduced to beggary, with the first sure, melting touch of his lips against hers.

And to chicanery. For it was not air that she needed at all. She would never need air again.

This kiss. This kiss was all that she needed. All she would ever need her whole life long.

The wonder of his languid, half-open lips devouring hers destroyed every certainty but that one. It drew a moan of pure pleasure from her throat and the heart from her body.

Tiana gave him back a kiss filled with such unabashed, innocent pleasure that he pulled her to him and crushed her in his arms. She trembled, helpless, against him, but the instant he'd captured her mouth, he was the one trapped. Her hot,

94

honeyed lushness fed a hunger he had never known went so deep.

His hand was shaking as it found the small of her back, supple and warm under his palm. He pressed her even closer.

Tiana lifted her arms, but before she could put them around his neck they fell, powerless, to lie along the tops of his hard shoulders. Because the slow, bold tip of his tongue trailed across her lips, which were already parted to imitate his, and sent a flame to strike at the very core of her being. It hollowed her body to emptiness.

Her own tongue dared to meet his. And Stand filled her up again: with a magical power as strong as that of a tree struck by lightning, with a wild, pulsing passion that came pouring from him into her.

It gave her power to move her arms again. She found the solid, warm column of his neck with her palms and clung to him while his lips and his tongue melted hers, and then, magic of all medicines, remade them again. His hard hand slid up her back and over her bare shoulder, caressing it, making every inch of her thrill to that touch, again and again.

He was lost, captured by her sweet response. Her skin was smooth as an otter's fur. Soft as thistledown.

"Cousin? Standingdeer? Could I talk with you?"

It was Bluford's voice. *Damn it all!*

Feet sounded on the steps of the veranda and then on the graveled drive.

"Standingdeer? Are you out here?"

Only then did Stand tear his mouth from Tiana's and let her go.

He stepped back and looked at her. Even in the dimness he could see that her eyes were ablaze.

Only when Bluford's heavy footsteps had

crunched to a spot within a few yards of them did he turn away from her.

He stepped out of the shadow of the tree and walked to meet him. "What is it?"

"I must go now, Cousin," Bluford said, with no sign that he had seen Tiana in the tree's shadow or their embrace there. "My headache has come back again with this long talk of Papa and his killer. Will you see to Maud and bring her home?"

"Yes. Take my horse and I'll bring her in the buggy."

"And will you come into the house to meet with Gray Fox and the others? They're writing a new memorial protesting the lotteries. It's to be sent to Washington City tomorrow, and they'll need you to sign for Pine Grove."

"I'll come in for a moment," Stand said. "Rest well."

Bluford gave him a weak wave and trudged along the drive toward the barns to get his horse. Stand turned back to Tiana.

She came farther out into the moonlight, away from the darkness of the big magnolia, to wait for him.

The moon washed her dress almost white, paler than the huge creamy blossoms gleaming thick in the dark branches of the tree. Their heavy scent filled the air, sweet as the taste of Tiana.

"You heard?" he asked.

"Yes," she said. "But before you go, Stand, I have something to ask you."

He took a step closer so he could see her face.

"What is it, Tiana?" The shape of her name was like honey on his tongue.

"Can we take Coosa to Ellijay?"

He felt as if the blade of a sword had passed through his body. After that kiss? What she wanted to talk about, after such a kiss, was a horse race?

"Please, Stand," she said softly. "I don't think it will hurt him, and I need the money."

Was this the reason she had kissed him? To soften his resistance to her plan?

"Why?" The word came out so hoarsely it hurt his throat.

She was silent for an endless time. "I'd rather not say," she answered in a small voice. "Could you please just trust me?"

That was the last thing he could do if all she had been doing was using her feminine wiles to get her own way. But, God help him, he *could* kiss her again.

He could reach out and pull her into his arms and down on the grass and take her right here, and to hell with the party and other people and Maud and memorials to Washington City.

And to hell with whatever scheme she was working.

She came away from the tree and walked toward him. The moonlight on her solemn face made it a perfect cameo. "It would give Coosa experience at an altitude much like Dahlonega's," she said.

His heart twisted. So she *was* manipulating him.

"Does that mean you're making a trade?" he asked cynically. "Are you agreeing at last that he should run in the Gold Stakes?"

"Yes."

And she gave him a smile as alluring as the heady fragrance of magnolias that filled the sultry night.

She was very near to him now, near enough to touch.

With every cell in his brain screaming for him not to do it, he reached out and took her fine

shoulders in his hands. He let himself pull her to
him for one fast, hard kiss on the mouth.

It sent a spiraling thrill straight to his groin.

"Do we have a trade?" she asked when he had
torn his mouth away from hers. "Ellijay for
Dahlonega?"

Her voice was a husky whisper.

"It's a trade," he said.

Bluford rode away from Running Waters at a
long, steady canter, spurring his mount into a gallop when he passed among the heavy stands of
birches that grew where the Tenkillers' driveway
met the Federal Road. Those trees shut out the
moonlight.

Tobacco Jack's spirit bothered him most in the
black dark.

A long sigh shuddered through him. He couldn't
live this way much longer—so tired all the time
that nothing gave him any enjoyment, not his
steamboat, not his horses or his gambling. Not
even the stunning, red-haired woman whom he
kept in a house in Augusta.

Was Willie Ragsdale really the guilty one? If he
wasn't, and Bluford killed him, then Willie's clan
would be out to avenge themselves by killing
Bluford. Hiding and running from them would
make him even more miserable than he was now.
To say nothing of the fact that Papa's spirit would
still be haunting him.

He followed the road east, refusing to let his
horse slow to a trot. If he was too late getting to
the meeting place, no telling what his stupid cohorts would do. One time they had ridden right
up to the house and asked Maud where he was.
When he had protested, they had threatened to tell
her about the other woman, knowing that Maud
was already notorious for her jealousy.

That was one of the reasons he had to get rid of them soon. If she ever found out, she would make his life even more miserable—unbearable, really: he'd have her raucous rantings in his ears all day, as well as Tobacco Jack's spirit whispers torturing him all night.

Two miles from where he'd left Running Waters, he turned off the road and doubled back onto his own plantation of Pine Grove, looking and listening for anyone who might have followed. No one had.

When he kicked the horse into motion once more, it lifted into the canter Bluford had been demanding, but this time he pulled the animal back and held it to a short, slow trot. He wished he would never arrive at the meeting place; he wished he were someplace else.

Finally, giving the low *hu, hu, hu* call of the owl, he approached the thick grove of pines that grew closest to the road. He hadn't wanted to use that as their signal, for the owl always called when somebody died, but the ignorant *yonegas* couldn't seem to imitate any other bird.

Oh, how he wished he'd never gotten mixed up with them!

However, the extra money *had* come in very handy.

Bluford gave the call again, and this time one of them answered. He set his teeth and rode in to see them, holding one hand up to keep the needle-laden branches out of his face. Thank goodness the moonlight was strong enough to filter in through the trees.

After tonight, he would set all of his energies to finding the murderer. Once he had killed him, Papa's spirit could go to the Nightland and leave him alone. It'd be worth giving up some of his luxuries, if it came to that.

He rode up to his partners, who were waiting on horseback in the shadows of the trees.

"This'll be our last raid," Bluford said briskly, trying to sound very much in command. "And it's a good thing we're planning to take stock from some of these plantations around here. There's suspicions now as to why this valley's always been spared."

"Aw, Blu, why don't you quit singin' that song about the last raid?" Sykes drawled. "Even that servant girl finding us with a penful of stolen horses didn't get us caught, did it? And you said she's dead now, so we're safe."

"Fawn may have told Tiana Tenkiller about that; they were very close. I need to get out of this now."

Walters silenced him with a harsh, harrumphing sound. "Who has suspicions about this valley being spared?"

"Etuwee Campbell, for one," Bluford retorted. "And Joe Raincrow, for two. They're smart enough to figure this whole thing out. We better take a couple of my horses tonight, too, just to be safe."

Sykes coughed, hawked, and leaned to spit on the ground beside his horse. "Main one I want is that silver runnin' stud of Gray Fox Tenkiller's," he said. "I aim to have that horse and make my fortune with him."

"Forget him," Bluford snapped. "He's too unusual—too easy to trace from hand to hand. I ain't about to keep *him* in a holding pen anywhere on my place, no matter how well hidden it is."

"So," Sykes said, "we'll take him all the way to Augusta tonight."

"The Tenkillers are having a party," Bluford said, biting each word out from between his teeth. "I just came from there. Half the Nation is there right now, do you understand? We *can't* risk that."

"You mean *you* can't risk it, Cherokee. Nothing they can do to us."

"You'd be surprised," Bluford retorted, suddenly loyal to his brothers he was planning to rob. "All they'd have to do is pretend there's no law just the same way you Georgians do."

"We pretend no such thing," Walters said smoothly, chuckling as he took up his reins and urged his horse to move along. "Stealing horses from Indians is quite legal in Georgia. Now, then, since we are sure of the master's whereabouts, exactly where is the plantation of this most astute thinker, Mr. Etuwee Campbell?"

Bluford told him, then rode behind them, unwilling to have the two white renegades at his back. They were getting to know this part of the Nation very well; they didn't really need him anymore. Except, maybe, for the use of Pine Grove to hold the stolen horses for a day or two.

And he no longer needed them. Now that Tobacco Jack was dead and he had control of Pine Grove, running it every day satisfied the craving for power that used to nag at him all the time. If Tobacco Jack hadn't held him on such a short rein from the time he was a boy, Bluford would never have gotten into this mess of thieves in the first place—if his fellow Cherokees caught him now, they'd run him out of the Nation or hang him, and he would lose Pine Grove forever.

Standingdeer's being back at Pine Grove made that an even stronger possibility; Papa had always said there wasn't much that got by without Stand's seeing it. But then, too, Papa had always been partial to Stand, even before he was called The Paint.

Not because he'd been a better boy and was a better man than Bluford, though. It was because

Stand's mother had been Papa's favorite baby sister.

Still, it wasn't fair for Papa to have loved his nephew more than his own son.

Bluford heaved a big sigh and glanced sharply sideways, as though Tobacco Jack's spirit were riding a ghost horse in the darkness beside him. He gritted his teeth as Sykes led them into an especially black patch of woods. From now on, these two renegades could carry on without him—he had a more urgent task to do.

This awful danger he was in was all Papa's fault. He would be rid of Tobacco Jack once and for all before the moon waned again.

The next morning Tiana woke just after Grandmother Sun peeked into her room, although she hadn't come to bed until long after midnight. And then, wedged between Cahtahtie and Sally, with two other girls whose families had stayed at Running Waters overnight giggling and then snoring on a pallet on the floor, she had lain awake even longer.

But trying to rest three in a bed wasn't the main reason she hadn't been able to sleep. Then, as now, the memory of Standingdeer's kiss was pounding in her blood, demanding to grow and multiply itself, begging to be repeated again and again.

She threw off the sheet and climbed over Cahtahtie to set her feet on the floor. She had to be alone to think about The Paint.

Nobody stirred as Tiana tiptoed across to her armoire, threw off her nightgown, and shrugged into her riding clothes. She left the house by the back stairs, ran across the porch and down the steps into the heavy, dew-laden air of the morning.

She avoided Moss, who was bringing an early-departing guest's horse up from the stable yard, and two of Dilcey's helpers who were going, yawning and stretching, into the summer kitchen. Soon the smell of woodsmoke and frying bacon and sausage would float over the plantation. With a sudden desire, so sharp that it twisted inside her, she wished that Standingdeer were one of the guests who'd stayed over, that she would see him at breakfast.

If he hadn't taken Maud home as soon as he'd finished with the letter to Washington City, would he have kissed her again? Would he have danced with her?

How could she have danced with him and not held her face up for his kiss for all to see?

And now they were going to Ellijay! Everything would be perfect: Coosa would win lots of money so that she wouldn't have to worry anymore and . . . Stand would kiss her again.

Surely one more kiss wouldn't matter. After that, she would be careful not to do it again. After that, she would make herself remember that her secret would always be a barrier between them.

Tiana hugged herself; during these past, awful weeks she'd almost forgotten how it felt to be happy, even just for a little while. She veered left to take the fork that led to the barns.

As she passed the well house, something reached out and caught her arm, so hard that it jerked her around.

She whirled, and when she saw who was holding her arm, her toes curled to the curve of the earth, even through the soles of her boots. Old Sudie!

It couldn't be. But it was.

The round, bent shape inched out from behind the stone wall of the wellhouse and into full view, holding onto Tiana's arm with a hard, shaking grip, like an owl's on a mouse. Sudie tilted her turbaned head sideways and fixed Tiana with an unrelenting stare.

"I've come for my freedom, Sister," she said.

For three or four long heartbeats, Tiana's brain refused to work. The cold shock numbed it. Finally it accepted the words.

"I don't have that to give you, Aunt Sudie," she breathed.

"Bluford will sell it," the old woman said, the brown glint of snuff flashing in her toothless mouth. "You give me the money to buy it."

"No! I can't! I don't have enough money to ... You see, my brother ..."

"Bluford won't ask much for me; I can't work no more," Sudie said hoarsely, as if Tiana hadn't spoken. "But I'll need fares to git me North and money to live once I'm gone. Five hundred dollars."

Tiana tried to jerk free, but Sudie's thin claw had the sinewy strength of a man.

"Don't try to run from me! Five hundred dollars. Or do you want Bluford to hear who it was took up a hoe and knocked his daddy dead?"

The cold spread from Tiana's brain down the back of her neck and into her spine.

"Didn't know I seen ye, did ye?" the old servant cackled. "Well, Old Sudie ain't blind, and she ain't dead yet."

Tiana felt her eyes widen, but aside from that, she couldn't move. Not even to speak.

"Cat got yer tongue, eh?" Old Sudie murmured. "Well, you jist wait, girl. Bluford'll cut th' heart from yer body to git rid of Tobacco Jack's ha'nt."

She squeezed Tiana's arm hard enough to bruise the skin through her sleeve, then dropped her own hand, pulled at her head rag, and eased back against the wall of the well house.

"Go on! Git!" she hissed in a piercing whisper. "You go find my money."

Tiana, panic beating a path through each vein in her body, turned and ran.

Stand looked down at the top of Tiana's head as she stroked Coosa's legs and picked up each of his feet one more time before the race. The last race of the Ellijay meet.

"Last chance to finish in the money," he said, surprising even himself by the hardness in his voice.

Her head jerked up, her beautiful face set in the mask she had worn for four days. "You don't have to tell me!"

"Why do you need it so much, Tiana?"

She turned away and examined Coosa's hock without answering.

He'd give anything, Stand thought, to be able to see straight through her shining black hair, confined in a braid as always when she raced, through her skull and into her mind. What in the name of Thunder was driving her?

And what was driving *him*, that he cared this much?

Finally she straightened up. "How do you know I need the money?"

"You've been like a mad person this whole trip, staying to yourself, not talking to anyone, agonizing over losing."

Never giving me a chance to be near you, to touch you.

"I *loathe* losing!"

"It's more than that."

"No, it isn't!"

Stand gritted his teeth. Why the hell had he come? She had only beguiled him with that kiss to get him to let her run Coosa in this race. Why was he hanging around, asking for more like a half-grown whelp of a boy?

Her high, full breasts rose and fell with the agitation of her breathing, straining at the buttons of what must be her narrow-chested brother's shirt. He ached to touch her.

"I don't see a thing wrong with Coosa," she said, a worry line between her eyes the only blemish on her perfect face. "Why he didn't win yesterday will forever be a mystery to be."

"He was sulking," Stand said. "He was acting spoiled. Which he is."

That put the fire back into her eyes. But not the fire he wanted to see.

"He is not! I don't know why you keep saying that!"

"Time, Miss Tiana!" Moss called, running uphill from the track toward the spreading ash tree where they waited. "Bettah gits this hoss to th' startin' line!"

She grabbed the reins and threw them over the stallion's head, then rushed back to his side to mount. Stand stepped in to pull up the cinch on the little racing saddle, to force it to buckle tighter.

"Hurry!" she said, and pushed at him a little. "Give me a leg up."

He did. And had to fight to make himself turn her loose; the feel of her dainty foot and the inward curve of her waist burned into his palms even after she was mounted and Coosa was dancing excitedly away.

He tore his eyes from her and saw the crop that had slipped from her wrist.

"Here," he said, remembering their old jest as he bent to pick it up. "You'll need this to threaten him."

She stood in one stirrup and reached out across empty air to take it from him. At the moment she touched the handle, as suddenly as a rabbit darting from a pile of brush, she smiled at him.

For the first time in four days. A quick, conspiratorial smile that would lure a hidden buck out of cover and into danger.

His heart turned over.

But she whirled Coosa and headed him toward the track without a word.

Moss ran to take the bit and Stand watched them trot downslope to the track, forcing his feet to stay rooted on the hillside. He was a fool, forty kinds of a fool, for kissing her in the first place. The girl was insincere; she used her smiles and her kisses to get her way. She was not only a woman, but a Tenkiller, and neither could be trusted.

Yet the sight of Tiana tugged at his heart. She looked like a doll so brittle that it was ready to break, even there in the saddle she was born to. Her delicate shoulders looked almost frail, so strange and stiff was the way she held them.

He narrowed his eyes to watch her as she tapped Coosa's side with one heel, making him sidepass to stand at the starting line beside one of the horses that would race him. Her hands trembled on the reins—Stand could see that even from this distance.

For the hundredth time he wondered what had happened since the night of the social. She was in a lot of trouble: that was why she had kissed him for the chance to come and win this money, and there was more to it now. But *what?* If she wouldn't tell him in four days and three nights of sleeping and eating at the same campfire and working the same horse, then when would she?

Not until she was forced to, like Elena. Like his mother.

An old woman peddling frybread tugged at his arm. Stand got a coin from his pocket and gave it to her. He took the bread, but a thought hit him and he forgot to lift the treat to his mouth.

If Coosa won this race, he would offer to lend his share of the money to Tiana. And before she got it in her hand, he would make her tell him why she needed it so desperately!

The minute the drum rolled, Tiana relaxed in the saddle and rode like a dream woman. Her long legs clung to the horse like a lover's embrace; her hands played his mouth like a song. *Uncle Jack had been right*, Stand thought. She was a natural.

And so was the stallion. He distanced his rivals without breaking a sweat and won the money going away.

Tiana rode Coosa away from the track, up the gentle slope of the hill, and over its crest to their camp at the edge of the trees. As the stallion splashed across the little stream that ran between their campsite and the Campbells', she looked at their fire pits, their carriages, the oak and black locust trees, the water flowing over the rocks, and the other horses staked all around there as if she'd never seen them before. The purse swinging from her wrist had brought her back to life.

She had lived here for four days and three nights, had eaten and slept and talked, a little, to The Paint and Gray Fox and Cahtahtie and Etuwee, but all that and the trip up here from Running Waters was nothing but a hodgepodge in her memory. What she did know, sharp and clear as stars shining down on snow, was that it had taken every ounce of strength in her body to keep from flinging herself into the safety of The Paint's arms and pouring out her panic to him.

It had taken every shred of her sanity to remember that his arms weren't safe—that they were the most dangerous place she could be. For if he held her, if he kissed her again, she would need him forever. She already did, after only one time.

She needed even more than the kisses, too. She needed him to be her friend. If he held her again, she would probably blurt out the story that Sudie was threatening to tell.

And then he would turn in an instant from a friend to an enemy. He would hate her forever. He most likely would kill her; he had sworn that he would.

That danger must stay uppermost in her mind a few minutes from now. She had avoided being alone with him for four endless days, but she couldn't any longer. Her only chance was to talk with him, and with Gray Fox nowhere about.

She rode Coosa up to the fire pit, told him, "Whoa," and swung down from his back. She ran to the carriage, looking for the safest place to hide the purse from Gray Fox.

But there wasn't any time.

"Sister!" his voice called from behind her. He was still across the creek, but not very far. "Tiana! Why didn't you wait for me?"

She didn't even glance his way while she ran back to Coosa and, standing on his off side, knotted the strings of the purse securely around her arm.

"The Paint will be here shortly," Gray said, loping his big roan horse out of the trees and across the creek into the open space with its circle of fire rocks in the middle. "When he gets here we can divide up the purse."

"You might as well take yourself right back to the track and all your good-time gambling friends," Tiana said icily. "I'm not letting you have one penny of this purse."

"Tiana!" he said, his tone deeply hurt. "You sound mean as a harridan."

He stopped his horse and stared down at her, slumped in his saddle as if she had taken away his last hope in the world.

"I am mean," she said, taking the bridle off Coosa and slipping his halter on. "I am mean as Spearfinger and forty *Uk'ten*'s put together, and don't you forget it. Go away, Gray Fox."

He sat there watching her while she unbuckled the girth and removed the saddle.

Finally he said, "Johnny Campbell and Edley Shoemake were talking a while ago about the latest pony club raids. Did you know that stock from nearly every plantation around Running Waters was stolen the night of our social?"

"The Paint told us on the way up here that Pine Grove lost three head," she snapped. "Changing the subject won't help you one bit, Gray."

The news struck fresh terror into her bones, though. What if a pony club were raiding Running Waters this minute, while they were gone? Could Gabriel and Ned, his other stable boy, hide the best horses in time?

Of course not. Those Georgians always struck fast as lightning.

She wouldn't let herself think about it now. The bundle of burdens weighing down on her head seemed to double and triple every day, and she simply could not take on another one to carry. Not when she had to have all her nerve for this talk with The Paint.

She picked up the grooming brush and stepped around to the other side of Coosa.

"I'm not just changing the subject," her brother said. "I'm trying to guess what's bothering you so much that you're acting like this." He was speaking in his sweetest, most reasonable tone. "I thought maybe you were worrying about things at home."

"I'm acting like this so you won't have a chance to use your charms on me," she said, drawing the brush in long sweeping motions down the horse's side. "To talk me out of this money."

"But I have to have three hundred dollars!" he cried. "You *know* that, Ti."

"*I'll* deliver the three hundred," she told him, studiously keeping her tone cold and calm. "Or as close to that amount as I can get. If you meet Sykes and Walters, you'll try to double it and lose."

"It isn't very kind of you to remind me of my failures," he chided. "There have been plenty of times when I've won."

She leaned one elbow on Coosa's croup and looked her brother straight in the eye. "Gray, here comes The Paint. I need to talk with him privately. Would you excuse us, please?"

He stared back at her. "You've been so unfriendly ever since that day you made me work in the hayfield," he said. "I hope you don't stay this way forever, Ti. Just let me know when you have a pittance to dole out to me."

He turned and left the clearing, greeting The Paint with a faint wave of one hand as they passed each other. Tiana pretended to be totally engrossed in grooming the horse.

The Paint dismounted beside her, but she hardly looked at him, just nodded and said, "*Osiyo.*"

He caught the light scent of her skin as he strolled around her to the tailgate of the wagon in which they had brought their supplies, then lifted himself up to sit on it. She stayed where she was, which she would never have done yesterday. Maybe winning had made her ready to talk.

Tiana stepped beneath Coosa's neck and started Mon his opposite side, circling the brush over his hide in short, hard strokes, every muscle in her body still drawn so tight that she looked as if she would snap. She needed help. This win wasn't enough.

"Congratulations," he said. "You two made a great run."

"Thank you," she said, and, to his surprise, she turned and looked directly into his eyes.

The only other time she'd done that during this entire trip was when he'd handed her the crop.

"Stand," she blurted at last, "I really need to talk with you."

His heart leapt. "What about?"

She bent to take a shaky swipe with the brush down Coosa's off foreleg, then raised herself to look into his face again. Her eyes blazed, huge and dark, almost as bright as they had after his kiss.

"I need to borrow your half of the purse."

"It's yours."

For a heartbeat she stood, not moving, as if she still waited for his answer.

Then she gave him a smile that tore out his heart, one that bared the pain to her pride this request had cost.

"Thank you, Stand. I ... I'll pay you when I can."

She looked away and snagged the brush in the stallion's mane. It knotted and tangled because her hand shook like a spider's web in a wind.

"Tiana," he said, trying to pull her to him with his voice, not daring to get up and go to her, not yet. "What's wrong? Why do you need so much money?"

She turned her face away. "I can't discuss it."

"You can with me." He used the quiet, soothing tone that had brought many a wild thing to his hand.

She dropped the brush and leaned both elbows

on the gray's back, laying her face on her crossed arms.

"What kind of trouble are you in, Tiana?"

She lifted her face to look at him, tears rolling down her cheeks. "I'm not! I'm not in trouble at all."

"Don't ever lie to your friends."

"Oh, is that right?" she stormed, her eyes flashing hot into his. "Is that some kind of wise rule of life or something?"

He nodded, keeping steady eye contact with her.

Finally she broke it and stomped around the horse to come and sit on the tailgate of the wagon beside him. Not quite close enough for their shoulders to touch, but near, as she would sit to draw warmth from a fire.

"It's Gray," she said. "He's way in debt from his gambling. It's ruining Running Waters. Soon there'll be nothing left."

He nodded, watching her face. She kept her profile turned to him.

That was part of it, true; the whole Nation knew how foolish Gray's behavior had been. But her voice had sounded brittle and her words had come too fast.

"That's why the stables burned, isn't it?" he said.

"Yes. And now they're threatening to burn the house."

"Will this purse be enough to stop that?"

She swallowed so hard it must have hurt her throat.

"Yes! Yes, thank you. Everything will be fine now."

But she didn't smile. There was no sigh of relief, no slumping against the side of the wagon—or against him—because she was saved from her fears at last.

Her supple body was still frozen too stiff. There was something else she was trying to hide.

She tossed her long braid over her shoulder and turned to give him a quick, sidelong look.

"What else?" he said. "Besides Gray's gambling?"

"Nothing else! Why does there need to be something else? Isn't that more than enough?"

Pure, hot anger cut through him. Anger at her, at whatever was making her keep her secrets, anger at life. Why, why the hell did it always have to be this way?

"Gambling makes Gray absolutely crazy," she rushed on, as if she could fill the distance growing between them with words. "I hate it! I don't see how anybody even remotely in his right mind can indulge in such a stupid . . ."

"You're a gambler, too."

"I most certainly am *not!*"

"Anybody who does anything with horses for profit is a gambler."

She turned around fast, tossing her head. The tip end of her braid flicked the skin of his neck like a whip.

"Is that another of your wise rules of life?"

"Right." He pierced her with his eyes, willing her to look at him and keep looking until she saw the frustration and fury that he would be damned if he'd put into words.

"And another rule is that Gray Fox can make debts faster than you can pay them," he said. But he didn't hear his own voice. A waterfall roared in his head.

Tiana Tenkiller was just like the trapper's wife he'd loved so long ago: she definitely had her secrets, too, even if she was young and openly naive.

No, it was he, Standingdeer Chekote, with all the hard experience of his long years of wandering and his wise rules of life, who was naive. How could he ever have hoped that she cared for him, even a little, when she kissed him like a fiery, innocent angel?

He must be getting old and lonely.

Chapter 6

The Paint swept his eyes away from her face and, in one scornful motion, stepped down from the tailgate so suddenly that the whole wagon rocked. Tiana grabbed the rough edge of her seat with both hands.

He stalked off toward his horse.

He was furious with her. "What else?" he had said, and when she had answered, "Nothing else," his eyes had repeated his rule: "Never lie to your friends."

But he wasn't her friend. She clenched the board in her hands until she could feel the splinters bite. A cold wind blew through her.

"I'll pay you back," she called, pretending that the money was the cause of his anger. *Wishing* that it were. "It's not as if you'll never get your half of the purse."

He didn't answer; he didn't even slow his steps.

She jumped down and ran after him, blinking to clear her vision. His broad shoulders, muscles bulging beneath his blue shirt, looked like the pale wall of a mountain against the dark green of the trees. Like a wall of granite looming between them.

"Wait a minute, Stand," she said loudly. "We

didn't talk about repayment. I'll sell some horses and pay you, but I don't have time for that now."

He whirled to face her and stood, legs apart, boots braced against the sloping ground as if he were trying to keep his balance in a storm. His eyes looked bleak as winter.

"Forget the money," he snapped. "Keep it." He turned on his heel and took hold of his reins.

His haughty disdain fired an answering anger in her.

"No!" she cried, jerking at the pouch tied to her wrist. "I *won't* be obligated to you! Take it! Give me your knife and I'll cut it loose—you can take it all!"

He flicked his reins over his horse's neck and, without even turning to look at her, stepped into the saddle and swung the buckskin's head toward the creek.

"I'll never ask you for help again!" she yelled to his impervious back. "And I'll pay every penny I owe you!"

The only answer she got was the splashing of the horse's hooves as Standingdeer rode into the water.

Oh, how she would love to leap onto Coosa and chase after the buckskin! To catch him and throw the money straight into The Paint's haughty face!

But she couldn't. She needed it too badly.

Instead, she walked to Coosa and sagged against his warm side. The Paint's contempt was a terrible thing.

But it was better to face his contempt than the hatred he would feel for her if she told him the truth.

Finally, when the strength came back into her limbs, she untied the money from her wrist, went to her reticule, and stashed the pouch deep in the pocket of the one dress she'd brought with her.

She made sure the horses were all right and then carried the dress into the woods to find a private spot to change into it. She wouldn't be riding anymore this trip, and the bulge of the money would be too obvious in her riding breeches.

Her prize safe, she came back to camp and threw herself into cleaning Coosa and his tack, caring for him and Danny and Switch, and gathering as much equipment into the wagon as she could in preparation for their leaving for home at first light the next day. She kept her mind on dividing the money she had between her salvation and Gray Fox's.

But when the sun slipped down behind Turkey Mountain and no one else came back to camp, when the locusts started buzzing in the woods and the night birds began to call, when wisps of mountain mist drifted across her campfire and darkness fell, her thoughts turned against her and clung to The Paint. It was for the best that they become strangers again, she told herself over and over. It was for the best.

Because if they weren't strangers, they would be much more than friends. One kiss from him had proved that.

And such a dream could never be, for he would hate her forever if he knew that she had killed Tobacco Jack.

Once I get myself and Gray out of this fix, she vowed as she slid into her quilts in the bed of the wagon and covered her ears against the sounds of singing and dancing down in the valley by the track, *I'll pay back every cent of this money to The Paint. I'll never ask him for help again.*

After dark the next day, when she and Gray arrived home, Tiana didn't even help put up the horses. She climbed down from the wagon in the barn lot, shook the travel dust from her skirts, and ran up to the house fast, as if Old Sudie were still lurking behind the well house to catch her. She waved hello to Dilcey in the kitchen, but she didn't stop until she had reached Papa's study and closed the door.

She locked it and leaned against it, panting for breath.

Gray wouldn't think of the safe again because he had emptied it once. That was why she had hidden Mama's brooch there. She would put the money in it, too, for tonight, and by this time tomorrow all the vultures would be paid.

That is, if Sykes and Walters would accept the brooch as their payment. It was easily worth three hundred dollars—anyone could see that by looking. She would give it to them and divide the thousand dollars in cash between Old Sudie and the note on the foundation mares.

Sykes and Walters would take the brooch out of the Nation where it wouldn't be recognized; no one would know how low Gray Fox's gambling had brought the Tenkillers. She would sell a horse or two at a decent price to pay back The Paint.

A knock crashed at the door; she shoved her hand deep into her pocket to cover the pouch full of money.

"Tiana!" Gray called. "Let me in!"

"I'm busy."

"Doing what? Hiding *our* money?"

Thunderation! He must have the second sight!

She didn't have time to hide the money; if she made him wait, he'd think about the safe and find the brooch there. So she thrust the pouch deeper into her pocket and opened the door.

"Well, at least we won one race," Gray said cheerfully, sauntering past her and across the room to drop down on the leather settee. "I suppose we can't expect Coosa to run his heart out *every* time."

He patted the place beside him, but Tiana shook her head and leaned against the jamb of the open door.

She bit her lip. "Couldn't we have rehashed the races on the way home, Gray, instead of waiting until we're both so tired we can't see? I'd like to get to bed soon."

"So would I," he said. "Let me have the purse money now so I won't have to wake you in the morning."

"That's funny, Gray Fox," she said wearily. "I'm at the barn by good light every morning and you seldom show your face before noon. I can't imagine *your* waking *me* up."

He chuckled. "Aw, that's not always true. Don't you remember the time I got up early to catch a frog and put it in your bed?"

The childhood memory and the charm of his smile coaxed an answering smile from her. "I remember. I just wish your pranks were still that harmless. Why do you have to get us into such trouble?"

But you got yourself into your own trouble, a small voice inside her insisted. *You can't blame Gray for that.*

"So that you can get us out," he teased. "That was smart of you to borrow The Paint's half of the purse. It's really our money, anyway—we do all the work and Coosa *is* our horse."

Tiana's stomach tightened into a hard knot. "He *was* our horse until you gambled him away. How did you know I borrowed The Paint's half of the money?"

"I slipped back through the woods and eavesdropped on you. What'd you expect when you told me you had to talk to him alone?"

"I borrowed his money for some personal business," she said. "Our half can pay Sykes and Walters."

His smile faded. "There'll be two hundred left over from that. *I* should have it."

"That'll go on the note for the foundation mares," she said sharply. "I'll get the rest by selling a two-year-old."

"You? Papa left *me* in charge of Running Waters."

"To his eternal regret," she said coldly. "I told you the other day I was taking charge."

"Now, Ti," he said, smiling again, trying to charm her. He got up and came over to her. "Don't be hateful anymore. Let me have the two hundred, and I'll make enough to ransom the mares without selling anything."

He patted her shoulder. "Just think, Ti. You could keep *all* your babies!"

For one insane instant she almost listened to him. Even after all his losses. But then The Paint's voice, low and sure, sounded in her mind.

Gray Fox can make debts faster than you can pay them.

"As I said at the Council Oak, Gray, you know me too well. But I'm not giving in. You get nothing."

Gray's smile faded into a hostile stare. The clock in the front hallway chimed; Tiana counted every stroke. Nine.

"Then I'm leaving."

"Don't be ridiculous! We have a cotton crop, and the second cutting of hay, and the corn . . ."

"*You're* taking care of everything, remember? *You're* selling horses and paying debts and even delivering the three hundred dollars I owe to Sykes and Walters. Surely *you* can get out a cotton and a corn crop!"

He sounded so hurt. All his life she had run to heal his wounds, no matter who or what had caused them.

But not now. She must be strong, stronger than she'd ever been, or he would squander the money she'd garnered by the skin of her teeth and this house would lie in ashes.

Cold fingers traced the length of her spine. "Look at it this way, Gray," she said softly. "I don't mean to hurt your pride; I mean to keep you away from temptation. If you have no money, you can't gamble it away."

He met her gaze for only a moment. "I'm leaving. If you won't let me be the master of this plantation, if you insist on meddling in my personal affairs, then I'm leaving."

She let the words hang between them for a long time, but he didn't take them back. He was threatening, bargaining, bluffing, trying to get the two hundred dollars. He didn't care what happened to the broodmares.

Well, she would call his bluff. "Where will you go?"

"To Dahlonega."

He stomped past her and out of the room.

"Dahlonega!" Tiana cried, turning to follow him. "Gray Fox, you're going into *Georgia*?"

"I know you worry about me, Sister," he said sarcastically from the foot of the stairs. "Please don't."

"But it's a gold-mining town!" she shouted as he ran up the steps. "It's a wild place full of gold-hungry whites!"

"I have friends there!" he yelled over his shoulder and disappeared down the hall to his room.

A cold breeze brushed through the hallway, coming from nowhere out of the hot summer night. Gray Fox was leaving her, leaving right now. He would ride out into the thick, black dark and be gone.

Who did he know in Dahlonega? No telling—he had gambled with every scoundrel in the Nation and had made many trips into Georgia. She couldn't protect him anymore.

And he couldn't protect her. He never had.

Tiana stood, listening to the sounds of his packing, his calling to Dilcey for some shirts, his shouting down the back stairs for her to fix him some food for the road. He was leaving Tiana here alone.

And not because she had taken charge, not because she insisted on paying Sykes and Walters for him. He was secretly relieved about that.

All he really wanted was the two hundred dollars. If she gave it to him, he would stay. He thought she was bluffing, too. He was calling her bluff.

She waited at the front door until he clattered down the stairs, a heavy bag in each hand. No telling what he had pilfered from the upstairs rooms to sell once he got to Dahlonega. That should give him enough of a stake to live on, at least for a few days, until he lost it.

He stopped in front of her. "You're always wanting everything to be the way it used to be," he said. "But it won't be if I don't live here anymore."

Then he just stood there, waiting for her to give in.

Her heart stopped. He was right. All her dreams of keeping Running Waters intact would be dead.

But she couldn't relent. She had to save whatever she could. Because she couldn't save her brother.

"Gray Fox," she said, "I wish you wouldn't go. But I won't give you this money to throw away."

Never in her life had she felt so strong and determined.

"While gambling in Dahlonega," she said, "you will not give a note on so much as one head of cattle or horse on this plantation. If you do, I will send straightaway for Papa to come home."

Thank God and Thunder, she thought, that the land was held in common by the Cherokee Nation. If Gray Fox could, he'd risk Running Waters itself.

"Tiana," he said in a pathetic, hurt voice. He shook his head sadly. "How can you misjudge me so?"

He stood still, waiting for her to give in.

"*You've* misjudged *me*, Gray," she said, as a hollow hole in her heart replaced the sympathy that she usually felt for her brother. "Don't make that mistake again. I will send for Papa. Do you believe me?"

He glared at her, and then nodded, grudgingly.

"All right, then," she said, and stood aside to hold the door for him. "Ride safe."

Once he was off the porch, she turned and ran for her room, hot tears pouring like a river down her face.

Tiana leaned deeper into her stirrup, careful not to sit down and back in the saddle, which would signal Coosa to slow his long trot, and took the embroidered cotton handkerchief from her pocket. The sweat trickling from beneath her hat down her temples had begun to drip onto her best riding habit.

"Grandmother Sun shines extra hot today," she muttered to the stallion, unwilling to admit, even to him, that the fear chasing along her nerves was another, perhaps the more potent, cause of her perspiration. "I wish I could've asked someone to come with us," she admitted to him, "but Dilcey can't ride, and I don't want anyone else to know we've sunk so low as to sell Mama's jewelry."

She wiped her face, then thrust the scrap of damp cloth back into her pocket, feeling all the way to the bottom to make sure the brooch was still there. It was, and now she wished that the comforting weight of Papa's pistol was, too.

But if she had left it in her pocket, where she had put it early this morning, by tonight she might have killed yet another man. Her conscience could not bear that burden.

She patted Coosa's neck. "I'm depending on speed instead of guns today, Big Rabbit. Remember that."

A hundred yards or so ahead, at a curve in the Federal Road, a huge sycamore leaned out backward over the way, its branches lowering so far that its hand-sized leaves brushed the ground on the opposite side. There, that was the marker. Sykes and Walters waited behind it, inside the woods that always before had looked so welcoming to her.

Tiana glanced ahead again, and then behind her. Coosa twisted his head, too.

"It's all right," she said, stroking his neck again, more for her own comfort than for his. "Nobody we know is around to see us."

Or to help. What if she needed help? After all, these men had set fire to the stables and had threatened to kill her brother and her.

And more. She could still hear Sykes' raspy voice saying, *After I sample what's beneath them boy's britches there.*

She suppressed the memory, as she had done a dozen or more times during the long morning's ride. After she had paid them, she would be rid of these two enemies for all time.

She straightened in the saddle. The men were nothing but cowards, sneaky barn burners, blustering about the country spewing threats. All they really wanted was money.

And the brooch was worth much more than three hundred dollars. Anyone could see that. If she gave it to them, they would go away forever.

Tiana touched her hat and the collar of her habit, then shifted her right leg slightly around the horn of her sidesaddle. Today they couldn't taunt her about any boy's britches. Mama had always told her that if she acted like a lady and looked like a lady, she would be treated like a lady.

She threw back her shoulders and sat up ramrod-straight. Tiana Tenkiller could do this. She could save her brother's life and her beloved Running Waters and she didn't need any help to do it.

Especially not The Paint's. She would never ask *him* for help again. She would never even *think* about him again.

She looked behind her one more time. Dust was rising in front of the herd of cattle she'd passed near Bascom's Ferry, and she could hear the voices of the drovers bringing them across the Nation from Tennessee to markets in Georgia or the Carolinas. The men were singing.

Grandmother Sun was shining. The rhododendron was blooming, pink and purple. The waxwings were calling, their wings flashing as they whirred from tree to tree. The woods smelled like summer and the mountains loomed blue above them. Everything would be all right.

She reined Coosa over and left the road.

Only a thin scattering of beech trees stood between the big sycamore and the clearing that lay behind it at the edge of the deep woods. Tiana eased Coosa to a quiet stop before she rode through the beeches, her eyes searching the roughly circular open space ahead through the crisscrossing branches and trembling green leaves.

Coosa snorted once and jingled the bit on his tongue.

"Where's yore brother?"

She grabbed at the saddle, getting a handful of Coosa's mane instead, as she whirled to face the rough voice. Sykes had stepped out from the shelter of the sycamore behind her.

"I came in his place."

The sound of her voice thrilled her. It sounded as though she was perfectly calm and in control. Sykes would never know how much he'd frightened her.

"Aw," he croaked, pausing to spit a stream of brown tobacco juice on the grass, "you Injuns is too crooked for that. Where's he hidin'?"

"I have brought your payment," Tiana said. "Let's get this transaction done."

He made a grimace of thin lips across crooked teeth. "Git down off that stud horse and bring it here."

She was not about to dismount; she had decided that before she left home.

"You come to me," Tiana ordered. "Keep one hand at your side and hold out my brother's IOU notes with the other."

She took the leather pouch from her pocket and dangled it by its strings. "There's a diamond-and-gold brooch worth at least five hundred dollars in here," she said. "That'll pay for every note my brother gave you."

Sykes chuckled, a scornful, rasping sound that grated along her skin. He began walking toward her.

"We ain't in the jewelry business," he said. "Wasn't nothin' said about no brooches."

"It's the very best quality," she said. "You won't

have any trouble getting far more for it than we owe you. Now show me Gray's notes; you did bring them, didn't you?"

"I'd rather have cash."

He was close enough that she could see shreds of tobacco in the corners of his mouth. However, both his hands hung empty; he didn't even reach into his pocket.

"I don't have cash. You'll have to take the brooch."

"We should at least *look* at it, don't you think, Sykes?" Walters' smooth voice asked. Tiana jumped. He was approaching from her off side.

For an irrational instant her fear lessened. She wasn't alone with Sykes anymore, and Walters seemed to be supporting her position.

"Did *you* bring the notes?" she asked.

"I beg your pardon?" he said as he walked up to her.

"If I'm paying off my brother's debt to you, you should return his notes," she said.

"He gave us no notes," Walters said. "Having an acquaintance with your brother is lucrative for us and we trust him."

"Not any more. Gray Fox has left the Nation. And I would suggest that once we have completed our business here, you two do the same."

Walters stopped too near the stallion's head. Tiana squeezed Coosa's right side; he edged to the left.

"Take this brooch and go. Your very presence here is illegal under Cherokee law."

Walters gave her a sad smile. "Unfortunately, my dear, Georgia law prevails. For three whole years. Or hadn't you heard?"

He extended his chubby arm and seized Coosa's bit.

Sykes ran forward, fast as a snake striking, and caught it on the other side.

"Git down," he growled. "I aim t' search yore pockets, *see* if you don't have cash."

He jerked a knife from a sheath at his belt and held its point to Coosa's silver neck.

Coosa stood still. Tiana didn't move.

"Now, sweetie," the ugly man croaked, "git down and come here to me."

Hot defiance mixed with cold fear in her veins; visions of Old Sudie and the bloodstock mares and the big white house going up in flames swam before her eyes. Why, *why* hadn't she had sense enough to bring the three hundred in cash? She could've ridden to Augusta and sold the brooch.

Walters said, "We have always coveted this magnificent animal, my dear. However, if you do not comply with our wishes, we shall cut his throat. My friend Sykes fancies you more than the horse."

Sykes gave her a cold, ugly smile of assent.

It sent terror leaping through her, fear that brought with it the instinctive urge to escape.

She threw the pouch straight into Walters' fat face and, pulling on the reins, yelled, "Ha! Ha! Go now!"

Coosa's great strength plucked his head from the thieves' hands, nearly taking their arms from their sockets as well. He reared and broke away, snorting his fear and disgust, to smash backward into the thin stand of beeches.

Tiana locked her leg around the saddlehorn as he whirled to face the other way, frantic to run. She ducked, lying close to his neck as they dashed through the beeches again, passed the big sycamore, and plunged out into the Federal Road.

Straight into the herd of Tennessee cattle.

Coosa's right foreleg struck a heavy body; then

untold numbers of bodies swarmed toward them, bawling and lowing.

"Hyah! Git, there, git!" one of the drovers shouted, and then the noise of the cattle drowned him out.

The dust blinded Tiana, choked her. But Coosa pressed on, relentless, pushing, forcing a path through the chaos coming at them from all sides. Tiana clung to him and let him keep his head.

The cattle sounded like Sykes' rusty voice bleating behind her: hurry, they had to hurry. She stuck her heels to Coosa.

He plunged on, shying from the clacking horns. As they emerged from the back edge of the herd, he jumped sideways. Tiana's heart stopped. Was he hurt? Had a cow hooked him?

Oh, dear Lord, what would she ever tell The Paint? There was no reason at all to have a running horse of Coosa's caliber anywhere near the horns of cattle. Pray God her darling stallion wasn't hurt.

She leaned as far as she could over the sidesaddle to look, but she could see no wound, and as soon as he was free, he moved out with all his normal smoothness and speed. Probably they were safe. Once Sykes and Walters had mounted, they, too, would have to contend with the herd in the way; and by the time they broke free, she and Coosa would be a mile or more down the road.

Toward home. *Home!*

The longing to be there, safe at home, at Running Waters, surged through her, a primal yearning so strong it made her limbs weak. Oh, if only she could ride up under the portico and slide off Coosa's back into Papa's protective arms!

Or Stand's.

Standingdeer's arms. That was where she wanted to be; she could still feel their incredible power, the circle of warm protection they had created around her.

Maybe he would be there, looking for Coosa, ready to see how he was after the races, eager to argue about his training and his treatment. Maybe he had forgotten how furious he had been with her for not telling him everything.

If she could believe that, maybe it would happen.

She took a deeper seat and smooched Coosa into his best gait, a long, ground-eating lope. Thank the Great Protector that she had brought him; Sykes' and Walters' mounts couldn't outrun him, even if they avoided the cattle herd.

A deep shivering ran through her at the memory of Sykes' eager eyes and ugly, leering mouth. But surely when he and his partner learned the real value of the brooch, they would leave her and Running Waters alone.

Or would they appear someday at the door, coal oil and torches in hand, threatening to burn down the house around her if she didn't accede to their wishes?

The vision froze her where she sat. If they came to Running Waters again, she would kill them both with her bare hands!

She glanced over her shoulder: still no one rode in pursuit. All of that was over—she had to believe it. Sykes and Walters were paid. She would never see them again.

And when she reached the plantation at Running Waters, Standingdeer Chekote, The Paint, would be there.

Someone was there, all right, but it wasn't Stand. Tiana sensed something wrong as soon as she rode onto the place, coming in off the road at a long, slow trot to let Coosa cool out. From the entry gate she glanced, as she did at every home-coming, up across the graceful S shape of the driveway to the front portico of the house, plainly visible at the top of the hill a quarter of a mile away.

This time an unusual mixture of vehicles and horses milled around it. None of them was familiar to her, at least not from this distance. She eased Coosa off the drive and into the shadows of the birches that grew along the road.

Maybe her eyes were playing tricks on her in the late afternoon light. Grandmother Sun already lay, rocking slowly downward, along the top of Hickory Mountain. She cast a reddish light over the earth, leaving some spots in deep shadow. But the front veranda glowed bright; it stood in the direct path of her long-reaching beams.

One wagon appeared to be piled high with something. *Furniture?* Tiana's fingers itched for Mama's opera glasses as her eyes strained to make out what they were seeing. That was a plow, she was sure, fastened to the sideboards.

For a long, long time she sat there, her fingers frozen to the reins, her legs and seat frozen to the saddle. The sweat dried all over her body, beneath her clothes, and on her face as the summer heat that had created it evaporated from every inch of her skin. Up there, on top of the hill, two men who looked no bigger than boys lifted a crate of flapping, white-winged fowls down from the wagon bed.

Were they taking chickens into the *house?*

Her house. Her mama's house. She hadn't ordered any chickens. And if she had, it would have been from someone with sense enough to take them to the chicken yard.

Where were her servants?

She smooched to Coosa, lifting the reins and

squeezing him at the same time; he leapt out of cover and onto the grass of the hillside like a wild horse, like a horse fresh out of the barn for the day. They took the quarter mile cross-country, fences and all, without one hesitation or one glance back, bursting into the yard between the two big magnolias that loomed across the driveway from the door. Coosa slid to a stop at the foot of the steps, spraying gravel in the drive, and stood still as a statue, snorting and blowing.

A half-dozen adult strangers and three or four children, all of them white, froze in the middle of their tasks and stared at Tiana. She stared back, unable to force her mind to absorb what she saw.

The chickens ran loose now, squawking and clucking. A stovepipe lay scattered in pieces on the sawed-oak steps.

From the corner of her eye she glimpsed movement around the barns and the burned stables, but she had no strength to turn her head and really look in that direction. Directly to the right of her, the overloaded wagon sat hitched to two mules; both had thrown up their heads at Coosa's arrival.

Tiana stared at them for an age, then managed to turn her head straight to the front again and look at the house.

The door stood open. Just inside, in the middle of the hallway beneath Mama's chandelier, every candle blazing, an enormous old woman sat, rocking.

She had brought her own chair. It, too, was huge, with a high, laddered back and wide, scarred arms. And rockers worn sharp on the edges.

So sharp they made marks on the floor. The polished cherry floor that Dilcey kept perfect and shining.

Every time the woman rocked, the marks cut deeper. Back and forth. Back and forth.

Cutting ruts like a wagon's wheels in mud.

Tiana spoke in a voice so brittle that she didn't know it was hers. "You are ruining the floor," she said.

The old woman didn't answer. She looked at Tiana out of tiny colorless eyes, as steady as a snake's, and rocked on.

Tiana turned back to the men and the other women closer to her. They were on the veranda and in the driveway. One big boy was still in the wagon; two little girls played beside the magnolia where she and The Paint had kissed.

Tiana was choking, but she said, "What are you doing on my place? Where are my servants?"

One of the women, not much older than Tiana and hugely pregnant, giggled. "Yore *servants* done run off." She nudged the man beside her. "Tell her, Harve."

The largest and oldest of the men, plainly the old woman's son, squinted up at Tiana and said, "Reckon this here ain't *yore* place no more, Injun girl."

"Of course it is my place!" Tiana said, still in that strange, splintery voice.

The big man wagged his head. "Nope. Not yore place a'tall. It be ourn now and we 'uns got the papers to prove it: Number seventeen-three-nought-six-nine-nine. The Harve Snider family done won this here plantation in the Georgia State Lottery."

Chapter 7

The words echoed against the wall of the house. They bounced off it and rolled, over and over, down the long driveway to hit the door of the hay barn. It stayed shut against them, but they wouldn't stop trying to get in. Over and over, their din echoed in Tiana's ears.

The Georgia State Lottery.

The Georgia State Lottery.

"Get that woman out of this house and those chickens off the veranda!" she screamed. "You *can't* win Running Waters! We didn't gamble it!"

"You 'uns gambled it when you never went West like the gov'ment said to do," Harve told her, and then gave a great guffaw in appreciation of his own wit.

Tiana made an earsplitting sound of rage and swung Coosa toward him, taking the ends of the leathers in her right hand, ready to hit him.

The pregnant woman picked up a shotgun from the wagon bed and handed it to Harve. He pointed it at Tiana's chest.

She sat still, squeezing the narrow strips of leather, but feeling nothing in her hands. *Why* hadn't she brought the pistol? But even if she had it in her pocket, she couldn't shoot these people, thieves though they were.

135

The Paint. The Paint would know what to do. He would take Harve Snider and the rest of his filthy, squatting clan by the napes of their necks and throw them out of her beloved house, off Running Waters, all the way back to Georgia!

She turned Coosa's head and dug in her heels; he carried her east at an in-hand gallop. He had taken the yard fence and the hay meadow fence before she came to herself enough to realize how much the stallion had already given that day. She slowed him to a trot, laid the reins against his neck, and sent him around the edge of the wood-lot onto the faint trail that led up over the hill to Pine Grove. Pray God The Paint would be there.

When she rode onto Bluford's plantation through the darkening dusk, she couldn't remember any of the trail in between. It was as if she had been plucked from in front of Harve Snider's shotgun by a giant's hand and dropped down here, by the stand of pines where she'd hidden Jane Hunt on that horrible day last February, sent from one horror to another.

Well, no horror on earth could keep her from finding The Paint. She set her jaw, tightened her aching leg one more time around the sidesaddle's horn, and smooched to Coosa. At a thundering gallop they crossed the field at the end of the quarters where Fawn and Tobacco Jack had died.

By the time she rode into the yard, the sound of Coosa's hooves was reverberating against the hills, the dogs were barking an alarm, and three silhouettes, lamplight shining through the open door behind them, were coming off the porch to meet her.

"Who is it?" Bluford's wavery voice called.

"It's the Coosa horse, Blu—are you going blind?" Maud said. "Is that you, Tiana?"

Tiana couldn't speak. She slid Coosa to a stop

beside The Paint. She would know his broad outline in the darkest dark. With a whimpering cry,
she fell off the horse into his arms.

"Are you hurt?" he rasped, and she felt his
breath on her cheek. "Tiana, has somebody
harmed you?"

She shook her head, but a chilling fear, and then
a heated rage, rushed through Stand, anyway. By
God, whatever it was, *whoever* it was, would answer to him!

He tightened his arms around her and turned to
stride back to the steps. He had to see for himself
how she was.

Maud fluttered into his way, calling for the servants, for a lamp, for a fan, for smelling salts and
cold water; he stepped around her. Bluford followed, saying over and over again, "What is it,
Tiana? What has happened?"

Tiana didn't hear any of that. She just clung to
The Paint's neck without saying a word.

In the parlor he laid her on the soft cushions of
the settee and went down on one knee beside her.

"Tiana? Can you talk? Talk to me!"

She tried to sit up, but she sank back down as if
all her strength had left her. "Coosa . . . he's run so
far . . ."

"Bluford, get somebody to see to the horse,"
Stand snapped over his shoulder, then turned back
to her. His heart stopped. Her face had gone pale
as cotton in the dusky room, and her eyes had
closed.

Sweat broke out on his lip. "Maud!" he yelled.
"Bring some smelling salts!"

The air was close and still as midnight. And the
way she was dressed! No wonder she couldn't
breathe.

His hands went to the buttons on her collar and
fought to undo them, his fingers made clumsy and

slow by the haze clouding his eyes. By Thunder, whatever it was ... her secret trouble, no doubt ... she'd tell him at last.

He got one button undone, then another and another.

Tiana's eyes fluttered open. They were huge and dark, full of fear as her voice had been. But the terror receded when he looked down at her, their faces only inches apart in the dimness. She gave him a smile filled with happy relief.

Whatever her trouble was, she had run to *him*. There *was* a bond between them; he hadn't just imagined it that day of the fire.

Pride, protectiveness swelled his heart, and then a surge of pure desire rose in his loins. His hands moved more slowly at their work. Tiana. He would give the earth to be undressing her now for another reason than to cool her skin.

The Paint's rough fingers brushed Tiana's throat; his forearm grazed her breast. The touch made its tip swell to a throbbing life of its own, even through her jacket and her shirtwaist.

Even through the panic still pulsing in her veins.

The intimacy of his movements turned her bones to jelly.

Then, too soon, he was done. He lifted her with one strong hand at the back of her neck while he stripped the sweaty jacket away and dropped it onto the floor.

His hand held her suspended in space, floating in a dim world of no time. She let her eyes fall closed again.

Then Stand slowly, very slowly, slipped the top button of her blouse through its loop. And, below that, the next.

Cool air wafted onto her throat and her chest, but the bewildering heat inside her grew with every unintentional caress of his fingers. How would she ever bear it if he *meant* to make love to her?

Then his hands were gone, and he was lighting the lamp at her head.

Yellow light flared onto the carved bones of his face. A warrior's face. Fierce, savage, *handsome* warrior's face.

The Paint would get Running Waters back for her.

"Now," he said. "Tell me."

She sat up. He rocked back on his heels and pierced her eyes with his.

"The Georgia Lottery," she said in a hollow voice that she didn't recognize. "Running Waters. Some awful settlers won it."

"No!" Bluford said, coming toward her from behind Standingdeer.

"Tiana, I am so sorry!" Maud called out, bustling into the room, brushing past Bluford to sit beside Tiana. She put an arm around her and offered a glass of cool water. "Drink this, dear."

The Paint didn't move. He couldn't move. The lottery. There wasn't one damned thing he could do.

Standingdeer's eyes burned at Tiana like coals in a fire. "They're on the place now?"

"Yes, until you throw them off." She clenched the water glass with both hands. "You have to make them leave, Stand. The old woman's rocking chair is ruining Mama's cherry floor!"

Poor darling. Poor, innocent darling. If only that cherry floor were all she had to worry about!

"Did they hurt you?"

"No. I didn't fight—there were so many of them swarming all over the place when I got home. A man named Harve Snider had a shotgun, and I didn't take Papa's pistol with me when I left this morning . . ."

"When you got home? From where?"

She looked away from his eagle eyes.

"You might as well tell me, Tiana," he said harshly. "Even in the dark, one glance at Coosa says he's been a lot more miles than from Running Waters to here."

"From the sycamore on the Federal Road."

"That's a hard day's ride. Why?"

She gave a great, trembling sigh. He was strong and implacable, and all her strength was used up. What difference did it make, anyway? Gray Fox was gone, and soon everyone would know it. And know why.

"To meet Sykes and Walters, to pay what Gray owed them. I took Coosa for speed because if I'd had the gun, I . . ."

She bit her tongue just in time. She'd almost said, *I might have killed somebody else.*

He made a strangled sound. "Dressed up like you are in a fancy riding habit? Riding sidesaddle? You took Coosa for *speed?*"

"They'd be more likely to treat a lady with respect than a tomboy," she said. "And I've ridden steeplechases in a sidesaddle. But I was scared Coosa might get hurt."

He stared at her, his eyes flashing hard, like swords' blades, in the mellow light of the lamp.

"*You're* the one who risked getting hurt! Great Thunderers, Tiana, a riding habit and a sidesaddle wouldn't deter men like that! I can't believe they didn't take you as well as your money."

"They tried. At least, they were trying to get Coosa, but we were too quick for them."

Stand's blood froze. God in Heaven, he thought, he could have lost her forever this very day.

Lost her? an ironic voice taunted from the back of his mind. *She isn't yours. This girl is a Tenkiller.*

Standingdeer Chekote is in agony because there is nothing he can do to save Nicotai Tenkiller's plantation.

"Coosa!" Bluford cried, his voice wavering. "They tried to take Coosa?"

For one fleeting moment Tiana wondered why he would have such concern for her horse.

"Yes," Tiana said. "But we broke away and outran them. I don't know if they chased us or not—there was a herd of Tennessee cattle."

"You have too much courage for your own good!" The Paint thundered. "Tiana, listen to me ..."

She put down the glass, leaned forward, and grabbed his shoulders. His muscles felt hard as rocks in her hands. Solid as rocks to cling to.

"No, *you* listen to *me!* I have no courage at all! I turned tail and ran like a rabbit when that horrible man took his shotgun and pointed it at me."

The memory of that moment came back so vividly that she had to stop and draw a deep, shaky breath.

"I need you to save Running Waters, Stand. But I'll help. I'll do whatever you tell me." She looked at him beseechingly.

His heart split into pieces. He was as helpless as she was.

All expression drained out of The Paint's face as he stared at Tiana; it turned into a smooth mask of stone. Her hope sank into the floor. Would he refuse to help her? Was he remembering her yelling at Ellijay that she'd never ask him for help again?

"You can't do a thing, Tiana," he said. "And neither can I."

Her ears closed. "I know I said I'd never ask you for help again," she said. "But I have to. I can't get rid of those people by myself. *Please*, Stand."

Such a look of hurt came into his eyes that she

loosened her fingers on his shoulders. Had they been digging into his flesh *that* hard?

"I can't take Running Waters back for you, Tiana."

How could he *say* such a thing?

"Of course you can! You're a hero! You're The Paint!"

The pain in his eyes deepened into agony.

He said hoarsely, "All the heroes in the Cherokee Nation can't give your home back to you; the whites would bring in the Georgia Guard and mow us all down like cutting oats in the field."

"No! Surely not!"

"Surely so! Don't you realize that the Principal Chief of the Nation has lost his own home the very same way? Wouldn't he have called warriors to fight if it would have done any good?"

"That's true," Maud said.

Bluford muttered, "Chief Ross and your father and the others say not to resist."

Tiana looked from one to the other, shaking her head. "I do not understand this!" she cried. "It's wrong!"

"It's our only protection against those sensationalist stories in newspapers all over the United States ranting about bloodthirsty Cherokees killing and maiming white people," Maud said.

"But who *cares* what lies they tell?" Tiana cried.

"Even lies can damage our bargaining position, you know that," Bluford said.

"No! Someone always will point out the truth, like Mr. Evarts does! And Chief Ross has retained the attorney, Mr. Wirt . . ."

"We don't *have* a bargaining position," Standingdeer said heavily. "And truth won't help. I told you. Someday every one of us will be walking West."

An awful silence took all their tongues. Somewhere in the room, above and behind Tiana's head in a corner of the ceiling, a moth fluttered. The summer-sundown breeze came to life, picked up the edge of the curtain, and then dropped it against the sill.

The Paint got up, turned his back on her, and paced to the window.

"I'll never go West!" Tiana cried. "I'm going home."

She leapt up and ran, but with his long strides he caught her before she got to the door.

A fearful fury at her own helplessness flooded through her, so fast and wild that it made her sick. She clawed at his arms and beat her head at his chest to get loose.

"You're wrong, Stand," she cried. "Wrong, wrong, wrong!"

But he was right, and she knew it, at least about the futility of fighting for Running Waters tonight.

Devastation swept through her like a tornado through a mountain valley, uprooting her faith in The Paint and her papa and Chief Ross like so many trees in its path.

Suddenly she sagged defenseless against him. "Turn me loose," she said. "I need to be alone."

Tiana paced back and forth in the room that Maud had given her, from the mantel clock to the window from which she had been watching the moon. It had gone out of sight straight overhead. Midnight. She would wait another hour—if she could contain herself—until the moon started sliding on its long trek downward. By then, everyone in the house should be asleep. Everyone in *both* houses should be asleep.

But when the clock read twelve-fifteen, she could stand it no longer. She slipped out of Maud's wrapper, which she had put on after bath-

ing and washing her hair, and climbed into the
soft, old deerskin breeches and shirt that she'd
found with matching moccasins in a bottom
drawer of the dresser. They must've belonged to
Bluford when he was a boy; they were so small
they fit tight as her skin. But for this job that was
good; the skirts of her riding habit would be an
impossible hindrance. She couldn't act like a lady
anymore, anyway. It would only hamper her.

And so would acting like a woman.

Her hands went still on the knot of her beaded
belt, and she stared through the window out into
the pale, shimmery night. Even without closing
her eyes, she could feel The Paint's fingers brushing her skin, unbuttoning the high collar of her
blouse.

New anger shook her, anger at herself now as
well as at him. How could she let herself remember those touches that were rough and tender at
the same time and that had, for an instant, torn
her loose from reality?

Well, it wouldn't happen again. Reality was the
fact that he had only meant to calm her down, to
cool her, to let the night's heat drift away from her
body. So that he could tell her he would not try to
retrieve her home for her.

She still couldn't believe that that was true. She
straightened her back and jerked the belt tighter
around her waist, then stepped into the moccasins
and tugged the leggings down to meet them.

What did it matter how tight they were or how
she was dressed? No one would see her, anyway.

If God and the Thunderers went with her.

She tied back her still-damp hair with a fringe
she had worked loose from the leggings and eased
open the door to her room. Treading lightly on the
balls of her feet, she made her way down the hall
and then the long staircase. The moccasins let her

pass all the way to the outside door without making a sound.

She stepped out onto the back porch and ran down the steps, through a patch of moonlight, to the house's long shadow that stretched toward the woods. Staying in its blackness, she picked up speed.

Locusts and other night insects buzzed, and in the distance a dog howled. The noise came from the direction of home. It sounded like Red Tickler, mourning. And why not? All his family had gone and left him. Well, she would steal him, too, from the Sniders.

This time as she crossed the field at the bottom of the quarters where Old Sudie lived, without Coosa's strong legs beneath her, she wanted to close her eyes. But she didn't dare. Her feet flew over the upsloping ground; her lungs barely expanded enough for her to take a true, deep breath. Until she had run, panting, past the spot where Fawn had died and she had killed Tobacco Jack, all the way through the pine thicket at the top of the hill and into the hovering protection of the woods beyond.

There Tiana stopped, hugging the rough trunk of a hickory tree for support while she took in gasp after gasp of the cooling night air, thick with mist from the mountains. Tobacco Jack's spirit must be haunting only Bluford, because she'd neither seen nor heard anything untoward.

The instant the thought had passed through her mind, she wished it back. No, she wished it never born.

For it had created the reality. Something had moved, not far from her. Something, or someone, *was* near.

Behind her. She prayed for the courage to turn around.

"Tiana."

Deep relief flooded through her. The Paint. Not Tobacco Jack's spirit, after all.

Then angry panic ripped her arms from the tree and whirled her around. "What are you doing out here?"

"Waiting for you to do something foolish."

He spoke from a shadowy place beneath a sourwood tree; the moon lit the chiseled bones of his face, but it didn't reach his eyes.

"Don't try to stop me," she said.

He stepped toward her, full into the moonlight. Directly onto the path to Running Waters.

"Stop you from what? Walking into the muzzle of the Georgians' shotgun?"

"They'll never see me. They're too busy ruining our floors and sleeping in our beds." Her voice broke.

"Which is better than you sleeping in your grave."

Tiana caught a ragged breath. "Don't try to scare me, either."

"I wouldn't."

"You would, too! You *are* trying, right now! But it won't work—I'm going after my horses. That's one thing of ours that the Sniders won't get, even temporarily, and when Papa comes home, we'll get everything back."

After a moment he chuckled. It was a dry, ironic sound in the quiet night, a sound that, without words, called her a foolish child.

Her fury grew. She wanted to rush at him and pound his chest with her fists, but she already knew how futile that would be.

"You'd fight a bear with a hickory switch, wouldn't you, Tiana? I should've known that telling you the dangers would only make you more determined."

"And I should've known *you'd* be lurking out here in the dark, ready to hold me back!"

He stood in the middle of the faintly defined trail; on both sides of him the underbrush grew thick, mostly thistles and sumac. It'd be futile to try to make a dash past him.

His legs straddled her path like two tree trunks growing there, his strong muscles straining against the tight twill of the pants he wore. His thighs looked as immovable as the mountains.

She said the only thing she could think of to remove him from her way, although the minute the words had left her tongue, she bit it in surprise.

"Why don't you go with me, instead?"

The Paint stood looking down at her, his rugged face limned by the moonlight. Several expressions passed over it like clouds, one following fast after the other.

At last, with a hard edge to his voice, he said, "Why not? Heroes ought to be good for something."

The passion pulsing underneath those words wiped away her anger as if it had never been. It opened a window into his heart.

He wanted to launch an attack on the Sniders just as much as she did; she could see that now, in the tension of his muscles and in the tautness of his stance. No, he wanted it even more than she did, if that were possible. For he was a warrior—he was meant to fight. Yet he, too, was powerless against the intruders and the notorious Georgia Guard.

In the old days, The Paint would have been war chief, the one the tribe turned to when the time for action against an enemy had come. Now he lived alone in a vast place where he had to act instantly on instinct, every day of his life. He wasn't accustomed to trying to solve his problems through lawyers and courts and negotiations, as Papa was trying to do in Washington City. He hated that as much as she did.

"Don't worry," she comforted him, then came out of the shadows and walked to him. "As soon as Papa and Chief Ross and the others have worked out a treaty, we'll get Running Waters back. We'd only hinder them if we tried it now. Tonight we'll get the horses."

Their eyes met and held, looking into each other's souls even through the shadows.

Finally Stand shook his head, a crooked smile tugging at the corners of his mouth. "I would believe you," he drawled, "if only you were carrying your riding crop."

"Next trip I'll bring it," she said. "Does that make you feel any better?"

"Yes and no," he said dryly. "I hadn't realized we were making more than one trip."

She laughed, looking up at him, loving the glint of mischief in his eyes.

"Oh, yes!" she said, her voice leaping with the excitement that ran with the blood in her veins. "We'll get the two-year-olds first—there are eight of them—and put them in that pen behind Bluford's barn. I don't think he'll mind, do you? Then we'll go back for the mares."

He grinned down at her, his face dark and gorgeous in the pale glow of the moon.

"Then by my reckoning, we'd better get started."

They moved through the woods single file, Tiana at The Paint's back like a shadow. He found their way faster than she could have done, and she marveled. How many years since he'd lived on this land?

They took the ridge trail at the long, slow running pace native to their people and maintained it without a rest until they had covered the two miles or so of Pine Grove and crossed onto Running Waters.

"Why didn't we think to bring a horse for this?" The Paint asked, throwing the teasing words back over his shoulder in a tone just louder than a whisper.

"Horses' hooves echo in the quiet of the night," Tiana whispered sternly back. "Horses can't slip through the woods. Horses tend to nicker when they see other horses."

"All right," he said. "You've convinced me. But you're going to have to let me rest pretty soon."

"You aren't even breathing hard yet," she retorted. "But as soon as all the horses are safe, I'll let you take a nap in the hay."

"So that I'll be at the barn for morning chores?"

"That's right. Bluford doesn't have enough servants for such an increase in the horse population."

"Do I get breakfast?"

"Only when your work's all done."

They stopped the teasing and ran some more. At last, when they'd reached the three-acre woodlot near the edge of the backyard, they slowed their pace and then stopped.

Tiana took Stand's hand. "Let's sit for a minute," she whispered, leading him to a large log. "Then we'll make our lightning raid."

Her hand, so warm and trusting in his, filled him with the close feeling of conspiracy, flowing like a warm drink into the empty space he'd only recently known was there. His hand tightened around hers and he sat very close.

"You must be exhausted," he murmured. "You've ridden hard all day, and now this run."

"Huhnn," she whispered in denial. "You've given me new strength."

The sweet words flew straight to his heart and he sat silent, holding her hand, listening to them over and over again, stretching out the moment until the bright moonlight found them. Then he stood and made himself say, "Let's go. It'll be daylight before we can make two runs."

They crept through the woodlot, darting from one bit of cover to the next, watching the looming outline of the house through the surrounding trees. Just looking at the shape of it in the night brought tears to Tiana's eyes. Those awful people were actually living in there, sleeping with their greasy hair on Mama's fine cotton pillowcases, inside those walls that had surrounded Tiana with safety all her life!

She blinked and forced herself to look at each window for a light, for any signs that someone was awake who might look out. There were none.

The Paint led her in a long half circle, from one spot of darkness to another down the side of the hill and across the graveled driveway, until they crouched in the darkness cast by the hulk of the burned-out stables. One of the Sniders' hounds began to bark. Another loped across the yard searching for them, looking huge in the white light of the moon.

Stand called the dog to him in a whisper and began scratching his ears. "Let's wait here a minute," he whispered. "Let the dogs quiet down."

From somewhere behind the house, Red Tickler gave a long, mournful howl. "Good," Tiana whispered. "There's Tickler. He'll be here in a minute."

Her gaze drifted back to the house and stayed there while the night settled around them and the acrid smells of the stables' ashes rose to fill her nostrils. She'd almost rather see the house in ruins, too, than to envision those horrid people inside it.

No, she wouldn't. *Yes*, she would.

No. Someday the Tenkillers would reclaim their plantation. Tiana had to have her home.

A thought struck her. "Wouldn't the Sniders be surprised if Sykes and Walters came and burned the house down around them?" she whispered to Stand.

His soft, dry chuckle floated to her through the darkness, saying that he never knew what to expect from her next. The affection she heard in it made her want to see his face. "It could happen," he whispered.

Yes. If they were angry enough about her escape with Coosa and about getting the brooch instead of cash . . .

Tiana's knees locked into their crouch; her hands flattened against the soot-covered ground. Old Sudie's money! It was hidden in Papa's safe!

She sucked in her breath fast and hard, as if she'd been hit in the stomach.

"What's the matter?" Stand whispered, moving toward her. "What's wrong?"

Her lips parted, ready to tell him. She clamped them shut. The Sniders' hound came to her then, thrusting its cold nose into her neck.

"The dog startled me, that's all," she whispered back, hoping he wouldn't notice that that couldn't be true. "Come on, let's find The Butterfly."

Another night she would come back for the money. Tomorrow. Tonight she had to save her horses.

She leapt up and ran across the barnyard to the pens behind it, half of them in moonlight, half in darkness. A horse came to meet her; another nickered. She climbed onto the first rail of the board fence, happy to see them, suddenly heedless of the fact that she'd deserted the cover of darkness for full moonlight.

"There you are, Butterfly!" she exclaimed softly,

hugging the filly's head to her. "I've come to get you, you know."

Tiana pulled back to stroke the silky neck and swept her gaze over the pens and the pasture, as much of them as she could see in the night. Her hand tangled in Butterfly's forelock; it stopped moving.

"Stand!" she called, too loudly, turning to look for him. He came out of the shadows and leaned on the fence beside her. She lowered her voice to a whisper. "Where is everybody? I'll bet there aren't a half-dozen horses here!"

"I noticed."

She tucked a stray wisp of hair behind her ear and strained her eyes into the dark. "Did they turn them out into the valley pasture, do you think? Or into the hay meadow? We just mowed it."

"If they moved in right before dark, they don't know where the valley pasture or the hay meadow is. You said that when you were here, there were men down by the barns?"

"Y . . . yes."

"They may've been horse traders. I've heard they travel with the lottery winners sometimes— that gives 'em quick cash to go with their new place."

Tiana gasped. "You mean my horses are gone? The traders bought them already?"

"It's likely. They'll drive them all night and be in Georgia or Tennessee by morning."

The words set the blood pounding frantically in her head. Tiana threw herself over the fence and moved among the horses, looking to see who was there, calling, "Go look around, Stand! Try the east paddock!"

He disappeared, but came back within what seemed to her seconds. "Nothing," he said. "Who've we got left?"

"Butterfly, thank God, and Thunder. And Tannassy Sundown. They're the only two-year-olds. They're mixed in with the broodmares—Jane Hunt is here, and three more."

"The best ones?"

"Yes," she said, her voice rising in wonder. "Why would the horse traders leave *these*? They've left the very best ones!"

"Must have a different market for them," he muttered. "Probably plan to come back tomorrow."

"Well, they'll be too late," Tiana declared. "Let's get them out of here. The tack the servants saved from the fire is in that loafing shed, remember?"

She had caught both Jane Hunt and New Chowa when he came out of the shed that backed up to the fence near the gate. All he carried was a halter fastened to a lead rope and a bridle with reins. "I could only find one bridle," he said. "No saddles at all."

"Filthy *thieves*," she said, her voice breaking as she took the halter and tied both ends of the lead rope to the sides of it to form makeshift reins. "My silver-trimmed saddle was there."

Her hands shook, but she managed to stick Jane Hunt's head into the halter.

"Listen!" The Paint said as he slipped the bit into New Chowa's mouth. "What's that?"

A loud howling, then barking and yipping erupted on the hill close to the house. "That's Tickler," she said, hurrying to slip the strap through the buckle of the halter. "He must be tied. If he keeps that up, he'll wake every one of the Sniders. O-oh, we've got to find him and take him with us!"

"What we've got to do is get these horses off this plantation," The Paint said. "I didn't come this far to let the *yonegas* shoot me and keep them."

"Go on," she said, throwing herself onto the mare's back. "Start them. I'll untie the dog and follow you."

The Paint vaulted onto New Chowa. "Forget that," he said as the barking grew louder and several other dogs joined in. "The dog isn't worth it. Let's *go*."

Tiana squeezed Jane's sides and rode her in front of him, out to the open gate of the pen. She sat there to block his exit.

"Tickler is Papa's favorite dog," she argued. "He's the only dog Mama has ever let in the house."

"Tiana, for God's sake, will you *think*? If you want to save your horses . . ."

The barking grew still louder and closer, flowing down the hill from behind the house toward them. Tiana turned to see Red Tickler streak across the moonlit driveway at the head of the pack, dragging a rope from his neck, coming straight to her.

She slid off the horse to welcome him. To pick him up and take him with her.

"Tiana! Dammit, woman, get back on that mare!" The Paint roared above the cacophony of barking and whining.

Tiana barely heard him, with Tickler licking her face and ears and all the others begging for her to pet them, too. They barked at the one dog who'd greeted her at the stables, and he whimpered and growled in return. All of them made so much noise she couldn't hear herself think.

But the shotgun blast sounded perfectly clear.

And extremely close.

The dogs went silent as stones.

"Well, well," crowed Harve Snider in an exultant voice, "little Injun gal done come back home."

Chapter 8

Harve stepped out into the moonlight across the driveway from the far end of the loafing shed, the butt of the gun against his hip, the muzzle pointing into the air, just as he had fired it. He had come because of the dogs, but from the opposite end of the house's big yard, ready to head off whatever they might have scared into running.

"Git up from thar, honey," he said, "and come over hyar to me."

Tiana felt, rather than saw, The Paint, mounted on New Chowa, off to her left just out of her range of vision. Evidently Harve hadn't seen him; he didn't turn his head in that direction. Thank God the shed stood between them!

The Paint had no weapon, except for the knife he wore at his belt. A shotgun volley at this distance would kill him.

Terror surged through her, stronger than any she had ever known. She had to protect Stand.

"Don't shoot," Tiana begged, pressing one hand to the ground to help herself up on wobbly knees. "Please."

She had to walk toward the horrid man. She had to keep his attention off Standingdeer. He must not see him.

"That's sweeter talk than you was makin' earlier

this evenin', anyways," the intruder said. "And I g'arantee it'll git sweeter yet. Come 'ere."

Tiana took a slow step forward. The pack of dogs surged with her, yipping and growling, tangling around her feet.

"Hyah! Git away from thar!" Harve said, and bent to pick up some of the gravel to throw at them.

Hoofbeats thundered behind her. Before she could turn her head, they were close enough to run her down and The Paint's strong arm had swept her off her feet. He dragged her up and across New Chowa's withers, holding Tiana's head down with one hand, bending over her to press his face to the horse's neck, yelling like a warrior crazy for blood.

Her hair came loose and poured across her face, swinging nearly to the ground; she fought to raise herself up so the mare wouldn't step on it. But she could only turn her face sideways and look under New Chowa's neck at their tormentor.

The Paint drove the mare straight into the blocky body of Harve Snider, who looked up at them from the bent position in which surprise had frozen him, too shocked to put his slow-moving limbs into motion. Tiana heard the hard whoosh as the air went out of him, and the grunt of pain as he fell. The shotgun flew out of his hands and forward, to go skittering along the curving line of the gravel.

The Paint swerved New Chowa down off the slope and around in a circle to follow it, pressing Tiana even harder against the horse as he slid halfway off the side of the cantering mare to pick up the gun. Then he was sitting on top of the mount again, giving a cry that chilled the night, a primitive war cry as old as the mountains around them.

He raised the gun toward the sky, fired it once,

and then threw it away so he could put both hands on Tiana to set her upright. She swung her legs over the mare's withers and clamped them tight. The Paint pulled her backward into the hot-blooded circle of his arms.

She molded herself to him, desperate for a place to hide, for comfort. No. Desperate for the feel of him.

He gathered her closer with a motion as intense as his cry, and bent his head to tuck hers into the safety of his shoulder.

Shouts sounded behind them, then two shots, and as New Chowa circled to go back into the pen, Tiana saw lights flare, upstairs in the house and down in the yard.

"Who's there?" a man's voice bellowed.

A woman screamed, "Harve ain't in bed. Is he outside? Did th' Injuns git 'im?"

"Maybe," The Paint muttered in an answer only Tiana could hear. "But it's *certain* they're getting the horses."

Butterfly and the others were huddled together at the far side of the enclosure; Stand swung New Chowa in behind them and started them into a trot, then immediately into a canter, moving out.

"Take the road!" Tiana shouted over the sound of pounding hooves. "They won't expect that!"

"They won't follow," Stand said in her ear. "That bunch is scared of Indians and they don't know how many we are."

The five horses clustered in a herd ahead of them, running scared, headlong into the night. Then, at the curve of the driveway just below the house, Stand urged New Chowa into a gallop, passed the horses, and turned them south, straight for the road.

They separated then and, one by one, jumped over the first paddock fence and then the other one, stringing down the hillside like clouds flying across the face of the moon, heedless of everything except the fear of being left behind.

Tiana balanced herself for New Chowa's leaps, and once the mare's feet had hit the ground again for the second time, she grabbed both of Stand's wrists and squeezed them in triumph. They were so big she couldn't reach around them. They were so strong and hard she couldn't turn loose of them. So real. So alive, thank God. His pulse beat under her fingers in a quick, triumphant drumming.

"We did it, by Thunder!" he growled into her ear.

He squeezed her tighter with his arms; he had both hands on the reins and his eyes fixed on the way ahead as he sent them all plunging down the hillside, his hair and hers whipping around their faces like black banners of victory. Mist covered the moon.

At the bottom they burst through the wispy fog, crossed the drive, and dashed out into the road, with Stand pushing New Chowa to her limit to get there first and turn the others east. Tiana caught only a glimpse of the white-painted wrought-iron signpost as they passed, but she could read its legend, ornately scripted in both English and Cherokee, as clearly as if it were engraved on a board beneath a lamp right in front of her eyes: *Running Waters, Tanta-ta-rara, N. Tenkiller, Plantation.*

It would always be the Tenkiller plantation, she vowed, clenching her teeth so hard that her jaw began to hurt. Somehow, someday, she would take *everything* back.

The Paint held New Chowa in the lead, slowing the pace, letting all of the horses blow and catch their breath while he kept them moving at a long trot. The night folded them into its arms.

"I'm so *glad!*" Tiana said, her hands still clinging to his wrists. "He didn't hurt you, Stand. I was scared that he'd shoot when he saw you!"

He made a rough sound deep in his throat and rocked her body back against him.

"And we saved six horses!" she continued to rejoice. "The best ones. I'm thankful that they didn't get Coosa, either."

"So am I," he drawled wryly. "You'd have had me chasing after the horse traders on foot to get *him* back."

"What do you mean?" she teased. "He would've been left there with the best ones. In fact, he *is* the best!"

"Since I've been helping with his training, yes," Stand said thoughtfully.

"He's *always* been the best!" she cried with mock indignation, and twisted in his arms to try to see his face.

But his body tensed and his grip on her tightened.

"Shhh!"

Tiana turned around again and peered into the dark night.

"What is it?" she whispered.

"Horses. A dozen or more."

Tiana listened, separating the sounds of her own horses' hooves from those of the others, still a fair distance away.

"They're on this road," she whispered at last.

"Yes. And coming to meet us."

She clamped both her hands around one of his huge ones, tangling their fingers together in the leather lines that he held. "Who could it be?"

"Somebody up to no good. We've got to get out of their way."

He lifted New Chowa into a short lope and

dropped her back a little to bunch the others together.

"The trees. Where the road narrows," Tiana said, and felt the short nod of his head that told her he'd already thought of that place.

They kept, as much as possible, to the loose, sandy soil at the side of the road for the next quarter mile, picking up speed, hurrying for safety past the open fields yawning out there in the dark. Then a scrap of moonlight caught the big thicket of hemlock and pines, and Stand was driving the horses off into it. The footing changed to spongy leaf mold and pine needles that gave back no sound.

The silence brought the noise of the horses on the road close, much closer. They were almost upon them.

Stand said softly, "Whoa. Whoa. Easy, now."

Their horses drifted to a stop, blowing a little, listening, too.

Tiana prayed they wouldn't whinny when the others went by.

There were more than a dozen. So many that the hooves striking the road rumbled for a brief moment like thunder. They were close enough that they could have seen one another through the trees, but the moon had drifted away again, into the fog. They seemed close enough to touch.

Close enough to reach out and snatch what few horses she had left. And her and The Paint as well.

The smells of many horses and of the dust beneath the dewy surface of the road floated in among the trees on the heavy, damp air. One of the drovers' voices rang out, in an unintelligible shout, dangerously near their hiding place. And then, in a mighty rush, they were gone.

Tiana sat desolately still in the circle of Stand's arms.

As the sound of pounding hooves died away in the distance, she said, in a voice so bitter he would not have recognized it had he not known it was hers, "A pony club. Taking some Cherokee horses to Tennessee."

"Has to be," he answered.

"Do you think they've been to Pine Grove?" she asked, her strange voice turning fragile as glass. "Suppose they got Coosa!"

Her whole body stiffened as she pulled away from The Paint. "Let's go see about him!"

Stand fought to keep himself from grabbing her sweet softness and holding it to him again, from trying to force the fear from her body. Damn the white-eyed bastards, Goddamn the thieves! They had stolen more than horses from the Nation tonight.

They had stripped a brave girl of what pathetically little happiness she had.

He gritted his teeth against the helpless rage that roared in his head. He was powerless to stop the sneaking pillage of this Nation that he loved—he had known that for fifteen years, ever since Andrew Jackson had betrayed the Cherokee after they had bled and died to win the Battle of Horseshoe Bend for him. Long since, he thought he had accepted that fact.

But he would be horsewhipped if he would let them get away with plundering Tiana's heart again tonight.

"Wherever they've been," he said, forcing his tone to be light, "I hope they go to Running Waters next."

She laughed. Still in that eerie voice, but she laughed.

Gently he started New Chowa moving, easing toward the nearest of the other horses.

"Maybe they'll steal Harve's team," he said,

continuing his imaginary jest. "And he'll have to walk everywhere he goes."

"When we take Running Waters away from him, he'll have to walk all the way back to Georgia!"

When. When horses could fly over the top of the moon.

When Chief Ross himself had moved his family into a log cabin over the Tennessee line because *his* plantation had been lost in the lottery. Did she really believe those places could be recovered?

He called to the herd, heading New Chowa back to the road, hoping the others would follow.

"Don't worry about it now," he said to the top of Tiana's head. She was holding it so straight it seemed her neck would break. "Call your darlings and let's get going. I don't aim for those horse traders to come back tomorrow and find them grazing along here."

New Chowa carried them out onto the road and the other horses followed, huddling together behind her as if for comfort. The wispy night mist whipped around them.

"Won't the horse traders be surprised when they see that empty pen and all the best ones are gone?" he said, and was rewarded by Tiana's chuckle. It sounded more like her this time.

The moon drifted out into the open again; it draped light across Tiana's shoulders like a long yellow shawl. They looked a little less rigid than before, but she rode leaning forward, agonizing to see her Coosa.

If the stallion was gone, dear God, what would she do?

And what could *he* do to help her?

Nothing. Absolutely, positively nothing.

His hands knotted into impotent fists on the reins. That fact had helped drive him from home in the first place, fifteen years ago, and he should not have come back now.

Tiana brushed his fingers with hers as she tangled them into New Chowa's mane and leaned still further forward. The mare picked up speed, and Stand let her. Better to end this misery as soon as they could.

They rode in silence onto Pine Grove and across it, driving the loose horses before them, not slowing until they loped up to the barn lot. The Paint bent to open the gate.

He wanted to say, *Look, the gate's fastened. If thieves had been last through it, they probably wouldn't have bothered.* But he bit back the words. What if he raised false hopes in her? She had been through enough.

He and Tiana sat on New Chowa, not moving, while Butterfly and the others flowed past them to mill in the lot and snort the smells of a new place into their nostrils.

Stand ran his eyes over the moonlit paddocks. He could see some shapes of horses grazing, and inside the barn he heard one kick. Probably Pine Grove had been spared this time.

Finally New Chowa followed the others in. Even after she stopped at the rail, neither of them made a move to dismount.

"Well," he said at last as he vaulted backward over the mare's croup, "let's get down."

Neither of them said anything else while he took Tiana by the waist and lifted her to the ground. They walked together into the wide doorway of the dark barn. She stood still and waited until he took the lantern from its hook and lit it.

The instant the light shone, she gasped.

"Stand! Look! Bluford's bay is gone!"

He held the lantern higher.

It was true. The big blood bay, for whom

Bluford had paid fifteen hundred dollars and whom he kept so carefully, always in the second stall in the row on the right, was gone. The square space, covered with aromatic new cedar shavings, gleamed open and empty in the circle of light.

"They've been here!" she cried. "Coosa!"

She ran headlong down the center aisle, looking from side to side to find her stallion. Halfway down, on the left side of the aisle, he nickered and kicked the wood wall in greeting.

For a minute Stand stayed where he was, holding up the lantern, not caring that its light wavered crazily on the floor and then on the ceiling from the tremor of relief that ran through his hand. And his heart.

Then he walked toward her. She stood on tiptoe, hugging the horse, her arms making a necklace of gold deerskin around his silver neck. Making a picture of happiness.

"Well, your sweet one is safe," he said.

"Yes!" She turned and threw Stand a brilliant smile, but when she let her arms drop, she didn't run to him. Quick as thought, she opened the stall door and slipped inside.

"Coosa is here, and so are lots of others," she said. "But where is Bluford's Bay Boy? It must be three o'clock in the morning."

She bent down, out of sight, to run her hands over Coosa's legs, to know through her skin as well as her eyes that he was truly here, alive and unharmed.

"Bluford probably rode off to a card game somewhere," Stand said. "Sometimes he plays all night."

He walked to one of the posts that ran down the center of the barn and hung the lantern on a nail. He couldn't seem to hold the damn thing still.

She finished inspecting the stallion and came

out into the aisle, fastening the latch securely behind her. She hugged the big spoiled baby again, but this time when she turned away from him, she came toward Stand.

He leaned on his heels to feel the post at his back.

Tiana walked forward to face him in the circle of light. "Thank you, Standingdeer," she said. "For my horses."

He looked down into her dark eyes. Her wide dark eyes, full of gratitude.

"You're welcome, Tiana," he said. "But you didn't need me." *I'm the one who needs you.*

"Yes, I did!"

"Not if you'd have carried your riding crop."

Standingdeer smiled at her. A lazy, sensuous smile that returned her hurting heart to her body.

I would have needed you if I'd had an arsenal and an army. I need you, Standingdeer.

"Do I look that fierce in my buckskins?"

His smile spread to his eyes and made them soft as brown velvet. They caressed her, from the fringes across her breasts to the long, tight leggings beneath.

"You look fierce. Like a Beloved Woman ready to go on the warpath," he said.

The rich tone of his voice stirred her soul.

"I thought you'd say I look like a warrior."

His heavy-lidded gaze moved lazily over her once more, then came back to her face. It lingered on her lips.

"Never," he drawled, "not even on a night with no moon."

The powerful pull of his dark-burning eyes lifted her feet from the floor. She took a step toward him. Then another.

Coosa made a lonesome little whickering sound.

The horse next to him answered. Somewhere outside the open doors, a night bird called.

But The Paint stood silent, looking at her.

Drawing her to him.

She took another step.

And he reached across the lantern light to cup her cheek in his hand.

To slide his hard palm upward and drive his fingers into her hair, to step forward and pull her mouth to his. To devour it.

With a trembling sigh she leaned into the cradle that his hand made for her head and opened her mouth to his with no holding back. She closed her eyes and came closer into the shelter of him, sliding her palms up his chest, feeling the thud of his heart beating there before she molded her body to his wonderful one and wrapped her arms around his neck.

He straddled her legs and drew her in harder against the rising heat in his loins, desperately drinking the sweet nectar from her tongue, nectar so strong he could live on it.

Her softness pressed against him like raindrops falling onto parched ground. The desert of his body absorbed its sustenance in one reckless instant and he drew her in closer, thirsty for more.

His hand moved in her hair; her hair caressed the back of his hand, smooth as silk drawn over his skin. The rest of his body yearned toward that touch. He thrust his tongue deeper to claim her and fell headlong, all over again, into the well of her sweetness.

He shaped the sweet roundness of her bottom with his other hand. The ache in him burst into agony.

He had to have her. God help him, he had to, no matter how dangerous it might be.

He broke the kiss and held her away from him,

clasping her arms, slender and firm, beneath the worn deerskin of her sleeves. She opened her eyes, her face still tilted up to his.

Her face. It was high-cheekboned and beautiful. Its delicate jaw and chin were as determined as a dust storm, as strong as sin. She had the hot power of the sun in her face, and the silent persuasion of the moon.

Finally he moved his still-starving mouth. "Tiana," he said hoarsely, caressing her, up and down, from elbow to shoulder. "Let's go up to the loft."

Her eyes were still glazed from his kiss. Her smile was a slow, loving one.

Without a word she nodded. He held her with one hand while he took down the lantern from the post; he kept his fingers around her arm while they walked silently toward the foot of the ladder. But he had to turn her loose when they reached it. She climbed it ahead of him.

When he stepped into the loft of Pine Grove's big barn, she was standing in its broad western doors, open to the flooding moonlight, waiting for him. He blew out the lantern and set it on the floor.

He strode across the empty space between them, wiping it out of existence in the time it took him to get his next breath.

"Tiana."

But he couldn't reach for her. Not yet. His eyes could not stop looking.

Bathed in the pale yellow light, she seemed to be The First Woman, a natural phenomenon, a living statue of woman sent down from the sky to step off a cloud of moonlight and into this loft that floated high above the ground. The supple, worn buckskins molded to every curve of her lithe body, their deep golden color blending with that of her

skin, yet staying startlingly pale against the black
of her hair and her eyes. The fringes across her
breasts swung free, up and down with her breathing.

She smiled at him then, a heartbreaking flash of
eyes and teeth. The ache inside him changed to an
agony.

He reached out to grasp her waist with one
hand. And to cup her soft breast in the other.

A new, trembling flash of pleasure ran through
her.

"Standingdeer!" she gasped, and turned her face
up, her mouth seeking his.

As soon as she found it, she wished that she
hadn't. For the hot thrill of his tongue and the
sweet ravages of his lips threatened to consume
her.

And she had to ignore them so she could feel
the magic of his hand! He was circling the tip of
her breast with his thumb, melting all of her body,
making it disappear, only to bring it back again,
crying for more.

She tore her lips from his, sliding her hand
along the muscles of his forearm, signaling him
not to move it away.

But he took it away, anyway. "Over here," he
said gruffly, and moved to the pile of loose hay beside the wide doors. She followed him, her body
screaming for his hands to come back, her heart
beating like a thousand racing hoofbeats in her
chest.

"Aren't you afraid maybe Old Spearfinger's up
here in the dark?" she teased in a trembling voice
as he stepped out of Brother Moon's light.

*That's not what I'm afraid of. What I'm afraid of is
that you will tear out my heart.*

But he no longer cared if she did.

"Aren't *you?*" he teased back, jerking the tail of his shirt from the waistband of his pants, ready to pull it over his head and spread it over the prickly, sweet-smelling hay to make them a bed.

"No. I'm brave," she said, standing close, but still in the edge of the moonlight, slanting her head to one side so that the black curtain of her hair fell as a backdrop to her face. Her perfect face. Her skin glowed like pale copper.

He lifted one hand and reached out to run the tip of his finger along the curve of her cheek. Down the side of her satin neck.

"Tiana, Tiana," he said, shaking his head in mock censure. "You're too brave for your own good, I've told you that. You scare me sometimes." *You scare me to death. You could make me want to belong somewhere, to someone . . . to you.*

She sent him a slanting, sensual look. "Are you scared now?"

"No," he lied. "But I was scared when you stood up and walked right at the muzzle of Harve Snider's shotgun. Maybe because it surprised me so—it wasn't like you to do as you were told."

They both laughed.

But then the whole terrifying scene came flooding back into Tiana's mind and she could see Harve's face leering at her in the stark light of the moon.

And his gun. The gun he could have used to kill Stand. His long, ugly gun waving in the air—with the graceful white columns of Running Waters looming behind it. The gun he had used to keep her out of her own home.

Tears sprang into her eyes.

"Oh, Stand," she whispered through lips gone stiff with pain, "that awful man and his people have moved into my *home!* What will I ever do?"

All the smiles and laughter vanished from her face. She held out her arms to him. "Hold me, Standingdeer," she begged, and broke down completely into great, racking sobs.

Stand let the fabric of his shirt fall from his hands and reached out to fold her, trembling, into his arms again.

She kept talking and talking through her sobs. "I need you so much, Stand. Let's sleep here in the hay and not go up to the house tonight. I don't want to go back to that room in Maud's house—I want my own room in my own home!"

Her tears soaked through his shirt to wet his skin.

"Oh, Stand," she wept, "what am I ever going to do?"

Somewhere, far away downstairs in the huge old barn, a horse stamped in his stall. A dove called, low, and fluttered its wings in the eaves. Tiana clung to Stand.

But not because she wanted to make love with him. Because she needed comfort.

The magic companionship had gone; she wasn't even thinking about him now.

A rushing, searing heat surged through every muscle in his body, stripping away his skin to leave him raw and burning. He wanted to punch his fist through the wall, break the posts in two and tear the barn down around them, thrust her away from him and ride through the night as fast as a horse could run, as far as the land could take him.

Stand took a long, shuddering breath. His nostrils filled with the smells of leather and cedar and horses, of the mist floating in at the doors and the pines on the mountains.

Of Tiana's fragrant hair and her smooth, soft skin.

And the salt of her tears.

He tucked her head into the hollow of his neck and rocked her in his arms.

Chapter 9

The sounds of birds, trilling and chittering and calling louder and louder, the way they do just before dawn, finally pulled Tiana up out of sleep. She opened her eyes to a high framework of crisscrossing rafters that lifted the roof out of sight in the gray morning dimness. It was after sunrise, though not by much. The noisy doves must not know that the world was already awake.

Where was she?

She sat up quickly and strained to see through the blue half-light. Wide loft doors stood open near her; she was in a pile of hay, one of many that loomed against the walls.

In a barn, of course, but not hers at home.

Home. The entire nightmare of the previous day came pouring back through her consciousness like scalding water over her skin, every horrible minute repeating itself, each connecting to the others in a sheet of hot torture.

Except for Standingdeer.

Standingdeer! He was the only good thing about yesterday.

She dropped back into the warm indentation made by her body and pulled the blanket—a saddle blanket, by the feel of it—over her. Her hands

172

clutched it tight. He must have covered her with it.

The last thing she remembered was sobbing her heart out in his arms while he rocked her back and forth and held her close against his body. She must have cried herself to sleep there. Had he slept beside her?

She sat up again and looked around, feeling the shape of the hay beside her. No. The hollow in the stack of hay just fit her. Only her.

A loud kick echoed up through the floor from below; a muttered curse followed. Then came the rattling of a latch on a stall.

Stand? Was he stalling and feeding her horses?

She scrambled to her feet, smoothing at her hair, picking the bits of hay from it as she pulled it together to hang down her back. Stand had slipped his fingers into it, just *there*, to cradle her head in his hand.

So he could kiss her. The taste of him still lingered on her lips.

And, oh! She could still feel his hand on her breast. That memory came back so strong it took the power to walk from her legs. And the power to move from her hands.

For a long time she stood there, her fingers loose around her hair, her whole being lost in remembering how it felt to be held in his arms.

Finally she brushed at the wisps of hay caught in the fringes of her buckskins, ran to the ladder, and began to climb down. Maybe she could slip over to the watering trough and wash her face before he knew she was up.

Halfway down she could see, through the rungs of the ladder, the dim figure of a man coming out of a stall.

It definitely wasn't Stand.

She stopped, gripping the sides of the ladder

with both hands, and closed her eyes. Where was he?

Finally she pried her fingers loose and made her foot reach for the next rung down. Then the next. At last she stood on the packed dirt floor and started down the aisle. Whether the man in the shadows was Bluford or one of his servants, she'd have to speak with him. She wouldn't be obligated to anyone here for doing her chores: that would just add to the burden of guilt she felt every time she looked into Bluford Tuskee's pitiful face.

The man stepped out in front of her, a flake of hay in his arms. He lowered it to look at her. Bluford.

"Mr. Tuskee?" she said. "I'll do my own chores."

He spoke at the same time. "What're you doing here?"

Tiana stopped in her tracks. "I'm sorry," she said. "Did I startle you?"

He took a sudden step forward and peered at her through the gloom. Silently, he came another step closer.

Her heart plummeted. Had Old Sudie already told him? Dear Lord, what was he going to do?

"I'm checking on my horses," she said quickly. "Standingdeer and I brought some of them over from Running Waters last night. I hope it's no problem; we ran them into the pen outside until we could ask where you wanted them."

"That's all right, Miss Tiana," he said, with a ghost of his flirtatious manner. "They're as welcome as you are."

"I'll pay you for their keep when I can."

"I wouldn't think of it," he said, and held the hay out to her. "But I *would* let you give this hay to Bay Boy while I bring him some water. I had a lengthy card game last night and I'm anxious for my bed."

"I'll be glad to." Tiana took the hay and went to the bay's stall. She stopped at the door, shocked by the sight inside. The new sunlight streaming in at the wide doors of the barn showed Bay Boy with sweat crusted all over his body, and his head hanging low from exhaustion. He was too tired to even look up when she slid back the door and went in.

This horse hadn't merely been to a card game and back. He'd been ridden into the ground.

He ignored the hay she held in front of his nose.

"Which way did you and Stand bring your horses?" Bluford asked, carrying the full water bucket down the aisle.

"Uh," Tiana said, wrenching her thoughts from the bay's condition to the question. "By the road. We brought them right down the road."

Bluford stopped in his tracks. Water sloshed out and wet his skin through his pants, but he hardly felt it. He stared at Tiana through the haze of his tiredness. The road!

He cleared his throat. "Did you . . . did you see anybody?"

"We heard a large bunch headed fast toward Tennessee, but we didn't see them."

Air came back into his lungs and he carried the bucket to the open door of the stall.

"You didn't even get a glimpse of them?"

"No. We didn't try; we assumed it was a pony club and we surely didn't want them to see us." She flashed him a questioning glance, which he ignored.

He went into the stall and started to hang the bucket from its hook. Tiana was still holding out the hay to Bay Boy, but Bluford could feel her eyes glued to his back.

"Of course you didn't want that," he said heartily, but the desperate need to ask whether Fawn had ever told her he was in a pony club was tearing at his tongue.

"Bay Boy seems too tired to eat," Tiana said. "Do you think he's cooled out enough to have so much water?"

"Oh, yes," Bluford said, forcing a pleasant tone. "I've been home for quite a while, puttering around the barn."

Then he bit his tongue. She'd know that was a lie; he'd already told her he was eager to get to bed. And she was right about the water. He could've ruined his best horse by being so addled by fear. He tipped the bucket and let over half of it run out as he hung it up.

"Did you have any trouble getting your horses?" he asked quickly.

"Besides being threatened with a shotgun, no."

She stuffed the hay into the rack and turned to glare at him as if he'd been the one with the gun. "It makes me so mad I can't see straight!" she burst out, her eyes filling with tears of frustration. "Someday, I swear, I'm taking *everything* back!"

It came to him then, in a flash of inspiration, how to get close to her, gain her confidence, and find out if she did know anything. If her friend Fawn had said anything to her before she died. He straightened his back and, despite every bone in his body screaming from exhaustion, leaned casually against the wall as if settling in for a chat.

"Why wait for someday, Miss Tiana?" he said. "I can call full-blood warriors down from the hills any day."

She stared at him. "But ... The Paint says we can't win. And last night, you and Maud agreed that we should respect Chief Ross's requests not to resist."

"The Paint," he said, lowering his voice, "is older now. Perhaps he has lost his youthful wild courage." He smiled at her. "Also, my cousin has no home, so he doesn't understand how you feel. I do."

Her shocked, hopeful gaze fastened itself to his. "Can you really get my home back for me?" she whispered.

"I certainly can." A twinge of guilt tugged at him for promising her something he never intended to do, but then it died. *Serves her right*, he thought, *for ignoring me last night and asking only The Paint to help her, as if he was a mighty war chief and I was nothing at all.*

"Oh, Mr. Tuskee, thank you!" she cried. "When? When can you do this, and what can I do to help?"

"We'll talk about it later," he said, weariness flowing through him suddenly, fast and swift as a river. "After I've slept, we'll make our plans."

He left her standing there and strode unsteadily out of the barn. Tiana's heart beat harder and harder as she watched him go. Now, if she could persuade The Paint to help them, Running Waters was as good as saved.

She turned back to the exhausted Bay Boy and curried and coaxed him until he ate a bit of hay and lay down to sleep. Then she went to feed her own horses.

She was almost done when, on her last pass down the aisle to get hay for the horses in the outside pen, she glanced into an empty stall and stopped stock-still in her tracks.

The Paint's horse was gone.

The hot bath and changing into Maud's split skirt and summer blouse made Tiana's body feel better, but they tore her spirit to pieces. She wanted her own bathtub in her own room in her own home. She wanted her own clothes. She wanted Dilcey.

Restlessness drove her immediately out of Maud and Bluford's house, the house that once had been Tobacco Jack's, and back to the barn. Bluford would probably have to sleep all day before they could make their plans. In the meantime, at least she had her own horses.

Butterfly was kicking at the walls because the stall was strange to her, nipping and squealing at her neighbors. Tiana slid open her door.

"You want to go home, too, don't you, Babe?" she said, putting her arm around the filly's neck and leading her out to the wall rack where she had hung the one halter and one bridle that, with the sidesaddle and Coosa's bridle, comprised the only tack she now owned. She took the halter down and slipped it onto The Butterfly's dainty head.

"Let's have a little ride and we'll both feel better," she crooned. "And soon we'll be on Running Waters again."

Once the mare was haltered, Tiana led her to the hitching post to one side of the barn door and tied her there in the warm sunlight. Then she went back into the cool gloom of the huge barn, turned immediately to the right, and stepped up over the sill to enter Pine Grove's crowded tack room. She was sick of riding sidesaddle. Surely Bluford wouldn't mind if she borrowed one of his saddles so she could ride astride.

The small room smelled like leather and Bay Boy's wet saddle blanket and dust.

Bluford should've shut the door when he put up his saddle this morning, she thought. If he'd get into the habit of keeping it closed, it would save bushelfuls of barn dust from drifting in and settling onto the tack.

She squinted in the dimness, trying to see which saddle would be her best fit.

The hinges on the door squealed behind her, and the room went completely black.

It became a closed cocoon, stale and still.

Tiana's breath left her.

But someone else was breathing. Slowly, with raspy pauses, not three feet away at her back.

Someone who smelled of snuff and dry sweat and old age.

"Missy!" hissed the voice she dreaded worse than the bite of a snake. "You got my money for me?"

Tiana closed her eyes. *Lord, please help me.*

She needed Sudie's silence a thousand times more today than a few days ago when her situation had seemed so desperate. Today her shelter, her food, her place to sleep where she could watch over Running Waters, *her keeping her horses,* depended on Bluford's not finding out that she had killed Tobacco Jack.

And her heart's life depended on Standing-deer's not knowing.

"Well?" came the hateful whisper again. "What you say? You brúng my money or not?"

Tiana peeled her dry lips apart and licked them. "No," she whispered at last.

"How come?"

"I got it," she said, turning around in a rush, but she could see nothing at all in the blackness. "But I hid it in my house and now some Georgians have moved in there. They won our plantation in the lottery."

Even in this dire situation, it hurt her throat to say that.

"You went in the night and got y'r horses, didn't ye?"

"Yes."

"Then go git my money."

"I ... *will*," Tiana said hesitantly. "I plan to. One night soon, I'll—"

"Y' better know I'll tell Bluford," Old Sudie interrupted, her cracked voice no more than an evil murmur floating through the sweltering darkness. "Girl, you got one week."

Standingdeer stayed gone for three long days, and Tiana thought she would lose her mind. Over and over again, she would find herself praying that he would come back and help her know what to do—the next instant she would realize that if he did return, she couldn't even *tell* him about Old Sudie's demands.

Then she would pray that he would *never* come back, so there'd be no chance of his finding her out.

Living this closely with Bluford caused her the same mind-splitting confusion. He, her sworn enemy—who was about to become aware of that fact if she couldn't get her hands on money for Sudie—had attached himself to her as firmly as moss to a tree. And she had encouraged him.

Sometimes, like now, with him sitting in the chair beside hers on the back veranda, rocking back and forth while reciting the pitiful details of his haunting, she felt terribly guilty about this strange, new friendship between them, as if she were a complete fraud and a liar. She gladly would *be* a fraud and a liar, though, if such behavior would get Running Waters back for her, and at the moment it seemed that it would.

"I'm so sorry that you can't sleep, Bluford," she said, glancing at him, trying not to meet his anguished eyes. It still seemed awkward to call him by his first name, but he insisted.

He also insisted on ranting about Tobacco Jack's

spirit and Willie Ragsdale until she wanted to scream. If he was going to organize an attack to recover Running Waters for her, he had to do it soon.

She only had four more days.

"One thing that might help you is trying not to think about your papa's spirit during the day," she said gently. "Let's put that out of mind for now and finish our plans for Running Waters."

Bluford narrowed his bloodshot eyes. "What do you know about Willie Ragsdale?"

"Nothing. I've told you that over and over. But I don't think he's a killer."

Bluford stopped rocking and planted his elbows on his knees while he squinted at her. "That night at your social you sounded mighty sure."

Tiana looked straight at him. "I was only saying what I felt in my heart."

"You can't prove he is innocent?"

"No."

He leaned back in the chair. "I believe you," he said, then started rocking again.

However, a minute from now he could be putting the very same question to her. Bluford changed his mind constantly.

The one thing he *couldn't* change it about was Running Waters. She wouldn't let him.

"I think we should plan to drive the Sniders out of Running Waters the day after tomorrow," Tiana said. "Are you sending a runner to the hills tonight?"

"Not tonight," he said. "We'll need time to plan before we call anyone in."

"We've planned for three days," Tiana said, trying to keep the impatience from her voice. "We must act—*now*."

"Of course," he said, as if she'd echoed his own sentiments exactly. "I'll send a boy first thing in the morning. When Grandmother Sun goes down the next day, we'll have you back in your own bed again, I promise."

"I'll be forever grateful to you," she said. "Do you think twenty men will be enough?"

"It'll be plenty. I have no doubt that, painted for war and giving the war cry, we can make the *yonegas* run over each other on the way back to Georgia."

The confident words lifted her heart. Everything would be put right, after all. She would move back into the big house at Running Waters, get the money from the safe, pay Old Sudie, and settle down to training Coosa for the Stakes. She would need that purse money desperately now—to repair and replace things the Sniders had destroyed. She couldn't bear for Mama and Papa to see home the way it was now.

"Tell me some more about your friend Fawn," Bluford said, taking a pipe and tobacco from his pocket. He filled the pipe's bowl without looking down because his bleary gaze was firmly fixed on Tiana. "Did you two always share your secrets?"

Standingdeer felt a tightening in his gut when he rode the buckskin onto Pine Grove. What a waste! Two hard days on the road and another, harder one, waiting to see Chief Ross—all for nothing.

And the devil of it was, he'd known the trip would be useless before he'd ever ridden the first mile. He shook his head. Not only was he getting old and lonely, he was getting old and *una-sti-ski*, crazy.

What was there about Tiana that did this to him?

He spurred the dun into a fast trot.

Nothing. The girl had no hold on him. He had

made this trip to try to get rid of her, in fact. He wanted nothing to do with any of the Tenkillers; he was trying to shift the responsibility for her from himself to Chief Ross.

He ignored the small voice that contradicted him. *No, you went to Red Clay to try to prove to her that, somehow, in some way, you can still be a hero.*

That was wrong, he thought as he lifted the horse into a lope. He never cared about other people's opinion of him, not even Tiana's. Especially not Tiana's.

Especially when she had come into his arms only to grieve for her home, he reflected. He caught sight of the big barn in the distance, and the feel of her in his arms scalded his memory. Tiana hadn't been thinking about him.

And she still wasn't. His insides tied themselves into a hard knot as he drew down his mount to a slow walk and rode up to the back veranda. Tiana and Bluford were sitting on the porch with their heads together, like conspirators, so absorbed in talking that they didn't hear him.

"*Osiyo*," he said.

Tiana's head flew up, throwing her hair over one shoulder. Just that quick sight of her face flashed a thrill through his body. He tried to ignore it.

"Standingdeer!" she cried, and sprang to her feet.

But she didn't dash down the steps to greet him. She stood in front of her chair as if the backs of her knees were glued to it. The chair beside his cousin.

Bluford stayed where he was, leaning forward in his chair with his elbows on his thighs, leaning toward Tiana.

"*Osiyo*, Cousin," he said. "We wondered if you had gone back West without saying good-bye."

Stand threw his reins to the ground and dismounted.

Bluford got up, finally, and walked to the edge of the porch. "Tooker!" he bellowed. A small servant boy appeared, to take Stand's horse.

Tiana stood still, fighting the light-headedness, almost dizziness, that the first glimpse of Stand had thrown over her. He had come back!

Stand let Tooker take the buckskin horse and, slapping the dust from his pants, started up the steps. Tiana tried to glare at him. She must remember: he'd refused to even *try* to get back Running Waters, when his cousin had *volunteered*.

But his wide, muscled shoulders moved with the wild grace of a panther. His sure feet, silent in his moccasins, took the steps as if he owned them.

And his dark, far-seeing eyes looked straight into hers.

"Tiana," he said, and swept off his hat.

His face. His square-jawed face was more beautiful, even, than the mountaintops at sunrise. It stopped the heart in her body.

They stared at each other while Bluford turned toward the house and yelled, "Akee!" and while the servant woman came out, already carrying a tray with the cool drinks her master was about to order.

From the corner of her eye Tiana saw Bluford sink back into his chair. "Sit down, Cousin, sit down," he said.

But Stand leaned against one of the porch columns at the top of the steps. Still looking at her.

"I've been in the saddle all day."

He took one of the tall glasses of lemonade from the tray and downed a long drink. Only then did his gaze move to Bluford. It flicked back to Tiana.

"Where's Maud?" he asked.

"Her sister, Susannah, took sick and sent for her," Bluford replied.

"I'm surprised she'd go off and leave you here alone with a beautiful woman."

Tiana caught her breath. He thought she was beautiful! And he was jealous!

Bluford said, "She didn't want to, but loyalty won out over jealousy. Maud's a very loyal woman."

Stand nodded. "A jealous one, too."

"Well, she needn't worry," Bluford declared expansively. "Tiana and I are becoming good friends, nothing more."

Stand turned up his glass and drained it. Nothing more? That didn't sound like the Bluford he knew.

"I went to see Chief Ross," he said.

Tiana was at his side in an instant, her dark brown eyes enormous with eagerness. He clamped his jaw shut, and his fists, too; he could have shaken her for rushing to him *now*, not to be near him, but because she wanted her home again.

But then, looking at the longing in her face which he would soon wipe away, he could have kicked himself for raising her hopes needlessly. He had started this conversation all wrong.

"You did? You went to ask the *Chief?* Did he say we should try and take back our plantation? Oh, Stand! I should've guessed you'd be doing *something* about those horrible Sniders!"

The pain of his failure shot all through his body as she looked at him with such naked hope.

"I can't make everything right in this world, Tiana," he said harshly. "Not the things controlled by the white men and the politicians."

He tore his gaze from hers and fixed it on the gable of the barn which was blending into the shadow of the mountain now that day was about to end. He could picture the hope fading from her face in that very same way.

Then he forced his feelings down and spoke steadily. "The Chief said that his policy holds, just as it did when his own home was lost in the lottery. He insists that any trouble caused by Cherokees can only undermine the bargaining that he and the negotiators are trying to do."

"The *Georgians* have caused all the trouble!" she cried. "Taking back what's ours wouldn't be causing trouble!"

"I'm just telling you what he said. He sends his deepest regrets; he knows exactly what you are going through. He wants his plantation back just as much as you want Running Waters."

She made a pain-filled sound that turned him around to face her again. He wished he hadn't. The look on her face bespoke unendurable loneliness, as blue as the mountains. How could he resist taking her into his arms? Even if she was only using him?

Even if she *had* been so chummy with Bluford.

He said softly, "The Chief is sending word today to your papa to come home and see about you."

She straightened her shoulders and raised her chin. Her dark eyes flashed.

"Well, *I'll* send word today for Papa to stay right there and get that horrid law repealed! I'll be living at Running Waters again long before Papa could get home."

She put her fists on her hips and whirled to fix her fiery gaze on Bluford.

"Isn't that right?" she said. "Tell him, Bluford!"

Bluford? Hadn't she always called him Mr. Tuskee?

Stand looked at his cousin. Bluford met his gaze; then his eyes slid away.

"I'm going to get some men together," he muttered, "and take Running Waters back from the lottery."

So. This time *Bluford* would be the big hero.

No, he would *talk* the big hero. Bluford didn't have the guts to attack a henhouse, much less bring down the Georgia Guard on his head. He was raising Tiana's hopes to make himself look good in her eyes; he never intended to do a thing he was saying.

"You'd better get your *brains* together," Stand ground out between clenched teeth. "And get a bridle on that tongue of yours."

"No!" Tiana cried. "We can do it! We're going to get Running Waters back, day after tomorrow. We thought you'd help us, Standingdeer," she added in a small, hurt voice.

"Help you what? Get your lungs blown out by Harve Snider's shotgun? Bring the Georgia Guard in to rape and beat you and throw you out of Running Waters again and burn every place for miles around to teach us a lesson? Rot in a filthy Georgia jail? Swing from an oak tree in Georgia?"

He glared at Bluford until Tiana thought the look would cut his cousin in two. "Come to your senses, Blu," he said. "You won't take that kind of risk and you know it. This is a homeless girl, not even twenty years old. You ought to be horse-whipped for this charade."

He turned on his heel and clattered down the steps, headed for the lighted door of the summer kitchen. Tiana caught up with him just as he took its stone doorsill in one furious stride.

"Stand!" she cried. "It isn't a charade!"

He ignored her and crossed the room to jerk out a chair from beneath the worn trestle table.

"Get me some supper," he barked at Akee, who turned, her body twisted in place at her pan of dishwater, to stare at him in surprise. "I haven't had a bite to eat all day."

Tiana sat down across from him, clasping her hands together, twining her fingers so tightly they hurt. She *had* to make him change his mind. If he kept saying such awful things to Bluford, he could make the indecisive man give up!

Akee appeared at the end of the long table, a filled plate in one plump hand, a glass of buttermilk in the other, and a sheen of sweat on her face. She wasn't accustomed to serving the masters where the servants usually ate.

"If you was to want to eat up at the big house, Mr. Stand, in the dinin' room . . ."

"I'll eat here," he said. "I'm not going up to the big house. I'll sleep in the barn."

He took a long swig of the cold buttermilk, then set down the glass. "Tiana," he said, "about Blu. You have to know he's better at talk than action—"

"He's *not* lying to me!" she interrupted, her eyes blazing at him. "Bluford plans to get Running Waters back and drive the Sniders to Georgia! He can do it, too."

And you can't, those enormous dark eyes said to him. *Or you won't. Whichever it is, you're not my hero anymore.*

If he ever was, he thought, picking up a piece of fried chicken and biting into it. Why did he care? She'd always been interested in him only for what he could do for her.

The other night in the barn, begging him to sleep with her, she'd only been softening him up for another request to retrieve Running Waters. Hadn't she kissed him before she asked his consent to take Coosa to Ellijay?

Her heart had never really been in one thing she

had done in his arms. Maybe she'd kissed Bluford, too, and more, to try to recover her home.

He allowed himself a bitter grin as he took a vicious bite out of the drumstick in his hand. Served them right—let them use each other. If he had the sense God gave a wooden goose, he'd be happy Blu was responsible for her.

Blu couldn't take care of himself, much less of her.

Stand swallowed and took a long, ragged breath of the close air of the kitchen, full of the sweet fragrances of woodsmoke and fried chicken and freshly baked corn bread with sourwood honey. And of Tiana. Sweet Tiana.

"How come you're calling him Bluford all of a sudden?" he blurted. "Always before, you called him Mr. Tuskee."

"He asked me to call him that. We've talked quite a lot these past three days."

Stand picked up his fork and laid it down again. He picked up his bread and spread it with honey.

"Tiana," he said, "my cousin Bluford is a married man, and Maud's the most jealous wife in the Cherokee Nation."

Tiana stared at him, her beautiful lips slightly apart. In spite of it all, an overwhelming desire to kiss them washed through him. He could remember their exact taste. More delectable than the honey in his mouth.

She leaned toward him as Akee brought a lighted candle and set it between them. The night mists were drifting in from the mountains.

"Stand," Tiana said, trying not to watch the soft light hitting the hard, handsome angles of his face, deepening the lines at the corners of his eyes. "Won't you please work *with* Bluford instead of accusing him of not being sincere?" she asked softly. "At least, don't discourage him. I really believe he means to help me, but I also believe he needs your help."

Stand picked up his glass and drained it of the cold buttermilk, then set it down on the table with a gesture as gentle, yet as dangerous, as his voice when he spoke.

"Tiana," he said, "use Bluford all you like, but leave me out of it. Just remember one thing: he's had a lot more years to practice at that game than you have. You'd better find out what he's wanting from you."

Then he pushed back his chair, got up, strode out of the kitchen, and left her sitting there.

Chapter 10

Tiana clutched the rope reins of the bosal harder, one in each hand, and tried not to let the jittery tightness tormenting every nerve in her body flow from her legs into Butterfly's sides. The filly broke into a too-fast trot, anyway. Tiana did nothing about it.

Just as she had done nothing about it when The Paint insisted on giving Coosa his morning workout. The Paint, at this very moment, was riding Coosa! When, for all the five years of the stallion's life, no one had been on his back except her!

And Coosa, the traitor, had done nothing to prevent him, either. Well, he *had* crow-hopped a couple of times when Stand had settled into the saddle, but he was accustomed to carrying extra weight in some races, and Stand's hands were exceptionally good. As good as hers, but she'd never admit that to him.

She glanced down the farm road into Bluford's cornfield, where the two of them had cantered out of her sight. However, she couldn't summon the strength to even care whether Stand was holding him to the best pace or whether he would ride him too far. All of her energy was funneling itself into fighting the fear of Old Sudie and her threat.

One week. In the tack room when Sudie had

rasped out those words, that had seemed such a scanty amount of time. Now it sounded like a fortune. For, as of now, there was only *one day* left.

One more day of no attack on Running Waters and both cousins would know that it was *Tiana's* death which could send Tobacco Jack's spirit to the Nightland. She would be not only homeless, but hunted, maybe dead.

What in the name of Thunder would she ever do?

The muffled sound of hoofbeats jerked her gaze from the black filly between her knees to the road again. Stand and Coosa came loping toward her.

The sight of them was so powerful that for an instant it took her mind. They looked like one being. Stand's tight gray breeches and white hunting shirt blended together would be the precise color of Coosa; his legs fit the horse's sides exactly; his hips didn't rise from his seat. His squared shoulders moved only with the gentle rhythm of the gait, the big sleeves of his shirt lifting and falling in the breeze.

His hair caught the sunlight like the wings of a raven.

He *was* a Raven, a warrior, yet he wouldn't lead men to take back her home! And he accused her of using him!

That furious resentment tasted acrid as alum on her tongue, but she couldn't stop watching him, loping toward her as serenely as if he and Coosa were part of the morning, a gray-white cloud floating across the green land in front of the high blue mountains.

The closer he came, the faster the bitterness in her mouth faded, replaced by the sweet honey of his kiss.

Just looking at him made her ache to taste his

lips again. She had to get her wits about her before she tried to talk to him.

He was coming toward the barn, but she was sure he wasn't done with Coosa. Not after all his ranting about pushing the horse harder. She'd keep a close watch, and as soon as he quit on him, she'd go in, too, so she could try once more to persuade him.

This time she had to make him agree, bite her tongue, and take the insults he might hurl at her. She'd admit he'd been right: Bluford would never get the job done.

If Stand clung to his stubborn refusal, then she had no choice. She would chance another raid of her own on Running Waters, into the house this time, into Harve Snider's lair.

Frustration and fear formed a tight, aching knot in the pit of her stomach; she sucked in her breath. The sudden sound sent Butterfly charging into a hard run.

Tiana's head snapped backward and her balance shifted. By the time she had recovered enough to give startled signals with her legs and hands, Butterfly was so far gone she ignored them. Even Tiana's sitting down and back as a signal to slow the pace was useless; she might as well have been a mosquito in the saddle on the two-year-old's back.

They raced around the pen once, and then again, picking up speed with every stride. Tiana's hair came loose from its tie-back and streamed into the wind.

Dimly she heard shouts above the noise of Butterfly's pounding hooves. And Coosa's. Then the vague sounds became words.

"Circle her, Tiana! Pull her around!"

She braced her foot in the stirrup, grabbed the left rein farther up toward Butterfly's mouth, and hauled on it with all her strength, hating, even in her panic, the mark the rope bosal would make on the filly's black velvet nose. But Butterfly didn't care. That nose stayed high in the air, pointed straight ahead. She ran even faster.

Tiana let go of the right rein and took the left in both hands, gritting her teeth, pulling hard. At last! Butterfly's head began to turn, slowly, slowly. The breakneck pace lessened. They started into a much smaller circle; Butterfly's head began to come around.

Then Coosa's hooves pounded louder, coming closer and closer; Butterfly jerked, trying to take back her head and run with him. Tiana gritted her teeth and held on. Thank goodness she already had the mare's body bent too far for her to go anywhere. She took a ragged breath, the first she'd had since the runaway started. It was over.

The next instant a force as mighty as a high wind ripped her legs loose from the filly. She flew out of the saddle, her body caught around the waist by Standingdeer's outreaching arm.

Holding Tiana tight in his burning grip, he reined Coosa to a stop, but he didn't have a free hand to reach for the filly. Butterfly began dancing in circles. Tiana's seat had just brushed the stallion's withers when the filly began to buck. The saddle shifted crookedly on her back; one flying iron stirrup hovered over her poll, then came crashing down hard, on her head.

The filly went crazy. She pinned her ears back, tucked in her head, and pitched in deadly earnest straight at them; the last thing Tiana saw, as Stand's other arm came protectively around her, was Butterfly's whirling change of direction, heels in the air, coming within a hairsbreadth of Coosa's shoulder.

He jumped sideways; if The Paint hadn't had

such a grip on her, Tiana would've gone right over his head.

If The Paint hadn't been such a fantastic rider, they *both* would have gone off on the other side of the stallion.

But she was in no mood to admire him now. She drew in a mouthful of air so she could scream, "*What* do you think you're *doing?*"

"I'll ask you the same," he ground out and brought Coosa to a jarring stop.

Tiana fought to get free, pushing at his hard chest, arching her back against the incredible strength of his arms. And against the flaring, insidious desire for him that filled her.

"I was *riding,*" she said, through a jaw set hard for the struggle. "Until you ripped me off my mount and nearly crippled her and Coosa, too!"

He brushed both her hands to her sides and held them there with one unconquerable arm slanted across her body.

"You'd better thank me that *you're* not the one crippled!" he said, tightening his hold on her.

She kicked at him, but, sprawled sideways as she was, the best she could deliver was a weak blow to his shin with her heel. He didn't even flinch.

"I was perfectly all right," she yelled, squirming in his arms, trying to see him, to glare at him. She succeeded in getting her seat under her, but with her back to him.

"I had her under control!"

"And I'm the Governor of Georgia."

All the colors of the rainbow rushed by in front of her eyes. The back of her head burned with the heat of her fury. She banged it at his chest.

"I'm not listening to another one of these insults. Let me off this horse this instant, do you hear me?"

"Calm down or you'll *fall* off."

He caught her head with his chin and tucked it into the curve of his shoulder, sliding his hands up her arms without loosening his fierce embrace. His palms flamed against her skin, even through the sleeves of her shirt.

A memory flooded through her, tearing through the curtain of her anger around her heart. He had caressed her this way that night in the barn, except then she'd been facing him. Lifting her mouth for his kiss.

She strained against his muscle-roped arms. Kissing him had been the biggest mistake of her life: it had made her want more. And more.

"Don't you dare say that I can't ride that filly!"

"I wouldn't think of it," he drawled. "I would simply say that you *almost* couldn't ride her."

She twisted, trying to hold her body stiff, away from his. He wouldn't let her.

"I wasn't in the least danger of coming off until you tore me loose!"

Her cheek pressed against his chest; she couldn't move.

"You were in danger of going into the fence or through it. Or over it."

"*You* put me in more danger when you . . ."

His heart was pounding hard and wild, like a drum beneath her ear.

Like her own heart was doing, there in the center of her body.

. . . appeared there, at Council Oak, beside Gray Fox, as if you'd sprung full-grown right out of the earth. When you won half of my horse and tied me to you.

When you held me and let me cry myself to sleep.

"You gave that filly way too much speed, way too soon."

"I didn't *give* it to her! She took it!"

Tiana bit her tongue as soon as she'd said the words.

"My point exactly," he drawled in his most infuriating way.

She racked her brain, unsuccessfully, for a tart answer.

"You nearly got yourself killed," he said very low, his rich voice rumbling in his chest, "Tiana."

Nobody, *nobody*, ever said her name the way Stand did.

The sound of it, lingering on his lips like a sudden sigh, wafted through her. She closed her eyes; her body went limp against him.

Her *treacherous* body, which shaped itself to his like water filling a pool. Her skin drank in his warmth through the two sets of their clothes, heating her blood all the way through her body faster than the sunlight beaming down.

Let me go, Stand. Let me go.

But she couldn't shape her lips to form the words. Coosa stamped and snorted. Neither Stand nor Tiana moved.

Until they heard the sound of a horse coming, fast.

It raced up the long driveway, then pounded off and onto the grass, finally starting to slow in bouncing hops as it reached them. Bluford sawed on the reins.

"Bring me another mount," he yelled toward the barn. "And send to the house for Akee to pack me some dinner."

"Yes, *suh!*" a voice called back.

Bluford rode up to and along the side of the pen where Butterfly, exhausted at last, was standing, blowing, beside the fence. Her saddle was loose and hanging to one side. Bluford looked at the heaving horse, then at Tiana and Stand. Mostly at Stand.

"I just heard at Horn's Tavern that the Lighthorse have jailed Willie Ragsdale for murdering Pa," he called, his voice shaking with excitement.

Stand's whole body tensed; one hand went to his hip as if reaching for an invisible gun.

Tiana sat up very straight, staring at Bluford's smugly satisfied face, a screaming *No!* rising to her lips.

His eyes met hers as he pulled Bay Boy down to a complete stop. "Tiana, you were wrong," he shouted. "Willie's guilty."

Goose bumps broke out all over her. What should she do? What *could* she do without turning the accusing finger on herself?

He dismounted and walked quickly around to the gate, coming into the pen without any change in his intense expression. The sight of the two of them on one horse with Stand's arm around Tiana, plus another disheveled horse in the pen, wasn't enough to divert him from his news.

"How do they know?" she croaked as he neared them.

Stand repeated the question loudly enough for Bluford to hear. "How do they know he's guilty? What's the evidence?"

Tiana pushed Stand's now loose arms away, threw her leg over Coosa on the off side, and slid to the ground. She stood there, rooted, at his shoulder, hiding her face while she ran her hand along the horse's neck and twisted her fingers into his mane.

She couldn't let Willie Ragsdale take the blame for what she'd done. But how could she stop it?

Bluford's voice rang in her ears like a bell of alarm.

"Tom Jolly went to the council," he said, "and swore that he saw Willie Ragsdale coming from

Pine Grove onto the Federal Road right after Papa was killed."

Stand made a sharp sound of disgust; Tiana felt, rather than saw, his body relax.

"The Jollys and the Ragsdales have been at each other's throats since before I went West," he said. "Ever since Ettsceu Jolly's killing all those years ago. Tom's lying."

"No!" Bluford cried. "The Lighthorse wouldn't have made the arrest without good suspicion. You know that."

He glanced away to see his stable hand leading a fresh horse out of the barn and up to Bay Boy, then turned back to Stand.

"Come on, Cousin," he said. "Ride with me. Let's save the Nation the expense of a trial."

Stand stood in the stirrup and swung down from Coosa. Tiana carefully didn't glance up at him.

"No," he said. "I'm not killing a man on Tom Jolly's word."

Cool relief surged through her. Maybe Stand could convince Bluford not to go, and she wouldn't have to try!

"But there must be more proof than Tom's word!" Bluford cried. "The arrest proves that."

"The arrest proves nothing," Stand said. "Except that politics can accomplish most anything."

"Well, I'm going alone, then!" Bluford said, whirling around to stalk toward his horse. "If you want to turn coward, that's your concern."

Stand strode up beside him, leading Coosa. Tiana followed in his shadow. If Stand couldn't stop Bluford, then she must. But how? *How?*

By telling the truth. But she couldn't.

"Bluford," she said, "couldn't this wait? I thought the attack on Running Waters was to take place tonight!"

"I'm sorry, Tiana," Bluford said, hurrying to his horse, "but that'll have to wait. This is too important."

He snatched his saddle from the stableboy, who was transferring it from one horse to the other, and snapped, "Run up to the house and tell Akee to pack me some clothes, too, and hurry. Enough for two days."

"Yassuh!" The boy headed for the house at a run.

"Don't ride down there and do something foolish, Bluford," Stand said. "Killing the wrong man will only make more trouble."

"But killing the right one will set me free of my misery!" Bluford cried, throwing the saddle on the fresh horse, a tall, lanky sorrel. He tightened the cinch and secured it, then stuck his hand into the pocket of his coat to pull out a pistol.

"Maud's coming back today," Tiana blurted. "Wait and see her, at least. She could give you her advice."

"I don't need anybody's advice."

Tiana's blood chilled. She had never heard the indecisive Bluford sound so resolute.

He cradled the gun in his hand, checking the action; then he opened the chamber and Tiana saw the bullets glinting in the sun. He closed it and pulled out the tail of his shirt so he could stick the weapon into the waistband of his trousers, out of sight.

The Paint stood still, watching him. "I'd better come with you."

"No!" Bluford cried, turning to glare at him as he arranged the shirt and tucked it in over the gun. "Now I know you'd only try to stop me. And after you swore to help free Tobacco Jack's spirit and send it to the Nightland!"

"Shooting Ragsdale won't send any spirit to the Nightland except poor Willie's."

Bluford's face twisted. "Times have changed," he said, "when a National Hero won't take revenge for his own blood."

"You'll be the one changed," The Paint retorted, "from master of a plantation to a jailed man when Tobacco Jack's real killer turns up."

Bluford threw him a hate-filled look. "Go ahead and admit you don't have the guts for it," he said. "I'll be the hero in this family now. I can damn well get the job done by myself."

Bluford tightened the cinch one more notch and mounted. He wheeled the horse, rode toward the house to meet the boy bringing his saddlebags, threw them across his saddle, and headed down the driveway at a fast lope without so much as another glance in his cousin's direction.

Tiana, the pit of her stomach on fire, watched him go.

What kind of coward was she? Would she stand here in silence and let an innocent man die in her stead?

She turned to The Paint, her lips parted to speak, her mind searching for words to tell him the truth.

But he was already gazing down at her, his narrowed eyes burning into hers as if he'd already forgotten about Bluford and Willie.

"You're not hurt, are you?" he asked. "I thought I got there before she pounded you against the fence."

Tiana let her lips drift closed and swallowed hard.

The Paint hadn't snatched her from The Butterfly's back because she was messing up the two-year-old's training. He had raced into the pen and folded her into his arms because he had panicked, afraid that Tiana would be hurt.

The Paint truly cared for her!

But the realization brought her no joy. Once he knew the truth, he would hate her forever.

"Go after him, Stand," she begged. "Bring him back."

His eyes turned hard in that instant, changed from brown fire into black chips of obsidian.

"He's a grown man," he snapped, and spun on his heel to return to the horses.

"But he's . . . not really responsible," she argued to his back. She followed him. "He's so . . . disturbed . . . from not being able to sleep, and all."

He grunted, and turned to glare at her over his shoulder. "How do *you* know he can't sleep?"

"It's all he talks about!" she cried. "You've heard him!"

"I've heard him making big plans to take back Running Waters, too," he said. "But has he done it? Are you living in your own home, sleeping in your own bed?"

"No, but . . ."

"So. He's nothing but talk where Ragsdale's concerned, either."

He walked up to the sweat-covered filly and began unfastening her saddle. He stared across it at Tiana, following him around like a begging puppy, unable to think what to do next. "Don't worry about your friend Bluford," he said sarcastically. "He won't do any shooting."

The cold terror grew in her heart. Bluford had sounded and acted different about Ragsdale than he had about Running Waters. The Paint was wrong. Shooting Willie Ragsdale was one thing his cousin *would* do.

A man would die a few hours from now, bleeding on the floor of a jail cell where he didn't deserve to be because she wasn't brave enough to own up to what she'd done. Another man, who already was haunted, would spend the rest of his life beneath a burden of guilt like the terrible one she bore.

If she didn't speak the truth.

The Paint stripped the tack from Butterfly and watched her venture out into the middle of the sandy pen to sniff out a spot in which to roll. He wasn't going to do one thing to stop Bluford.

Unless she could persuade him. She swallowed a few times and walked over to lean on the fence, fighting to keep the panic out of her voice.

"Bluford sounded different this time," she said. "I think he really will shoot Willie Ragsdale."

The Paint sent her a look of irritation so strong it singed her skin. "He may *try*," he said with a shrug. "The Cherokee officials will stop him."

Panic got the better of her. "They may not! I don't understand why *you* don't stop him! If you don't believe Willie is the one who killed . . . your uncle, then why don't you ride after Bluford?"

The Paint stood very still, holding Butterfly's saddle in his arms. He stared at her. "What's going on here, Tiana? This is a man's business, our family's business. What stake do you have in it?"

Her cheeks flamed hot and her gaze dropped away from his before she could stop it.

"What stake do you have in it, Tiana?" he repeated.

Her lips parted, to answer him, but her brain wouldn't tell her a single word to say.

"If you're that frantic about Bluford, then you and he must be more than good friends."

His hard, bitter tone tore at her heart even more than the awful words.

"No!" she shouted. "We aren't! Bluford . . ."

"Don't waste your breath," he said, his voice so

cold it made her shiver. "A mole could see that you're hiding something."

"I am *not!*" she yelled, but even she could hear the tinny sound of the lie in her voice beneath the loudness. As a distraction, she hurried on. "I know the Constitution revoked the old brood law, but the District Sheriff or one of the Lighthorsemen might believe in it still. If so, they might sympathize with Bluford and deliberately let him get to Willie."

She dared to look at him then, but she couldn't find one particle of feeling in his eyes.

"That's not very likely," he said.

Her hands began to shake and she clutched at the top board of the fence to steady them. The blood pounded so loud in her head she thought surely Standingdeer could hear it.

"I think you should go see about your cousin," she insisted with stubborn desperation. "His nerves aren't good enough to get him through a situation like this."

Stand stared at her for an endless time. Raw pain dried out his eyes and drew his skin down so tightly over the bones of his face that he thought it would tear.

"And neither are mine!" he roared. "Since you're so damned worried about Bluford, Tiana, why don't you go see about him yourself?"

Her dark eyes flared wide, then narrowed into shining arrow points of anger.

His heart beat once, dull and slow as the tolling of a bell.

"I will!" she shouted. "I will do exactly that!"

Then she whirled and ran for the pen where her mares were kept.

Stand turned the other way, amazed that he could still walk, that the horses still stood, blow-

ing and fidgeting, in the middle of the pen.
Amazed that the sun still shone.

What the hell had he ever expected, anyway?

The question repeated itself viciously behind his
blurring eyes as he grabbed hold of Coosa and
swung up into the saddle. No woman and no
Tenkiller could be trusted. Tiana was both.

Chapter 11

The next day's ride from New Echota back to Pine Grove with Bluford was the quietest trip Tiana had ever taken in company. Her mind was on Old Sudie and on The Paint. Bluford's, she supposed, was on the bedeviling ghost of his papa since he'd learned that Willie Ragsdale wasn't guilty.

Almost as soon as she had that thought, though, he proved her wrong. As they reached the edge of his plantation, Bluford suddenly urged his sorrel to come up beside Jane Hunt and said, "You know those two *yonegas*, Sykes and Walters?"

Tiana shivered. "How could I forget them?"

"Do you know them well enough to give me some advice about them?"

She shot a sharp glance at his sheepish face. "Are they still lurking around here?"

"Yes, and I want to get them out of the Nation."

"Bluford," she said slowly, a tired feeling of helplessness drawing her down into her saddle, threatening to pull her right into the ground, "if you can't drive those two away, how do you ever hope to take back Running Waters?"

"That's different!" he blustered. "I can ask for help for Running Waters! But those two are a private matter."

"If they're the ones you're out gambling with all night," Tiana said tightly, "then I'd advise you to stop. They're dangerous men."

"I know that."

"*I* know that I must have Running Waters back today," she burst out. "Bluford, we have to do it *tonight.*"

Then she lifted Jane Hunt into a lope and rode on ahead so she couldn't hear his fumbling excuses. For a few more minutes she had to believe that she could still stop Old Sudie, buy her silence for one more day—for today was the day the ancient woman threatened to tell her secret.

Tiana saw Standingdeer as soon as she and Bluford came in sight of the house at Pine Grove. Grandmother Sun rode high overhead; her light, even at this distance, outlined his silhouette on the front veranda. It was unmistakable.

He sat in a corner of the balustrade, leaning back against the post, one foot on the floor and the other on the ledge in front of him. The bend of his long leg, the powerful slant of his shoulders, the very position of his body held the tense, wild grace of a panther waiting for prey to pass by.

Her fingers twisted into the reins. Was he waiting for her? Had Old Sudie told him the secret, since Bluford wasn't at home this morning to hear it?

Surely not. Bluford was her master; Sudie didn't know The Paint well at all. Tiana squeezed her tired mare into a faster trot. She must find the old servant and beg her to wait.

But she could no longer keep her mind on that problem, dire as it was. The Paint was watching them ride toward him; she could feel his eyes on her even though she couldn't yet see his face. She could feel his arms around her, too—her body remembered yesterday afternoon and, above all, that night of the raid on Running Waters as clearly as if he had just this moment let her go.

And in spite of his angry accusations, her lips could still taste his kiss.

But he didn't appear to remember any of that. He sat unmoving, no longer looking at her as she and Bluford rode up to the veranda steps.

"Well?" he said at last, his eyes passing over her to rest on Bluford. "Did you drop Willie Ragsdale where he stood?"

Bluford gave a great, weary sigh. "He was gone when I got there." Nobody spoke while Bluford dismounted.

Tiana looked at Stand, straight into his hard, expressionless face, but his gaze never left his cousin.

She said, "You were right, Stand. Tom Jolly admitted to lying. The Lighthorse had to let Willie go."

The Paint didn't reply. He didn't even glance at her.

Bluford said as he trudged up the steps, "Tom admitted he only wanted to cause Willie a spot of trouble for him preaching removal and all. He wasn't ready to go so far as to lie under oath."

"I don't know why we think the *whites'll* destroy the Nation," Standingdeer said bitterly, "with that kind of brotherhood among us."

"At least nobody got killed," Tiana said.

"That's right," Bluford said. "Which means I still won't be able to sleep."

He crossed the porch heavily and opened the door. "Maud's coming home today. Is she here yet?"

"No," Stand said.

"When she comes, tell her I'm trying to rest."

He disappeared into the dimness of the hallway, calling for Akee to send Tooker to care for the horses.

Tiana sat on Jane Hunt and stared at The Paint's hard profile. He didn't move.

He was still angry with her. And an answering anger began to rise in her. He had no right.

"Are you not speaking to me?"

Slowly he turned to look at her, his dark gaze on fire beneath his lowered lids. It was the only sign of life in his face.

"We spent the night at your aunt Lottie Turnip's," she offered, hating herself as she spoke. It was none of his business.

"It hadn't occurred to me to wonder."

His tone was as flatly neutral as the look on his face.

"I just thought you might like to reassure Maud," she flared, "since you're always so concerned about how jealous she is."

A muscle jumped along the square line of his jaw. His sensual lips flattened into a straight, wooden line. They barely parted when he spoke. "You'd better go see about Bluford. He appeared to be a bit overtired."

Pure, honest fury rushed all the blood to her head. And with it, the real reason she had chased after Bluford rushed to the tip of her tongue. She bit it back.

"Standingdeer, if you would only trust me . . ."

The words hung in the air between them, mocking her. Mocking him. He couldn't trust her.

"I had to stop Blu from becoming a murderer," she shouted. "*That's* the only reason I followed him!"

"Just like your father was only driving my mother home from making some medicine when she was killed," he said.

Tiana stared at him. His eyes were black stones.

"What on earth are you talking about?"

"Your father and my mother were lovers before

you were born," he said. "I guess it's a Tenkiller tradition to come to Pine Grove for such as that."

The horrid words dropped into her heart and hung there like a frozen waterfall.

"You lie!" she cried. "And you have a dirty mind. If you'd been staying in the house instead of living in the barn like a ... a *skunk*, a stinking, striped skunk, you would know that I have not been sleeping with Bluford!"

Her impassioned words didn't move one muscle in his hard, indifferent face.

"I would know nothing of the kind," he said.

"You low-down liar," she said, "don't you ever speak one word to me again."

Then with a cry of frustration so horrible that it hurt her own heart, she swung Jane Hunt around and headed for the barn, determined to reach its concealing walls and put them between her and Stand.

"He *is* a skunk," she croaked aloud to Jane Hunt as they pounded down the driveway toward the barn. "He's a *snake* to say such things about me and about Papa. And his own *mother!* I never would have believed it of him—I never knew him at all."

Tiana stayed in the barn for what seemed hours, her mind numbly refusing to think, her body and spirit longing to go home.

She threw her borrowed saddlebags onto a nail on a post, took off Maud's English saddle and put it away, and groomed Jane Hunt to a fare-thee-well. Then she led her out to the paddock, let her go, caught Coosa, and fastened him into the crosstie in the wide center aisle.

She couldn't bear to be outside, either, with the sunshine warm on her back and the locusts and the bees fussing in the fields like old friends. The quiet dimness of the barn, with its smells of hay and horses and manure and cedar shavings, felt more like home. If she closed her eyes, she could almost believe that it *was* her own stables—before they had burned. Before Stand had saved her and Butterfly. Before she'd ever *seen* Standingdeer Chekote.

But she kept her eyes open and started with Coosa's mane, pulling the soft brush slowly downward through its shiny black thickness, willing the motion of her hand and the warm closeness of the horse to soothe her. He turned his head from time to time to look a question at her, but she worked on in silence, her throat so full she couldn't even speak his name. She couldn't cry, either. She would never be able to cry again.

"Well, would ye looky here!"

Tiana whirled toward the sound of the eerily familiar voice, a strange shudder passing all the way through her in the space of a heartbeat.

In the shadows, just inside the doorway, was a half-grown, disheveled boy. To one side of him stood Sykes and Walters.

She went light-headed with fear. Her fingers closed hard around the brush, ramming themselves between the tufted bristles like rabbits running for cover.

"Yes!" Walters exclaimed. "I can hardly believe our good fortune."

Their eyes seemed to devour Tiana and Coosa.

"That Bluford!" Sykes croaked. "Ain't he th' cagey one, though? Never said one word 'bout havin' that silver stud horse in his barn."

"We must remonstrate with him quite severely," Walters chortled.

Tiana stared back at them, trying to slow her racing pulse, trying to think once more, trying to understand. Why should Bluford have told them anything about Coosa?

They didn't look at each other, but, at the same moment, they began to walk toward Tiana.

The fullness drained out of her throat to make way for a scream. But her voice failed her.

Her feet took a step away from them. But her legs couldn't run. They could barely hold her upright.

Her hand ached for a weapon. But the brush was all she had.

"Git 'im brushed up all shiny pretty for us," Sykes said. "We'll take 'im, now that we know where he is."

Walters smiled. "I must agree. Bluford has put us off for the last time."

"What do you *mean?*" she blurted. "What does Bluford have to do with Coosa?"

"Bluford always says we mustn't abscond with your gray stallion," Walters explained in his schoolmaster's tone. "Too unique, too eye-catching, too easy to trace from one hand to the next."

He gave her a wink. "I'm afraid Bluford's a bit of a sissy, don't you? What's a small risk when you're already immersed in a large one?"

Sykes chuckled. "Right," he said. "Might as well be hung for a sheep as a lamb."

They walked up close to her, too close. Sykes laid his hand on Coosa's neck.

One part of Tiana's mind ordered her to take the thick wooden back of the brush and break his filthy fingers. But the clamor arising in the rest of her brain drowned out that command.

From that long-ago, horrible day, she could hear Fawn's strange shout: *Listen!* And then her dying voice saying, *Bluford ... pony ...*

Club. She would have said "pony club" if she had had another breath.

Bluford had ridden Bay Boy into the ground the

night she and Stand had seen and heard the pony club raid.

More horses had been stolen the night of her social than at any other one time. Bluford had left Running Waters early that night, knowing that most of the neighbors were away from home, at Running Waters.

Which the raids did not hit. They *had* hit Pine Grove, though . . . but that could have been to cover up.

This was the reason Bluford had been muttering and worrying this morning about Sykes and Walters!

Bluford couldn't sleep at night or carry on a sane conversation in the day because he was obsessed with more worries than his papa's ghost.

He had better worry. If it became known throughout the Nation that he, Sykes, and Walters were running a pony club of horse thieves, stealing from the Cherokees, Bluford would be hanged.

Bluford Tuskee was a horse thief. And a traitor to his people.

And to think that she'd wasted all that sympathy on him! She had felt guilty that *she* was the cause of his misery! Instead of Tobacco Jack's spirit, it was probably his own conscience that was haunting him!

Sykes waved his hand in front of her staring eyes. "Hey, honey, we scare you so bad you can't talk?"

Tiana looked at him, really seeing him this time. His narrow eyes held no depth at all. He did scare her; he scared her right to the bone.

But she would die before she let him know that.

"Bluford is at the house," she said clearly. "If you came to see him, you'll have to go up there."

Maybe The Paint would see and hear them talking to Bluford. *That* would serve all three of them right—since he was already in a righteous rage.

"That's what we come for," Sykes said. "You and your stud horse wait in this barn for us, hear?"

He turned to the boy behind him. "Watch her close, Morris. Holler if she tries to run off into the woods—I ain't about to start tracking her amongst the ticks and the bears and the panthers."

Walters chuckled. "The boy's too simple to even do that, Sykes; he's certainly not the most valuable thing you ever won in a card game. But if she does run, we'll make Bluford track her down."

Then he looked at Tiana and smiled his oily smile. "You are too intelligent, my dear, to run from us twice. To do so would force us to take you to Georgia, or perhaps even to kill you . . . eventually."

His face went suddenly solemn. He ran his eyes all over Coosa and his hands the length of the stallion's long, sleek neck. Then, without another word, he and Sykes turned and left by the east doors.

She ran to the west ones to watch them.

But one glance up the hill toward the house froze her eyes and her thoughts on a different danger. Bluford wasn't in his room, lying down, not at all. He was standing in the shade of the grape arbor, his head bent, listening.

To Old Sudie.

For the longest time, for the whole time that it took Sykes and Walters, unaware of Bluford and Sudie, to walk up the hill and along the side of the house opposite the thick, brushy arbor, Tiana remained as helpless as if she'd stuck her tongue to an iron fence in the wintertime.

Then she came free and alive again, her body already moving before her mind had realized what she must do.

The Paint. Oh, dear Lord, she needed his help. The yearning came out of pure instinct, out of her heart's memory. Then she remembered. She was alone. She would have to save herself.

A slight movement to her left, at the edge of the orchard, caught her eye. Lidy, Akee's kitchen helper, was filling a basket with apples.

Tiana glanced over her shoulder. "Morris?" she said, praying that the boy was indeed as simple as Walters had said. "Would you please come here?"

He frowned at her, but he came. "If you'll go tell that girl that I said it was all right," she said, pointing at Lidy, "you can have some apples to put in your pockets. And eat some now. Eat all you want."

He nodded and smiled, then ambled away to the orchard.

Tiana ran back to Coosa and unfastened him, throwing the lead rope over his neck and tying it to the other side of the halter with shaking fingers. She hoped God would forgive her for tricking a half-witted child and that Morris wouldn't be punished too severely, but she was in worse trouble now than he could ever be.

This must be what the spirits had been telling her early that morning at *Tanta-ta-rara*. The big gray horse did indeed hold her destiny, for once again his speed and his strength would determine whether she kept her life or lost it.

Tiana threw herself onto his back and then, just as quickly, off again. She dashed to the ladder that led to the loft and scrambled up it, crossing the yawning space straight to the blanket she'd tossed aside on the hay. Her blood pounding in her ears, she snatched it and fled down the ladder.

She threw herself onto Coosa again as she

started him moving, loping him out of the gloom of the barn and into the bright heat of the day. In the paddock behind the barn, Butterfly raised her head and nickered. Tiana kneed Coosa toward the gate and bent down to lift its latch.

She could do nothing about her broodmares in the other pasture, but she'd not hand these two-year-olds to Sykes and Walters and to that sneaking, traitorous Bluford on a silver platter. She called to them, low, and both Butterfly and Tannassy Sundown came through the open gate to follow her.

Without even a glance back at the house, she turned Coosa for the woods, heading due east into the thick of the trees, avoiding the cotton fields as well as the quarters. Some of the servants would see her, no doubt, here in the plain light of day, strung out with three horses. But that couldn't be helped. She simply had to believe that Sykes and Walters, and even Bluford, were no match for her in the mountains.

But Stand was. He was known as a tracker as well as a warrior. What would happen when Bluford talked to him?

She wouldn't let herself think about that.

She urged Coosa into an easy canter and the others lifted into that gait as well. When they reached the protection of the trees, Tiana plunged into them without even looking for a path. Once deep into the shade, she bent double to avoid the low-hanging branches, scooted back onto Coosa's loins and spread the saddle blanket over his back for a seat.

It had been a foolish risk to take the time to go up to the loft and get the blanket; every moment would count once they realized she was gone.

But she had needed it to protect her skin and Coosa's from the soaking sweat during the long ride to come, she told herself. There had been no time for a saddle.

Somewhere deep inside her, though, a tiny voice insisted on another reason. She had taken a terrible chance to get the blanket, that voice said, because now it was all she had left of The Paint.

Stand spent the whole afternoon in the woods, wandering through thickets of thick-growing birch and buckeye trees, looking up into their branches and the far-reaching ones of the sourwoods, searching for a sign. He supposed.

He couldn't imagine why else he was there, caught in the closest, most humid air of the valley, cut off from what little breeze might filter down from the mountains. Unless the truth might be that he wanted to torture himself.

Because when he looked down, the fire pinks and the purple foxgloves and the wild blue phlox filled his eyes and reminded him of Tiana. In her blue-violet dress showing the perfect, smooth curve of her shoulders. And the soft, silky rise of her breasts.

He heard her name in the lonesome whirr of the jarflies' humming and smelled the scent of her on the air where the sunlight broke through to warm the moist earth. He heard the unearthly cry of pain that tore from her throat as she rushed away from him.

Damn him for a heartless scoundrel! He'd had no call to say that about her father! What was it about her that pulled his deepest feelings out of his gut and poured them over his tongue? He had wanted to bite it off when he'd seen the devastation that had come over her face.

They were true words, yes, but there was no reason she would ever have had to hear them. He had simply let fury and jealousy take him over, after learning for eighteen years on the plains and in the high mountains that letting his emotions rule could get him killed.

Finally, just before sundown, he tramped out of the woods and went back to the house.

She wasn't there. Neither was Bluford.

"Miss Maud, she come home to this 'ere sit'ation," Akee said, "and she done pitched a hissy fit and taken out after 'em."

"Bluford and Tiana went somewhere together?" Stand asked, astonished by the bitterness he heard in his own voice. Why wasn't he used to this idea yet?

"W-e-e-ll, not 'zactly," Akee said on a long sigh.

He gripped the back of the chair she had pulled out for him at the supper table, pushed it up onto two legs, and thumped it against the floor.

"Tell me what you know, woman," he snapped.

Akee recited a bizarre story of the afternoon: the house servants had gone to pick blackberries in the woods, so "they didn't know nothin'," but the field hands had seen Tiana on the big gray stallion riding catercorner, at a lope, toward the woods, trailed by the young black horse and the young red dun.

Master Bluford had come to the cotton fields on his Bay Boy a short while later, "terribl' upset," asking if anyone had seen her. Once the field hands had told him which way she had gone, he had "took out after her like his head was on fire."

An hour or so later, Miss Maud had arrived home and joined the procession into the hills.

"Tiana was leading the two-year-olds? Did she take saddlebags or food?"

Akee grunted. "Nothin' fr'm this house. I be knowin' that. An' Sebastian, he say them fillies *follows* her. No lead ropes."

"She didn't leave a message with the stableboy or with the field hands?"

"Nope. She never say nothin'. Just be ridin' away."

Stand dropped the chair onto all four of its legs. Dark or no dark, he would find the little horse thief and the stallion tonight. His money had paid the entry fee in the Dahlonega Futurity, and his interest in that racehorse was all he had left in the world.

At least, all that was of any good to him. Why he felt that, he didn't know, but it was the truth and he didn't intend to sit still and be robbed of it by a sneaking Tenkiller.

"Pack me food and water for three or four days," he told the startled Akee. *"Now!"*

He took the stairs two at a time and strode down the hallway to his room. Jerking his saddlebags from the armoire, he raised both flaps and made sure that his ammunition was there beneath the clean shirt and the set of buckskins he carried. He slung the bags over his shoulder, strapped on his pistol, picked up his rifle and bedroll, and jammed his hat on his head.

He paced out into the hallway, down the stairs, and out of the house. Akee came from the summer kitchen with his food and he took it, then headed for the barn and his faithful, big buckskin. There wasn't much moon, but he could take a lantern with him. Tiana with three horses, Bluford, and then Maud were bound to leave a trail that the greenest *yonega* could read.

His anger at Tiana grew with every step he took. She had no call to take his horse away without telling him. Had she been planning this ever since they'd rescued her horses?

If so, though, why hadn't she taken them all?

Maybe her primary purpose was to get Coosa

away from him, probably as revenge for what he'd
said about her precious papa. Yet from the very
beginning, she'd fought the idea that he had a half
interest in the stallion.

Or maybe she needed *all* the Dahlonega purse to
pay Bluford for recovering Running Waters for
her. If he demanded money instead of . . .

Or maybe she left because of a lover's quarrel.

Even though Stand had accused her, something
deep down in him hadn't truly believed that she
and Blu were lovers, not after the way she'd
kissed *him*. Fool that he was. Even though he
knew for a fact that she'd been after something
from him every time she had lifted her lips to his.
Even though she was Nicotai Tenkiller's daughter.

Even though she'd followed Blu to New Echota
like a shameless hussy!

And hadn't Bluford, *terribl' upset*, ridden right
out after her today, dammit all to hell?

Stand had never let himself believe she was a
horse thief, either, but she had proved that she
was.

He caught his buckskin out of the pasture next
to the barn lot and saddled and bridled him, ignoring the fact that he usually brushed his back
first. Then he rode to the door and stopped to take
down the lantern that hung just inside.

The last time he'd lit it, it had created a circle of
gold with beautiful Tiana standing in the middle
of it. In its glow he had reached for her. By its light
he had taken her up the ladder and into the loft.

Into that brief heaven.

And now she was going to take him into hell.

He set his jaw and wrapped his reins around the
horn of his saddle. Holding the lantern with one
hand, he fumbled in his pocket with the other; finally he took out a match and struck it against his

leg. He opened the lantern, lit it, and rode out of the barn into the close, sultry night.

No telling where Tiana had got to by now—from what the servant had said, he was calculating she had maybe six hours' head start. By now she could be afoot, or worse: every renegade in the Nation, including her old enemies, Sykes and Walters, coveted that gray running stallion. One of them was bound to get him now, and probably Tiana, too.

Well, it would serve the little jade right if they did.

Bluford reined in and turned back while there was still plenty of light to last until he got home. He sighed and slumped in the saddle, making himself small enough to pass beneath the low-hanging locust tree branches, letting Bay Boy pick his own way.

Tiana's escaping was the ending to be expected to this bitter, disastrous day. Killing her, though, likely wouldn't have brought him any sleep, anyhow. Even if Papa's spirit *did* go on to the Nightland, Sykes' and Walters' threats were enough to keep him awake forever.

If they started talk about him at Horn's Tavern, he was a dead man. He was a dead man, anyway. If he couldn't give them the gray horse, they would kill him. Or so they said. And the gray horse was gone, long gone, somewhere over Chenowee Mountain.

Halfway back down its western slope, Bay Boy stopped to drink out of Walking Creek. Bluford sat him impatiently while he drank, rinsed his mouth, raised his head, and let the water dribble, then dropped his head and drank deeply again. Bluford wanted the horse to drink his fill, but he also wanted to be home before dark.

Then Bay Boy raised his head again, higher this time, and nickered in a high, loud call that made Bluford's mouth go twice as dry as it already was. The horse confirmed Bluford's fear. He pricked his ears, stared into the trees on the western bank of the creek, and nickered again. Someone was coming.

Sykes and Walters? Had they followed Bluford after all, in spite of commanding that he must ride alone through the hot, steamy woods to bring back The Coosa?

Tiana? Had she doubled back somehow? Was she planning to kill him before he could kill her?

He took the pistol from his pocket, aimed it, and tried to hold it still in his shaking hand.

When the horse and rider came out of the trees and into view, his grip loosened and his hand swung the gun down, almost dropping it into the water. For the horse was his wife's dainty mare, Brown Belle, and the rider was Maud.

"Bluford, stay right there!" she called and splashed into the creek, moving straight toward him, her sharp eyes scanning the bank all around him. "Where is she?"

The simple sight of her had turned his mind into mush. He couldn't remember how to speak.

She had to repeat the question before he could say, "Where's who?"

"Tiana Tenkiller, that's who!" Maud shouted. "Akee said Sebastian said that you tore out after her when you heard she was gone."

"She got away," he said.

"Oh? So you admit it, do you?" she said, throwing him a piercing look as she rode past him up onto the bank. She turned the mare to face Bay Boy. "You tried to take advantage of the girl and she ran away?"

"No! Nothing of the kind!"

"Then what?" she demanded, her eyes gleaming with that jealous look he knew so well.

"I'm after her, not for pleasure, but for revenge," he said. "Old Sudie told me today that Tiana is the one who killed my papa."

Maud's busy mouth gaped into stillness and her eyes glazed over with shock. But only for a moment.

Then they filled with fury.

"Don't say such a thing! Bluford Tuskee, now your papa's spirit will *never* leave our house because you've used it in such a lie!"

The jumble of tracks looked clear enough, even in the meager light of the lantern, until Stand reached the hard clay trail that led up the ridge directly east of Pine Grove. He followed it over the top on faith, knowing that it was the easiest way through the thick piny woods and that Tiana had been in a tearing hurry.

Halfway down the other side, he stopped and dismounted, kneeling between the close-growing brush to look at the ground. Sure enough, five different horses had passed that way within the past few hours.

When he swung up into the saddle, he heard the first roll of thunder, already as near as the mountain at his back, loud in his ears like the rumbling of rocks in a slide. Perhaps it was a good omen, since the Cherokee called themselves Friends of Thunder.

He smooched to the buckskin and took the hill at a long trot all the way down, heedless of the branches scraping his hat and catching at the sleeves of his shirt. But the rain swept in, hard and fast, close on the heels of the thunder, and by the time he reached the soft earth at the bottom, his shirt was soaked through and water ran in rivulets off the brim of his hat.

Worse, though, much worse, was the running stream the storm had already created in the little draw. Every trace of a track had been washed away.

Rattling Gourd. The thought came to Tiana from above, dropped into her mind from the overarching black sky full of clouds and their curtain of rain.

She huddled farther back under the rock ledge that sheltered her and hugged the idea to her mind the way she hugged the saddle blanket to her body. All during the frantic ride of this endless afternoon she had racked her brain for some action, something she could do. For she would hate herself forever if she simply ran away from that loathsome pony club.

Yes, they would be on her trail, but this rain would wash it away. If they did kill her, though, then Bluford would get away scot-free; he would tell Stand what Sudie had said, but not about Sykes and Walters.

She drew in a long, trembling breath, filling her lungs with the mixed fragrances of horse from the blanket, wet earth and pine, fresh rain and old mountains, letting her body go limp into the bed of needles and moss she had hastily made. Yes. She would take a chance and ride many miles out of her way.

Because Rattling Gourd would know how to stop Bluford.

And he could make medicine for her protection.

Chapter 12

A short time after Morning Red had faded into gray, while the cove still swam with shadows, Tiana gathered the horses and left the ledge. She led Coosa and slipped out of the mouth of the creek on foot, studying the damp ground both east and west of it. It would take a miracle for anyone to have trailed her here, even if there had been no storm, but she couldn't be too careful. No one must see her: word traveled throughout the Nation like the breeze in the trees.

She stopped behind a giant birch and, laying her cheek against its peeling bark, looked down the valley the way she had come. The mountains gathered tighter here than around the river bottoms where Running Waters lay. They caught the growing sunlight on the tops of their thick mantles of trees, light green on the ridges closest to her, darker green behind, and then dark blue and pale, pale blue in the far distance. Fog filled the low places.

Tiana sent her gaze searching, slowly, around the valley and along the closest foothills at its edge. Nothing moved in the early morning. She mounted Tannassy to let Coosa have a rest and started her little procession moving to the northwest.

They stopped only once, when Grandmother Sun was high overhead, to drink from a stream. Tiana filled her empty, growling stomach with cold, sweet water, then snatched a handful of blackberries from a bramble nearby, scratching her hands in her eagerness to eat. But she didn't take time to pick very many. Rattling Gourd would give her food when she arrived at his cabin.

She mounted Butterfly and, with the other two horses trailing, rode along the rocky path beat out by the deer and bears coming to water. Tonight she would stay at Rattling Gourd's; then tomorrow, if she pushed, she might reach *Ulisi* Tahnee's old home. She should have gone there instead of to Pine Grove the minute she'd found the Sniders on Running Waters.

She shouldn't have run to The Paint. Now she had too much to remember: the adventure of their raid for the horses and the feel of being held in his arms, the honey taste and the marvelous floating magic of his kiss. The devastating touch of his hand on her breast. Those memories only served to make her all the more miserable now, mingled with his horrid, vengeful lie about Papa.

And with her imaginings of his anger when Bluford told him her secret. He was, most likely, already trying to track her.

She glanced behind her and smooched to the horses.

The old shaman, the *dida:hnvwi:sg*, the Curer-of-Them, sat in front of his house at the edge of the spruce-and-fir forest which crowded in on two sides of it. The green leaves and white blossoms of wood sorrel covered the ground around his feet and reached up on the legs of the two straight-backed chairs he had placed beneath the overhang of the porch. He and they looked to have grown

there; the only movement about them was the
fringe on his turban, ruffling now and then in the
barest breeze.

At first Tiana thought he didn't know she was
there. Then he raised a hand in greeting and let it
fall back to his lap. "*Osiyo*, Daughter," he said.

"*Osiyo*, Grandfather." Tiana reined to a stop and
dismounted, clinging to Butterfly for a moment
until her feet became accustomed to the ground.
"Were you expecting me?"

Coosa and Tannassy came up behind her; they
and Butterfly drifted wearily off toward the creek
that burbled behind the cabin. Rattling Gourd
squinted at them.

"In the crystal rock I saw a woman coming," he
said, "but not a herd of horses."

Tiana laughed and went to sit beside him. For
several long minutes they spoke only greetings
and inquiries and answers about her family's
health. Then the old man stood.

"You have ridden a hard trail," he said. "Come.
Eat."

Inside the cabin's dimness, he gave her tea—
sumac, from the taste of it—poured from a clay
pot into a tin cup and some frybread from a cloth
sack. Tiana ate and drank hungrily, in spite of the
lump growing bigger by the minute in her stomach. She could tell him about Bluford's wrongdo-
ing, but how could she confess her own?

When she had finished eating, he said, "Speak,
Child. You come to give warning. And to ask for
something."

His small, sharp eyes captured hers and held
them.

Tiana set the cup onto the rough surface of the
table with a soft thump. His powers truly were
great.

She nodded. "People are losing animals they

need and love to pony club raids, Grandfather—
someone may get killed trying to defend his stock.
Good horses may be mistreated or hitched to a
plow. One pony club is run by a Cherokee, Bluford
Tuskee of Pine Grove Plantation."

His bright eyes went dull. "You are certain?"

"Yes, I am certain." She told him the whole
story, including Sykes and Walters and Gray Fox.
Except for the fact that she had killed Tobacco
Jack.

When she repeated Fawn's dying words, and
when she told of Bluford's haunting, and especially, in the end, when the old medicine man asked,
"Is that all?" she longed to tell it.

She wanted, she *needed* to pour out her heart
and have that wrinkled, wise face turn to her and
say that she would be forgiven.

That The Paint would forgive her.

But fear held her tongue.

Until he said, in a tone that drew the words to
her lips, "Daughter, you haven't asked what you
came for. You have given only the warning."

She stood up and walked out of the cabin onto
the porch. He followed her. And then, staring off
into the growing dusk, fast forming itself from
fragments of mist that swirled through the trees
like spirits low to the ground, she told him everything.

"It was not intentional," he said at last. "You are
not *di-hi'*, killer."

She whirled to look into his face. "But Tobacco
Jack's family may not know that. Or believe it.
Make medicine for my protection, Grandfather,
please. Bluford now has two reasons to kill
me, and his cousin, The Paint, has sworn *tsu-tsa'si*,
vengeance."

"At first light," he promised, "I go to water for
you."

"Thank you," she whispered. "At first light I ride for *Ulisi* Tahnee's old home cabin."

She took off the jacket to her riding habit which she'd worn tied around her waist all day and offered it to him.

"This is the only cloth I can offer you to gather herbs for me."

"This propitiatory gift is for regaining Bluford's goodwill?"

No. The Paint's goodwill. Use it to make The Paint never hate me anymore.

Instead of speaking those words, she said simply, "If that can be. And that of his ... family."

She forced herself to swallow around the lump in her throat. Fatigue beat on her head like a stick on a drum.

The old *dida:hnvwi:sg* heard it. He said, "Sleep there tonight," and gestured toward a gnarled dogwood tree at the edge of his creek. "Let the small Long Man carry away your fear."

By the time she woke the next morning, most of Tiana's fear had indeed gone. But it had been replaced by a pulsing desire to be at her grandmother's cabin. To ride into the clearing and go in through the door, even though her *Ulisi* had been dead for more than ten years. To rest there, in the place her papa had stayed during many hunting trips. To be at home.

She rose from the bedroll Rattling Gourd had lent her and collected her horses, not going to his cabin, even for food. Once she reached *Ulisi*'s, she would be hungry again, she thought as she mounted Coosa and turned him south, toward the trailhead. Once she reached that cabin, she would feel like herself, she would come alive again.

She rode away at a trot, not looking back. Rattling Gourd would still be at the water, saying the incantations for her; in addition, she must do what she could for herself. She must ride so far up into the hills that neither Bluford nor The Paint could ever find her.

Tiana spent one more night in the open, eating wild muscadines and persimmons to assuage what little appetite she had. Listening for the sounds of another human being on the same mountain. Looking for a fire that might be that of someone in pursuit.

Late the next afternoon she swam the horses across near the head of the Keowee River and began to climb the western slope of *Tsuda-yi-lun'yi*, Lone Peak Mountain. Water poured from her pantaloons and her boots and even from the skirts of her habit, which she had removed and wrapped around her waist to try to keep dry. But she noticed no discomfort, nothing except the welcome coolness of the breaths of breeze against her skin. Nothing could distress her now; she didn't even bother to keep watch at her back. The closer she got to Papa's hunting cabin, his mother's old house, the faster the blood beat in her veins and the safer she felt.

For an instant, as Coosa carried her around a tangle of loganberry briars and onto a deer trail that led up through a piny woods, as Butterfly and Tannassy snorted gently behind her and the bluebirds and thrushes flashed their wings in the trees, other pictures overlaid them in her mind: a glimpse of Mama's prized cherry floors, a glance at Papa's portrait in his study gazing toward the safe that held the money for Old Sudie, a peek into her own room with the lace canopy over her bed.

The Paint, his heavy-lidded eyes so compelling in the light of the lantern that they had drawn her to him without a word.

Tears welled up and blotted out everything, imagined and real.

But she hunched her shoulders and wiped them away on her sweat-soaked blouse. At the cabin there would be some clothes she could change into. At the cabin there would be food and a fireplace to cook it. At the cabin she would still have three of her horses and the means to keep them fit.

At the cabin she would have a home.

Her heart felt almost easy as she topped the last ridge and started downhill through the hot, sticky woods. The deer trail here was so wide that she could see down it into the clearing and across the deep-running creek. There sat the little house, nestled high into the wooded side of the next rolling hill like a secret treasure.

Home. At last.

All of it, its weathered logs and native stone underpinnings for the porch, and the two square windows winking in the sunlight, the smoke coming from the chimney, the graying boards of the fence, and the lines of the shed nestled farther down in the open clearing toward the bubbling branch, shouted comfort and safety to her, even from across the creek.

She broke the horses into a long trot and kept them there until they'd crossed the fast-running, singing water. But as they came out onto the bank and started up the slope to the cabin, she brought them to a halt so sudden that their wet hooves skidded on the grass and clicked against one another.

Tiana sat as still as prey, staring at the cabin, the blood pounding up into her head like a hot-water spring bubbling out of the ground.

The smoke coming from the chimney ...

Some trick of her mind had hardly noticed it at first, making her imagine Papa or even her grandmother magically inside the walls, as if in a dream. But the smoke was real, curling gray and white against the peaceful blue of the sky.

Someone was in there. Someone had beaten her to her only refuge.

A movement in the trees to her left became a person as she turned. Her fist flew to her mouth to stifle a cry.

He materialized out of the shadows at the edge of the woods, the low-slanting sunlight gleaming all at once from his tight tan buckskins, the black hair flowing loose down his back, and the silver metal of his rifle. Sweat broke out on Tiana's palms and her mind raced in circles like a squirrel in a trap. The cave! She could run to the cave in the hillside behind the house.

No. Of course she couldn't. That gun would drop her before she'd gone two yards.

She looked into Standingdeer's face.

No, not Standingdeer's face. The face of an angry, vengeful god. A god who had no favorites. A god who never dispensed forgiveness.

Bluford must have told him what Old Sudie had said! He *had* come to kill her.

"Get out of here," she managed to say through the strangling tightness in her throat. "This place is mine."

The expression on his face didn't change in the slightest. "So you're still trampling on the tradition of Cherokee hospitality."

Would he say that if he had come to kill her? Instead, wouldn't he say, *No, as a matter of fact, I've come to kill you so my uncle's spirit can go to the Nightland?*

The rifle slid through his hands until the butt rested on the ground and the muzzle pointed straight up.

She cleared her throat and said, *"You're* one to

talk about hospitality, jumping out to meet me with a gun."

He shrugged. "Horse thieves ought to expect to be met with a gun."

Her knees, her whole body, began to shake, so that Coosa moved nervously beneath her. Horse thief. Thank goodness he had called her that instead of murderer.

"I'm no horse thief."

His eyes glinted black fire into hers.

"I grant that you never admitted, deep in your stubborn little heart, that half of The Coosa belongs to me," he growled as he strode toward her, the fringe on his sleeves and leggings swinging. "What do *you* call it when you take someone else's property and secretly carry it away?"

She felt her cheeks flame hot. "I left in a hurry."

"As all thieves do," he retorted. His massive muscles rippled beneath his shirt as he crossed his arms over his big chest. He growled, "The horse will not race at Dahlonega,' you said. 'He will not.' But now that I've signed him up and paid that exorbitant entry fee, you've begun to think about that rich, rich purse."

He was so close now, close enough to touch. But farther away than the Western Nation. His eyes blazed into hers.

"I did not . . ."

"You didn't think I'd come after him, did you? Because I said money never meant that much to me. Couldn't you know, though, that I would find you at the race?"

"Your ownership of Coosa and that Dahlonega race were the last things on my mind when I left Pine Grove!"

The fire in his eyes died to cold ashes.

"Was it Bluford on your mind, then? Does he want money now, in addition to your . . . companionship, for launching an imaginary attack on Running Waters?"

Tiana's lips went stiff around her mouth; she could hardly move them to speak.

"How can you still be harping about me and Bluford?" she cried. "Don't you know me at all?"

"Evidently not." His scornful tone scraped her soul like a rock's edge dragged over her skin. "Maud came home that day. Did she run you off?"

Her unshed tears became tiny cats with claws, ripping at Tiana's frozen face from inside, yet she kept her voice even. "Where were you? You ought to know."

"I was in the woods until nearly sundown."

Ah! So he probably *hadn't* talked to Bluford! Maybe he truly didn't know what Old Sudie had said!

In that moment, though, the hurt of his oft-repeated accusation went deeper than her relief. She set her jaw and squared her shoulders.

"If I had stayed at Pine Grove a moment longer," she said, matching his withering look with her tone, "Coosa would have been stolen and I would have been killed—and *not* by a jealous wife. I had no choice but to run."

He came closer, balancing the rifle in one hand as easily as a feather.

"What the hell are you talking about?"

Her face was pale in the dimming light of the afternoon, her eyes huge and dark as the sky over the plains at night.

"*Who would have killed you?*"

"Standingdeer," she said, "I hate to tell you."

"Tell me anyway."

"Sykes and Walters threatened to take me to Georgia and kill me . . . eventually."

She stopped, but he knew that wasn't all. That couldn't be what she would hate to tell him. And there was that secrecy in her voice again. Always, always there was another secret.

He set the rifle on its end and reached out his hand, but he laid it on Coosa instead of on her, petting the stallion instead of stroking Tiana's soft skin.

"Where the hell did you see *them* again?" he asked, his voice hoarse as a frog's croaking.

"At Pine Grove."

"What were they doing there?"

"That's what I hate to tell you. They're in a pony club with Bluford."

His eyes narrowed in disbelief.

Quickly, before she could lose her nerve, Tiana blurted out what Sykes and Walters had said. Then she slid quickly to the ground and ran up the slope to the house. She couldn't bear to witness his silent pain.

Tiana ran across the porch and in through the open door, past the table and chairs to the north wall of the room. She took the tin dipper that always hung beneath the shelf there, splashed it into the bucket of cool water, and drank from it as if she were dying of thirst. She dipped it in again.

The dimming light that had followed her into the room disappeared. She turned to see Stand's rugged body filling the doorway.

Grief was carved into the bones of his face.

In a quick, helpless gesture of consolation, Tiana held out the dipper.

He stayed still as midnight for one endless heartbeat; then he reached up and, with a vicious sweep of his powerful arm, hung the gun in the rack overhead. Then he crossed the room to her.

"Blu's my cousin; he's Cherokee," he said, his tone so harshly argumentative she thought he might strike her. "Sykes and Walters're nothing but low-life scum *yonegas*. You surely can't take their word to ruin a man's life."

He snatched the dipper as if it held the proof.

"Think about it, Stand," she said through the tears clogging her throat, and made herself recite the damning clues. Fawn's dying words, Bay Boy's absence and then his exhaustion, Bluford's insomnia and obsessive worries, his asking her about Sykes and Walters on the way home from New Echota, his angry exclamation about them the night she'd been thrown off Running Waters. She ticked the reasons off on her fingers, one by one.

"Blu lost horses, too," he said. "The night of your social."

"I thought of that," Tiana agreed. "It was, no doubt, a distraction, an attempt to cover up Bluford's involvement. Remember, before he left Running Waters that night, Mr. Campbell and the others had been remarking how strange it was that no horses in our valley ever got stolen."

The Paint stood quietly in the low beams of the sun, his eyes glistening, one huge hand cradling the cup of the dipper, the other wrenching its handle.

Tiana's heart hurt for him. First he had lost his uncle, and now his cousin.

Outside the open door, the buckskin whinnied. Coosa whinnied back.

"Tiana," Stand said at last, "why didn't you come to me with this?"

"Because you were so hateful to accuse me of being lovers with Bluford and told that *despicable* lie about my papa *and your own mother*, and I swore I'd never speak to you again!"

The handle of the dipper twisted in his hand in an echo of the pain writhing in his eyes.

"You must admit that you followed him to town

like a common wanton!" he answered harshly. "I couldn't believe you ran after him after we had . . ."

"I followed Bluford into town on business!" Tiana cried. "Urgent business! I swear to you, Standingdeer Chekote, that I never cared a whit about Bluford! And he never touched me. Never!"

She took two steps toward him.

"Can't you believe that, Stand? Can't you trust me? Especially after we had . . ."

He didn't say a word.

"I've needed you so," she said, to her own shocked surprise, her voice breaking. "Oh, Standingdeer. I would have died if you hadn't come!"

And then, as thoughtlessly as she had spoken, she lifted her arms and held them out to him.

He turned his head so that he looked full into her eyes. The last of the red sunlight glowed on his skin like copper on fire.

But the warmth of it shattered against the cold, icy mask of his face.

Chapter 13

He looked at her that way for one silent moment. Then he threw the dipper clattering to the floor and closed the space between them. With a little cry, she went into his arms, clinging to his shoulders, rising up on tiptoes to press her cheek to his.

"Tiana." He gave a great, shuddering sigh and held her hard against him. "Tiana."

She loved him. The knowledge came to her heart through the palms of her hands clasped flat to the back of his neck, through the tips of her breasts crushed to his chest. Through the flesh of her flat belly cleaving to his. Through the very strength of her cheekbone, nuzzling against his to bring the silk of his hair against the skin of her face and the scent of him into her blood.

Whatever spiteful lie he had told about her papa had come of his agony because she and Bluford had spent the night in New Echota. He cared for her. He had ridden hard miles to come to her.

She loved him. That was why she would have died if he hadn't found her and why she had said such a thing to him when she didn't even know it was on her tongue.

"How did you know I would come here?" she asked, her heart singing because he *had* known.

"I used to hunt from this cabin," he said. "When I was a boy. With your papa and Uncle Jack."

The name sent a quiet shiver through her. Thank God and Thunder that Stand had spent that awful afternoon in the woods, that he hadn't seen Bluford after Sudie had told Tiana's secret. If only he would never hear it! Now she really *would* die without him.

Tiana sent the eternal worry away. For the moment, for this precious time, her love was safe. The truth of that was flooding in through the window on the deepening dusk.

She drew back her head just enough to look into his eyes. "But how did you know that I had come here *now*?"

He laughed. The low, rich sound melted her bones. "Because, in spite of what we said out there, I do know you, Tiana. I can *feel* what you will do."

She laughed, too, the joy of loving him rising inside her, and pretended to struggle to get out of his arms. "Oh? I'm predictable? Well, I suppose that's better than being easy to track."

He tightened his arms around her waist to hold her against his chest.

Easy or hard, I would have tracked you to the ends of the earth.

The thought came to him like water flowing, to his great surprise. And with a slight uneasiness. He'd better be careful; his heart, unleashed, loved too hard, too deep.

But he couldn't suppress the smile that kept clinging to his lips. Or the urge trembling along the muscles of his arms to hold her even tighter.

His gaze wandered from her eyes to her mouth. Her luscious, curving, slightly parted mouth. He couldn't quite remember what he had meant to say.

Her breasts pushed softly against his chest.

"Standingdeer," she murmured, not believing she would say the words even as she said them, "Standingdeer Chekote, I love you."

The heedless, sweet declaration, so softly spoken, yet so sure, raised goose bumps along his arms. She loved him?

She loved him.

A sharp realization ran his soul through like a lance thrown from a hilltop. He had been longing to hear her say that; he had been trying to force her to say it by accusing her of caring for Bluford.

The lift and fall of the breeze rising toward night became the only sound in the room. Until he whispered, gruffly, from deep in his throat, "Tiana."

He captured her face in both his hands and took her waiting mouth with his. She met him with an equal passion, as if she were trying to prove with the kiss that her words had been wholeheartedly true; a groan tore loose from somewhere inside him.

As his tongue twined with hers like a wanderer coming home, her throbbing lips opened to its ravenous settling-in with a need so deep that it brought her weak against him, limp as a doll in his hands. His mouth lifted, then slanted in unspoken demand across hers, bringing every inch of her body to press against his.

His heart became a wild, flying eagle, trapped in his breast. He couldn't let it loose to soar, to follow the urge, the aching need to have more of her that leapt and grew in his loins. Because her kiss, strongly sweet as sourwood honey, kept his fingers captive in the crumpled silk of her hair and his hapless body melted to hers.

The thickening air of the coming night surrounded them, threatening to carry them out into the growing dark like leaves in a storm. Tiana wrapped her arms around the solid column of Standingdeer's neck and clung there, helpless, breathless, terrified to move the slightest bit lest he take his marvelous mouth away.

When he did so at last, she had no strength to prevent it. And no power to walk or to talk.

He scooped her up off the floor and shifted one arm beneath her useless knees. She drove her fingers into his hair and clasped him to her.

Then he wrested his mouth from hers to look for the bed. Remembrance stirred in him. Yes, there. In the far corner, like a gift sent from heaven.

He crossed the cabin in four long strides, kissing her again in rhythm with each step—fast, sweet kisses that she returned so eagerly, his very soul opened to her. His heart turned over.

She *was* his.

Wasn't she?

Beside the bed, he let her go and set her on her feet, dropped his hands to her hips, and crushed her against his growing hardness. By the Thunderers, he would *make* her his. At this moment he didn't care *what* her name was.

"Stand?" she said.

In answer, he planted one long leg on either side of her. His thighs heated hers like a fire in a snowstorm. His eyes glittered, brilliant in the faint dimness of the room, like dark stars lit by an unwavering light.

"Tiana," he said, "I hope you meant what you said."

"I did," she replied, while the richness of his voice and the heat of his manhood turned her to sweet, shaking jelly.

He buried his face in her hair, asking hoarsely, "Do you know what we're doing . . ."

She went up on tiptoes to trail her lips up his

cheek, to brush them against his temple, to smell the fresh cedar scent of his hair. "I know I love you," she vowed again.

He groaned and took them tumbling headlong into the welcoming softness of the bed. Their mouths found each other again and struck fire.

But it wasn't enough. Not nearly enough.

The Paint shifted her higher onto the pillows to bury his face between her creamy breasts. His lips went straight to her skin, at a spot where a button had come undone, and worked slowly sideways, pushing away the shirt as he went, burning a row of fiery kisses up the side of one of her breasts toward its tip, taut and aching with the new, desperate need to feel his lips around it.

Tiana trailed her fingers slowly into his hair, her wrists so weak with wanting she could barely move her hands.

And then his hands were there, too, at her breasts and he swept open all the buttons of her shirt, drew it off her shoulders and down over her arms. Halfway, he stopped.

Tiana opened her eyes. His gaze flicked to them, then back to her bare breasts, pale as clouds in the dusky room.

"You are as beautiful," he said hoarsely, "as a light in the dark."

The mountain air caressed her, centering its coolness on the wet heat that his mouth had left on her skin. Then Stand bent his head; his lips and his tongue took possession again. They laved the standing bud of her breast with an impossible flame.

She glimpsed the bone-melting sight of his head at her breast through her half-open lids; then she let them drop closed. She couldn't look at that vision any longer. Not at the same time his mouth was sending such dancing delight through her veins. Both together made too much pleasure to bear.

When he had drawn all the breath from her body and filled it again with a torturing, overpowering desire, he stripped her shirt completely away. He untied her breeches and swept them down and down while she pressed kiss after uncontrolled kiss to the rippling surface of his chest.

She let him slip off her moccasins and then the hindering breeches. Stand came back to her then, rolled onto one elbow, and lay looking down at her. The mask was gone, forever, from his face.

She sat up fast and tugged his shirt loose from his pants, starting at the top to unbutton it. His eyes moved to hers and stayed, smoldering in the dimness, sending smoke into her blood that stopped its flow. But it could not stop her hands.

She finished with the shirt and threw it heedlessly away; then, her fingers trembling with their own boldness at touching the hardness straining beneath them, she started on the lacings of his breeches. When she was done, he rolled away from her, as far as the side of the bed, to shrug out of boots and pants. After an endless moment he turned back to the caress of her hungry hands.

And she came to his.

Their lips found each other's again.

All the world stopped except the slow, haunting calls of the night birds outside, and inside, the marvelous pull of his mouth. She dug her fingers into his muscle-bound back and clung to him to keep from drowning in the roaring river of wanting that threatened to wash her away.

And then they were twining together, tumbling deeper into the soft, cradling embrace of the bed, farther into the dark corner of the room. Where no one and nothing could find them.

Except the sweet, forest-scented air of the mountains and the wild, pounding need for each other.

He rolled to lie over her, to cover her, touching her everywhere with his hands and his mouth, his hot flesh pushing against her, finding its home. He entered her with a swift, untamed passion and she whimpered deep in her throat, clasping her arms around his neck and arching to meet him, taking him into her as fully as she had given her heart.

But her own, unaccustomed flesh resisted as pain shot through her beneath all the pleasure. Standingdeer murmured a wordless apology before he smothered her cry with his kiss.

And then, mesmerized by the voluptuous delight created by his body and hers, she forgot the hurting in her hunger. She forgot the fear that had driven her here and the secret that she still held away from him. She gave everything else to him except that: her heart and her soul and every inch of her body, learning to move with him in that instinctive rhythm older than the misty blue mountains around them. She let it carry her out of herself and into him, taking and giving, bringing him into her until at last, swirling dizzily together out into its mindless wonder, they created a place of fire and cool peace that would forever be theirs.

A place where they stayed for a long, precious time, lying so close only silence could come between them.

Night gathered outside on the porch and drifted in through the wide open door.

"There won't be any moon," Tiana said.

"There'll be one, but we won't be able to see it for the fog."

She lifted her face and rubbed her lips along the hard line of his jaw.

"You contradict everything I say," she teased. "You've done it since the minute we met."

"No." He stole a kiss as solemn as his tone. "Since the minute we met, *you've* contradicted *me*. The first thing I said to you was that Coosa would run at Dahlonega, and you said he would not."

"No, no!" she said, laughing. She trailed the tip of her finger down his bare arm, tracing the winding rise and fall of one bulging muscle.

"Your recollection is faulty, sir. The *first* thing you told me was that I was an awe-inspiring rider, the best jockey that you, in your travels all the way to the Western lands and around the entire world, had ever in your whole life seen."

He laughed, too, a delicious sound of pure joy rumbling up from deep in his big chest. "I didn't say that. I'm sorry, miss, but I'm afraid *your* recollection is faulty." He tapped the tip of one finger on the end of her nose for emphasis.

"Well ... maybe not those words *exactly*, but that's what you meant." Her finger retraced its path and continued along the wide, square line of his shoulder. "Didn't you?"

He caught her wrist in his hand and held it so tight that she turned in his arms to look up into his eyes. It was too dark for her to see.

But his voice told her all she needed to know. "I didn't know then how truly awe-inspiring you are," he growled, and wrapped her tighter into his arms to really kiss her.

Even in the dark his lips knew exactly where to find hers.

And even after all they'd just done, she felt him begin to harden again.

"You're rather impressive yourself," she murmured against his mouth as she reached down to touch him. "Hero is the perfect word for you."

He shifted his hip so that he'd go more fully into her hand.

"Perfect is the perfect word for you," he whispered, letting the feather touch of her fingers fan the flame in his belly. His hand found the delicate curve of her hip.

She closed her hand around him and kissed his bare chest.

"So you admit that I'm the perfect trainer of running horses?" she said. "And, therefore, that I should be given full control of the horse?"

He cupped her hipbone in his hand and circled his thumb into the hollow there, then slid it up to the inward curve of her waist and upward still to find her breast. His thumb captured its high, swollen tip.

"You *have* full control ... of me ... right now," he muttered. "I can't even breathe when you do that to me."

"Neither can I," she managed to whisper just as his mouth took the place of his hand.

His mouth. It lavished his care on every inch of her skin, following the circling, sweet heat of his hands like a shadow follows the sun. He warmed and he fired that breast, then the other, before kissing a round ring of flames onto the trembling thin skin of her belly.

After that he moved lower, down along the inside of one thigh, then back up and across to the other, barely brushing against the edge of the mound between her legs.

She cried out, "Stand!" and arched her back in a silent plea for more.

His wet mouth traveled all the way to the inside of her knee, where it lingered for an unbearable time; then it retraced its path, but just to one side of the trail that was already burning, up and up to the crying triangle waiting for him. His tongue and his lips took her by storm.

A cry rushed to her lips, but although they were parted, it couldn't come out. Her hands stretched toward his head, but they couldn't drift down. Her legs took in the touch of his hands and melted away.

And then, when she believed that she could not live through one moment more of such bliss, he lifted his head and took her into his arms, sliding his open mouth up her skin until he reached hers and, in one earth-shattering, tender thrust, he was above and inside her, firing her blood to blazing, like a dance to a drum, filling her emptiness like a wild primal cry. She was skimming the earth and possessing the sky.

They soared like tall trees of the mountains reaching for heaven. They trembled like leaves, like needled branches on the wind, while the power of the ancient, unutterable magic held them fast and took them spiraling, up and up to the tops of the towering cliffs until they rushed over the edge like a roaring waterfall.

But instead of crashing to the rocks below, they took flight across the sky, riding ridge after ridge of delight unfolding, until they burst into the heavens like a vagabond star.

Stand threw back his head and called, "Tiana!" like a great shout of victory, then dropped his face to lie cradled in the curve of her neck. She clasped him to her, wrapping him closer, and took her own safety in the cove of his arms.

Stand woke to light streaming in at the east-facing door. It washed across the room in a golden glow, like a wide road of sunshine leading straight to the rough-hewn bed. To Tiana.

She lay huddled on her side, beneath the rumpled covers, facing him, one of her soft hands clinging to his. The old quilt tumbled up around her head, its faded reds and blues made pale as water by the shining black of her hair and the vibrant, peach-colored radiance of her skin.

He cradled her hand in his palm. Tiana.

She loved him!

His heartbeat caught and stopped for an instant, then started again in a rough, uneven rhythm. No one had loved him since he couldn't remember when. He had forgotten this warm trusting, this feeling of safe shelter in the midst of a storm.

And to think that he had found it with Tiana! Never in the history of time had there ever been a woman like her.

He stretched his legs to their full length and snuggled deeper into the straw mattress, careful not to wake her.

Watching her breathe in and out deeply, slowly, he smiled. She was so far gone into her dreams that her shoulder never moved beneath the patterned quilt. Was she dreaming of him?

Of last night? He lifted her hand and pressed a kiss to the tips of her fingers. Last night. The most precious night of his life. The night he would never forget.

He frowned at that unwanted intrusion of a thought of the future. This moment. This moment was all he had. He had lived by that rule for fifteen long years, from many an End of Fruit Moon to many a Corn-in-Tassel Moon. Especially since that mockery of a home with Elena. He had held off all thoughts about the rest of his life while he slept alone on the ground from the great Shining Mountains to the Western Cherokee Nation.

But now, in this bed in a cabin at the Center of the Earth with this brave, beautiful woman beside him, he could no longer keep his long-buried dreams at bay. A home. A real home. It was what he had always hoped would be out there ahead of him, someday.

Wouldn't it be fine to have Tiana in it?

He smiled. She had been so spontaneous, so sincere, when she told him she loved him. He could still hear the breathy, sweet sureness in her voice.

But then his mind took him back over the whole memory of yesterday's sundown and his spine stiffened. Tiana had explained why she had taken Coosa and run from Pine Grove. Neither Blu nor Sykes and Walters would want her loose and talking now that she knew about their pony club.

But that explanation told him nothing about what she'd been doing the night before and earlier that day. What "urgent business" had she had in New Echota?

He forced his memory to bring back that horrible morning that she had ridden in from town side by side with Bluford. *I had to stop Blu from becoming a murderer*, she had shouted.

How did she know that Blu's killing Ragsdale would have been murder?

She hadn't been lovers with Bluford, he knew that now. In some instinctive way, he had always known it. But at this moment, lying with her in their warm, cozy haven, that knowledge did not hold all happiness.

Tiana still had a secret.

He let go of her hand and brushed back her hair. She slept on. She looked so innocent. There must be a good reason; all she had to do was tell him.

He cradled her cheek in his palm. "Tiana?"

"Mmhmn?" she said, but she didn't stir.

Stand took hold of the quilt, yet he couldn't bear to pull its warmth away from her. He trailed his thumb along its edge, on the unbelievable satin surface of her skin, then slipped his hand between the quilt and her bare flesh.

Sudden fire sprang up in his loins.

God help him, all he wanted was to have her again.

But he wouldn't. Not without knowing.

He shook her gently. "Tiana. It's morning."

Her legs stretched out to their full, lithe length, tickling his with her toes on the way. She yawned and lifted her arms to stretch them, too, making the quilt billow and settle again.

Cool morning air crept into the cocoon of their warmth. Her full, high breasts brushed his chest. She opened her eyes and smiled at him.

Desire rose in him like a rolling river.

"Tiana," he said, ignoring everything but his tormenting suspicions, which he couldn't seem to stop. "You never did tell me. What business did you have in town?"

Her huge dark eyes opened wider and she stared at him for one endless instant. Then she lowered her lids over them like drawing a curtain. Her long, curly black eyelashes, thick as poplar seedlings, lay against the curve of her cheek.

"Tiana."

She yawned again and nestled deep into the whispering straw of the mattress as if sleep were calling her back.

He raised himself onto his elbow. The ropes of the bed creaked beneath them.

"I have to know, Tiana," he said in a voice so raw he could hardly realize it was his. "What business?"

She squeezed her eyes more tightly closed and prayed for the right words to come. Not now. Dear Lord, he couldn't be asking her this right now. She couldn't tell him the truth and she couldn't think of a lie. She couldn't think, she couldn't talk.

All she could do was go into his arms again.

But he wasn't touching her at all anymore. He lay propped up on one elbow, looking down his aristocratic nose at her like a judge.

"I couldn't bear to think of Bluford killing Willie," she muttered. "I had to try to stop him."

"And why did you take such a task on yourself?"

Her eyes flew open and glared into his.

"*You* refused to try to stop Bluford from killing an innocent man, so *I* had to do it!"

He stared to the depths of the dark pools of her eyes and knew that she had told him the truth.

But not all of it.

She watched his face. His handsome, rugged, chiseled face. Her heart went through the floor.

He wasn't going to let this pass.

"Why were you so positive that Willie was innocent? How well do you know *him?*"

Shock froze her mind at first, and then her gaze, fastening it on his.

"Not well at all! I ... I *wasn't* sure!"

But his slanting lids drooped and his sensual lips flattened into a straight, hard line. A spark of remembrance lit his narrowed eyes.

"You must've been. At your social, when you heard him accused, you nearly pitched a fit."

"I did *not!* I merely pointed out that ... that he ... perhaps he was only in the vicinity ..."

"You merely pointed it out in a voice that shook like a tree in the wind."

"I can't bear injustice! I ..."

"You have a secret."

She sucked in her breath between her parted lips; her face went pale.

He waited for a lifetime, but she didn't speak. She simply stared at him with those enormous eyes, dark brown and as full of fear as a hunted doe's.

Tiana. Brave Tiana, who was afraid of nothing.

"Goddammit to hell!" he shouted.

He threw back the covers and swung himself off the bed. Snatching his pants from the floor, he jerked them on without bothering with any but the top button. He grabbed up his boots.

"I should have known," he said, his tone low and hard. He jammed his feet into his boots and threw her a look that shriveled her soul.

"Women never tell a man everything."

Then he turned his back on her and stomped out of the cabin. He had lied yesterday at sundown when he told her that he knew her.

He didn't know her at all.

Chapter 14

Tiana lay there and shivered. She couldn't tear her gaze from the open door, that hard rectangle of spurious sunshine which held no warmth and no light. Her lips were pressed so tightly shut that she couldn't have spoken if she'd tried, but her heart cried and cried, "Stand, come back! I'll tell you my secret."

But she wouldn't, of course. Even if she did, it would change nothing. He would still be hating instead of loving her—only for a different reason.

Loving. Loving her.

Last night he had been loving her.

Slowly, carefully, every muscle aching as if she'd just been beaten with a stick, she slid downward, one hand feeling for the edge of the quilt. She didn't want to move any more than she had to. She didn't want to let go of the memory of Stand, lingering in the warmth of the bed they had shared.

She pulled the quilt all the way up, over her head, and lay in the shadowy semidarkness, smelling Stand's scent. She curled into the spot where he'd lain, soaking his warmth in through her skin. And forced herself not to think.

For a little while she succeeded. But then her eyes came open and she stared into the dimness, seeing the daylight only as a faraway paleness through the worn cotton batting of the quilt.

Stand had never said that *he* loved *her*. Not once during their magic closeness of the night.

And he didn't. He couldn't, or he wouldn't let one secret drive him from her. He was, no doubt, at this very moment out at the shed saddling his horse, getting ready to leave her. After the night they had shared!

He was as much a deceiver as she—no, he was worse. His body had only been pretending when it said that he loved her; hers had told him the truth. Her love for him went so deep it twisted her body and her mind into knots that she could never untie.

She scrambled out of bed to look for her clothes. She had to get away; she couldn't just sit here in the same room where they'd made love and hear him ride out.

Her garments lay in a heap on the floor where Stand had tossed them. The hunting shirt and breeches that he had pushed urgently down and off her body so that their skins could touch. So that they could lie together and make sweet, sweet love.

She picked them up, then sat on the side of the bed holding them limply in her hands. They were so soaked with morning dew they were impossible to wear. There must be something here she could wear!

Tiana ran to the corner cabinet, her bare feet cold on the rough wooden floor, and fumbled among the old clothes folded there. She jerked out a thin cotton dress of *Ulisi* Tahnee's and slipped it on over her head.

It mocked her: the long skirt swirled daintily around her feet; the bodice held her breasts full and high. She had no use to look like a woman now. She never would.

With only a quick brushing of her hair, and a quicker splash of water on her face at the washstand, Tiana turned and ran outside, deliberately facing away from the horse pen, desperately rushing for the wall of the woods to put it between her and Stand. She never wanted to see him again.

A junco, flying low to the ground, darted along ahead of her and a squirrel, leaping from a branch in a red oak tree to one in a black locust; both chattered to her as she entered the trees. She couldn't answer; her throat was too full and her heart was too hollow.

Grandmother Sun was burning away the last wisps of the fog. It would be a beautiful day in the Mountains of the Blue Smoke—this ugliest day of her life. The trees spattered her with beads of water as she passed beneath them, flapping their leaves at her like an old woman flapping her hands in dismay, scattering dousings of dew onto her head and her dress like showers of teardrops. The woods were crying because The Paint didn't love her in return.

But she didn't cry.

And she wouldn't.

But the yearning for Stand dogged her every step of the way as she wandered through the close, hot woods. She fled from it until late afternoon, then finally gave up and headed back toward the cabin.

Perhaps she could banish it there. She would walk straight into the cabin and smooth out the bed, erase every trace of Stand. She would face her memories of last night head-on and then set them to rest in some faraway part of her mind. When she was an old, old woman like *Ulisi* Tahnee had been, then it would be safe to remember them.

But when she came out of the woods into the edge of the clearing and saw Stand, the hurting for him, the aching for him, filled her thoughts. She stood still, staring, while all her frantic feelings broke through the barriers she'd built.

He was still here! He hadn't left her after all! Did this mean he'd forgiven her for not sharing her secret?

But what was he doing? He was astride, not Coosa, but The Butterfly. He had taken a second one of her horses!

Tiana picked up her skirts and ran toward them.

"What do you think you're doing? Get off her. Get off now!"

He was trotting Butterfly around the opposite side of the pen; he seemed not to hear.

Tiana turned her eyes from the sensual way he sat the horse and climbed up on the fence. "Do you hear me? Dismount from that filly this instant!"

The Paint didn't even look her way.

When they came around by Tiana, she stood on the bottom rail, on tiptoes, and grabbed at the bridle. She missed, but Stand did stop the filly and turn her around. He brought the reins together and folded his hands on the horn of the saddle as calmly as if he'd been waiting for Tiana to snatch at the mouth of his mount.

"Her disposition's as fiery as Coosa's," he said. His voice had lost its bitterness, but it held no trace of friendliness or warmth. "She's not too hard to handle, though, if you take the time to get to know her. She's smart as a wolverine."

"I know that!" Tiana cried, all her pent-up frustration pouring to the tip of her tongue in a flood. "I ought to—*I'm* the one who's breaking her! And I never said you could so much as touch her. Dismount!"

Standingdeer slumped in the saddle as if her order had meant just the opposite.

"Sorry," he said calmly. "But she needed riding and I needed something to do. Coosa and building my lean-to only used up the morning."

"*I'm* riding her! I was just waiting until the cool of the day."

"You still can. I'm only slowing her down for you."

"I can do that *myself*. I've never lost control of that filly—I don't care what you say about that day at Pine Grove!"

Then his earlier words hit her consciousness like a rock falling from the side of a mountain. *His lean-to?*

"What did you mean about building a lean-to?" she blurted out.

He inclined his head toward the creek, his face set in haughty, chiseled lines that cut at her heart in spite of her anger. "I put one up down there by the ford. I'll stay there while the two of us together get Coosa ready to run."

Tiana grabbed the rough top rail so hard that its sharp edge cut into her hands. Stand was *staying*? No. *No.* She hadn't wanted him to go, but it would be twice as much torture if he didn't.

Strangling on the words, she said, "Get Coosa ready to run where?"

"At Dahlonega, of course. You agreed to that, if you remember." He sounded sure and immovable, as he had the day they had met. As he had the first time he'd told her that Coosa would run at Dahlonega.

"*But not now!* That was before everything . . ."

His lips formed a blade-thin line. "Aren't you as good as your word?"

Yes, God help me. I was as good as my word when I told you I loved you.

Her heart beat a warning like the throbbing of a war drum. She must drive him away. She must drive him away. She couldn't live in this agony for a whole month, until that race began.

Fighting for control of her thoughts and her voice, she said, "I'll bring Coosa in by myself." She cleared her throat against the hoarseness there. "You can meet me in Dahlonega."

"You go in alone and you'll never make it to Dahlonega. Sykes and Walters'll be waiting to see if they can take Coosa before he runs. That is, if Bluford doesn't think of this place and come here."

He glanced toward the shallow ford in the creek, and for the first time she realized that he had built his lean-to between her and the natural entrance to the cabin's clearing. He had put himself between her and danger.

Somehow, that made everything worse.

She cried, "I've taken care of myself this far!"

His eyes, hard as agates, met hers. "With my help and the grace of God."

She stared at him, struck by the careless arrogance—and the truth—of his words. Cold fear raced through her, like the burbling creek through the rocks at the bottom of the hill. She couldn't live with him here. Not with this awful distance between them.

And not if that awful distance disappeared. She must never touch him or let him touch her, not ever again. If he would leave, by the time of the race she'd be strong enough to see him one more time.

"If you'll go away now," she begged, "I'll meet you in Dahlonega without fail. If you're that determined to go through with this."

"I am."

The fence rail dug into her palms. "Why? You said money isn't important to you."

"It is now. I want to buy a ranch."

"You don't need money for that. You can claim land without paying in either Nation, East or West."

The bitterness returned to his voice, tenfold. "For how long? Until the whites push through our borders again? No. I want land bought and paid for that no one can take away. Land outside any government grant."

"All right," she said desperately, "Coosa will win it for you. I'll meet you in Dahlonega."

His sharp black glance pierced her soul.

"Trust me, Stand!"

"Seems I've heard that before."

"I promise!"

"I promise not to touch you again, if that's what you're worried about," he said, shooting every word at her like an arrow released from a bow. "Because I can't trust you, Tiana."

"Yes, you can."

"Then tell me your secret."

He sat there on Butterfly, staring straight through her, and waited. She clamped her lips shut and met his hard gaze for an interminable time. Until he swept his eyes from hers and turned Butterfly's head away, starting her going again at a trot.

Tiana intended to get down from the fence and walk back to the cabin, to make her way inside it and close the door. When Stand had gone to his lean-to, she would come out and ride her horses.

Instead, to her own disbelief and dismay, she clung to the fence like a drowning child, watching him. He had promised not to touch her again. Wasn't that what she wanted?

He was ignoring her. Wasn't that what she wanted?

He was staying here. And that had better be what she wanted. If he left, he would most likely go back to Pine Grove—where Bluford would tell him what Sudie had said.

When he and Butterfly came around in front of her, she said, "If you insist on staying here, Standingdeer, I can't make you go. But I *won't* turn Coosa completely over to you. I'm his only trainer and I intend it to stay that way."

He slowed the mare and grinned. He actually gave her that lopsided, unexpected grin of his, and even though it was full of harsh irony, it sent heat all the way through her to the soles of her feet. "What did I tell you?" he said. "Once more you're contradicting me."

The taunting words brought the entire night of their lovemaking sweeping back through her like a hard, swirling wind. It scared her more than the worst storm she'd seen.

"You are the bossiest, most overbearing man I ever saw in my life!"

"Butterfly doesn't think so," he said, slowing the filly all the way to a stop, stroking her glossy black neck. "Do you, girl?"

Tiana couldn't drag her gaze away from his square, copper-skinned hand. It called to her skin—she could feel it on her—strong and compelling, yet honeyed as the sweet-mouthed copper of the bit he had slipped into Butterfly's mouth. At the same time, it was as magically gentle as his voice.

How could she live this near to him—how could she live *anywhere*—and not have his touch?

He petted the filly again.

"Besides that, she likes me," he said.

Tiana's heart turned over. *So do I*, it said. *Oh,*

Stand, so do I. I love you. I can't help myself—I love you.

Stand stood up, suddenly, in the stirrup and dismounted. For one tumultuous heartbeat, Tiana thought he meant to come to her.

But he walked around Butterfly. He ran his hand over the filly's elegant neck again and down her chest; then he bent and slowly, slowly stroked the length of her leg.

Tiana's breath stopped. *Oh, Stand,* it whispered as it flew away and dissolved against the side of the fragrant mountain, *please do that to me.*

"See?" he said. "She's already letting me handle her all over."

He obviously liked Butterfly; he would ride her without harming her in the least. But to Tiana's chagrin, at that moment she couldn't care less about how he treated her favorite filly. Her only concern was the question carried by the blood pounding hot in her veins.

Would she ever again feel The Paint's hands on her? Would he hold to his vow that he wouldn't touch her anymore?

The mare took her foot from his hand and stepped away from him.

"At least she lets me most of the time," Stand said ruefully. "She's going to be fast. One of these days she'll beat her daddy's time."

"No, she won't," Tiana declared, hardly knowing what she was saying. She only wanted to make Standingdeer meet her eyes with his. *"Nobody'll* be faster than Coosa, not even her."

Stand's head whipped around and his gaze met hers. "You're the one who first predicted she would!" he said. "How come you're going back on it now?"

"I . . . I've changed my mind," she muttered, willing him to walk closer to ask her why.

"Why?" he asked, but he stayed where he was.

"Because I've realized that there's never been another running horse as good as Coosa, not in the whole Nation. And there never will be. Not in our lifetime."

He laughed. But it was a bitter sound, not that deep, rolling laugh rich enough to make the whole world happy.

"You're loyal, Tiana, I've got to hand you that."

And then, like a shifting stab to the heart, he said, "At least to your *four-footed* friends you are."

The dry, accusing irony of the words changed the sweat on her skin into crystals of ice. It brought back her fear, full-blown, to blot out the foolish desire. She had no more sense than a goose to let herself be drawn to him as she had been. Stand was bound to hear the truth from Bluford. Then his accusation would be awful indeed.

She lifted her chin and set her jaw; she would kill the affinity she felt for him. They would live here together but separately until it was time for the race; maybe then Papa would be home for her moment of reckoning.

Stand saw in her face that he'd hit his mark. Good. The more anger between them, the easier to keep apart.

"I'm loyal to *all* my friends," she shot back obstinately, her dark eyes flashing. "Some of them just aren't smart enough to see it." She kept her gaze defiantly locked with his.

I can make you close those beautiful eyes, he thought, fighting to keep from taking a step toward her. *I can kiss you and change that challenge into sweet surrender.*

But he wouldn't. He'd known the first time he ever kissed her that he'd be better off to leave alone. Even if she weren't tarred by her father's brush by having a secret love, she did have a secret, just as his own mother had done. Just as Elena had done.

Even though she'd said that she loved him, keeping her secret was more important to her than he was. He would never waste another thought on this beautiful girl/woman with the treacherous heart.

He turned back to the filly and held out his hand. "Come on, girl," he crooned. "Come to me."

She didn't move, so he took a step forward, then another, talking softly, urging her to come.

The Butterfly sidled a little farther away.

"Damn it," he said in that same gentle tone, but deep down inside he was yelling the words. The filly's huge dark eyes held the same stubborn, yet beckoning, look as Tiana's.

In the middle of the night, Tiana woke, so suddenly that she could hardly breathe. Listening.

The noises came again: a high screech, like the sound of an owl, and then a loud thump. The wind whistled around the corner of the cabin.

The screech sounded yet again, more piercing and longer this time. The thud came harder; it shook the wall. A sigh of relief trembled through her.

The shutter. The wind had risen and was catching the shutter on the west window.

She reached for her covers and huddled beneath them, scooting in deep so she could feel the scratchy, worn wool of the blanket through the thin hunting shirt she wore for a gown. In spite of its warmth, she shivered.

The very air seemed cold, but how could that be? What had happened to the sultry summer night that had smothered her skin when she finally left her front porch and came in to bed?

From far away thunder rumbled, long and low.

The house shifted, feeling as if it had moved on its foundation, and then she could hear the wind pushing and calling in earnest now, rushing down the slopes of the mountains into the protected valley. The trees surrounding the cabin creaked beneath its force.

What if it became a terrible storm? Could Stand's lean-to withstand it? Or an overflow of a rain? Would the creek rise far enough out of its banks to wash the lean-to away?

Tiana wrapped the blanket more tightly around her shoulders and pretended that it was his arms. Why couldn't she have thought fast enough to tell him a lie when he asked for her secret? Then he would be here with her tonight instead of somewhere out there on the other side of the wind.

But she was a hopeless liar—no one ever believed her when she lied. Besides, that would have been, somehow, a sin against nature. It would have been as bad as killing a deer for food without asking Little Deer's pardon; her feelings for The Paint raging like a war in her heart went too deep for lies. Better not to tell him anything than to lie to him.

Even if he would never love her in return.

The cold wind pushed against the wall like a hand pressing on her back. The slab door moved on its hinges.

Stand had better come in. He would, wouldn't he? Stubborn as he was, he surely wouldn't stay out in a storm.

He would run to the cave, though, instead of to the house—if he knew that the cave was there. She smiled at her own foolishness. He knew it. If he could lead her over the trail from Pine Grove to Running Waters in the dark without one hesitating step, he would remember *Ulisi*'s cave from the time when he was a boy.

The first drops of rain hit the porch, blowing so hard that it sounded like hail. Tiana's eyes flew open to stare at the door, its rough shape barely visible in the erratic flashes of lightning.

Stand would come in. He'd have to pass the cabin to get to the cave; surely he wouldn't do that.

So she must get up. It wouldn't do to let him find her this way—she was likely to hold out her arms and beg him to climb into bed and snuggle under the covers with her. But her heavy limbs refused to move.

The rain thickened in a trice, slamming into the cabin on a wind that cried and squalled down from the tops of the mountains. It tore at the walls like the claws of a panther.

It turned to volleys of hail.

Where was he?

Lightning flashed white in the small square of one window, pointing a crooked, accusing finger at Tiana. The crack of thunder which followed shook the earth beneath the cabin. It jerked her up straight, clutching the blanket to her chest with both hands.

The wind swelled and grew, coming from every direction at once, fighting to tear the walls from around her. Its noise, and that of the thunder, and of the bending, creaking trees, filled the world. Even from this distance she thought she could hear the waters rising in the creek, roaring like a river.

Closer at hand, the banked embers of the fire began to hiss. How could that be? Was water coming down the chimney? That had never happened before.

She threw off her covers and ran to the hearth, intending to cover the fire to protect it. But rain lashed at her, finding her face in the dark, riding the wind into her lair. It froze her to the middle of the floor.

The roof! It was coming through the roof! A great gust of wind and scattering hail blew into the room, hitting Tiana, gathering fast around her to close her into a cold circle of ice.

A scream rose from her heart. "Stand!"

Another realization tore its way loose from the mush her brain had become. Stand couldn't hear her in this uproar.

She turned away from the fire and ran to the door, which was moving back and forth in its jamb as if from the breathing of a monster. If it blew open, everything in the room would be ruined.

Rain slashed at her face through a crack in the door and at her back through the hole in the roof. She caught a quick, deep breath from the shock of its coldness and pressed her body against the door to try to hold it steady. A terrific force hit it and knocked her back.

"Tiana!"

She would never have heard Stand's shout through the crashing of the storm if he hadn't been so close. Even so, it had sounded like a whisper.

With stiff, trembling hands she undid the latch and he rushed into the room. A great flash of lightning lit up the cabin. The center of the roof lay open to the black sky, the bare timbers crisscrossing overhead like desperate fingers trying to hold the house in one piece.

She saw Stand's face for an instant, its bronze color made pale by the brightness of the lightning, his eyes dark and wild as the storm. He grabbed her arm and pulled her to him, pressed his wet lips to her ear.

"Come on! Let's get to the cave!"

He was moving her out the door as he spoke, with a force so strong she was helpless to resist.

"No!" she cried. "The corners still have a roof! We'd be safer in the house, in the corner!"

But he pushed her ahead of him as if he didn't hear, which, indeed, he probably didn't, holding her around her waist, running so close his leg moved against hers. Out into the full force of the wind.

When it hit her it took her breath, and what little sight she had disappeared in the constant blinding flashes of lightning. Rain filled her eyes and her ears, drenched her hair and her skin in one instant. She tried to gasp, but she couldn't get enough air.

The horses!

Her heart broke, but she didn't even try to say the words. Stand couldn't hear and her lips couldn't move; even if they could communicate, she didn't know in which direction the horse pen lay.

For an eternity they ran, ahead of the wind and into it, buffeted to one side and then to the other, with Stand's solid body behind her, around her, the only stable thing in the world. Her bare feet had long since gone numb with the shock and the cold, passing over grass and rocks, water, moss, pine needles, and smooth ground with the same quick impunity because Stand held her up.

After an age of their staggering uphill, the lightning stabbed down to meet them, to show them the black mouth of the cave. A sudden quiet fell.

The wind stopped; an ominous stillness permeated the valley.

"Hurry," Stand said. "It's a dancing devil storm, as the plains peoples say. It'll be here soon." His long legs pushed harder, reached farther. He was practically carrying her now.

The next instant they were out of the awful silence that filled the world and into another, smaller one. Into the cave. Out of the sporadic stabbing light and into the darkness.

Into peace.

Stand held Tiana hard against him with one arm as they bent down for the low ceiling. She felt the lifting of his other arm, extended to feel for the walls. They moved slowly, carefully, a few feet farther in from the entrance, into the musty, cool air that felt as if it hadn't moved for a generation, and collapsed into a heap, clinging to each other, gasping, while the water ran from their bodies in rivulets and streams; their wet clothes stuck them together as if they were glued.

Then a terrible roaring noise filled the night, blasting its vibrations even into their sanctuary.

"*Is* it a dancing devil?" she choked.

"Yes."

The sound was terrifying enough to close her throat on any more words, but then a strong, strange feeling of suction, sneaking in toward them like a snake through the mouth of the cave, threatened to pull them apart. Tiana wrapped her arms around Standingdeer's and clung to his hands. The storm was trying to snatch them back out into the open because they had escaped.

Stand scooted further back against the wall, straddled his legs, and folded Tiana closer to him, pulling her body into the shape of his like a spoon into a spoon. His face pressed against her hair.

Her whole body trembled.

He hugged her harder.

"It'll be gone in a minute," he said comfortingly, his voice rumbling in her ear. "It can't last long."

The roar continued for what seemed to be a lifetime, and then, as he had predicted, it was gone. Silence followed, but only for a moment, until the cave filled with the sound and smell of the rain. And the returning hail.

Tiana began to shake, from the top of her head to the soles of her feet, her body trembling and shivering, desperate for more warmth to drive away the cold that went clear to the bone.

"I . . . I wish . . . we . . . need a fire," she said between chatterings of her teeth.

"We've nothing to build one," Stand said unsteadily. "But don't complain. Thunder was with us, or we'd have lost our lives."

Tiana held onto his left hand with both of hers. Thank God he had come for her.

"What happened to your lean-to?" she asked, to get her mind off her shivering.

"Flattened," he replied with a self-mocking smile. "Went down with the first gust of wind."

"I still can't believe it took the roof off the cabin," she said. "*Ulisi* Tahnee was born in that house."

"No house can last forever."

She let go of his hand and made fists out of hers.

"Don't *say* that! The cabin's the only home I have left! That tornado better not have taken it!"

A worse thought struck her then; she gasped and twisted her face to try to see his, although the cave was black-dark. "Oh, Stand, the horses! What if they were killed or hurt?"

She pushed at his arms as if she were going to jump up and run out to see about the animals. His grip on her turned to one of iron.

"They're likely all right. They can get in the shed."

"But what if lightning struck them, or some pieces of the roof?"

"We'll see about them as soon as it's light," he

told her soothingly. "That won't be too long from now."

"I pray it won't," she said, but the quiet acceptance in his voice drained some of the tension from her. The warmth of his body was beginning to soak into hers.

"Did your *Ulisi* Tahnee live in that cabin all her life?" he asked.

He was only trying to distract her from her worries, and she knew it. But the rain was pounding down, and even if she could get loose and go out, she wouldn't be able to see to find the horses.

And it felt so good to get warm.

It felt so good to be held in Stand's arms.

"Yes," she said. "Except for the times she came down to Running Waters. When Papa first built the plantation, she moved into the big house, too, but they always argued. Each time she got mad at him she went back to her cabin."

"Did you ever go with her?"

"Yes. She died when I was eight, but I can remember all about it."

"I remember her, too."

"Wasn't she fun? She was like a child herself."

"Yes," he said. "*Ulisi* Tahnee was my favorite person in the Tenkiller family."

Something in his voice caught at her.

"When we first met, you made some taunting remarks about us Tenkillers," she said, searching her memory as she spoke. "And that day of the fire, I got the feeling you wouldn't have come in to breakfast if Papa had been home. Do you have something against us, Stand?"

He didn't answer.

"I know you were upset when I followed Bluford to town, and that's why you told such a spiteful lie about Papa. I can't believe you hate the

Tenkillers so much you'd tell an awful lie about your mother, too."

She twisted as if to look at him, even in the deep dark.

His arms tightened around her to hold her still.

"It wasn't a lie," he said. "My mother was with your father when she was killed. I've always held it against them both."

The quick intake of her breath stirred the air against his hand. "*With* him?"

"Yes. Your father says they loved each other."

She did turn in his arms then.

"But my mother . . ." she said in a small voice, and let the rest of the words trail away.

"Was sick with childbed fever," he answered. "For almost two years after having her first child, the one who died."

She didn't speak.

"I'm sorry, Tiana. I shouldn't have blurted that out that day just because I was angry. Otherwise, you need never have known."

"When did you and Papa talk about . . . it?" she asked, and her voice trembled a little.

Stand tightened his arms around her again. "At the Council Oak. When I refused to go to Washington City with him."

He explained the whole story then, to himself as well as to her. "For years I blamed Nicotai for killing my mother," he said at the end, amazed that he had been speaking of this without the old anger twisting his gut. "But somehow, without really knowing I was doing it, I've let it go. When I'm really honest with myself, I remember how grieved he was the day she died and I know he would have saved her if he could."

"It's just so hard for me to believe," she said.

"It was for me, too. My mother and I were

close—I never dreamed she'd keep such a secret from me."

Waves of incredulity and anger and betrayal of her mama broke somewhere deep inside Tiana. Yet the rich rumble of Stand's voice and the immediate, fascinating power of his body holding hers smoothed them, sent them and the past into the far, far distance.

Tiana gripped the mighty muscles of his forearms where they crossed at her waist. "Is that why you said women never tell everything?"

"Partly it is," he said, his voice turning forbiddingly harsh. "But other women have kept secrets from me, too."

The words hung heavy in the air over Tiana's head, echoing against the walls of the cave and the curtain of the driving rain, ready to drop down and crush her.

To hold them back, she said, "Who?"

The hard muscles of his chest rose, pushed against her back, then fell away from it as he heaved a deep sigh. His arms stayed crossed in her lap, but he loosened his hold on her. Cool air came between his warm hands and her flesh.

"A woman I loved," he said slowly.

The words snatched the air from Tiana's lungs with a quick force greater than the sucking pull of the storm.

They filled her breast with a roiling, liquid jealousy. No, a fear. Did he still love that woman?

She waited to hear.

"It was many years ago," he said.

Slowly, slowly, she pressed her fingertips into the flexing muscles of his arms. "Where?"

"Deep in the mountains some call the Shining Mountains and others call the Rockies. They have a whole different spirit from these of the Blue Smoke."

Thunder crashed and crashed again, going away from them over the ridges, rolling and rumbling, coming back again, calling to them. Then came another flash of lightning.

"What was her name?" Tiana whispered.

"Elena. A Spanish woman come up from Santa Fe."

"So far into the mountains? By herself?"

The Paint gave a wry, bitter chuckle.

"I questioned that as quickly as you do," he said. "She told me she came for adventure. And solitude. Since those were *my* reasons for wandering, I believed her."

"But you are a man . . ."

His chin brushed her hair as he nodded. "But I realized a woman could want those things, too. I admired her for being so brave to go out and get them."

Tiana held herself very still. He'd always said *she* was brave. Did she remind him of this Spanish woman, Elena?

Was that the only reason he admired her? Was that the reason he couldn't love her?

"I was catching and breaking wild horses," he said. "I thought I could do the same with any woman. But she caught me, instead, and broke me."

"She left you?"

"I left her," he said, his deep voice turning hard as the wood of a hickory. "It turned out that she wasn't brave, or alone, at all. She had come to the mountains with a trapper named Perez. Her husband."

He sat as still as if he'd turned to stone.

So did Tiana, trying to imagine it all. "But you had some happiness with her," she said finally.

"It wasn't worth it if I couldn't keep it."

She sank back against him and he held her. Morning sneaked into the inside of the cave.

"I've forgiven her, too, I suppose," he said slowly, obviously deciding on the truth of his words as he spoke. "People have to live as much as they can in each present moment; I've been trying to do that myself for all these years since."

They didn't move, not for ages, while a terrible clap of thunder crashed right at the entrance, while the rain drummed down, while their wet skins cleaved together everywhere they touched and their shared heat drove the cold from their bodies at last.

But inside her, Tiana's heart was made of hailstones, frozen together into one big lump. The Paint's feelings went so deep and lasted so long that they terrified her. He had taken years to forgive his mother and her father and Elena for keeping their secrets. And those secrets had been *nothing* compared with hers!

She gritted her teeth. He would never forgive Tiana if they both lived to be a hundred.

"About the Tenkillers, though," he said thoughtfully, "I admit I tried to stay away from you at first because you were Nicotai Tenkiller's daughter, but I know, deep down, that you and your father are two different people; you aren't necessarily going to behave like him."

He bent to brush his cheek against hers and then rested his chin lightly on the top of her head.

"And not all women are the same," he went on in a lighter tone, his old teasing voice that made her smile. "You aren't my mother and you aren't Elena. You are the brave, sweet Tiana, champion horsewoman of the Eastern Nation."

She let him rock her back against his chest; she let him drop a kiss against her temple. She let him believe in her.

Although she was also champion among all the treacherous women he had ever known.

The marvelous feel of his iron-muscled arms sliding gently against her shoulders took the soul right out of her body. She loved him so much she could die for it.

Before he found her out, couldn't they have a bit of happiness, like the time he'd had with Elena? They had one month, one moon, one *Tsa-lu-wa'nee*, Corn-in-Tassel Moon, to be happy together. It was the only chance they would ever have.

The thought stopped her breath. What was she doing? Hadn't she promised herself, just last evening, that she would never touch him, never lie with him again, if that happiness couldn't be forever?

Yes. But then, those few hours ago, she hadn't known the lesson she had learned this night: that in one wild moment her whole world could be reduced to a small circle in a damp, dark cave with Standingdeer's skin hot against hers and his breath stirring in her hair.

Chapter 15

T he rain stopped. Tiana and Stand sat in the silent darkness for a short time more, until the arching entrance of the cave began to show its shape against the light.

Then he took her by the arms and put her away from him, bending his legs so he could get up. "We'll be able to see now," he said.

She stayed still, in spite of the clammy feel of the cave floor against her bare legs. "I don't want to see."

He didn't want to see, either. If Coosa was hurt or dead or if the cabin was gone, how could he comfort Tiana? But they had to find out; it might as well be now.

Instead of creeping in, gray and misty, the way most mountain mornings began, this morning's dawn burst over the mountains like a striped warbler's song. The instant he and Tiana stepped out of the cave and straightened their backs, the sunrise broke open the sky and poured pinks and reds and then yellow light and more light into the valley.

"Grandmother Sun can't wait to see what the storm has left and what it has taken," Tiana murmured.

She brought her other arm across her body to

cling to his hand with both of hers, and he felt the
fear vibrating through her. She wasn't looking toward either the cabin or the horses, though, and
he knew without being told that she was waiting,
working up her courage to do so.

The sight she had chosen, however, was enough
to drain every ounce of mettle from the bravest
warrior: the storm had cut a swath a half mile
wide up the side of Chilowee Mountain. It had
ripped huge beeches and pines, and even the hickory trees, out of the earth by their roots and left
them tangled together like twigs of kindling for a
giant's fire, ludicrously awash in green leaves.

"It looks like a fresh trail stomped down by an
Uk'ten'," she whispered.

The ground left bare shone in the sunlight, covered with a chaos of debris, ugly as an enemy's
smile. It was in a direct line from the cabin.

Tiana gasped. Stand turned, thinking the house
was gone, but she was staring toward the horse
pen, where he saw what she had seen: a glimpse
of Coosa near the shed.

She dropped his hand and then she was running straight down the hill, black hair streaming
out behind her, long bare legs flashing in the sunlight beneath the thigh-length hunting shirt she
wore. Her feet dipped into and out of the wet
grass like a hummingbird's work; her hands
stretched out in front of her to meet the cool wind.

The breeze lifted and carried her, white shirt,
creamy legs, and black hair against the green of
the near mountain. Stand stayed very still and let
the sight take him.

She would be all right, now that she knew
Coosa was safe. But would *he*? Nobody, *nobody* in
all of his life had been able to walk into his very
soul the way she did. Never, with no one else, had

he shared all the deepest feelings in his heart. With Tiana, it was as natural as rain.

When she reached the pen, she threw herself over the fence and her arms around the stallion's neck. Then, in an instant, she was darting to Butterfly and into and out of the shed, from one horse to another.

He stood still. He couldn't tear his eyes away, not even to look and see whether the cabin was gone.

"They're all right!" she called, her happy tones echoing against the granite cliff on Chilowee. "All four of them!"

The sound of her voice freed his feet; he ran down the hill, too, then, just to be near her again.

"Everybody's alive," she sang out, smiling at him, watching him come to her. "And nobody's hurt."

She dashed out of the pen to meet him, grabbed his hand, and bolted toward the house, pulling him behind her. "And the cabin! The tornado didn't take it! Look, Stand!"

He laughed. The pure joy bubbling up in her made him laugh; it wiped away every thought in his head.

"I wish we could say the same for the roof," he said.

The door stood open, as they had left it. However, the early sunlight pouring in to fill the house came not through it but down through the rafters that loomed bare in pointed peaks against the sky and the mountain.

The faded red-and-blue quilt hung crazily from a tree near the porch. Pieces of a chair and a lamp lay scattered, broken, along with some clothing, in the yard. Tiana didn't even seem to notice.

She let go of his hand, ran across the porch and into the tumbled, sodden room. "There *are* a few shingles left," she said, pointing to the corner. The one above the bed.

Stand followed her inside.

"Did it blow away the cooking pots? I just realized I'm starving."

"I'll fix you some breakfast if you'll build me a fire," she said, smiling and tilting her head to one side so that her hair swung loose, calling to his hands. "Since the roof is gone, we can have a picnic without leaving the house!"

He looked down into her tantalizing face, wanting nothing so much as to take her that instant. He had no control anymore, no character at all—he had lost it somewhere. Most likely right here in this room, in this bed, which was still standing, tousled, mostly dry, and infinitely inviting.

"I'll find some dry wood," he said gruffly, and turned away to step over the mess on his way back to the door.

When he had gone, Tiana hurried to the kitchen end of the cabin, to *Ulisi*'s meal box, where she kept the supplies. The wind had dragged it out from its corner and turned it over, but the lid was still latched. She set it upright and opened it. Wonderful! The tin of cornmeal Papa had left from his last hunting trip had stayed dry.

She closed the lid and scooted the meal box back into place, then took the iron pot from its hook and started out to the creek for water. Hot mush would be good for breakfast; later in the day The Paint could go hunting for a squirrel, and she would fry it to make their supper.

Halfway down the hill the glint of metal caught her eye. The water pitcher lay upside down, turned over a stalk of bitterweed as neatly as if two hands instead of the wind had done the deed. A few feet farther toward the creek, nestled right side up in a clump of grass, lay its battered matching bowl, full of rainwater, sticks, and leaves.

She picked them up and took them with her, her heart lifting high as the wind in the trees. The storm had left them everything they needed; she and The Paint together could do anything. He was building a fire for her, she was cooking for him. They could pick things up and repair them, carry the bed outside to dry, if indeed in its protected corner it had gotten wet, and replace the roof. Together.

The overflowing creek roared like a waterfall; as she came closer to it, it drowned out the chirpings of the awakening birds. Spray from the rushing water soaked her face and the front of her shirt as she began to fill the pot and the pitcher. She had never seen this water run so high.

They certainly couldn't cross it to leave, even if they wanted to, and no one could come to them. She shivered with sudden excitement. This whole valley, and all the mountains around it, belonged only to her and The Paint!

For one moon. One Corn-in-Tassel Moon.

Then The Paint would find her out if Bluford came to the race. If he didn't come, The Paint would leave her, anyway, to go West.

The roaring water danced over her hands, freezing them, filling and overflowing and refilling the vessels. Tiana looked at her face reflected in the shining side of the pitcher, her eyes huge and dark with happiness. And with lurking guilt.

She truly was the most treacherous of all women. Standingdeer had opened his soul to her, yet she had still kept her secret.

Fighting down her conscience, assuring herself that four more weeks wouldn't matter now, pleading with the spirits of the forest and the mountains that she and Stand deserved at least a few days of happiness, she carried the full containers back up the hill, one in each hand, with the bowl tucked under her arm. The cool breeze plastered the wet shirt to her body and the tops of her legs, hindering her steps.

She glanced around to see if Stand was coming. If he wasn't at the cabin and if *Ulisi*'s dress hadn't blown away, she would change into it.

But when she came back into the yard and saw him through the open door, squatting on his haunches in front of the hearth with his shoulders wide and massive beneath his blue shirt, his black hair shining in the sunlight, all thoughts of guilt and of her own appearance went right out of her head. Standingdeer Chekote filled her eyes.

And her heart. She could not believe how much she loved him, in spite of the hurtful way he had left her bed.

Oh, please God, couldn't he love her, too, just for a little while? Couldn't he tell her that in words so that she'd have it always to remember?

His shoulders flexed beneath the still-damp cotton of his shirt as he arranged the wood and blew on the kindling; their wide, square line tapered to his waist, where the narrow tunnel of his backbone hollowed out and disappeared into his tight pants. Her fingers screamed to follow it.

His small, round hips rested on the heels of his boots.

The black raven's wings of his hair were beginning to dry; they fell forward so that she couldn't see his face.

Silently, on bare feet, she crossed the porch and the room, walking in the path he had cleared through the storm's debris. She didn't pause until she stood beside him.

He knew she was there, for his busy hands went still for a moment. Yet he didn't look up.

His square, dark-skinned fingers moved again with the easy power, the sure skill, of a man long accustomed to the fire-making task. As they had moved over her body one night with that very same intention.

He opened the tin, took out a match, struck it on the hearth, and held its flame to the kindling.

The twigs caught and flared. The blaze licked at the logs.

Tiana's blood rose and beat like thunder in her veins.

For an endless moment she and The Paint both watched, staring at the burning wood as if they'd never seen fire, motionless as if they'd never stir again.

Then he dropped the match and stood up, turning to face her in the same flowing gesture. His dark gaze met hers. He reached for the pot and the pitcher in her hands. He took her burdens and set them down.

"While the water boils," he said hoarsely, "we should get out of these wet clothes."

But still he didn't touch her.

"The water won't boil if it isn't on the fire," she answered in a whisper.

"That's true."

But he didn't move to pick up the pot and put it there.

Neither did she.

"Stay here," he said, and then he was gone, past her, moving so close to her that he left the faint fragrance of his damp skin in the air.

She took a long, trembling breath. If she had any strength left, she would turn her head and look for him. Her eyes were empty, her *soul* was empty, without the sight of him. But her body had so little power.

The next instant the warmth of the blanket came

around her back. And through it came the deeper heat, the harder feel, of his hand.

"Get out of that shirt," he murmured. "Before you catch cold."

Her fingers went to the buttons, slipped them through the holes; both of her hands lifted to pull the damp cloth out to her shoulders and off. The shirt slid to the floor at her feet.

Stand wrapped the blanket tighter around her bare skin. Through it, the feel of his arms took the last of her energy.

Except for enough for her to whisper, "You'll get me wet again."

He let her go.

She turned to see him.

He was standing on one long leg, his head bent, tugging off his boot. His hair obscured his face again; she longed to see his features, read in them what he was feeling.

He shifted his weight to the other foot and disposed of the other boot. It dropped to the floor with a muffled thud.

Then he shook back his hair and lifted his head. The look in his eyes stopped her heartbeat.

She reached out and touched him, just with her fingertips, trembling, following the line of his cheekbone and brow. Then, with her palm, she stroked back his hair. It shone in the sunlight, black as the nights they'd spent apart.

His breath left his body, drawn out by the touch of her hand like water from a well. But he had no need of it.

Not while her gaze clung to his, her eyes wide and enormous, black as her thick, curling lashes. Dark as the summer-night sky over the plains; he could rise into them and fly. He could crush her into his arms and never let her go.

But he didn't. He lifted his hand and caressed

her hair as she had done his, mirroring her gesture as if returning a vow.

With his other hand he unbuttoned his shirt and his pants; then, finally, hating the parting, he let her go and stepped away to strip off his clothes. The instant he was done he reached to take her back again, enfolded her instantly close in his arms.

"Ah," he breathed with his cheek against her hair, wanting to speak, wanting to say her name, but his heart was too full.

She raised herself up on tiptoes and brought her lips to his ear. Her warm breath made him shiver.

"Standingdeer," she whispered. "Take me to bed."

Her sweet boldness made him smile. He pulled back to look at her.

"I would love to take you to bed," he said, "but you seem to be wearing it."

She smiled at him, too. A seductive smile that took the heart from his body.

"Then we're already there, aren't we?" she answered, and raised her mouth for his kiss.

She tasted sweet as wild strawberries, warmed by the sun. The ravening hunger for her spiraled hard in his belly and spread, raw and needy, down into his loins.

He lifted her against him, pressing her to the length of his body as he deepened the kiss. Then he knelt to lay her down on the sun-washed floor, in front of the fire. Its heat seared her cheek like the touch of a fever.

"Tiana," he whispered as he drove his fingers into her hair and found the tip of her tongue with his, "I'm glad that it stormed."

"So am I," she managed to say just before she closed her eyes and let the melting magic of his kiss send a rainbow of sparkling colors spiraling, dancing, across the backs of her lids.

He rolled onto his side and freed one hand to search for the edge of the blanket.

She broke the kiss.

"I love you, Standingdeer," she whispered against his lips.

He groaned and buried his face in her neck, raining kisses down the side of it onto her shoulder, but that was his only answer.

No, he answered, too, by thrusting his fingers into her hair, lifting her with his other irresistible hand to free the mass of it that was caught beneath her hips, arranging it on her makeshift pillow while he smiled into her eyes.

And that was answer enough.

"Stand," she whispered. "Oh, Standingdeer."

He took her face in both his hands while his mouth came home to hers.

With an impatient, desperate sound that she hardly recognized as coming from herself, she kicked at the cloth confining her legs, arching her back to try and free them. His hands moved downward to help, then returned, too soon, to cradle her head again while he increased her torment with his lips and his tongue.

She moaned in protest and twisted against him again. He made a soothing sound of compliance, deep in his throat, and began to caress her neck, leaving it with a last, reluctant trailing of his thumbs along her collarbone to take her breasts into his hot, callused hands.

Tiana tore her mouth from his.

But he wouldn't let her move any more than that.

He captured her eyes with his heavy-lidded ones and held her still as a dream while his rough thumbs circled on her taut, straining nipples.

Then, with the suddenness of a cry, his hands were gone, moving lower, and his fingers began to trail along the edges of the blanket, everywhere it touched her, setting her skin on fire, melting every bone in her body that hadn't already dissolved from his caresses and his kiss.

His blunt, rough fingertips brushed the insides of her thighs, once, then again, and he stripped all of the blanket away. It lay gathered around them like a warm pool in a river.

She felt the hearth's fire on one side and the cool, penetrating air from the mountains on the other. She trembled.

Until Standingdeer made her warm.

Until his rough hands and his hot mouth seared her skin and stirred her blood to a pounding heat.

Until he took her breast into his mouth and stirred the depths of her being with the gently turbulent circling of his tongue.

Until he cradled her in one arm and looked down at her.

His eyes moved slowly, slowly over every inch of her, all the way down to her feet, and then made their possessive way back to her face.

"I know you're acclaimed throughout the Nation as the best horsewoman," he drawled solemnly. "But you are also the most beautiful woman. In *any* nation."

And then he smiled.

Pure pleasure rose in her. From the smile. From the look in his eyes.

"Thank you," she whispered. "And you are the most wonderful, handsomest man."

His smile widened, deepening a dimple at the corner of his mouth.

"Then we must be meant to be together," he whispered back.

And he lowered his head to place his mouth everywhere his gaze had just been.

His hands underneath her back, his mouth on her skin, Tiana floated before the fire and let him draw out her soul from her body and take it for his to keep.

Finally she gathered the strength to thread her fingers into his hair and hold his head, to keep his sweet, burning lips pressed to her flesh at every spot until the next one, crying out for its turn, could no longer be denied.

Then, when she could bear it no longer, this marking of her skin for his own, she threw back her head and cried out.

"Stand," she begged. "Standingdeer, please."

He enclosed her then with his huge, powerful arms and slid his hands up under her shoulders. He lifted her, brought her close, so he could kiss the hollow at the base of her throat, so he could nuzzle his face into the curve of her neck. So he could nestle her into his arms as if he would never let her go.

He threw back his head to look into her eyes as he entered her. Gently at first, and then with all the force of the storm that had just passed and the one raging within them.

He caught her mouth with his in a kiss that struck her soul with lightning. She wrapped herself around him and clung to his shoulders to escape from its flames, but he carried her headlong into their glory.

The burning rhythm took them and she moved with him, arching to each of his thrusts, until they were melded into one eagle being, soaring together up through the open roof and into the billowing breeze, flying out fearless and strong over the mountains. They dived into the hearts of the hills and swept through them; they rose above the highest mountains with a medicine power greater than that of wood struck by lightning.

Until, at last, they broke through into the sky itself and came to rest above the treetops.

She tore her lips from his and pressed them to that sweet hollow where his magic muscles met in the middle of his chest. He buried his mouth in her hair.

For a long, precious time they lay there, sated, tangled in each other's arms, basking in the heat of the fire.

The wind picked up and swirled its coolness into the room. Tiana turned and hid her face against the bulge of Standingdeer's arm.

She pressed her lips to the salty sweat on his skin.

She would never move again. And neither would he. They would lie here, wrapped around each other like the limbs of trees broken in the storm until they grew very, very old and became part of the earth. They would love each other this way forever and forever.

Shadows from the rafters crisscrossed above them like a blessing from Grandmother Sun.

At last Stand drawled, "If you had put the pot on the fire, we could have breakfast now."

Tiana raised herself up, fast, and looked at him. "Me!" she protested, laughing. "Why didn't you do it? You took it from me!"

He propped himself up on one elbow and grinned at her, his eyes glinting with mischief. Leisurely mischief. And teasing affection.

"You *gave* it to me. Because you wanted your hands free to . . . pounce on me."

"What!" Laughing, she playfully hit at him. "You make me sound like a wanton!"

He caught her flailing fist.

"Don't try to deny it," he growled with mock severity. "All of us here know the truth."

His hand slid up her arm.

"All of us?" Still laughing, she looked over her shoulder. "Who is all of us?"

"Coosa and Butterfly and Tannassy and my buckskin," he said, "and the black-throated warblers nesting out there in the locust tree."

He pulled her closer to him with a hard, hot hand she pretended to resist, but could not.

He drifted down onto his back with the blanket for a pillow, drawing her with him. She bent over him. Her hair swung forward and fell across his shoulder to form a curtain around them.

"Now those nosy ones outside can't see us," he said, his eyes burning more intensely than the fire at her back.

"I don't care if they do," she teased. "All we're going to do now is cook breakfast, remember?"

"No, we aren't," he said when her lips were only inches from his.

"You said you were hungry."

"I am," he growled, and slid his hands up her back to hold her in place so he could take her mouth with his.

It was noon before they could sit apart, not touching, and eat their cornmeal mush swirled with molasses from the jug that had fallen, miraculously unbroken, from the shelf on the wall. Nothing, ever, had tasted so good to Tiana as that hot gruel and the sweetening. Except for The Paint's honeyed kiss.

Grandmother Sun had never shone so bright; the breeze in the summer had never been so delightfully cool and pine-scented. The air had never been so light in her lungs to make her feel she was floating. Except for this morning she had spent in Standingdeer's arms.

She feasted her eyes on him, sitting cross-legged on the opposite side of the fire, bare-chested, in the one pair of Papa's old pants she'd found intact, pants two sizes too small that left his ankles bare. She hoped his shirt would never dry. And that his saddlebags had blown away across the highest mountain so he wouldn't have another.

For the immensity of his shoulders, the huge muscling in his arms and his chest, the solid column of his powerful neck were sights she could never tire of exploring. *Why* hadn't she run the palms of her hands over every fascinating inch of them again and again, and why hadn't she memorized all of him while she had been in his arms?

Tonight she would do just that. For tonight he wouldn't be in his lean-to; tonight he would lie with her.

The first thing she would do was spread all the bedding out in the sun to dry, although, like the blanket, some of it was hardly wet. She wanted it to soak up the scents of the mountains to perfume their cozy lair. The smells of sunshine and cedar and pine—and the feel of each other's arms—would surround them both tonight.

A great, growing happiness burst into life inside her. Three and a half weeks. Almost the whole of this Corn-in-Tassel Moon. Surely during that time Standingdeer would tell her that he loved her.

Because he did. His body had just told her so. He would tell her with words soon.

And she wouldn't think beyond that.

Chapter 16

They were hardly apart during the days and nights that followed. All through the hours of daylight they worked at the endless tasks required for simple survival.

And they talked. Especially at sundown each evening, when a little breeze would rise to cool them and to bring the scents of *Ulisi*'s honeysuckle wafting from the side of the house.

Sometimes the subject was nothing more than plans for the next day.

Stand would say, "Was that the last of the meat at supper?"

And Tiana would say, "Yes. But there're greens left, and I'll look for birds' eggs and hickory nuts to make *connuche*. You don't have to hunt tomorrow if you want to split some more shingles."

He would say, "I probably should. Never know when it might rain."

The low, contented sounds of their voices were like touches, like long, slow caresses of skin against skin. Finally, before the moon came out, those murmurings would pull their bodies up from the steps or out of the cane-bottomed chairs and bring them together, trembling, to walk with their arms wrapped around each other, out through the floating mists to make love on the grass. Or on a bed of pine needles farther back in the trees.

Other times, they shared long-forgotten memories of their childhoods or dreamed aloud about things they wished they had done. Stand offered his confidences in such an unpracticed way that Tiana treasured each one. He wasn't accustomed to opening his heart, his manner said clearly, but he would do so for her.

One night, a good while after dark had settled over them and brought a silence, she murmured, "What are you thinking?"

"About my uncle."

A trembling shock ran through her. It had been days and days since the thought of Tobacco Jack had intruded into this perfect, private world of theirs.

"He was so good to me," Stand rumbled on, "even when he was drinking."

Past him, somewhere out in the trees, a lightning bug flashed.

"You must really have been a favorite of his," Tiana said, as the vision of Fawn's battered face floated between them.

"I was. I went with him hunting and fishing, to town, to the neighbors', to the horse races, everywhere."

"You and Bluford?"

"No. Blu's mother kept to the old ways and sent him to her brothers to raise—farther back, even, than Cloud Mountain. I think that's when he began to resent me—when he came back, he said I'd taken his father."

"Did Tobacco Jack beat Bluford when he'd been drinking?"

"Yes. With everyone but me he changed from a good man to an evil devil as soon as he got full of liquor."

"You must have hated that."

"I did. I wouldn't let myself ever think about it while I was a boy, but as I grew into a man I began to admit to myself that my hero wasn't perfect."

"Is that when you went West?"

"Yes. When he tried to stop drinking and found out he couldn't. That's when Blu started drinking heavily, too, and I realized they both were very weak men. I had to get away and prove that I wasn't."

A long silence fell. The wild honeysuckle scent lay heavy on the air, and the rasping of the night insects rasped loudly in the trees.

"I wish he hadn't loved whiskey so much," Stand said at last, and Tiana could hear tears in his voice.

He cleared his throat. "If it hadn't been for that and Andrew Jackson turning traitor to us *Tsa-la-gi* after we won the Battle of the Horseshoe for him, I would have spent many more of my years here at the Center of the Earth."

"And we would have met many years before we did," Tiana teased, trying to pull him back from the agony that was taking him away from her. "I would have taught you the right way to train horses from the beginning, and we wouldn't have to have all these arguments now."

She was rewarded by his rich, low laugh and the warm touch of his hand. "Let's go in," he said, "and I'll teach *you* a thing or two."

They went into the cabin and to their bed. They made slow, sweet love, and Standingdeer slept, but Tiana lay staring into the darkness for hours, feeling his hand lying heavy at her waist like an accusation. He had opened his heart to her, he had trusted her with the deepest feelings he had, and she, as treacherous as Andrew Jackson, was still keeping from him the secret that would destroy them.

As the sun-washed days and the deepening nights flowed on, Tiana fought down her guilt and pretended that this summer moon would never end. But the moon grew smaller and smaller, until only a narrow, curving slice, like the sharp blade of a hay hook, showed over the tops of the mountains in the dark.

Stand began working Coosa harder, pushing him farther and faster each day. And Tiana's heart began to break.

One morning, early, when they went out to start working the horses, she said, "I'll give you Butterfly for the next few days and I'll take Coosa. I think he needs my lighter weight for a while; he's acting lame."

Stand stopped with his hand on the circle of rawhide that fastened the gate. He held it above the round, rough pole for an instant, then dropped it to one side. "No," he said shortly, "he isn't. And he'll have to carry more weight than yours in the race."

The word hovered in the misty air between them, spoken at last for the first time since the storm.

A terrible pain tore into Tiana's stomach; she thought she would be sick. Her lips went stiff, but she managed to mutter, "So. You're still determined to take him to Georgia?"

"I am. I told you, I intend to win and buy land that no one can take away from me."

"Land a thousand miles away!" she cried, appalled by the pain in her voice, but powerless to conceal it. "You'll leave me, Standingdeer!"

He whipped his head around to look at her. "Not if you'll come with me."

He waited, but she didn't, she couldn't, answer.

"Come with me, Tiana," he said at last, and his voice was so rough and his gaze so hot that she could see what it cost him to say it again. "I never thought I'd ever say that to another woman, ever, but I'm asking you."

His battle-scarred heart couldn't quite let him say, *I love you*. Not yet. He would say it, he would shout it from the tops of the smoky blue mountains if she would agree to go with him.

He watched her face, wishing he could reach out and touch her softly curving cheek. But he couldn't lift a finger, couldn't take a step, couldn't have run if a mountain lion had attacked. His whole life, his entire being, teetered on the edge of an abyss, while he prayed to Thunder to be saved from falling by the words she would speak.

Tiana clutched the lead rope she held until the rough hemp burned her hands. All she had to do was say *yes!* She might even talk Stand into leaving from here, right now, and going away where Bluford could never find them. She might live with her beloved Standingdeer for the rest of her life without his ever knowing that she had killed Tobacco Jack!

Her love for him, her wanting, her *need* for him flowed through her, washing away her strength like silt from the bottom of a river. Yet there was one big rock left, right in the middle of her leaping, pounding, stupidly hopeful heart. *She* would know.

She could not live with The Paint under a lie.

He was too honest and she loved him too much ever to trick him like that.

"I can't leave my home, my Nation," she said, holding his gaze, although she would have given her life at that instant not to have to see the hope disappear from his eyes.

But she made herself watch it die, smothered by inches by the pain that gradually crept in to kill it. Her stomach clutched in upon itself, and she wanted to bend over and be sick on the floor of the shed.

Dear Standingdeer. Every woman in his life had broken his heart over a secret, and now she was doing it, too.

His eyes turned cold as spear points boring into hers. "I'm certainly not staying here to watch the Nation crumble."

"Well, I am!" she cried, willing herself to keep looking into his eyes so that he would believe her. "I mean, I'm going to stop the *yonegas*. It wouldn't crumble if you and all the other so-called warriors would stay here and ... if you would ..."

"Hold it together with my bare hands?" he drawled sardonically. "Throw my body as a human sacrifice at the guns of the Georgia Guard?"

She grabbed the gate from his hand and pushed past him, running to Coosa, lifting his halter and slipping it onto his head in a blue haze of tears. "Then go on and leave now!" she yelled through porcelain-thin lips that threatened to break in her face. "Traitor! Remember Chief Doublehead, who ceded territory without permission of the people? Giving up our land is punished by death!"

She threw herself at the stallion, calling for him to move before she even landed on his back, riding for the gate as if she would run Standingdeer down.

He watched her gallop off the hillside with eyes that stung with scalding tears.

Traitor! Punished by death! He would gladly die a dozen deaths if that would hold back the stampeding herd of whites from the Center of the Earth.

He turned away and slammed the gatepost with

his fist. *If it would make Tiana love him as much as she loved this mountain land.*

The next morning Tiana walked out of the cabin into the early, fragrant coolness, crossing the porch without seeing its boards beneath her feet. Her eyes didn't work anymore. All night they wouldn't sleep and now today they wouldn't see. The only thing to be thankful for was that they didn't weep, on top of everything else.

No. There was one other thing. The Paint had slept away from her. She had started learning to do without him.

She moved slowly to the edge of the porch and lifted her leaden arms to wrap them around one of its posts. She laid her cheek against it.

After a moment or two, the sounds of movement drifted to her, feet brushing through the high grass, it seemed. She turned toward the horse pen to look.

The Paint was coming through the gate, leading Coosa out into the clearing. The sight stiffened her back and set her blood coursing like a slap to the face.

He might leave and go to Dahlonega, and to the West, but by the Thunderers, she would keep Coosa here.

"Leave him be today!" she called wildly. "He's acting half lame—he needs to rest!"

Her voice rang through the valley, echoing off the mountains nearby with its strange, nervous intonation intact. The stallion threw up his head and flared his nostrils to find her; then, with The Paint whirling to face him and hold onto his rope, Coosa reared, rising up and up into the morning mist, it seemed almost to the sky.

Standingdeer slid straddle-legged to the end of the lead, bulging muscles standing up along the tops of his bare shoulders and working in his back and arms. He got to one side and began trying to calm the horse.

The sight snatched Tiana's breath. Sweat broke out on the palms of her hands. She remembered exactly how those muscles felt to the touch: smooth as calm water on the surface, hard as living granite cliffs underneath.

His feet slipped a bit wider apart on the dew-laden grass, reaching into it to try and find purchase against the ground, working the saddle muscles that ran, long and lean, in the backs of his thighs beneath his tight-fitting breeches. He gathered the rope and brought it down with a jerk of the halter across Coosa's nose.

The stallion threw up his head, high, still higher toward the sky, and whinnied. The sound rang through the woods, clattering through the trunks of the trees to float out over the valley, a call of challenge to the whole wilderness. It came back to them in an echo resounding off the wall of Chilowee Mountain.

A thrill raced through Tiana's blood.

Followed instantly by a fear so chilling that she couldn't swallow.

For right behind the echo of Coosa's voice came a shout. *"Osiyo!"* someone called. "Hello this place!"

Tiana's hands stuck to the post she was holding. Her feet took root in the floor. All her instincts screamed for her to run to The Paint, but she was helpless to make the slightest stir, or to form a rational thought. Her mind jumped and scattered, throwing out names. Who could have found them? Bluford? Sykes? The shout had been too loud and rough, surely, for it to be in Walters' smooth voice.

Gray Fox? Maybe he, too, had remembered *Ulisi's* valley. Oh, pray God.

Standingdeer stepped away from Coosa to the very end of the lead; the horse dropped onto all four feet and circled him once, then stopped and pricked his ears in the direction Stand was looking, toward the creek.

A movement flashed behind the trees. Then the visitor appeared, out in the open, walking onto the narrow approach to the creek. Mist lay heavy over the water, but Tiana could discern a short figure wearing a dark red turban.

Rattling Gourd.

Relief took the strength from her knees. And then apprehension sent it flowing back through her in a pulsing stream. Before she knew she would move, she was down the steps, running past Stand and Coosa toward the shaman.

"*Osiyo*, Grandfather," she called. "Welcome."

She splashed into the creek to meet him. He crossed it slowly, punching his tall walking staff into the sand at its bottom with each step he took through the shallow ford. By the time he came out on the cabin side, Standingdeer and Coosa had joined them.

Tiana moved to put Rattling Gourd between her and The Paint, but he was already keeping to the opposite side of Coosa. They all walked together up the open slope.

"We are honored, Grandfather," Tiana said. "This is Standingdeer Chekote, The Paint."

Rattling Gourd stopped and turned his head to one side, eyeing Stand like an interested bird.

Stand inclined his head. "We have met," he said.

Rattling Gourd grunted. "I know this one. I scratched him for ball play and for battle when he was but a boy."

"A long time ago," Stand said.

"A long time ago," the old man answered.

He looked at Tiana. "Child, I would sit."

"Come into the house," she said.

"No. I have farther to go, and soon."

While she ran to the porch to bring a stool, Stand and the shaman walked to a black locust tree. Once she had returned and Rattling Gourd had sat, she sat and The Paint squatted on the grass at his feet. Coosa grazed, upslope a little, his shiny hide now and again catching the sunlight as it struggled through the fog.

Rattling Gourd let out a long breath and laid his staff down, carefully, onto the ground. His face sagged into an even deeper patchwork of wrinkles; suddenly he looked a hundred years old and entirely exhausted.

"Do you need water?" Tiana asked. "Let me bring you food and drink."

He waved the suggestion away.

"Later," he said. "When we have spoken."

He looked at The Paint and then at her.

"It is good that you are here," he said to her. "Forgive my rudeness, but I must immediately say why I have come. My medicine for you has been turned back."

The apprehension she had felt on the porch returned in a rush, multiplied a thousandfold.

"Turned back?" she whispered. Even through her dread she could feel Stand's questioning eyes upon her.

"Yes," the shaman said, and his kind voice shook a little. "The black bead was much more lively than the red. And then, in sleep, a vision came to me. Death stalks the accomplishment of your desires. Death begets death."

He closed his eyes. "I have tried; I cannot see whose."

Tiana couldn't swallow. Her throat had turned to paper.

It was fear making her light-headed, making her dizzy in this cool early morning, as if she'd been too long in the midday heat. But also it was guilt. Was she to cause *another* death?

"What are you talking about?" Stand asked, so harshly that the old man turned to stare.

"She can tell you if she cares to," he said, just as sharply. "I won't linger long. A stomp ground has called me for tonight."

"Where?" Tiana whispered, suddenly panicked at the thought of his leaving.

But what good would it do for him to stay? He couldn't even tell who would die, much less prevent it.

"One ridge away on the side of *Tsuwa'tel'da*," he said, nodding at the mountain opposite Chilowee. "A dance to pray for the Principal People to keep the Center of the Earth."

"But this . . . death! When will . . ."

"I cannot see," Rattling Gourd said, his voice heavy with frustration. "It is stalking now. When it will strike . . . or whom . . . I cannot see."

He placed both hands, palms down, on his knees. "Now I will eat," he said. "And drink. Then I will go."

Tiana didn't remember getting up or starting to walk, but halfway up the sloping grass between Rattling Gourd and the cabin, Stand caught her shoulder and turned her around.

"What the *hell* is he talking about?" he demanded. "What medicine?"

She jerked away. "I told him about the pony club. I asked him to stop Bluford so there wouldn't be killings over his thefts. I couldn't wait for Papa to come back."

"When did you do this?"

"On my way here."

His piercing eyes fixed her where she stood.

"You might have mentioned that to me."

"Why? What difference would it have made?"

"Is that the only reason you rode two days out of your way to go to Rattling Gourd's place?"

She hesitated. That look came into her eyes: the look that made him want to tear trees up by their roots and rip the granite cliffs off the mountains. The look that told him as loudly as if she'd shouted the words that she was hiding something.

"Yes. I . . . told him my life was in danger from them. I asked him to make medicine to protect me."

He stared at her through narrowed eyes.

She lifted her chin and met his gaze without wavering until he turned away and strode back to the old shaman.

Rattling Gourd drank the cold water and ate the last of the mulberries Tiana had stewed the day before. When he had finished, he handed the bowl back to her and drew out a large purple handkerchief to wipe his mouth. That done, he stood up abruptly.

"I have failed," he said, "but I try again. Until the red bead becomes more lively, take care, Little Sister."

He turned to Stand. "Take care, He-Who-Is-Called-The Paint. The death I see is that of a man."

With those words he began to walk with a rhythmic thumping of his staff, straight into the woods toward *Tsuwa'tel'da*, ignoring the fact that there was no path. Stunned by his last remark, Tiana watched him go without saying good-bye.

Grandmother Sun was driving away the mist in earnest now. The leaves on the trees floated, shimmering, among the beams of sunlight that shot through the still air like shafts of golden arrows.

She turned to Stand.

"What if it's you?" she whispered. Could it be, somehow, that Tobacco Jack's death would lead to that of The Paint? What had she done, that horrible long-ago day when she'd tried to save Fawn?

"What are you *talking* about?"

"The man. The one who will . . . die! What if it's you?"

Her beautiful dark eyes glistened with tears. She truly was frantic about him. Yet she didn't love him as much as she loved these mountains, as much as she loved a home she didn't even have in her possession anymore.

For one bright, flashing moment, he hated her with all the heart in his body. Almost as much as he loved her.

"He doesn't *know* somebody will die!" he snapped. "I'm surprised he didn't say it would happen within the next seven years. That's the way the Curers-of-Them usually protect their reputations when they make a prophecy."

His scornful tone made her furious. And even more fearful. She could not *live* if The Paint were dead.

Oh, *why* had she ever asked for this medicine in the first place? All this was on her head.

But giving way to the hysteria crowding into her throat and onto her tongue would not be the way to convince him to be careful. She knew him well enough for that.

So she fought for sensible words and a calm tone.

"Don't go to Dahlonega," she said. "You'd be safer here."

He made a gesture of disgust and glanced around to see where Coosa had wandered in his grazing. "We're going."

He turned on his heel and went to pick up Coosa's dragging lead rope.

In a strange, tight voice, Tiana said to his back, "It's dangerous in Dahlonega. We've known that from the start—that's the reason I never entered Coosa in that race. This warning from Rattling Gourd is a sign that I was right!"

"This warning is a sign that Rattling Gourd doesn't know how to stop Bluford and his bunch without causing a big uproar any more than you do," Stand said. "Reconcile yourself to it: we're going to run this horse in that race."

He led Coosa toward the shed to saddle him for his morning workout. Tiana set her jaw and followed.

"You don't have full control of him," she said. "I still own half, remember?"

"Not quite," he said over his shoulder. "Gray Fox is another one who'll be waiting for us at the track. If he's survived all these weeks in dangerous Dahlonega," he added scornfully. "He'll vote to run him."

Tiana ran ahead and snatched their only saddle and bridle from the racks in the shed. "I'll ride him this minute," she said, gritting her teeth against the fury and frustration she wanted to yell out into the mountains. "And you'll see he isn't ready to run, and he won't be two days from now, either!"

"You'll make him *look* not ready," Stand said, leaning back against one of the poles to watch her saddle Coosa. "But I don't care if you hold him to a walk: he's going to the Stakes."

Tiana jerked the cinch tighter and fastened its buckle. Then she clutched the sides of the strap and checked it one last time.

"So you want to get killed, is that what you're saying?"

"What I'm saying is that you're making yourself miserable listening to a bunch of superstitious nonsense. I thought you were braver than that."

She whirled on him. "I am! It is not superstition. I'm just trying to save your life, Standingdeer, and you're such a stubborn mule, I have no idea why!"

He gave a bitter laugh. "Whatever murky vision Rattling Gourd saw is the least threat we face. Every renegade in Georgia wants this horse, you know that."

"So! You see!" she cried. "You *admit* it's dangerous! All the more reason we should stay here."

"We can't stay here forever," he said.

Just like that. With not the least sign of regret. Nor of any other feeling at all. All the days that had once been magic for her meant nothing to him just because she had refused to go West with him.

Well, she could forget them, too!

She touched her heels to Coosa, bent over his neck, and rode him out of the shed. "Don't bother to time him!" she called. "Leave us alone!"

Grandmother Sun settled into her gray-white lair and remained in hiding the rest of the day while the air grew more sultry and close.

Stand and Tiana both stayed near the cabin, as if expecting another storm. The late afternoon of this day was almost as still as that time during the night just before the tornado had hit the valley.

The tension vibrating between them, though, was anything but still. They had argued ever since she returned, every time they spoke to each other, even about the simplest of chores.

"You needn't feel you have to hang around here," she snapped at him over her shoulder. He was sitting on the porch, watching through the open doorway while she cooked greens and wild onions. "I have sense enough to go to the cave if another dancing devil comes."

"Oh, I don't know," he drawled. "I had to carry you there the last time."

She whirled around to face him, the long wooden stirring spoon in her hand. Infuriating, overbearing tyrant! She ought to march right out there and hit him with the spoon.

He cocked one arching black brow. "Besides, what makes you think I'm here to take care of you?"

Tiana felt her cheeks flame hot. Arrogant, insulting turncoat that he was!

"You must be," she retorted, trying not to show her chagrin. "Why else have you been watching me all afternoon like an owl with a mouse?"

He grinned crookedly and gave a little nod, as if to say he appreciated her quick wit.

That fanned the flames of her anger into a blaze.

"You're just waiting to ambush me, that's what!" she cried. "If we run your stupid race, we must leave in the morning, so this evening you're lurking at my back, trying to figure out how to convince me to go!"

His grin broadened, but it didn't touch his dark eyes. "There's no 'convincing' to it," he said flatly. "You're going, I'm going, the horses are going."

"If I refuse, what're you planning to do? Tie me to my mount, kicking and screaming?"

He shrugged. "I wouldn't bother with that. No, if you're *that* determined to stay, I'll leave you here and take Coosa myself."

"You wouldn't dare steal him!"

"Why not? You did."

"I did not!" she said, crossing the room to the door.

"You did. And I wouldn't be. If I have to take him myself, at least you'll know where he is."

The Paint's words rang hard, like iron on an anvil. He meant that. The realization sent fear flowing through her, cold as a mountain waterfall.

"All right," she said bitterly, "I'll go. And I'll ride him—to keep you or anybody else off his back."

He favored her with a short, haughty nod that brought her blood to boiling. "Good."

She stalked out onto the porch, holding her spoon like a weapon. "Since you're being so open and honorable with me," she said sarcastically, "I feel obliged to warn you that I may deliberately lose the race. It would serve you right."

He chuckled, but the sound held no humor. There was something about it that gave her scared goose bumps.

"Losing's the last thing I'm worried about," he said. "You're too proud of both your reputations, yours and Coosa's, to ever deliberately lose a horse race."

Then he grew completely solemn and gave her a look that went through her all the way to her bones. "That's the *one* thing I do know about you, Tiana."

She stared at him for as long as she could, then she burst out, "Oh, go away and leave me alone! Cook your own supper!"

"Not tonight," he drawled, to her dismay, his gaze still fastened on her face. "Since we've agreed that this is our last night here, I'll help you use up the leftovers."

He stayed where he was while she finished cooking the meal and put it on the table; then he came in to eat. Tiana sat in silence, keeping her eyes on her plate, pretending to be hungry, trying to pretend that he wasn't there.

During the meal, clouds gathered on the mountains until they had wiped both Chilowee and

Tsuwa'tel'da out of existence, and then they began filling the valleys. They were low and blue and full of rain, but still they didn't turn it loose.

After a lifetime, no, two lifetimes, Tiana thought, the day slithered into evening. And the sound of the drums began.

"They'd do as well to save their energy," Stand growled, pushing his chair back from the table and stalking across to the dishpan with his plate and cup. "Or use it to try to bring back Grandmother Sun to shine all night."

"Don't *say* that! It isn't true!"

"It's true."

Instead of going outside to sit on the porch, as their ritual was, he walked stiffly to the hearth and dropped down, cross-legged, in front of the fire. Tiana put her full attention to the dishes and tried to ignore the fact that he was still there. She gritted her teeth as she scrubbed the tin plates with sand.

Why didn't he leave, get away from her?

A steady pattering against the window glass proclaimed that the rain had begun. For a long time no one spoke except for the fire, The Ancient One, popping and crackling in its bed.

The sound of the rain deepened. It beat slow and sure, like the drums across the ridge. Good. Perhaps the creek would be too high to cross tomorrow.

No, that wouldn't be good. She'd be trapped here with The Paint, probably blurting out her secret just to get rid of this awful feeling of pressure.

But oh, dear Lord, what if they left here and somebody killed him?

"They're out there in the rain, dancing and drumming," Stand said suddenly. "It's hard to believe."

"It's *because* they believe!" Tiana cried, turning

to cross the room toward him. "That dancing's the same as Papa's negotiations: both together will get the Removal Act repealed."

"Both together will do as much good as stomping on one grasshopper when there's a cloud of them blacking out the sun. There's a cloud of settlers hovering over us."

She lifted her chin and straightened her back, although she wanted to sink tiredly down in a heap. It was too much to think about on top of all her other troubles. Too much to face, this worry that was forever scratching at her insides like a raccoon in a cage.

"That act is unjust and sinful, and the good men in Congress won't let it continue to be law!" she exclaimed in desperation, grasping for hope.

"Forget the good men in Congress," Stand ordered harshly. "Who's the President of the United States, Tiana?"

"Andrew Jackson."

"The same Andrew Jackson who let us swim the Tallapoosa for him to steal the Creeks' canoes, who let us fight and bleed and die and defeat the Red Sticks for him at Horseshoe Bend with the understanding that we could keep our land forever?"

"Yes," she admitted.

"Tiana, that same Andrew Jackson, at the close of that war, suggested that while the United States troops were still on the field, they might as well go ahead and force the cession of all our Tennessee lands."

"He's just the President, not the King."

"Whatever his title, he has most of his people behind him. Every landless white man and every greedy soul who dreams of gold is with him, and they are going to win. The sooner you can make yourself face that fact, the better off you will be."

"It is *not* a fact!"

"It is," he grated. "As you well know, lots of things can be kept secret, but that isn't one of them."

"You *let* Andrew Jackson run you off!" she taunted, wild with anger that he could say such a thing, but wilder yet with grief that if what he was saying was true, her home, Running Waters, and her life with her family and the Nation would never be the same.

"You let him run you out of your own home," she cried. "And now you're doing it again. You'll risk your life to try and win a race so you can go West, but you won't risk it to try and save your Nation!"

He stared at her while the rain beat down above them, the fire in his eyes burning steady as coal. Relentlessly, from far away, came the sound of the drums.

Finally he said, "If you were a man, I'd take your scalp for that remark."

In one liquid motion, without touching the floor with his hands, he rose to his feet.

"Get to sleep, Tiana. We have a long ride tomorrow."

He left her, closing the door behind him. Tiana walked slowly toward the hearth and dropped down to sit where he had been, but even the leaping fire couldn't drive off the chill from her skin.

Chapter 17

Morning Red found Tiana awake. She must have slept, surely she had slept, but she couldn't remember it. All she could remember was staring into the black night overhead, her head spinning with the comings and goings of the stars from behind the moving clouds. And with Stand.

The night before they had left the cabin had been misery, sitting in front of the fire all night long, finally falling asleep on the floor with her head on her arm, but never feeling warm. She would never feel warm again.

Traveling with him was a misery, too.

The sky streaked slowly, a tattered scrap of ribbon at a time—one of pink, a torn bit of mauve, a thread of rose, then another of red. In the next instant the colors spread and grew, reaching out for one another, swelling from ribbons to banners—great swaths of crimson lit from within. They destroyed the blackness. Grandmother Sun struck fire.

This was the day. All the rest of her life would be set on its course by what happened today. If Bluford was waiting for her to show up in Dahlonega for the race, it would be only a matter of hours until Standingdeer knew.

As if he could hear her thoughts, she glanced

over her shoulder at the place across their woodsy campsite where he'd been keeping watch when she finally fell asleep. His bedroll lay there, still tied.

He was gone.

She turned to look for the horses. Through the light fog floating in the low place around the rope corral, she could see only Butterfly, Tannassy, and Hiwassee. No Coosa.

A sickening fear filled her. Had Walters and Sykes or another enemy come in the night? Could they have taken the horse and ... killed or kidnapped Stand without her knowing?

Had Rattling Gourd's prophecy already been fulfilled?

She stepped off her blanket and ran into the dew-wet grass. It soaked her bare feet in an instant, but she hardly noticed the cold water washing her skin. The fear in her stomach blotted out everything else. It made her dizzy, made her stop and look frantically around, unsure of exactly which clump of trees separated her from the small meadow they'd ridden through the evening before.

There! On the other side of that line of ashes and poplars, she was almost certain.

Running again, her breath coming short and fast, she reached those trees and passed halfway through them.

Yes! There was the open grass of the meadow and there, on the far side, was some movement.

It was Standingdeer, thank God, astride Coosa, circling the open area at a slow lope.

Her heart began to beat again. She reached for the nearest tree trunk, wrapped her arms around it, and leaned her cheek against the rough, peeling bark until all her breath came back.

The Paint had certainly taken Coosa out early; it

hadn't been light enough to see for very long. He was anxious to start this day. And to win.

So he could go West. Without her.

Bitter sadness, cruel hopelessness, rose in her throat. She watched Stand's perfect seat, the golden buckskin of his leggings never moving from one spot on Coosa's silver back, the square line of his broad shoulders holding as still as the air of the early morning.

Tiana ran the palms of her hands up and down the rough trunk of the tree. It didn't help. She remembered sliding them over the muscles of those powerful shoulders, and yearned for them to feel him again.

When Coosa had cantered to the far side of the meadow, she tore her gaze away and ran back to her bedroll. She sat down and pulled on her moccasins, silently making a vow. She would get ready for the day, too, just as coolly as Standing-deer had done.

Jerking up her makeshift traveling bag and feeling around in it for her comb and a bit of leather, she told herself to take one moment at a time. She would go to the creek to wash and tie back her hair for the race. She would go to the water.

To face the east, the direction of bravery and power, to formally greet Grandmother Sun.

She clutched the bag to her and hurried toward the creek. Once she was done there, she would take Coosa from Stand and ride him around a few times herself to learn his mood for this race. She was already dressed for it; she had slept in the set of Papa's old clothes she would ride in.

Coosa had no saddle, no bridle, no bit. At the track she would have to borrow those things for him if she could find a horseman she knew. There was bound to be someone—she seemed to remember that Mr. Danforth from Augusta had entered his mare in the race.

From now on, all day long, she would think of such details as that. She would think of nothing but Coosa and the race. *Nothing* else.

She took a deep breath. The mountains smelled fresh in the early morning, yet, at the same time, very old. They had seen everything, they had seen many days as fateful as this one would be. They were still there, still the same. Everything would be all right.

A dozen early-morning birds chittered that it was so. One of them, a wren, began a fine song of affirmation.

The sunlight caught, pink and shining, on every leaf of every tree along the creek bank. Tiana darted beneath them, hearing their whisperings below the music of the birds as she headed toward a wide opening between two clumps of maples where the bank sloped down to the water. It shimmered, too, like the leaves.

She took off the clothes she was wearing and walked out slowly, because the rocks hurt her feet, to stand waist-deep in the creek. She stooped to fill her hands with the cold water of Caney Creek, dashed it onto her face and looked for sand to scrub away yesterday's sweat. There was none. This creek was more narrow and deep than the one that flowed by the cabin; its bed was covered with small rocks and sharp stones.

When she felt as clean as she could make herself, she turned her face to the east and held up her arms, letting the red sunlight bathe her in bravery and victory. Then she climbed out and got dressed.

After her breeches and shirt she pulled on the moccasins, which she liked best to ride in, braided her hair, damp on the ends from trailing in the water, and tied it close to her neck with the leather thong from her bag. She put on her hat and leaned out to look at her crooked reflection in the water.

Good. The renegades in Dahlonega would take her for a boy. If only she could disguise Coosa as well!

She picked up her bag and slipped it over her shoulder. She would go back to camp, unwrap the last of their rations, force herself to eat because she had to have her strength, and then take The Coosa from Stand. It was time to begin to meld herself with the horse again, to become one with him for this day.

It was time to forget Standingdeer Chekote.

When Tiana began to walk up the sloping bank between the maples, she caught sight of movement on the other side of the low-hanging, tangled branches. Not a small animal, but something large.

Tiana stood still and squinted against the light.

Had Stand ridden Coosa down from the meadow to see her? Perhaps to talk to her?

The shadow moved again and separated itself from a body. The body of a man on a horse. But not Coosa.

Bay Boy. And Bluford!

She couldn't think of what to do.

Bluford rode toward her, fast. He stopped on top of the bank, directly in front of her.

"Miss Tiana," he said, his voice so strained that it trembled, "I want you to know how much I hate to do this."

His hands twitched; one held the reins, and the other touched his belt because of the way his arm was bent by his side.

"Do . . . what?"

"I have to kill you," he said, and the bent arm jerked, then plunged into the front of his wide,

woven sash. "So Papa's spirit can go to the
Nightland and stop haunting me."

He plucked out a pistol and pointed its muzzle
straight at Tiana's heart.

Behind her, the creek burbled on, chattering
among the rocks.

A hawk cried down at her from somewhere
high overhead.

Tiana wanted to scream for help. Didn't *anything*
care? Didn't anybody see that this man was about
to shoot her?

"I hate to do it, Tiana."

She couldn't speak, she couldn't even part her
lips.

Never would she have imagined that she would
die here on a creek bank so close to the border
with Georgia. At least they hadn't crossed over yet
and she would die on the soil of the Nation.

She forced her gaze to move up, to search his
face.

His bloodshot eyes showed even more sad pain
than usual.

A wild, quick hope flashed through her, shatter-
ing the ice that had frozen her lips.

"Bluford, I did kill Tobacco Jack," she said, trying to put enough regretful sympathy into her
tone to cover her fear. "But I didn't mean to—I
only wanted him to stop beating on Fawn. It was
an accident, Bluford."

"But Papa's dead, just the same," he answered
gloomily. "And his spirit won't leave me alone until I kill you."

Her hope died as fast as it had been born. She
swallowed hard and tried to think.

"Accidental killings don't fall under the blood
law anymore, Bluford, remember?" she blurted,
just for the sake of knowing she had tried. Like
many full-bloods, the Tuskees had always been

bound far more strongly by traditional law than by more recent rulings of the council.

She swallowed hard and went on. "Not for a long time now—wasn't it 1797 when the People decided that such killings shouldn't be punished?"

"No!" Suddenly his face flushed dark and he was shouting. "No! I *must* be free of his spirit! The ancient law prevails!"

His hand began to twitch again. His finger touched the trigger. He would shoot her any minute, so it didn't matter what she said.

"Your papa's probably haunting you because he's so *ashamed!*" Tiana shouted back at him. "Think of it: his only son a horse thief and a betrayer of his own people!"

The pointing muzzle grew steadier and steadier. She couldn't outrun its bullet if she tried, so she held her ground.

"The only way you'll ever be free of his spirit, Bluford Tuskee, is to disband that pony club of yours and turn yourself in to the law so you can take your punishment! *Then* Tobacco Jack can go to the Nightland."

Bluford flinched, then sat very still, relentlessly careful to hold the gun in exactly the same position.

Into the silence that fell, the musical voice of the wren trilled louder and closer. It must have followed her.

Go and bring The Paint to me. Go, little bird friend, and bring The Paint.

But what would The Paint do then? He'd help Bluford kill her.

Find the eagle, Sister Bird. Find the eagle to save me. Or fly into Bluford's face and distract him so I can get the gun.

Tiana longed to turn to look for the bird, to look at anything except the round black hole in the end of Bluford's gun, but not one muscle in her body would work.

As suddenly as he had produced the pistol from his belt, Bluford shoved it back in. He slumped in his saddle.

"You may speak truth," he said. "Sometimes Papa rides, frowning, beside me on the raids. I can feel him."

Hoofbeats pounded beyond the line of trees. Bluford snatched out the pistol again and whirled Bay Boy toward the sound.

Stand, his beautiful face and burning eyes set on his cousin, burst into sight astride Coosa. Bluford put the gun away.

For an instant, Tiana's heart sang, for Stand had obviously come to save her. But then she remembered. Bluford would tell Stand. In another minute, he would tell Stand that she had killed his uncle.

Coosa thundered up to Bay Boy and stopped. "Cousin, what're you doing here?" Stand demanded. His gaze flicked to Bluford's gun.

Tiana closed her eyes. She couldn't bear to see his face when Bluford told him; she could not.

But Bluford's words made her eyes fly open again. He said, "Cousin! I've come to warn you."

"About what? Spit it out, man!"

"Sykes and Walters, they're planning to steal Coosa and race him today themselves."

For one long heartbeat, Tiana's ears couldn't take in the words. She fastened her gaze on Bluford's face as if watching his lips would help her understand. Wasn't he going to tell Stand she was a killer?

What was he talking about?

"They've got a forged bill of sale written up," Bluford's voice went on. "They think that's a fine joke, since you couldn't testify against a white man in a Georgia court anyhow."

The Paint growled, "They'll need more than a piece of paper . . ."

"They've *got* more: a half hour's ride from here they can call on all the rascals in Dahlonega and the whole state of Georgia besides," Bluford said. "Your only chance is to hide the stallion until right before the race."

"He's hidden now. We aren't going in until later this morning."

"Listen to me and go!" Bluford cried, reaching across to push at Standingdeer's arm. "They're coming now! Hide the stallion; I'll bring Tiana and follow."

"You think I'd trust a horse thief with Tiana's safety?"

Her heart twisted in her body. The Paint still cared for her, even after she'd refused him.

Bluford wilted in his saddle again. He ducked his head and stared at the neck of his horse for a moment, then raised his gaze and dragged it to meet Stand's.

"I admit I've been involved with the pony club," he said, "but only because Papa never let me boss anything. You know that's true, Stand. *You* were the one he trusted."

"Forget all that nonsense. You're a grown man now!"

Bluford's hand twitched. "I know—I'm master of Pine Grove. After that, I didn't need the club anymore, but I couldn't stop what I'd started."

"The hell you couldn't!"

"I tried! I tell you, I tried!" Bluford yelled.

"You didn't try hard enough," Stand said. "You've disgraced our family's name, our kin, and our clan."

Bluford's face, lined by misery, flushed dark

with shame. He ducked his head again and stared
at his horse's mane.

"When this gets out," Standingdeer said, "*none*
of us will be able to hold up our heads. I'm glad
I'm going West."

Bluford lifted his head then and slowly, pain-
fully, brought his eyes up to meet Stand's. He
squared his slumping shoulders.

"I may be remembered as a horse thief," he said
in an eerie, low tone, "but I won't have it said I
was a party to murdering my own kin. Just now I
was trying to send you into a trap, Cousin, by telling you to go hide the horse."

"What!" Stand stared at him long enough to see
that he truly had meant this last thing he'd said.
Then The Paint swung Coosa around and rode toward the woods, looking from side to side, his
own pistol drawn, trying to see into the trees.

Tiana's whole body strained after him. He was
getting farther and farther away from her.

"No! Don't go!" Bluford screamed at last. "You
can't hide. I tell you, Cousin, I was lying. It's a
trap!"

A gunshot cracked.

Bluford's Bay Boy gave a long, screeching
whinny and reared.

Instinctively, Tiana jumped back to get out of his
way, trying to keep her eyes on Coosa and Stand,
who now looked to be as far away from her as the
sun. Yet her mind rushed frantically back to
Bluford and to the cracking sound that came again
from inside the grove of maples.

Then all her consciousness settled on one thing.
Directly in front of her, slowly, like a shock of oats
falling off a wagon, Bluford came out of his saddle. He twisted loosely in the air and, arms up-
raised, dived forward to fall to the ground at
Tiana's feet.

His cheek plowed into the muddy earth as if he were giving it a kiss; his arms flopped onto it in a grotesque hug. Then he lay completely still.

Blood poured from his back, but nothing else about him moved at all.

"Shoot the Indian, get the stud!" a familiar smooth voice called from the maples on Tiana's left, and an answering high-pitched, raucous yell echoed from the right.

"First I'm gittin' the girl!"

She tore her eyes from Bluford to look. Walters, mounted on his tall gelding, was riding fast out of the trees, holding a gun and pointing it at Stand.

Her heart stopped. Oh, dear Lord, she had escaped Bluford's gun only to see The Paint shot by Walters! No! This could not be.

She stood stunned, although she was aware of Sykes pounding toward her from the right. Walters and Standingdeer fired, but missed, with both horses moving so fast. Walters angled farther away from The Paint. Who was heading toward her. To protect her.

Tiana watched him come, her eyes blurring with tears, powerless to move until Sykes was upon her.

She turned then and tried to run into the creek, but after only a short distance he snatched her off the ground. She kicked and struggled as he dragged her up and across his saddle, but he held her helpless, facedown, pushing the heel of his hand into her back with the force of a boulder crushing the breath from a bird. The saddle horn dug into her breastbone; the ground moved beneath her eyes.

Sykes stopped his horse in the open area between the lines of maples. He jammed his hand into her hair and jerked the top half of her body up, twisting her back, wrenching all of her body out of line in the iron trap of his hands. She couldn't turn her head, but she could breathe now. And she could see The Paint. He was sliding Coosa to a stop, facing them, but too far away. Too horribly far away.

And he had no gun.

"Looky here, Big Warrior," Sykes shouted. "Look who's got yore woman now."

From the corner of her eye she glimpsed Walters riding out of the woods, where no doubt he had run to hide from The Paint. Then she saw nothing but Sykes' ugly face as he pulled her head higher and leaned over her. His foul breath whistled against her cheek and froze the blood in her veins.

Stand's body flooded hot with the quick desire to kill. He squeezed Coosa as a signal to charge at them, but, just as quickly, he loosened his legs and rescinded the order. Coosa backed and threw his head in protest.

The Paint's own heart, too, screamed for him to go ahead. But Walters could drop him before he got halfway to Tiana, and without him she didn't have a chance. Why the *hell* had he thrown the pistol away when it misfired? He might at least have been able to run some sort of bluff with it!

He watched as Tiana struggled helplessly, and suddenly the world went blindingly bright before his eyes.

He had to save her. He had to have her for his to keep.

The thought came over him like night swallowing the prairie. *He loved her so much he would fight this land for her. These stupid* yonegas *were nothing compared to that enemy.*

"You won't have her for long," he yelled back at Sykes, letting Coosa edge forward, looking at Walters from the corner of his eye, judging the distance to his gun. "And as soon as she's free, you're a dead man."

The weakness of having only words to use for a weapon sent bitter gall rising into his throat. If he'd had a good pistol, he could've emptied it into both of them before they could've blinked.

Sykes. He especially wanted Sykes. He hadn't felt this way since the Battle of Horseshoe Bend.

"Think again," Sykes called, and the hateful words echoed twice from a bluff somewhere across the creek. "I been waitin' might' near two whole moons, as you greasy Injuns say, to git my hands on this little squaw. I aim to keep her till I'm done with her!"

He meant it. His arm around her tightened until the breath left her again. She wasn't getting any air at all.

With an instinct older than her mind, Tiana lifted her leg over Sykes' and angled her body sideways to kick at his horse's flanks. The gelding went crazy.

Sykes held onto her through the first two jumps, but when the horse flung himself sideways, her body came free. She hit the ground and rolled downhill toward the creek, choking and gasping for breath.

A shot cracked, then another and another. The Paint shouted—oh, dear God, was he hit?—and Sykes' horse bucked over her, his hooves sucking mud on the soft bank, their glinting shoes missing her head only by inches. The instant he was gone, she scrambled to her feet, looking for a rock, a stick, anything to use to defend herself against Sykes.

She grabbed a fist-sized stone from the edge of the creek and then, frantic, looked around for the scoundrel. He lay on his back a short distance away, his mouth and eyes wide open, trying to suck in air. His fall had knocked the breath out of him.

He looked helpless, almost as if he were dead.

The rock in her hand grew heavier and heavier as the awful memories of Tobacco Jack came flooding through her head. Could she carry another death on her conscience?

But she had to do something. More shouts sounded from above her on the top of the bank, and one more shot. Stand might be in trouble. She couldn't let Sykes get up and help Walters.

Clamping her teeth against the fear and revulsion rising in her throat, she made her feet carry her to him. He was already beginning to stir, so without giving herself a chance to hesitate, she knelt beside him, jerked out the handkerchief protruding from his pocket, and began tying his hands together.

He gasped and moved them apart. Tiana fought to keep the fabric wrapped around them: she put her knee on his thigh and pulled the ends of the fabric together with all her might. But he still tugged loose and grabbed at her; she jumped away, but he caught her by the wrist.

She lurched backward, against his hold, got loose, and scrambled around in the mud, trying to get to her feet, trying to run. Sykes rolled over and snatched at her. He got her ankle.

She began to scream over and over again, "Stand! Standingdeer!"

Like magic he came, running down the bank on foot, his face set hard as granite. He reached them just as Sykes stood on his knees, Tiana's ankle in the air.

The Paint slid into him with a force that made the brigand turn loose of Tiana; he grabbed his shirt at the neck, dragged him to his feet as he himself got a footing and stood, and hit him in the

face with his fist, all in one motion. Sykes
dropped.

"Tiana! Are you all right?" Stand shouted.

"Yes," she said. And that took all the breath she
had. She lay on her back looking up at him, wishing he would pick her up and hold her in the remembered safety of his arms.

Instead, he bent, caught hold of Sykes' collar,
and, walking backward, started dragging him up
the bank.

His eyes went straight to her, though. Eyes of a
vengeful warrior, burning black as a Ravenmocker
streaking fire across the sky. Like that legendary
bird, those eyes said, he would tear the heart out
of the man in his hands.

"I thought that saddle horn would go right
through you," he said.

How could his voice be such a marvel of gentle-
ness when he had that look on his face?

"It didn't hurt me much."

"*Much*," he growled. "This son of a bitch'll find
out all about much hurting."

"What are you going to do?"

Stand didn't answer. He just kept dragging
Sykes toward the top of the bank.

Tiana got to her feet to follow them. She tried
again. "Where's Walters?"

"Up there, tied to his horse and a tree. I rammed
him into it with Coosa."

"What happened to your gun?"

"Jammed. So I threw it away."

They reached the top of the bank and Stand
dragged Sykes over to the maple where Walters
was waiting, almost comically entwined in one
of his bridle reins, which Stand had knotted
around his saddle horn. The other encircled the
tree and his body, being buffeted back and forth
with each motion of the nervous horse.

"Get me loose from here," Walters demanded.
"Take me to town to a doctor. I can feel blood on
my head from hitting the bark of the tree."

Stand glanced at his forehead. A small scraped
spot held a few drops of blood.

"Bluford bled a lot more than that," Stand said,
without any trace of emotion. "Tiana, would you
catch Sykes' horse and bring him here?"

She ran beneath the whispering maple leaves
into the deepening light of the sun to do as he
asked. The birds began chittering again. A light
breeze lifted from the south. The noisy wren flew
past Tiana and shouted one last message as she
disappeared into the woods. Behind the trees
loomed layer after layer of blue mountains. Tiana
could hardly believe she was still alive.

She caught the horse and led him back to Stand
and the *yonegas*. He took a knife from his boot, cut
the reins from Sykes' bridle, and, standing the
now-conscious, yet uncharacteristically silent, man
up against the trunk of one of the bigger maples,
lashed his hands together on the opposite side of
it and his entire body to the tree. He took Walters
from his horse and began to repeat the procedure.

"I assure you that all this effort is totally unnec-
essary," Walters said. "We need to be on the way
to town, instead, so that I can find a doctor."

"You need a shaman with a powerful medicine,"
Stand said. "A doctor can't help you."

"Why not? What are you going to do?"

The Paint took his knife from the waistband of
his pants and held its shining blade beneath Walters' nose.

"Did you ever hear the expression 'hair and
horses'?" he asked calmly. "A few years ago, when
I lived in this country, you hardly ever heard one
of those words without the other."

Tiana's blood stopped in her veins. He wouldn't.

He couldn't. Not the wonderfully gentle Standing-deer who had made sweet love to her.

But he held his knife very still and looked from one of his captives to the other, straight into their eyes.

Walters' pale face blanched even whiter. Sykes made a strangling noise deep in his throat.

Stand nodded. "That's right. I already have your horses."

"No!" Tiana cried. "I can't bear it! Stand, don't!"

"Go back to our camp," he ordered. "And wait for me."

His voice was cold as a frozen river. His hand never moved. His face was that of a stranger.

"They didn't really hurt me," she pleaded.

"Sykes laid his hands on you," he said. "That's enough reason for killing him right there. And Walters killed my cousin. My blood kin."

He sounded, and looked, as dangerous and implacable as the tornado had been.

"But the blood law's been rescinded!" she blurted. "We can turn them over to ..."

His eyes met hers. "To whom? How long do you think we'd last, two Cherokees armed with one rifle—assuming they didn't find it in our camp and throw it in the creek before we saw them—riding into Dahlonega with these *yonegas* tied to their horses?"

He was right. But oh, Lord, she couldn't bear to be responsible for, or even to know about, any more killings. Her mind whirled at a feverish pace.

"We can take them back to the Nation!" she said. "And try them there. It's only justice, Stand—think how many of our people have been put on trial in Georgia!"

He stared down into her earnest face. Her lips were slightly parted. Even in the midst of his cold fury, the taste of their warm sweetness sprang to his lips.

And he saw in her huge brown eyes that this agitation went deep in her; this dread of killing was shaking her to her bones.

He had to get her out of here, away from these scoundrels, away from Bluford's body. She had been through enough. The deaths of these worthless bastards shouldn't be added to the terrible memories she would always carry with her. She need never know what had happened to them.

"Go turn our other horses loose," he said, "so they can get to water. They won't wander far. Then we'll take Coosa to Dahlonega and find your brother to watch out for you. If he's not there, surely some horsemen we know will be there."

He put the knife back into his boot and tested all his knots and the strength of the leather reins one more time.

"I'll be back soon, boys," he said to his sweating captives. "Think about that while you're waiting."

Then, without looking back, while Tiana took down the rope corral, he went to the renegades' horses, stripped both them and Bay Boy of tack, and turned them loose.

When she returned she asked, "Shouldn't we take all the horses? And Bay Boy?"

"I'll get them when I come back," he said as he helped her onto the stallion's back. "I want Sykes and Walters taken care of fast, so it won't be long."

He vaulted up behind her, sliding close to fit his body to hers, and for the first time in what seemed an eternity, she felt safe. The Paint's arms were around her.

He took the reins and turned Coosa's head to the south, toward Dahlonega. He asked him for a fast trot and headed him straight at the creek. The horse changed to a lope, then to an in-hand gallop.

"It'd take too long to go around," The Paint called out. "We'll jump the creek!"

Then Tiana grabbed the mane with both hands and held on. It was too far! Coosa couldn't make it to the other side!

And in between was nothing but a hock-deep layer of rocks and stones!

She gritted her teeth. Coosa, her darling, would break his fleet legs and would have to be shot. She could not live through it.

So she clamped her legs to his sides, pasted herself to The Paint to let them balance as one weight, and squeezed her eyes shut.

Dear God in Heaven, Great Protector of the Principal People, let us fly. Give us the spirit and the wings of the Eagle!

They flew. When Coosa gathered his great, powerful haunches and left the bank, the sunlit morning air took them into itself and held them up. For a jump that lasted forever.

She was riding Coosa through the sky as she had always dreamed. She was with The Paint, flying through the air like a Raven.

The ground claimed them again with a perilous lurch. Coosa caught the soft bank with his front hooves—only the awe-inspiring power in his forelegs and The Paint's skillful shifting of their weight brought the rear ones far enough forward. Even so, his hooves struck rock and he heaved mightily beneath the strain.

And then he was balanced on all four feet and climbing up the sloping embankment, cutting through the grass at the top to the wet earth itself. Once on top of the bank, he stopped to blow.

The Paint swung him around to look back.

Bluford's Bay Boy stood absolutely still in the middle of the opening between the maples, his head hanging sadly over the body of his master. The sight burned itself into Tiana's mind.

The Paint made a low sound of regret, then turned Coosa in the opposite direction and urged him into the woods.

Tiana said, in a small voice, "Do you think we could have helped him? Bluford? Right at first, I mean, if Sykes and Walters hadn't been after us?"

"He was dead when he fell," Standingdeer said. "His blood was pouring so, he couldn't have lived."

"I feel sorry for him."

"So do I," he said, as Coosa crashed through a patch of purple-flowered rhododendron. "But he did it. Same as if he'd shot himself."

His arms tightened around her. He blurted, "Mainly, though, I wasn't thinking about Bluford. I was worried about you."

Tiana went still in his arms. She wanted every pore in her body to drink in his words, every nerve to listen.

Coosa plunged on, through a thicket of beeches and onto a deer trail.

"You were?"

She barely breathed the words, but he heard her. "Yes," he said.

His iron-sinewed arm crushed her back against him.

His breath came hot in her ear. "I love you, Tiana," he said. "When I saw Sykes manhandling you, I hated myself for not telling you sooner. You could've been killed never hearing that I love you."

The words sounded like a song to Tiana.

A song more beautiful, even, than that of the wonderful wren. He loved her!

"I'll do everything in my power to take you

West with me," he said. "You'll learn to love that land, too."

He let her go and reached out to hold back an oak branch until they could pass by. Her heart stopped and didn't beat again until his arm came back around her.

Stand bent over her and clucked to Coosa, who followed the command to turn left, leapt a fallen log, and long-trotted ahead, directly into the woods.

"The road's in through here about a quarter of a mile," he muttered, hunching his shoulders around Tiana to protect her from the slapping branches of the trees.

"How far from town are we?" she murmured, to give herself time to let the sparkling gladness dance through her veins.

"No more than five or six miles."

She hardly heard him or herself, her ears were so full of his earlier words.

And then the truth hit her, with the force of a blow to the back of her knees. The threat to her life had died with Bluford!

And so had the threat to Stand's life. A man had died, as Rattling Gourd had seen in his vision, but it hadn't been Stand.

For one flashing moment she stared at the heart-shaped green leaves of a redbud as Coosa cantered past it. Every drop of dew on each leaf stood apart from the others, round and glistening, like tiny glass bowls turned over separate small worlds.

As separate as her and Stand's old world was from their new world.

The fear that had haunted her waking hours ever since that cold, cutting day last February left her. She was free.

The knowledge surged in her heart like a horse chafing at the bit to start in a race.

The Paint loved her.

And she would never have to tell her secret now.

Chapter 18

A moment later they crashed through a line of hickory trees and out onto the road.

Even at this hour of the morning, several people were using it. One was a man driving a team hitched to a shining buggy with a black thorough-bred tied to the tailgate. The horse was a gelding, and very tall, but it reminded her of Butterfly. A boy on the seat beside the man wore purple-and-yellow racing silks.

Race day in Dahlonega. She was going into Georgia at this very moment. And her beloved Butterfly was wandering in the woods with no one to take care of her. But neither thought moved Tiana now. Stand had said that he loved her.

She would remember that moment and the sound of his voice saying those words for the rest of her life.

"Stand," she said, turning sideways to see his face, but suddenly feeling too shy to meet his eyes, "I love you, too."

"Ah-h-h," he said with a deep sigh of content-ment, and dropped his head to nestle hers into the hollow of his shoulder. "Tiana."

She melted into the hard curve of his body. His voice, saying her name, was all the caress she would ever need. Except for his cheek pressed against her hair and his arms around her.

He hugged her, then pulled the reins up across her legs so he could place his hands on her hipbones and move her even closer to him. They burned their shape into her skin through her thin breeches like a claim of possession.

His leg muscles flexed gently against hers as he gripped the sides of the horse; each movement sent a tingling thrill up her spine.

His lips brushed her ear and he murmured, "I want you to know, sweet Tiana, that you can tell me anything. Whatever it is that you've been afraid to talk about, you can tell me now. I won't let it come between us."

Whatever it is ... I won't let it come between us.

Dear God in Heaven and all the powerful Thunderers! If only he knew!

Despair flooded through her like a river rising out of its banks, washing away the happiness that had such a fragile hold on her soul.

Coosa hit a long, fast trot for which Tiana didn't even try to keep her balance. *How* could she answer?

Stand was waiting, but she couldn't speak. She couldn't even part her lips—they had begun to tremble.

"If you love me," he said softly, "and I love you, then we won't have secrets from each other. Now's the time to tear *that* old barrier down."

A burning sickness swirled in the pit of her stomach.

He was right. They couldn't live and love together under an unspoken lie—she'd known that the day he asked her to go West with him. Her secret hadn't died with Bluford after all.

The Paint lifted Coosa into a lope that brought them still closer to the fancy buggy. Tiana fastened her eyes on its shiny black walls, on its spinning, gilt-painted wheels. Stand could run Coosa straight into the rear of that vehicle, he could ride crashing through the back of it and send him floundering in panic up into the seats or tangling into the whirling wheels, and she wouldn't feel a thing.

"Tiana?"

"I . . . need some time to think," she said. "Let's talk about it later, Stand, all right? I can't think after what we've just been through . . ."

She clamped her lips together. She was babbling; what was she saying?

Stand took his hands away and held one on the reins above Coosa's withers, letting the other hang down by his side. Long inches away. Not touching her. Loneliness flooded her.

"Later, then," he growled. "But soon."

She sat up straight, away from his hard body, which had gone stiff as wood.

"I think we ought to run Coosa after all," she blurted, grasping for a safe subject, desperate for something to talk about, something to pull him back to her. Something to hold them together until she could decide what to do.

"If he runs around noontime, he'll have quite a bit of time to rest before his race," she said. "Usually the young horses race first, and I know there are several three- and four-year-olds entered."

His only answer was an unintelligible grunt.

Stand had said he would leave her with someone she knew and go right back to Sykes and Walters. But if Coosa *did* run, surely he would stay to see the race. Sykes and Walters were tied so well they couldn't escape, and as Stand had said, the loose horses wouldn't wander far.

In that instant, Tiana decided that Coosa *would*

run if he was at all fit. That would give her several hours more with Standingdeer. Surely it would.

The road became more and more crowded from there on in, and by the time they had crossed the Chestatee River, which separated the Nation from Georgia, and had topped the ridge overlooking Dahlonega, Tiana felt that she was drowning in a river of humanity. How could they ever hope to find Gray Fox, even if he was still here?

Worse, how could she ever hope for enough peace to be of good mind?

People, white and Indian, were everywhere, on horseback, afoot, and in wagons and carriages: in the muddy street, all over the rickety board side-walks, flowing in and out of the haphazard build-ings whose signs read: *Gen'l Merch. Toady's Tavern. Doc. Wm. Breen. Lawyer's Office. Billiards Here. Assay Office.*

Tiana tried to look around, to think about her surroundings and let her frightened mind rest for a moment, but it wasn't easy with Stand tense as a waiting panther at her back.

She did glance around, though, at the crowds gathered for this day of racing. There were too many people for her to comprehend. Most of them were men. Scruffy, dirty miners, prospectors or mule drivers, or clean and polished gamblers and dandies, they all had a hard, mean air about them.

Or maybe the hard meanness was coming from this place, this valley of ugliness in the middle of the beautiful blue mountains. This place that had belonged to the Principal People and had been called Licklog because the deer came to lick the salt naturally found here—until that fateful day when the little boy found a gold nugget in the bed of a creek. Then the name had changed to Dah-lonega, gold, yellow money.

That one word, *gold*, had filled all the mountains with greed. The greed that had cost her her home.

And now her secret would cost her Stand's love. She would have nothing.

She shivered and tried to shut the noise of the town out of her ears. But she couldn't close her eyes. Coosa, dropping into a slow trot now, attracted more attention than she liked. But not nearly so much as was usual in a race town on a race day.

She smiled wryly to herself. He was in disguise! Instead of coming prancing into town, perfectly groomed and blanketed behind the Tenkillers' gleaming buggy, he was sweat-soaked and carrying two disheveled riders, bareback, tired before the race had even begun.

He had to get rested. He *had* to run this race—at the end of it, somehow, she would know what to say to Stand.

Stand's touch, his arm against her leg as he reined Coosa to the side of the street, made her jump.

"Somebody in here'll know if Gray Fox is still around," he muttered, nodding toward a log building marked *Toady's Tavern*. "Your brother can keep you safe while I do what has to be done. We'll make those arrangements and then, before I go, you and I will talk."

She went cold to her bones. Not yet! No special words had come to her.

"I . . . I won't be safe here in Dahlonega," she mumbled, searching for the right words to make him stay. "This place is full of people like Sykes and Walters."

"If Gray Fox has survived here this long," he said, riding Coosa to a spot on the hitching rail beside a mule tied there, "he'll have made some kind of friends."

"Yes! The kind that'll fade away at the first hint of trouble! Gray thought Sykes and Walters were his friends. Anyway, Gray's probably in Mexico by now."

"We'll soon find out."

Stand scooted back on Coosa, farther still away from her, so he'd have room to reach into his pocket.

Stand motioned to a small, dirty boy playing around a barrel beside the tavern door and tossed him a coin.

"You know a gambler name of Gray Fox Tenkiller?" he asked. "Fancy clothes, Cherokee?"

"He be at the Eureka," the child said in a scornful tone implying that anyone in his right mind should know that. He pointed to another saloon two doors down.

Stand kneed Coosa along the hitching rail in that direction as he tossed the lad another coin. "Go bring him out, will you?"

With only a businesslike nod for an answer, the boy ran to do Stand's bidding.

An unreasoning relief filled Tiana: Gray Fox was alive! He was all right! Her gaze clung to the swinging doors of the Eureka.

Gray Fox came out almost before they had stopped in front of the place, booming, "Sister!" and then "Standingdeer!" with no more surprise than if he'd been expecting them.

He stepped aside to allow two women carrying full marketing baskets to pass, his white grin flashing. He looked older, more like a man. He looked happy and healthy, not at all like the harried youth who had stormed out of the house at Running Waters. Now that seemed a lifetime ago.

Tiana slid down from the horse and ran to meet him. He folded her into his arms.

"I'm happy to see you've forgiven me, Little Sister," he said, and held her away to look into her face. "You have, haven't you?"

She laughed, shaking her head in wry despair. His bold charm had not diminished one whit.

"I suppose so," she said. "How have you been?"

"Working like a field hand, trying to make you proud!"

"You have a *job?*"

"No, no! I haven't entirely lost my mind! But I'm prospering."

She leaned back in his arms to study him. He wore an obviously expensive suit and his face looked filled out. His skin and hair gleamed and his eyes sparkled.

"You look prosperous," she said. "But whether I'm proud depends on what you've been doing."

"Betting and staking miners," he replied. Stand finished tying Coosa to the hitching rail and joined them. "My assistants are down at the track right now, but I waited here for the champion racehorse to arrive."

"Your assistants? You *are* prospering!"

"Lately I've been picking the *right* bets," Gray said, giving her another hug before he let her go and turned to include Stand in their circle. "My luck has changed, Little Sister, so I know Coosa'll win. I've wagered a whole sack of gold dust and some nuggets on him today."

"The horse may be too tired to run," Stand said as he and Gray shook hands. "Gray Fox, you need to take care of your sister—"

Tiana interrupted him. "No, no! He'll be able to run. And you must stay and see him, Standing-deer."

"Where else would the man go?" Gray asked jovially, laying his arm around Stand's shoulders. "Dahlonega Racetrack is the place to be today."

"I'd be burying and avenging the dead," Stand snapped.

"What!" Gray exclaimed, putting his other arm around Tiana again to draw their little group to the relative privacy of the edge of the sidewalk. "What happened?"

Together, while the town's traffic flowed by on both the sidewalk and the street, Stand and Tiana told him the story.

When they'd finished, Stand said, "Gray Fox, I want you to take care of Tiana and the horse. When his stakes race comes up, you two can decide whether he's fit to run or not."

"No," Gray said somberly, "I'll go with you. I have unfinished business with Sykes and Walters, remember?"

"You stay with Tiana," Stand repeated. "Bluford's my kin. I'll bury him."

"Then what?"

"He's taking Sykes and Walters back to the Nation to put them on trial," Tiana said, stepping closer to her brother to lay a hand on his arm.

But her eyes met his for only a moment; then her gaze flew to Standingdeer's face. It lingered there, moving over his features like a questioning caress. Gray watched her. It was almost as if . . .

"And I think we should all go," she said urgently, "whether Coosa runs or not. We need to stay together."

The way she spoke brought the full realization to Gray. His sister had fallen in love with Standingdeer Chekote. A man who, obviously, had lost his mind.

"On *trial?*" Gray said, his loud voice rising incredulously as the full impact of the words hit him. "You're taking those bastards back for a trial after they've manhandled Tiana and killed your cousin?"

Stand gave him a long look. "I'm taking them back to the Nation," he said slowly. "Tiana thinks a trial would be justice since so many of our people have been jailed in Georgia."

"And usually killed in those jails!"

"Right," Stand said.

Gray Fox gazed back at him as if he, like Tiana, was trying to read the closed look on The Paint's face.

"But we're forbidden to hold council or court or have any other function of government in the Nation," Gray said slowly.

Stand nodded. "Right."

"By the illegal order of the state of Georgia imposing her laws on us!" Tiana burst out. "When Papa gets back, that won't be true anymore. For now, take them across into Tennessee, to Red Clay, to Judge Ross's place."

"It's a lot of hard miles to Red Clay *or* to New Echota," Gray said.

"And the day's nearly half gone," said Stand, "so I'd like to get started. Can you find me a mount?"

Tiana managed to drag in enough air to speak. "Wait," she pleaded. "Look! Coosa's not even tired. We really should run him and save that thousand dollars' forfeit. Let's all go to the track now—Sykes and Walters and our horses will still be at Caney Creek after the race."

She stopped and cleared her throat, looking from one man to the other, trying to find her real voice again, trying to think of what else she could say to convince them.

Gray patted her shoulder, but he didn't even glance at her. He spoke to The Paint.

"*You* stay with Tiana," he suggested. "Burying Bluford, rounding up the extra horses, taking . . . care of those two thieving sons of bitches—it's all a job for more than one man. I have some friends here who'll ride with me."

He smiled at his sister then, willing her to smile back. But she couldn't. As soon as Gray left them, The Paint would expect her to talk to him. To tell him her secret.

"I hereby give you my vote to cast on whether to run Coosa or not," Gray said to her.

"He needs to run. The forfeit fee's a thousand dollars," she repeated, again glancing from one of them to the other, hardly knowing what she was saying. The confused hope that the race would take Standingdeer's mind off her secret mingled in her heart with the despair that sooner or later she would have to tell him the truth.

Gray turned to The Paint. "Sykes and Walters are mine," he insisted. "I owe them. I'd like to take my friends and ride out there, if that's all right with you."

The Paint nodded in reluctant agreement. "You're sure of your friends?"

"Sure and certain. They're some white and some Cherokee, but I can trust them."

"Will you take Sykes and Walters to Red Clay?" Tiana asked.

"I'm taking them into the Nation," Gray said in a tone that chilled her. "And that's where they'll stay."

Suddenly she knew what he and Stand had said in that long look they'd exchanged. She opened her mouth, then closed it again. There was not one more thing she could do. Sykes and Walters deserved justice.

But she didn't want to think about it. So she said quickly, "Which way is the track?"

Gray turned and nodded toward the south end of town. "At the bottom of the hill there, in the bend of the river. It's in perfect shape today, dried out a lot in two days. Should be just the way Coosa likes it best."

He took her arm and turned her to look in that direction, too, as he thrust his hand into his pocket. "See that boardinghouse over there?" He indicated a two-story frame building, its pristine white-painted clapboards gleaming bright between its dull brown log neighbors. "The two rooms at the back of the first floor are mine. Here's the key—feel free to use whatever you need."

As her fingers closed around the warm metal, he squeezed her hand, then turned back to Stand.

"I'm gone," he said. "'Good luck if you run Coosa."

He left them. When he had disappeared into the crowded street, Tiana said, "I can't get used to it. Gray Fox is a completely different person."

"Because he's winning now," Stand said.

She nodded, watching the spot where Gray had last been, afraid to look up at The Paint. If only her brother's new luck would run in the family today!

At last she said briskly, "Well, we'd better get down to the track and tell the officials we're here."

She stepped off the sidewalk, untied Coosa with fingers that trembled, and turned to wait for The Paint.

But Standingdeer didn't follow. Tiana's eyes met his, and the dark look in them nailed her feet to the ground. Each chiseled feature of his face was thrown into relief by the rays of the climbing sun. The strong nose, the hard, prominent cheekbones, the square line of his jaw, the high arch of his brow. He looked like a warrior on an adversary's trail.

"Forget the race," he said. His implacable tone sent a chill up the back of her neck. "We'll take him down by the river for water. We can talk there."

Without answering, she vaulted onto Coosa's back. *Help me*, she prayed to all the spirits in the air and the earth, *help me to know what to say.*

In two long strides Stand was beside her and then he was mounted again, his long, hard body brushing hers, his arms around her to take the reins. Every inch of her body yearned to lean back, to feel him against her once more.

She knew now that it would be for the very last time.

Stand sent Coosa down the crowded street at a fast trot, guiding him around a team of ponies pulling a peddler's brightly painted wagon and in between two flashy pleasure carriages full of noisy fans headed for the track. He didn't speak and neither did she.

What could she ever say to him? Oh, dear Lord, what should she do?

She could not bear to lose him. And lose him she would, if she told him or if she didn't.

They passed a heavy wagon creaking loudly beneath a load of equipment for one of the gold mines. The teamster cracked his whip over the four mules pulling it and shouted, "Hyah, mules!" and then a stream of curses.

Tiana and Stand couldn't have heard each other if either had spoken. But neither had.

A thousand meaningless words crowded into her throat, jamming together until they couldn't come out. Which ones would she say when he finally forced her to speak?

The street widened and poured over the top of a long, sloping hill. At its bottom lay a large, open meadow in the same crescent shape as the bend in the river. Trees grew along the edge of the water—

huge locusts, birches, and oaks. Between the river and the side of the mountain lay the oval grass track, surrounded by spectators, hawkers, gamblers, and horsemen milling in all directions. At the moment Stand and Tiana rode Coosa by, there were horses on the track, but only for practice.

The Paint took them straight toward the river, through the trailing scents of horses, tobacco, and fragrant fried pies. The smell of food reminded Tiana that she hadn't eaten for many hours, but she didn't feel hungry.

He kept Coosa at a trot the entire width of the meadow and through the straggling line of tents near the trees where people were camped. Too soon, far too soon, they were into the trees themselves and riding down the shallow bank to the water.

When Coosa was hock-deep in the river, Stand slid off his back and Tiana did, too, fast, and on the opposite side so he'd have no chance to help her. She could not bear it if he touched her now. She could not bear it.

Coosa dropped his head and began to drink, moving out from between them farther into the coolness of the river.

Stand's eyes burned at her as he called her name.

"Tiana," he said, and once again, just as it had come over her the first time she had ever heard him speak, she had the overpowering sensation of his callused palm running over her skin.

But now, unlike that first time, she knew exactly how that felt. The mere memory of it made her weak.

How would she ever do without the *reality* of it for the rest of her life?

"Maybe I surprised you out there in the woods this morning," he said slowly. "So I'm going to say it again. I love you, Tiana. I love you, and you say you love me. Do you?"

His gorgeous, solemn face broke her heart.

"Yes," she whispered. "I love you."

"Then will you trust me? Will you marry me?"

With his question, the brutal truth of what she'd had, and lost, came crashing in on her.

"No!" she blurted, choking on the word. "No, Stand, I can't."

Turning away, she ran out of the water, heedless of the rocks on the bottom cutting at her feet through her moccasins, numb to the coldness of the shaded water. She dashed up onto the bank, into the shelter of a spreading locust tree, and, sobbing, threw herself to the ground beneath it.

Stand was there the next instant. He caught her by the shoulders and pulled her up to a sitting position. Caught, trapped, in the crook of his arm, Tiana lifted her chin and looked away from him, letting the tears pour freely down her cheeks.

"Why can't you trust me? Why can't you marry me?" His voice was so harsh that it jerked her head around, forced her eyes to meet his.

Never, ever, had she seen such raw pain. And she was the cause of it. Oh, Lord, why hadn't she just told him the truth from the very beginning?

"Standingdeer . . . my darling . . . I do love you," she choked, between the sobs that she had no power to stop. "But my . . . secret, the thing I haven't been able to tell you, it's too terrible. If you knew it, you wouldn't *want* to marry me."

She bit her lip, hard, and turned her face away once more.

He took her chin in his callused hand and turned it back again.

"Nothing can be that terrible."

"Yes, it can! If you knew, you wouldn't even *love* me!"

"Try me and see."

Chapter 19

Her is low voice was rich as thick honey, his hot eyes as compelling as a high wind. Her lips parted.

But the awful words wouldn't come.

Instead she cried, "Wait, Standingdeer. Please. Let's race Coosa first, and then, I swear, I'll answer your questions."

He dropped his arm away from her and stood up.

"I've done all the waiting I'm going to do," he said, and walked past her as if she weren't even there.

Tiana turned to watch him go, sitting stock-still with her palms flat against the cool ground, not even breathing.

He walked beneath two oak trees that reached out their branches to try to catch him, the same way she wanted to reach out her arms. He strode past the birches that lifted their roots to snatch at his feet, as she would have done if she could. He stepped into the embrace of a flowing, drifting willow tree and disappeared.

Tiana didn't know how long she stayed there, staring at that blurred green place where he had last been, holding her body upright against the pulling of the earth.

Finally a shout pierced the empty roaring in her ears.

"Miss Tenkiller, your horse!" someone was yelling. "Your Coosa horse!"

She had sat there long enough for Coosa to drift back to the bank and wander into the trees, grazing, up the river a quarter of a mile. So she ran to catch him, and with her father's old friend Mr. Timson, who had noticed Coosa's wandering and had recognized him and then her, helping and giving her advice, she began to get him ready for the race without one thought of whether she should run him or not. She was long past that kind of thinking.

She brushed Coosa's mane and tail without feeling the coarse hairs running through her hands. She rubbed his sleek coat without any awareness of the spirit and strength in the flesh underneath. Not one of the familiar tasks brought her the peace that it customarily did.

Mr. Timson's voice rumbled behind her, and she made an effort to hear what he said in case he required an answer.

"Run to the officials and bring Coosa's weights," he was saying to one of his servants. And then, more loudly, as if he knew that Tiana's eyes were filled with unshed tears and her real self was floating somewhere far away, he said, "I'm leaving you now, Missy, to go lay a wager on this horse of yours. Make sure he wins it for me, now!"

"I will," she replied, hardly knowing what she was promising. "I will, Mr. Timson, and thank you so much for the loan of equipment."

"I'm loaning you Jasper here, too," he said. "He'll get you to the starting line all right."

Tiana stopped brushing and turned to smile at him. "Thank you, sir," she said.

He tipped his hat and left her just as another of

his servants came running back from the track calling, "Seven Race, The Dahlonega Stakes, be next. That Coosa horse be next up."

With the help of the excited grooms, Tiana threw herself onto Coosa and let them take each side of his bit and lead him at a trot toward the track. She saw and heard nothing of what went on around her.

She looked desperately around for Stand but saw him nowhere. He was too hurt to even watch the race. She had broken his love for her; she'd thrown it away.

Wooden from her head to her toes, Tiana made her legs grip Coosa's sides and her hands hold the reins while Jasper walked him around and waited for the other horses to get into the starting position. Then he led them into place. She sat the horse and waited, next to the three other horses and their riders.

She didn't know whether Coosa was behaving well or not.

She didn't know whether her opponents were beside her or not.

All she knew was that The Paint wasn't watching. He wasn't even at the track.

She had lost him.

Somewhere far away, the starter's stick hit the drum. Without any signal from Tiana, they were off.

To her surprise, the race made her come fully alive. In the instant Coosa flattened out beneath her to run, her body changed from wood back into flesh, bone, and muscle: her thighs clasped his sides to melt her safely to him; her hands leapt on the reins to search for control.

But he didn't want to give it. He wouldn't give it. Shock replaced the surprise scattering along her nerve endings and she gave him more rein while she tried to get the feel of the bit, new to both of them. Two regrets flashed through her: that she didn't have her own equipment and that she hadn't been paying attention before the start of the race. Coosa always wanted to be the front-runner, and in such a long race that would be his undoing.

Then there was no more time to think. The three other horses pressed in closer and closer, two on one side, one on the other, racing, hooves flashing, almost mashing her and Coosa between them. Panic tightened his muscles and shot from him into her.

She shifted in the irons until she had recovered her balance, then rose and bent over his neck. He broke out of the crunch like a cannonball speeding toward a target; the wind tore at her face as fast as their rivals ran behind.

In a blur, she glimpsed the turn and leaned Coosa into it, trembling with relief when he responded to her hand and leg. The others came up on his heels, though, and bunched around him again, swiftly relentless. They were so close Tiana could smell the different horse scents of their sweat.

As they finished the turn and pounded down the far side of the oval, Coosa escaped them again. But almost before Tiana realized they were free and on the outside rail, she glimpsed a quivering movement behind and to her left. A slashing blow cut at her leg and she jerked around to look.

A blur of grulla horse, a mouse-colored buckskin, was pressing up on them, its nose even with Coosa's shoulder as it came up on the inside. The jockey was lifting his arm to reach ahead to hit at Tiana again.

He missed and got Coosa in the flank.

The stallion broke stride to whip his rear end sideways, away from the pain, and let out an angry squeal of protest. Instinctively Tiana tightened her hold on his mouth, calling to him, trying to soothe, in spite of the searing anger that flared in her stomach.

Coosa danced sideways, snorting, slowing nearly to a trot, letting all three of the other horses pass him by. Tiana crooned and talked to him and finally straightened him out, squeezing with her legs, driving him forward.

They *would* win, by the Thunderers! She would not let that cheating lowlife be rewarded for such behavior! Who was that jockey, anyway?

Coosa began to canter again, but slowly, sulking, tossing his head. The three other horses strung themselves out ahead on the inside rail, the guilty one in the lead.

"Don't let him win!" Tiana cried, and clutched Coosa's sides again with both legs in spite of the rushing ache across the calf of the left one where the other rider had hit her. For a heartbreaking instant, while the others drew fifty and more yards ahead, he wouldn't respond.

Then he answered with a burst of speed that made her whole body lurch for her seat, and she knew that he would give the race all he had. But if he ran full out now, could he go the distance?

They had completed only one mile of the four-mile race. Coosa had already used a lot of himself today. The heat and humidity were building in the air of the valley. How much could he safely give?

The stallion took out after his rivals with no thought of such things. That mouse-colored mare would rue the moment she had jostled and passed The Coosa Evening Star. And so would her rider.

Tiana bent over Coosa's neck and they leapt ahead, his body floating beneath her like a powerful cloud. He gave no indication he felt her hands on his reins or her weight on his back; they had blended into one being once more.

Before Tiana could believe they could have caught their rivals, they were gaining on the last two, passing them effortlessly, one by one. They came up on the grulla mare faster than thought.

The mare's jockey glanced over his shoulder and raised his arm to strike the mare again and again in a desperate try for more speed. In spite of all he could do, though, when they passed through the stretch for the second time, Coosa was breathing on her flank.

They entered the third round neck and neck. Going around the first turn, Tiana eased Coosa toward the outside to put some distance between them. The grulla's jockey might try lashing at Coosa's nose if they were close enough together, thinking himself fairly well hidden from the majority of spectators.

Coosa pushed on, faster than Tiana would've liked, pulling for more speed, champing to take the bit for himself. Tiana's feverish mind and sweating body chilled into desperate awareness.

She had to get control and keep it or the stallion would run through himself before the end of the heat. She shortened her reins and adjusted her balance. If she could hold him right there until the last part of the fourth round, she could ask for whatever he had left at the end.

He gave in to her commands reluctantly, and they raced around the oval track one more time. When they straightened away for the run down the backstretch, she came up high onto his withers and gave him his head. He took her through the air like a rushing wind, thundering down the stretch faster than he had ever run in his life, galloping so fast that Tiana feared his heart, and hers, would burst.

They passed the mare.

And the magic came, but not in feeling, as it always had before. It came in a thought, rolling into her head on the tumultuous shout of the assembled spectators and bettors crowding up against the track: she would win this race, but not for revenge on the other rider, infuriating cheater that he might be. She would win this race for Stand.

As expiation for leading him on and breaking his heart. As restitution for killing the uncle he loved, the only parent he had had. She couldn't give him her love for a lifetime, nor could she give him back Tobacco Jack, but she could give him the ranch that he wanted. The ranch bought and paid for outside the Nation, the ranch no government could ever take away.

She glanced back. The other rider was using crop and spurs freely, and the mare was giving him all she had, trying her heart out, but Coosa pulled farther and farther away from her nose every second. He crossed the finish line four lengths in the clear.

When he had galloped on to slow himself and had swung around to canter back to the winner's circle, jubilation rose and surrounded them. People whose faces Tiana somehow couldn't quite see crowded around, calling to her. Someone pressed a heavy pouch into her hands, while someone else dropped a wreath of flowers onto Coosa's neck.

They had won. They must find Standingdeer to tell him.

Tiana didn't dismount. When Mr. Timson's groom ran up to take Coosa's head, she waved him away and rode out through the throng at a walk with her eyes straight ahead, looking, always searching.

Was The Paint still here? Had he gone into town

for a mount and started back West? Or was he on his way to Caney Creek or to Pine Grove?

Wherever he was at this moment, she had lost him.

Once she'd woven her slow way through the crowd, Tiana got down and led Coosa, keeping him moving so he could cool out, heading in the direction of the river. Avoiding Mr. Timson and his ever-flapping tongue, she started downstream, toward the willow where she had last seen Stand.

She stumbled through the line of trees to the bank of the river, where Coosa dropped into an even slower walk, picking his ambling way along the edge of the water, over roots and rocks. He kept trying to drink, but she let him have only a mouthful because he was so hot. Her palms went wet with sweat and she pulled him along faster to keep his muscles from tightening up too fast, her eyes straining for a glimpse of The Paint.

He was nowhere in sight. The green and brown of the trees, the dangling bunches of white blossoms on the flowering locusts, the sprinkling of red-orange of the fire pinks growing in the shepherd's cress along the bank were the only colors there. No pale blue hunting shirt that fit across broad shoulders like a second skin.

Suddenly she saw him. He was squatting on his haunches beneath the branches of a thick maple tree, its limbs so long they dipped down at the end of their arch to drag their leaves in the water. Stand was watching those leaves as if, at any second, they could turn into hands and pull something rare, something magical, out of the water.

He didn't move when she came up behind him.

"Standingdeer," she said. She marveled that her voice wavered only a little. "We won."

He didn't answer.

She looped Coosa's reins around a branch of the

tree. "Stand? Here's the money for your ranch out West."

He still didn't answer. And he didn't look at her.

She clutched the pouch in both hands and, on trembling legs, walked around in front of him. Thousands of leaves whispered to her, everywhere above her head, but Standingdeer was silent.

He moved his head half an inch to look past her.

She might as well tell him the truth and be rid of this horrible burden. He already had withdrawn his love. He already hated her. What difference would it make?

If The Paint still wanted revenge, let him kill her. She didn't care. She had lost him.

Her shoulders straightened; she twisted the strings of the pouch in and out between her fingers.

She said, "The terrible secret I have is about Tobacco Jack's killer."

He sprang to his feet, his eyes searching hers, the bleak look gone in a flash from his face.

"You know who did it? You've known all along?"

"Yes."

His eyes lit with hope. And relief.

"Thank God that's it! No wonder you refused to marry me. You thought if I found out, I'd take revenge and end up dead or in a Georgia prison, didn't you?"

If only she could agree, let him always think that those words were the truth!

He took a step forward and reached for her. She stood like a spineless coward and allowed him to fold her into his arms.

She knew it was wrong to let Stand, in his ignorance of her guilt, embrace her like this. It would be the last one, but it was more than she ever thought she'd have again.

He drew her head to his chest, slipping his hand beneath her hair to cradle her cheek.

Then, weak with the deliberate betrayal of the act, she lifted her arms and put them around his waist, hugging him gently, trying to tell him without words that she truly did love him.

He held her closer. "It's all right, my darling," he said. "I'll forgive you for keeping it secret. And you needn't have worried.

"But tell me, Tiana," he continued. "Who killed him?"

Would God that she could lie!

She hugged him harder, just for a heartbeat, then let him go and stepped back to get free of his arms. He dropped them to his sides even as his eyes devoured hers.

"Tiana, who killed him?"

"I did."

The words came to her tongue as calmly, as smoothly, as if she'd always known she would say them.

"*You?* No! That can't be!"

He towered over her, his eyes blazing dark as a summer midnight in the paleness of his astonished face.

"Tiana! You?"

"Yes." She took a step backward. "It was an accident, Standingdeer. I never meant to kill him."

He folded his arms across his chest, flexing the muscles below his rolled-up sleeves as his hands gripped his upper arms hard. A strange, guttural sound of mixed pain and anger came from his throat.

"He was beating Fawn!" she cried. "I had to do *something!* He was drunk and he had already beaten her badly, really badly, the night before. Then when I tried to take her home with me to doctor her, he forbade it, ordered me off the place, and started beating her again."

She paused to take a breath, to try to make the words stop tumbling over one another so fast. She had to make him understand. She had to!

Stand stayed silent, simply looking at her with that same terrible stare.

"Tobacco Jack wouldn't stop hitting Fawn with his fists, and he was killing her," she began again. "He *did* kill her, Stand—she died right there on the ground by the quarters at Pine Grove!"

"*You* hit him with the hoe?"

"Yes. But before that, I screamed and screamed for him to stop. I *tried* to make him quit without hurting him."

She squeezed her fingers tighter together by wrapping the leather cord of the pouch around them. It cut her flesh.

"I hit him with the blunt side, Stand. Even in my panic I thought not to use the sharp edge!"

"Did he suffer?"

"No. He fell without a sound."

Stand's eyes burned into hers for another lifetime. Then he whirled away and strode to the river.

"Here's your money, Stand," she called, to his back. "It's all I can do to make reparation. That, and to tell you again that I am so sorry!"

The tears began to rise in a boiling rush, filling her eyes and her throat. "Take Coosa, too," she yelled, before they drowned out her voice. "You can have everything. I'm sorry, Stand. I'm just so sorry."

He kept going. Nothing she could say now would bring him back. He would never come back to her.

Frantically she ripped at the stubborn rawhide string, forcing it over the ends of her fingers and out from around them. She threw the pouch at the foot of the maple tree's trunk, turned toward the track, and began to run.

Stand went straight to the edge of the water and walked upstream along the bank without once feeling his feet move. He didn't see the river to his right or the trees and the people to his left. He could only hear two agonized voices: his saying, *Tiana, who killed him?* and hers answering, *I did.*

That absolutely could not be true. Tiana could not have killed his uncle Jack. Even hearing it from her own lips, he could not believe it!

She couldn't have. Why, Tiana Tenkiller was one of the gentlest people he'd ever known! Just this morning she was begging him not to kill those plundering, raping, thieving, conniving *yonegas!*

Yet she had killed his uncle Jack!

She had tried to save the white intruders but had killed Tobacco Jack?

Hot, twisting anger rose in his gut and he whirled, grinding his heels into the soft earth; he began to pace in the opposite direction. How could she? How the hell could she?

When he got his hands on her, he'd shake that answer out of her! Fury chased along his veins and jumped from nerve to nerve in every inch of his body. He began to run full out along the riverbank, needing speed, needing pain.

Needing escape from the next thought looming. He raced as if he carried magic to someone dying, fire to the freezing. He leapt bulging tree roots and pushed branches out of his face with both hands. But he wouldn't leave the narrow riverbank for the open meadow where the ghost thought could catch him.

He stopped at the tree where Coosa was tied, where he had been standing when Tiana spoke, reached up to grasp a limb in each hand, and let the truth burst into his brain.

She had made love to him knowing this.

Tiana had made sweet love to him holding her terrible secret closer to her beautiful body than she had held him.

Tiana had killed the only parent he had ever had and still she had come into his arms to love him like a deceitful, lying angel.

And she had called *him* a traitor and a coward!

His stomach tied itself into a knot that would never come undone. He broke the branch he was holding in his right hand, ripped it away from the tree, whirled, and threw it as hard as he could into the middle of the river.

How could she *possibly* have betrayed him so?

He turned to Coosa and began to strip him of his tack, not thinking about what he was doing, simply moving his arms and his hands and his legs at some familiar task in the hope that it would keep him from tearing the world apart.

He lifted the saddle, pulled out the weighted pad, and hurled it to the ground.

She had known this awful secret while she'd held him in her arms and made him fall helpless into her marvelous, huge dark eyes. She had known it when she'd huddled with him in the cave during the storm and listened to *his* deep secrets.

She had known it every single time she had told him she loved him.

It was too terrible to tell, she had said today. *If you knew, you wouldn't love me.*

His hands went still on the saddle. He grasped it, cantle and pommel, as desperately as if he were adrift in the Tennessee River, being carried into a current of the mighty whirlpool terror, the Suck, about to be pulled into its bottomless depths. His shoulders slumped, he laid his forehead against the slick-worn leather of the saddle seat.

Tiana had been wrong about that. He did love her. God and The Apportioner help him, he still loved her.

What a mess! He knew, this minute, in his bones, in the same way he always knew the spirit of a country the first time he rode across it, that he would never love another woman. Now that he knew he wanted a home, now that he had the money to buy one that the whites couldn't give and then take away, now that he had learned to trust a woman at last, she was telling him this!

Coosa turned and nosed at Stand until he looked up to stare past the stallion's silver head into the masses of white blooms, dangling in bunches from the flowering locust tree that grew upstream from the maple. On their delicate pale blossoms, trembling with them in the breeze, he saw his uncle Jack's face. Not the kindly face that he usually wore, but a red, fierce mask of drunken rage.

The face he had worn that day when Stand was ten or eleven and the field hand, Ned, had suggested a different way of unloading a wagon. Uncle Jack had pulled his pistol and shot the man dead on the spot.

The boy, Stand, had pushed that memory from his mind.

As he had done the memory of Tobacco Jack whipping a servant, who had stolen some sugar, until the woman's skin hung in ribbons from her back. It had taken him so many years to admit that a bottle of whiskey could change his kindly, easygoing uncle into a true *asgina*, Devil.

But now, of all times, he had to remember and to admit it. Tobacco Jack Tuskee had been the ter-

ror of the Nation when he was drunk, and everybody who'd known him said so.

Of course Tiana hadn't stood idle while he beat
her friend! If she would, without thinking, dash
into a burning stable to save her horse, she would
just as instinctively grab a hoe and use it to try to
save Fawn. After all, Jack had been beating the girl
to death.

What a horrible thing for Tiana to go through!
And then, on top of that, she'd had guilt to carry
besides the awful fear that someone would find
out.

Great Thunderers! He and Bluford had stood
right there in front of her that day at the Council
Oak, swearing blood revenge!

Stand dropped the saddle atop the weighted
pad on the ground and went to untie Coosa.
Hardly aware of what he was doing, he began
walking him up and down the bank of the river,
cooling him out some more, fighting through the
storm of thoughts and feelings still raging in his
head.

Yes, Tiana had made love to him while keeping
this secret. Yet no matter what she had done, he
loved her.

Abruptly he turned and strode back the other
way. But no matter how much he loved her, could
he actually make a life with the woman who had
killed the only father he had ever known?

Coosa came on faster, trotting past Stand's
shoulder, making him lengthen his pace to keep
up, leading him back to the locust. Stand began
gathering up the borrowed tack. He had to go and
find Tiana. If only he'd watched her to see who
had lent her the equipment! She might be with
that person right now, or they might know where
she had gone.

A blob of yellow deerskin in the green of the

grass caught his glance as he turned to leave. The pouch! Tiana had yelled something about the money. He went back, snatched it up, and held it to his cheek. Her scent was still on it.

Or it was still in his nostrils and in his blood. It always would be.

He stuffed the bag into his pocket and ran across the grassy, open space, the saddle and pads in his arms, the horse coming on behind him. A servant emerged from a green tent, glanced at him, and then came to meet him, holding out his hands to take the tack from Stand's arms.

"Mighty race, warn't it, suh?" he asked. "This 'ere Coosa Star hoss, he the best."

"Have you seen Miss Tenkiller?" Stand demanded.

"Naw, suh. Not since she ride in the race jist now."

"Who's your master?"

"Massa Timson. Four Pine Plantation, suh."

Stand glanced at the tent, which bore that name in flowing white script. "Is he here?"

"Naw, suh. One o' *ouah* hosses runnin' now."

"Tell him much obliged for the loan of the tack," Stand said. He crossed the reins over Coosa's neck and threw himself onto his back.

Of course Tiana would want to be alone in her pain. But she wouldn't be down by the river, because that was where he had been. Perhaps she was wandering in the crowd.

He rode slowly among the spectators on the near side of the track, hating to burden the tired horse, but determined to be able to see over and into the crowd. Tiana wasn't there, on either side of the racetrack.

Stand went looking for the officials at the starting line, but the men had no idea where she'd gone. He asked two other people, chosen at random, with the same result.

The knot in his stomach returned. What if some renegade had grabbed her?

Or what if, because of his anger, she had left him forever? What if she'd caught a ride out of Dahlonega with someone she knew, or didn't know, and was several miles down the road by now, on her way to God knows where?

She had no home, so where would she go? To Caney Creek to try and catch her brother? She had nobody else.

He put his heels to Coosa and turned him, riding out of the crowd and toward the road that led up the hill into town. She could have tried to find transportation at the livery stable or the stage stop or even at one of the mining companies with wagons always coming in and out of town.

Stand threw himself off the horse and, holding him out of the path of a gig that was barreling down the hill, started up toward town at a ground-eating run, the stallion moving easily behind. Pray God he wasn't leaving Tiana behind him somewhere in the crowd.

At the top of the hill, he swept his gaze along either side of the street. Narrowing his eyes against the bright sunlight, he tried to see the whole town at once.

No girl/woman, round-bottomed in breeches, hair tied in a braid. No delicate shoulders moving like wings beneath a man's thin, white-colored shirt as she ran.

No Tiana.

"Where's the livery?" he shouted to a teamster sitting slumped on his wagon seat in front of the store marked *Gen'l Merch*.

The imbecile took an age to answer, but finally

he yelled, "Around the corner," and pointed the way.

Stand looped the lead rope around his hand and dashed with Coosa through the crowded street until he found the livery, running into the dim hallway so fast the dust rose thick as a storm. The livery owner shouted from where he was working in one of the stalls, "Slow down out there!" He shook his head mutely when asked if he'd seen Tiana.

He did say, though, that the stage stopped at the other end of the main street, and then roared out a torrent of curses when Stand leapt onto Coosa, rolled him back, and rode out of the stable faster than he had come in.

He didn't slow down as he wove his way through the traffic in the street, passing a freight wagon hitched to a mule team that went on and on forever, without even glancing over his shoulder to see if he had room to slip back in among the mess of vehicles and animals. He kept up the pace to the end of the street and skidded Coosa to a stop in front of the glass door with its ornately scripted legend: *Augusta-Milledgeville Stage Company. Gold Leases. Inquire Within.*

In an instant he was off the horse, onto the ground, and across the sidewalk, his hand reaching for the doorknob.

The stage stop was closed.

Gone to the Races, a smaller, hand-printed sign declared, dangling on its black cord in Stand's face like a taunting, waving hand.

"Goddammit to hell!" He doubled up his fist and hit the doorjamb. He turned around and stared down the dusty street.

What he would give to know just one person in this town! Just *one* who knew how to help him.

He'd give every ounce of gold that was in the bag in his pocket.

But wishing for help was hopeless and a waste of time. He had to find her himself. He had to think.

She couldn't have found a way out of town from here, unless a stage had left and the office had closed within the last ... how long had it been? An hour? That wasn't likely.

But where would she go? She had no home.

Not back to Pine Grove, surely. And if she returned to the cabin, she'd have to walk.

She was on foot or she had stolen a horse. He wouldn't put it past her—she was *so* upset.

Or she might've been able to buy a horse and saddle on credit by signing her brother's name. Gray knew people here. He was known at the Eureka Saloon.

Stand ran across the sidewalk, his heels drumming on its boards like a song, and leapt onto Coosa. They were already heading for the Eureka at a fast canter when the thought hit him.

The boardinghouse! Great Friends of Thunder, how stupid could he be? How could he let the turmoil in his heart paralyze his mind like this?

Tiana had the key to Gray Fox's rooms. He had pointed out the building to her. She wanted to be alone. Of course that was where she'd gone!

Hope shot into his blood, pounding like a hammer into his veins, and he sent Coosa galloping at a long angle down and across the street. A rider coming from the other direction swerved to give them room; Stand thanked him with an absently lifted hand. Thank God he had thought of this!

He had been forty kinds of a fool to turn away from her the way he had done—she would naturally be thinking that he would never forgive her. She *had* to let him talk to her!

Stand stopped Coosa at the rail, wrapped the reins around it, and left him, bounding across the sidewalk and up onto the porch of the house in four steps. The double front doors stood open to show a wide hallway. He burst into it, his eyes searching for a door to rooms at the back.

He glimpsed a parlor, immediately inside to the left, with a closed door across from it; farther back, an arched opening on the same side as the parlor revealed a dining room. The door across the hall from that was closed, too.

Hadn't Gray Fox said the rooms at the back of the first floor? Stand banged his fist on that slab of polished pine.

"Tiana! Are you there? It's Stand."

Only a deep silence answered him. He banged again.

"Leave me alone!" she called. She sounded miles away.

He grabbed the glass doorknob, his knees going weak with relief. She was in there. And she was safe.

"Let me in! I have to talk to you!"

"No!" she called back. Her voice broke on the one simple word. She was crying.

He squeezed the knob until the points of its carving bit into his palm. He tried it, but it wouldn't budge.

"Tiana!" he shouted. "Open this door!"

"Go away," she yelled in a voice full of tears but no weakness. "Talk can't change one thing."

Chapter 20

"**O**pen this door or I'll break it down."

His voice had changed to low and dangerous from loud and angry in one heartbeat.

Tiana clutched the towel she was holding in both hands and stared at the door. He would do exactly that.

She forced her feet to move, to walk all the way across the room. She forced her hand to take hold of the key she'd placed in the inside lock and twist it.

Stand turned the knob and burst in.

His eyes seared her. His face was terrible; had he come for revenge, after all?

She held the towel up to one of her damp cheeks, like a baby with a blanket, wishing she could make a curtain of it that would shut out the sight of him. "Why are you here?"

"I need to talk to you."

A tiny tendril of relief relaxed and curled out inside her, before the stone of her despair dropped down and crushed it again.

"It's too late for that." She dropped the towel and walked away from him, away from the magic hands clenched at his sides, away from the marvelous arms that used to hold her.

He followed right behind her.

She kept moving, all the way across the big, spacious room, onto the braided rug and off it onto the oak floor again, walking slowly, straight to the window, wishing she could step through it and drop out of this misery forever.

The Paint stopped when she stopped. She could feel the exact place where he was standing as accurately as if she possessed antennae, like a butterfly.

But she would not turn around. She would not look at him again. Looking at him would only make everything worse. Would nothing, *nothing* make her lose this yearning to run into his arms?

"Tiana," he said, and now his voice was as raw as scraped skin. "I can't believe you could lie with me, make love with me, knowing that you had killed Tobacco Jack."

She whirled on him. "Don't you know it was torture for me?" she cried. "Don't you know that? Every time that thought intruded on my mind, I wanted to die!"

His eyes widened, flaring with new feeling, but she couldn't stop trying to make him understand, no matter how mad he got.

"Can't you ever, for one minute, imagine how horrible this has been for me?" she went on, the words pouring off her tongue in a torrent. "I didn't *intend* to kill him and I didn't *intend* to make love with you! I certainly didn't intend to fall *in love* with you. I hated myself for keeping it from you, but I couldn't tell you!"

"I know," he murmured.

And he did. Suddenly he could feel all the agony that she had gone through: the panic that he would find out and kill her—or leave her. For she did love him. All those weeks she had dreaded to lose him just as he now dreaded to lose her. He knew that, with the infallible instinct for truth which had kept him alive in the wild for so long. He knew it beyond a shadow of a doubt.

As well as he knew that he could never make a life without her.

"Well, you didn't know down there at the river!" she cried. "You wouldn't even let me say I was sorry—you turned away from me as if I'm some kind of *Uk'ten'*!"

"I was shocked, Tiana. Stunned past thinking. You yourself said that I didn't know how bad your secret could be."

"Well, now you do know," she said through lips that trembled so, she couldn't control them.

"Yes," he agreed, his hands lifting of their own will to cradle the delicate bones of her shoulders. "I know how bad Uncle Jack could be when he was drinking. I know you were only defending your friend."

She drew back, away from his touch. His heart sank.

He had waited too late to talk. Hadn't that been true all his life?

But this time he would share his heart, anyway, and Tiana would have to listen. That was only just—wasn't she the one who had taught him how?

"I'll always miss Uncle Jack," Stand said slowly, letting his hands drop to his sides, empty as the hollow growing inside him. "I'll always love him and the memories of our good times. But, Tiana, I love you more. I still want what I wanted at the cabin—to spend the rest of my life with you."

Tears, a hot, rushing river of tears, swelled into her eyes and poured down her cheeks.

"I've been thinking so hard, all this time," she said, swallowing to keep from choking on the words. "And I don't believe that you can ever still love me, now that you know."

"Believe it," he said softly. "I forgive you, Tiana. I love you. I want you to marry me and live with me for the rest of my days."

He meant it. The rich honey of his voice had never been more temptingly sincere. She had been wrong—he *could* forgive her. He *could* still love her, now that he knew.

She smiled. His heart leapt back into his chest, whole again, fluttering, fighting for its life.

"Oh, Standingdeer." Her voice broke. "I love you, too. I will marry you."

She lifted her arms, as if in surrender, and he reached out and folded her to him. Her hot tears soaked his shirt in an instant, pasting her cheek to his chest through the thin cotton cloth. Nothing had ever felt so good to him.

They held each other for a long, silent time. Then she lifted her face for his kiss.

But he put his hands on her arms and held her away from him so he could see her face.

"We have a sack full of money and that running horse out there in the street," he said. "What do you want to do with them?"

"I want to take them West," she said. "After we travel to Washington City to tell Mama and Papa. I don't care if it's on the great plains you tell about or in the Shining Mountains, but I want us to build a home and a ranch. With bloodlines for running horses that'll bring breeders to us from as far away as the Eastern Cherokee Nation."

Stand's blood sang through his body all on its own, for although his heart was whole again, it had stopped beating. An ore wagon from the mines rattled by, just outside the window, wheels shrieking, driver shouting.

After it had passed he said, "Will you really do that for me? Will you really leave your home Nation for me?"

As soberly as if she were making the solemn vow of their wedding, Tiana answered. "My home isn't in the Nation anymore. It's wherever you are, Standingdeer Chekote. You're the only home I'll ever want."

Avon Romances—
the best in exceptional authors and unforgettable novels!

The WONDER of WOODIWISS

continues with the publication of
her newest novel in rack-size paperback—

SO WORTHY MY LOVE
☐ #76148-3
$5.95 U.S. ($6.95 Canada)

**THE FLAME AND
THE FLOWER**
☐ #00525-5
$5.50 U.S. ($6.50 Canada)

ASHES IN THE WIND
☐ #76984-0
$5.50 U.S. ($6.50 Canada)

**THE WOLF AND
THE DOVE**
☐ #00778-9
$5.50 U.S. ($6.50 Canada)

A ROSE IN WINTER
☐ #84400-1
$5.50 U.S. ($6.50 Canada)

SHANNA
☐ #38588-0
$5.50 U.S. ($6.50 Canada)

**COME LOVE A
STRANGER**
☐ #89936-1
$5.50 U.S. ($6.50 Canada)

THE COMPLETE COLLECTION AVAILABLE FROM
AVON BOOKS WHEREVER PAPERBACKS ARE SOLD